VOODOO FOR TWO

A Cajun Magic Mystery
Book 2

ELLE JAMES

Twisted Page Inc

Voodoo For Two

Cajun Magic Mysteries Book #2

New York Times & *USA Today*
Bestselling Author

ELLE JAMES

Ebook ISBN: 978-1-62695-047-4

Print ISBN: 978-1-62695-048-1

Manufactured in the United States of America

First Edition April 2013 – Entangled Publish, LLC

Second Edition – Twisted Page Inc

This book is dedicated to my son Adam, who reminds me all the time that life is an adventure to be lived to the fullest. Love you, Adam!

Author's Note

Enjoy the following books by Elle James:

Cajun Magic Mystery Series
Voodoo on the Bayou (#1)
Voodoo for Two (#2)
Deja Voodoo (#3)

Bayou Brotherhood Protectors
Remy (#1)
Gerard (#2)
Lucas (#3)
Beau (#4)
Rafael (#5)
Valentin (#6)
Landry (#7)
Simon (#8)
Maurice (#9)
Jacques (#10)

Visit www.ellejames.com for more titles and release dates

VOODOO FOR TWO

A Cajun Magic Mystery

Book Two

New York Times & *USA Today*
Bestselling Author

ELLE JAMES

Chapter One

Bayou Miste, Louisiana

Nothing was blacker than nighttime deep in the swamps. Stars couldn't penetrate the cypress canopy, laden with long tendrils of Spanish moss, dripping down over land and water.

Silence reigned as if all the creatures of the murky waters and dense underbrush held their breaths for something—a cue, a signal, a happening—

A drum thrummed to life, stirring the night air with an ancient rhythm. The gentle sway of a breeze wafted through the gossamer moss, dancing in time to the placid swishing of the breeze through the trees, urging the insects and frogs into song.

"Breathe the air, touch the earth, stir the waters, and play with fire."

Just when Lucie LeBieu thought she couldn't stand still for another moment, the scrape of a match cut across the gentle hum of the night. Bright flame slashed through the darkness, illuminating the faces of three women standing in a circle.

This dark and mysterious place in the midst of the Atchafalaya Basin, on the edge of Bayou Miste, just happened to be home to Lucie, her twin sister Lisa, and her grandmother, the locally infamous Madame LeBieu, Voodoo queen of the surrounding bayous.

"Do you feel de rhythm of de night?" *Mamère* LeBieu's voice caressed the darkness, the sound an extension of the drum's beat.

Lucie shifted, not liking the creepy feeling she always got when her family did these kinds of things. "Gran, this is silly."

"Shh!" The older woman, dressed in a flowing red caftan, set the flame to a fat candle, then an incense stick, and placed them on the ground at the center of the circle. "We must commune wit' nature, become one wit' de power, de energy present in de darkness." Her grandmother's accent was as thick as the humid air and tepid waters of Bayou Miste.

Lisa and Lucie had been raised in New York City for the first eight years of their lives. Any accent they might have acquired in Louisiana since then was out of pure self-preservation, and it wasn't anything to talk about, in their grandmother's book.

"Feel de magick," her grandmother insisted, tipping her face back as if soaking in the moonlight that wasn't visible through the canopy of trees.

"*Mamère*, I never do it right." Lisa tried to shake off the sense of impending doom.

A hand reached out and pinched her arm. "Shut up and listen, Sis," her twin grumbled. "Can't you feel it? It's hot, alive, and sensuous."

"Lisa! Dis is not da time," *Mamère* LeBieu admonished.

Lisa snorted, but kept any further comments to herself.

Lucie stood still, closed her eyes, and tried.

She really tried, but all she got out of the beating drums, the chirping crickets, and the croaking frogs was a healthy case of the heebie-jeebies. "It's no use. I'm not cut out for this Voodoo nonsense."

"It isn't nonsense, Lucie," Lisa said. "I've used it to get guys all hot and bothered on several occasions and it worked great."

"You don't need potions to get guys all hot and bothered, Sis. I'm just not cut out to do this. I mess it up every time." Lucie slumped.

"Den be quiet while I work de magick," her grandmother demanded.

When *Mamère* LeBieu took that tone, Lucie obeyed. The woman didn't get angry often, but when she did, woe be unto whoever roused her ire. The woman had a wicked mean streak. Though Lucie didn't believe in her own version of Voodoo, she'd seen what a dose of *Mamère's* special powder could produce. Maurice Saulnier had the wickedest itch a man could have for two solid weeks after he'd trampled *Mamère* LeBieu's favorite azalea bush.

She itched just thinking about it.

Mamère closed her eyes and swayed in rhythm with the drum. "Ezili Freda Daome, goddess of love and all dat is beautiful, listen to our prayers, accept our offerings, and enter into our arms, legs, and hearts."

"Here we go," Lucie muttered. "Another spell." She exhaled a long breath. Why couldn't she have been born into a normal family, with normal parents and grandparents?

Her grandmother swayed with the candle's flame.

"Goddess of light and stars from above,
Help dose who lost de way to love.

Grant dem de courage to open de heart
De intelligence dey need to make a new start
De humility to admit when dey been wrong
De determination dey need when dey mus' be strong.
Ezili Freda Daome, goddess of light
Bring dis misguided woman de love tonight."

Lucie backed away from the circle, holding up her hands, anger swirling in her gut. "You did *not* just work a love spell on me. Tell me you didn't, *Gran.*"

"What do you care?" Lisa taunted. "You don't believe all that Voodoo anyway. You said you didn't."

"I don't believe in mine, but *Mamère's* is a whole different pot of trouble. And it's the principle of it. I don't *want* to fall in love." Lucie crossed her arms over her chest and glared at her grandmother.

The older woman ignored her protest, waved a filmy scarf, and sprayed perfume over the candle's flame.

"You know the story. Been there. Done that. Have the scars to prove it," Lucie mumbled. "For the love of cypress knees, don't mess with my love life." *Or lack thereof.*

"Mouthy tonight, aren't we?" Lisa grinned at her. "That's usually my job. But really, you need to get laid. How long has it been? *Mamère* magick is the best. Let her help you."

"Wow, you make me sound downright pathetic. Has anyone considered what *I* want? Doesn't anyone care?" Lucie spun on her heels and marched back toward the little shack she shared with her grandmother and twin sister. "I'll be at work until two. Hopefully, by the time I return, you two will be in bed and not out here playing Voodoo games."

The drum still beat from the back porch of the faded gray house. "Oh, go home, Remy!" Lucie shouted. "Your drum-thumpin' days are over."

The dark-haired, dark-skinned boy hit the drum hard. "Miss Lucie, you gotta learn ta chill."

"Chill, my fanny." She stomped through the house and up to her old room. There she changed into the miniskirt and grabbed the high heels she'd brought with her from her apartment. Jean Dupree insisted his "girls" dress like Hooters waitresses as part of their jobs at the Raccoon Saloon. Lucie didn't mind too much. When she wore jeans, she didn't get nearly the tips she got when she wore the miniskirt. And Lord knew, they needed the money.

Seemed her grandmother never got ahead of the mortgage payment. Speaking of which, wasn't she due to pay another one soon?

A loud knock echoed up the wooden stairway from the front door, rattling the screen against the doorjamb.

"Keep your shirt on, I'm coming," Lucie called out.

Carrying her high heels, she raced down the stairs, eager to get away from her grandmother's meddling.

Paul Renault, one of the two deputies employed by the parish, stood with his head down, scuffing his muddy black shoes on the faded deck.

"Paul? What are you doing out here at this time of night?" Lucie had gone to high school with Paul. She'd actually turned him down once when he'd asked her to go out. The man was just as shy now as he'd been all those years ago.

She regretted turning him down. How much courage had it taken for him to ask her out? And how long had it taken for him to get up enough courage to ask another woman? The man was still single, for the love of swamps and alligators. What would it have hurt for her to go out on one date with the man? A lot. At the time she'd been head over heels for one low-down, lying swamp rat, Benjamin Franklin Boyette.

"I'm sorry, Miss Lucie. I have a document for Madame

LeBieu. I'm real sorry." He didn't meet her gaze, but instead looked over her shoulder. "Is she home?"

"Sure. Why don't you come in while I round her up?"

"No, it wouldn't be right, no." He tapped an envelope against his hand. "I'll just wait here."

"*Mamère!*" She yelled as she turned toward the back of the house.

"You don't have to yell, Lucie. I'm here." Appearing out of nowhere, her grandmother stepped to the door, followed by Lisa, whose face paled, her dark eyes as big as ripe persimmons.

Gran LeBieu opened the door and held out her hand.

"Madame LeBieu, I didn't have anything to do with this, I just want you to know," Deputy Paul blurted. "It's just part of my job. That's all. Please believe me."

What was wrong with Paul? Lucie had never seen him quite this nervous, not even when he'd asked her out. "What is it?"

Paul handed the older woman the envelope, immediately backing away. "Consider yourself served, Madame LeBieu. I'm really sorry." With that, he spun and dove for the police cruiser, peeling out like his pants were on fire.

Her *Mamère* stared down at the envelope.

Lisa slipped an arm around her grandmother in an uncommon show of affection. "What is it, *Mamère?*"

"Somet'ing terrible, I be afeard." Her hand shook as she ripped the envelope open and stared down at the typewritten sheets.

Lucie stared at her grandmother's face, her light mocha skin blanching in the light from the porch. The paper slipped from her fingers, fluttering to the floor. "It can no be." The woman aged ten years in that one moment, her face graying, the wrinkles deepening in her care-lined face. "It can no be."

Her heart hammering in her chest, Lucie snatched the

papers from the floor, blinking back tears as she read the legal document.

A sob rose in her throat, and she fought to swallow past it.

"What is it, Lucie?" Lisa snatched for the letter.

"Talk about being up to our ears in hungry alligators," Lucie whispered. "It's a foreclosure notice on the house."

***

"Whaddya gotta do to get a beer around here?" A mountain of a redneck slammed a meaty fist onto the table behind Lucie.

The loud smack made her jump. "Keep your shirt on, LeRoy. I'll be with you in a minute," she shouted over her shoulder. To the ladies at the table she was waiting on, she said, "I've had it. I'm tired of this bar, tired of the bugs and alligators, and tired to death of Bayou Miste." More than anything, she was tired of living from paycheck to paycheck, worrying about money and the possibility of losing everything, including the roof over her head.

The foreclosure notice sealed the deal. She had to do something and do it soon.

"Girlfriend, you want some cheese with that whine?" Alexandra Belle Boyette beckoned with her fingers. "Gimme that beer."

Lucie balanced the heavy tray in one hand and, with the other, set longnecks on the table in front of her two best friends. "Really. No matter how hard I try, I can't make enough money here to pay the bills, much less start fresh somewhere else."

"Good! We don't want you to leave." Calliope Ostelet sipped her beer and then ran her tongue across her lips. "Ummm. Nothing like a tall, dark one to whet the appetite."

Lucie glanced around the Raccoon Saloon. Mounted and stuffed raccoons grinned down at her from shelves lining the bar's faded wooden walls. If she never saw another raccoon again, that would be just fine with her.

She sighed. "I've been wasting my time. There's nothing for me here." As soon as the words left her mouth a pang of guilt followed, pinching her heart. Her sister, grandmother, and the best friends a girl could ever hope to find were in Bayou Miste. But the burden of providing for her little family weighed heavily on her. Lisa was too much like their mother to help. She drifted from dead-end job to dead-end job, rarely contributing to the family coffers. *Mamère*'s income consisted of barter and trade for her services as a Voodoo queen, but rarely did she get paid in cold, hard cash. "No offense, but you know what I mean."

Alex's dark brows dipped together. "You say you have nothing to keep you here. Do you mean nothing or no one?"

With a shrug, she loaded the empty bottles onto her tray. "Same thing."

"You know what your problem is?" Alex set her beer on the table. "You haven't had a decent date since my brother left. Admit it."

Warmth stole up Lucie's neck, and she thanked the poor lighting for disguising the color in her cheeks. "I haven't had a decent date in Bayou Miste, period."

"Hey, Lucie, you gonna flap yer jaw all night? I've been waiting for ten minutes for one lousy beer. You can forget any tip."

She swung around and glared at the man, the empty bottles on her tray teetering dangerously. "LeRoy, you never tip, so what's the difference?"

"Well, if I did, I sure wouldn't leave *you* one." He returned her drop-dead look with one of his own, drumming his stogie-sized fingers on the table.

Lucie raised an eyebrow at Alex and Calliope. "See what I have to choose from?"

"Oh, come on," Alex said. "LeRoy's married. Besides, he isn't the only man in Bayou Miste."

"No, but the rest are just like him—loud, obnoxious, and ugly enough to make a swamp gator look good to me." Lucie lifted a mug of half-foam, half-beer from her tray, walked over to LeRoy's table, and slammed it down hard enough that the foam slopped over the side. "Here's your beer. Now quit yer moanin'."

"I'd rather be moanin' with you beneath me, sweet thang." He leered at her.

"In your dreams, LeRoy." Lucie turned her back, content —well, maybe content was stretching it—to ignore his rude invitation. As if!

A sharp pain zinged her right butt cheek.

"Ouch!" Adrenaline shot through her veins and she spun, fists balled, ready to take on the tank of a louse. "Tell me you didn't just pinch my ass, you bottom-dwelling alligator-turd."

"Lucie, don't lower yourself to his level," Alex warned. "Breathe deeply. Inhale, exhale."

Through a blur of red, Lucie heard her friend's calming words. She inhaled, then blew steam out her nose, repeatedly. When she could see straight, she forced words through her tight lips. "Don't...*ever*...do that again."

"Ah, sweet thang, face it." LeRoy spread his arms wide. "You want me."

"The man really doesn't know when to shut up," Lucie seethed.

"LeRoy, stuff a sock in it." Alex stood, positioning herself between the two, providing a barrier neither dared cross. "Lucie, Jean wants you at the bar. I suggest you go before you do something you'll regret."

She stood her ground. "He deserves to be taught a lesson."

"Be real," Alex said. "He weighs three times what you do."

"Move, Alex." LeRoy licked his lips and rubbed his hands together. "Me and Lucie's gonna have us a little rumble."

But Alex didn't budge. "Go on, Lucie. Jean's waiting."

She glanced from Alex to LeRoy. The idiot was practically drooling, wanting her to respond to his taunts. And she wanted to, with all the bottled anger and disappointment she'd been collecting for over seven years. But Leroy wasn't the problem. "You're right, Alex. He isn't worth the trouble." She turned an icy glare at him. "I'll let you slide this time. But don't touch me again. Or else!"

"Ooooo, I'm scared." LeRoy's laugh implied that he was anything but. "Or else what? You'll give me a lap dance?"

"I'll kick your butt!" She lunged forward. "Then I'll serve your balls as shooters to Mo's alligator."

Alex caught her in a clothesline snag around her shoulders. "Don't go there. LeRoy isn't worth it."

A couple deep breaths, followed by a slow count to thirty, cooled Lucie's temper, and she actually laughed. "Alex, you take all the fun out of waiting tables, do you know that?"

"You gonna be all right?" Alex peered into her eyes.

She still wanted to flatten the bag of hot air, but she had tables to wait and plans to make. With a parting glare at LeRoy, she got back to work.

While she distributed alcohol and snacks throughout the crowded room, worry built into an angry itch, simmering below the surface. What the hell was she still doing in this dead-end town? And how the hell was she going to earn enough money to pay off the mortgage and get the hell out?

Hard work hadn't gotten her anywhere. The factory wasn't hiring and tips were getting more scarce with the economic downturn. She'd have to resort to something she had never considered in her past. Something drastic, life-changing. Something she would never in a million years have considered if things weren't as bad as they were now.

When she'd satisfied her customers for the moment, she returned to Alex and Calliope to pick up where she'd left off. "Okay. I've made a decision. If I can't work my way out of this two-bit town, I'll have to bite the bullet and resort to a little of the V-word."

"V-word?" Calliope's pretty brow wrinkled.

Alex hissed, "Voodoo, dummy!"

"Cool! I love Voodoo." Calliope drank long and deep from her bottle of beer, apparently unconcerned by her friend's rash declaration.

"Maybe Gran LeBieu's Voodoo, but not..." Alex gave Lucie a sheepish grin. "Sorry, honey, but your brand of Voodoo never seems to work out just right. I don't think it's a good idea."

She flung out her hands. "I gotta do something soon, or I'll explode." And *Mamère* would lose the only real home she's ever known.

"Yeah, but..." Alex pinned Lucie with an intense stare. "We've seen your...uh...Voodoo before. You're likely to turn us all into two-headed toads. You may be willing to risk having toads for friends, but I'm not keen on eating flies the rest of my life."

Calliope snorted beer through her nostrils, slammed the bottle back to the table, and choked, her eyes filling with tears. With a big gulp, she managed to gasp and then dissolve into a fit of the giggles. "I've got to agree with Alex on this one. I don't want to end up being a frog like Craig Thibodeaux. Can you imagine hopping around Bayou Miste? If he and Elaine hadn't fallen in love, poor Craig would have been a frog for life. Talk about your wicked Voodoo spell."

Alex reached across the table and pinched Calliope's arm.

"Ouch!" Calliope rubbed the spot, a frown denting her brow. "Why'd you go and do that?"

"Lucie didn't cast that spell," Alex said. "Madame LeBieu did. And she knew what the hell she was doing."

"Oh, yeah." Calliope rubbed her side and nodded across the crowded bar at a couple sitting in the far corner, their heads together and holding hands. "He seems to be just fine now."

"That's exactly my point. Madame LeBieu's the Voodoo queen for a reason. Not so, our Lucie. No offense."

"Alex is right." Calliope smiled at Lucie and patted her arm. "Last time you tried to turn Maurice's alligator into a dog, you only gave the poor beast a bad case of puppy love. T-Rex hasn't been the same since."

She winced. Part of the problem had been and would always be that she really hadn't believed in Voodoo, her own at least, and still wasn't quite sure it would really work. But desperate times and all that...

"Yeah, and Maurice's grandmother has been beside herself trying to keep T-Rex from eating her poodle." Alex squeezed Lucie's hand. "You'd be crazy to try it."

Calliope shook her head. "Poor FeFe."

"FeFe, Schme-fe." She stomped her foot. "That was only one spell gone wacky. Not all of them go wrong."

"Lucie, be serious." Alex set her lips into a straight line.

"Don't give me that look," Lucie warned. "I'm not one of your little brothers or sisters."

"Then don't act like one." Alex crossed her arms over her chest. "Lucie, you can't do it."

Fighting the urge to stomp her foot again, she couldn't stop her words. "I can, and I will."

"Hey, didn't I ask for oyster shooters with my beer?" LeRoy scraped his chair back. "I'm not paying for this beer until I get my shooters."

In unison, all three women yelled at the man. "Shut up!"

"Lucie!" Bartender and owner of the Raccoon Saloon,

Jean Dupree, as wide as he was tall and as bald as a cypress knee, slung a towel over his shoulder, grabbed a mug from below the counter, and filled it from the tap. "Quit pissin' off de customers and get back to work." He smacked the heavy drink on the counter, sloshing beer over the side.

She marched back to the bar. "I got the tables covered. LeRoy's just bein' his usual jerk self."

"Well, you missed a table." Jean nodded to a stranger dressed in a leather jacket, seated as far away from the music as possible. "If you have time in yer busy social calendar, could you deliver dis beer to dat table?"

"I don't know, Jean, we swamp debutantes have appearances to keep up." She loaded the heavy mug onto a tray and swung around. "I can't be associating with the riffraff."

"Darlin', we only serve riffraff at de Raccoon Saloon." Jean chuckled behind her. "And I wouldn't be havin' it any other way."

"Someday real soon I'm gonna blow this town and leave you and your precious riffraff behind." As the last word left her mouth, she set the beer on the stranger's table and turned in time to see Eric Littington enter the bar alone.

Lucie's eyes narrowed like a hawk's as it homed in on its prey. Eric Littington, the blond-haired, blue-eyed attorney and son of the richest man in the parish. He and his family had enough money to pay off hundreds of mortgages like *Mamère* LeBieu's. *And* he was running for the U.S. House of Representatives—a position that would take him away from Bayou Miste, away from the parish, and away from Louisiana altogether.

Bingo.

She'd just found her ticket out of all her troubles.

"Oh, and Lucie?" Jean said behind her. "Before you blow town, don't be forgettin' ta give dese shooters to de jerk."

After a long assessing look at her target, she worked her

way back to the bar and piled the plate of oyster shooters onto her tray. With growing determination, she lifted the load onto her shoulder and wove her way back toward LeRoy. And just in case Eric should notice, she emphasized the sway of her hips. Wolf calls and shouts followed her through the crowded room.

"Hey, Lucie! If I had a swing like that, I'd put it in my front yard!"

How original. Lucie snorted, but kept a smile plastered to her face. Same old Raccoon Saloon, same old patrons.

Except one.

To hell with financial worries and to hell with this town. I'm getting out.

Laissez les bon temps rouler. Let the good times roll!

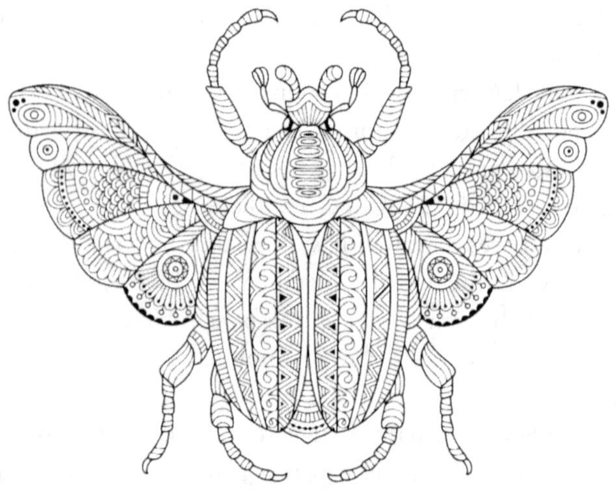

Chapter Two

Benjamin Franklin Boyette noticed her the moment he slipped into the Raccoon Saloon. That sexy way her midnight-black hair hung down her back to brush across her butt, and the way her hips swayed, made her unforgettable. Damn, how in hell had she gotten even more beautiful in the past seven years?

Ben groaned inwardly. This assignment would be a lot harder than he'd anticipated with Lucie LeBieu around. As much as he'd tried, he hadn't been able to shake her from his mind. And wouldn't, short of a strong dose of Madame LeBieu's Voodoo. Lucie was not an easy woman to forget—all five-foot-three inches of Louisiana hot sauce.

As if in auto-drive, his jeans tightened to the point he had to readjust before he could take another step. Had he known the luscious Lucie would be there, he'd have ignored Alex's advice and suggested another meeting place to conduct his business. He should never have trusted his sister. She'd always had the crazy idea that he and Lucie would end up together.

Didn't she realize that Lucie had been the one to dump *him* seven years ago? When he'd gotten the letter of acceptance from the Louisiana Police Academy, he'd crumbled the paper and tossed it in the trash, telling himself he didn't care anymore. Lucie had agreed to marry him and he was determined to stay in Bayou Miste and spend the rest of his life working to make her happy.

The next day, the world crashed in around his ears when Lucie had given his ring back and said she'd reconsidered. When he'd argued with her, she'd told him flat-out he wasn't good enough for her. She wanted a man who could take care of her, provide for her every need.

He had been willing to try, but apparently trying wasn't enough.

He'd been out of his mind, hurt and angry, saying things he didn't mean. Later, when he'd had time to cool down, he wished he could take back some of those awful things he'd said. But he'd realized the futility. Lucie hadn't wanted him.

His chest tightened at the memory. He'd fallen hard when he'd fallen for Lucie. But he'd had seven years to get over her. Now he was immune to her brand of infection.

That's what he kept telling himself, anyway. Somehow the idea never stuck.

Damned woman. She shouldn't have that kind of hold on him anymore. Not after all this time. Anger surged through him as, with a little more effort than he cared to admit, he pried his gaze from Lucie's swaying hips. Here on business, he didn't have time to reminisce about a flame blown out.

As planned, he'd arrived five minutes after Eric Littington, hoping to give their get-together a look of coincidence versus the planned meeting that it was. He scanned the interior of the bar. Despite being gone for seven years, he recognized just about everyone there. Except the woman in the corner with Craig Thibodeaux and the man in the leather jacket hunkered down in a seat in the shadows by the rear exit. He made a mental note to check out the strange woman and the leather-clad man.

Eventually, his gaze landed on the man he was looking for. Eric smiled as if seeing him for the first time in years, and waved a beckoning hand.

Ben covered the distance to the dark corner in a few easy strides. When he reached the table, he hid a grin.

If Eric planned to blend in at the bar, he'd missed the boat entirely. His khaki slacks and polo shirt were too sharp of a contrast to the standard jeans and T-shirts the rest of the crowd wore. Somehow, khaki didn't go with zydeco music and oyster shooters.

When they'd been growing up in Bayou Miste, Eric had already stuck out among the other children running barefoot through the bayous. He'd had the best of everything, while Ben had to be satisfied with secondhand clothes and toys. Now Ben shook his head, amazed at how the rich kid and the shrimper's son had become the best of friends. As a teenager he'd envied Eric, until he'd realized that no matter how much Eric had, he'd always been lonely in the small community, isolated by his father's wealth.

Ben wouldn't have traded places with Eric for all the oil money in the swamp. Even with the constant noise and confusion in the cramped four-bedroom house he'd shared with his brothers and sisters, Ben loved his family and had felt sorry for Eric being an only child.

He'd befriended the privileged teen and invited him home to dinner on more than one occasion. He could still picture Eric's face the first time he'd entered the Boyette house. The poor little rich kid must have felt like he was at Mardi Gras, with all the Boyette children gathered around the table.

"Hey, Ben." Eric stood and extended a hand. "Heard you moved back from Baton Rouge." He winked.

"Eric." Ben grabbed the extended hand and pulled him into a hug, like he was family. "It's good to see you." He scooted a chair up to the table opposite Eric, his detective instincts kicking into gear. He studied the fine lines around the other man's eyes. "So what's up?"

His boss had briefed him on the case before he left the Special Criminal Investigation Unit in Baton Rouge, but he wanted to hear the story from Eric himself.

His friend leaned closer. "I need you to be on the lookout for anyone trying to sabotage my campaign for Congress."

"Why? I thought that's how the game's played."

Out of the corner of his eye, Ben saw a flash of long black hair. Lucie bent to pick up a napkin off the floor and all his attention zeroed in on the frayed hem of her shorter-than-short skirt.

He gulped. She made it hard to concentrate.

He returned his attention to his friend. "Eric, you're in politics. You should expect some problems with your campaign."

"I understand that, but someone broke into my house in Baton Rouge and tapped all my phone lines. Not to mention, someone's been stalking me for the past month. No attempts on my life. But I'd like to know who it is, who hired him and why."

"And let me guess. You found that hard to figure out in a big city? Too many people, too many possibilities," Ben finished for him.

"Yeah," Eric said. "I guess that's why your boss thought it would be better if we did this here in Bayou Miste, where you know all the locals. We'll have a better chance of finding the guy if he follows me here."

With every fiber of his being on Lucie-alert, Ben fought the urge to glance around the bar again, knowing it would be for her, not potential suspects, no matter what he told himself.

Instead, he concentrated on his friend. "So, what's your excuse for being here when you should be out campaigning?"

"I'm here on the pretext of a quasi-vacation with my parents for the next two weeks. My campaign manager is setting up a few public speaking engagements while I'm home, complete with television coverage to keep me in the public eye."

"What about the environmental groups? Aren't you afraid they'll raise a ruckus after the chemical dumping stink in these parts?"

Eric pushed a hand through his blond hair. "My father promised to pay for the cleanup. There might be a protest or two, but I don't expect it to be major. The community knew it wasn't totally the fault of Littington Enterprises."

"Maybe so, but the tendency is for the media to make an example of the big industries." Without realizing he'd been looking, Ben spied Lucie and all his attention shifted to her. And she was one hell of a distraction with her thick, dark curls hanging down to her waist and the neckline of her T-shirt dipping low, exposing the full, rounded tops of her breasts—

"The only people who are supposed to know you're here on police work are my father and me." Eric's voice pulled Ben back to the business at hand.

"Beautiful." Ben replied automatically. But his response could just as well have been a commentary on Lucie's breasts or her rounded bottom. A derriere he'd known all too well, a lifetime ago.

"But what about you?" Eric asked. "Won't it seem coincidental that you and I showed up at the same time?"

Lucie swatted a customer's hand when he got too friendly. Just like her to look good enough to eat, but play hard to get.

Get back to business, Ben. She's not interested. Nor are you. Now what was Eric saying? *Oh yeah.* "I've got that covered." Ben grinned. "I applied for a job with Bug Tugsley Extermination. He owed me a favor."

"Do you think the townspeople will buy the story that you're back to start over as a bug exterminator after being a state police detective?" Eric leaned across the table, his voice low enough not to carry to casual eavesdroppers but loud enough to be heard over the music.

"Huh?" He purposely avoided looking at Lucie and forced himself to focus on Eric. "Oh, yeah. All I have to do is tell a few folks that I'd had enough with playing cops and robbers and wanted to get back to family." Which was true in a way. He needed a break from Baton Rouge. After his partner's death, he'd been driving himself too hard. "Word will spread through the grapevine. And what's not to believe? Everyone in Bayou Miste knows the importance we Boyettes place on family."

Then why had it been years since he'd been home?

His gaze drifted to the reason. Lucie.

"That they do." A wistful smile lifted Eric's lips. "Whatever you have to tell them. I just don't want the public to know that you're here to help me. I don't want the other candidates, including the incumbent Richard Gasson, to think I'm getting paranoid. And I don't want whoever's doing this to me to know I'm actively pursuing them."

Ben focused on his friend. "You can count on me."

"Thanks." Eric's gaze swept around the room. "It's good to be back."

"Uh-huh." Coming home had been a bittersweet ordeal. His mother had cried, along with half of his sisters. "Yeah, it's good to be home." He allowed himself another glance around, his gaze zeroing in on the dark-haired Cajun beauty.

With her head cocked at a haughty angle, Lucie swayed through the tables, stopping along the way to drop off full drinks and load the empties. When she reached LeRoy Le Due's table, the man openly leered.

Ben's hackles rose. From what his mother had told him, LeRoy was a married man now. He had no business eyeing Lucie like that.

"Got me my shooters?" LeRoy's voice rose above the crowd and the zydeco band, his gaze on her breasts, not his order of oyster shooters.

Lucie set the plate on his table and shifted the big tray from her shoulder to directly in front of her, two full mugs blocking LeRoy's view of her chest. "Here are your oysters. Now maybe you can be quiet and behave yourself."

"I got anything but behavin' on my mind." The drunkard lunged and grabbed Lucie around the waist.

Thrown off-balance, Lucie's tray tipped. The two full mugs and all the empty bottles slid off, landing with a loud crash on the hardwood floor, splattering beer and shattering glass in a million directions.

But that didn't slow LeRoy down. He hauled Lucie into his lap and ran his pork chop hands over her body.

Lucie struggled to keep the octopus's hands at bay. "Let. Go. Of. Me."

Ben was out of his chair and pushing his way across the crowded room before he could think through his reaction. Adrenaline pumped through his veins, lending fuel to his anger.

"That's it! That tops the charts," Lucie shouted. She breathed deeply several times, but unfortunately the rise and fall of her chest only incited more fondling by the hulking fool. "Your wife doesn't deserve this, LeRoy. Someone's gotta teach you a little respect."

Ben cringed. He'd never known Lucie to back down from a fight, even when the odds were stacked so heavily against her.

Unable to break loose from his roving hands, Lucie dove for the floor, toppling him from his chair.

His grip eased long enough for her to scramble free and shake the beer off her hands.

A high-pitched screech pierced the air behind Ben. He turned in time to avoid being trampled by a crazed woman leaping from table to table to get to the center of the fray. Ben recognized her as Eunice, LeRoy's wife.

Oh, boy. The show was about to get even rowdier. He'd better snag Lucie before Eunice did.

While he shouldered his way through the amassing crowd of betting Cajuns, he lost sight of Lucie for a moment.

Eunice screeched again, followed by what he could only guess was Lucie's yelp.

By the time he managed to get through, Eunice was on Lucie's back, her arm crooked around the Cajun beauty's neck, squeezing the breath out of her until Lucie's face had turned a bright shade of blueberry.

"Stay away from my man, you two-bit hussy! I married him, fair and square, and you got no bidness jumpin' his bones."

"But—" Lucie wheezed around the wiry forearm clutching her throat.

"No buts! I didn't give up the best years of my life with this bastard for no Cajun swamp princess to steal him away in a barroom."

"Now, ladies. I'm sure there's been some misunderstanding." Ben reached over, hooked Eunice by her bony hips and pulled.

Eunice refused to relinquish her hold on Lucie's neck.

Lucie would pass out soon if the other woman didn't let her breathe. She was already going from blue to an alarming shade of purple.

As a cop, Ben had been called out to break up fights every

bit as ugly as this one, but not ones involving Lucie. If he didn't do something quick, Eunice could kill her.

He applied his best negotiating voice, honed from years of responding to domestic violence incidents. "Eunice, let go of Lucie. She doesn't want to take LeRoy away from you."

For a moment, the woman's arm loosened.

He seized the opportunity to lift her off Lucie. Before he could set Eunice to the side, she grabbed onto Lucie's hair and yanked her along with her. "This bayou bimbo has got to learn she can't have someone else's husband."

Ben loosened his hold on Eunice to ease the strain on Lucie's hair roots. But she wrapped her legs around Lucie's waist and rode her back, holding onto the hank of hair for all she was worth. "You bitch! I should have known better than to let my man come to this shameful bar with the likes of you workin' here."

"He came on to me," Lucie rasped. "And I'm not a bimbo."

"My LeRoy wouldn't do anything wrong when he's got a wife sittin' at home, wouldja, sweet thang?"

"No, ma'am. I surely wouldn't." LeRoy gasped beneath the weight of the two women.

"So that leaves you lying like the whore you are." Eunice pulled tighter until Ben thought Lucie's hair would fly out in hunks.

"Ladies, this is no way to settle an argument." He tried to pry Eunice's fingers out of Lucie's hair and nearly got an elbow to the groin.

LeRoy scrambled away from the fighting pair and lurched to his feet. He rubbed at his crotch, a grin spreading across his face. "*Whoo-weeee!* Let the good times roll! My money's on you, honey cakes." He pulled out his wallet and started counting bills.

Ben grabbed LeRoy and jerked his arm behind his back,

high up between his shoulder blades. "Call her off or I'll tell her the truth."

The smile slipped down the bully's face and then back up again. "Who's she gonna believe, her husband or one of Lucie's ex-squeezes?"

He tightened his hold until sweat popped out on LeRoy's face. "Call her off or I'll do worse than Lucie did to you." Ben lowered his voice to be sure LeRoy got his message. He remembered LeRoy's bullying as a kid, but as an adult, Ben didn't have the time or patience to put up with it.

"Okay, okay," the bigger man squealed.

Ben let up on the pressure.

"Let her go, Eunice," LeRoy said. "She ain't worth it."

Her breath coming in short gasps, Eunice glanced up from beneath Lucie. "You sure? I got her right where I want her."

Lucie reared up, her temples straining against Eunice's hold on her hair. She slammed Eunice back against the floor. "Let me go, you moron! You should be kickin' your husband's butt, not mine."

LeRoy chuckled. "Ain't never seen her so mad. Kinda like it."

With a jerk of his arm, Ben reminded the larger man who was in charge.

"Lighten up, will ya?" LeRoy squirmed against the force on his wrist. "Eunice, let the swamp princess go. You and me got better thangs ta do."

With one last tug, Eunice released Lucie's hair, shoved her to the side, and stood up as if fighting in a bar were an everyday occurrence for her. "Come on, sweetie. Supper's ready and waitin'."

Ben released his hold on LeRoy.

The hulking man wrapped a thick stump of an arm

around Eunice's skinny shoulders and turned her toward the door. "Didja make my favorite?"

Eunice smiled up at him, dwarfed by his bulk. "I sure did. Mudbugs and rice. I caught 'em fresh today in that ditch alongside the road to our place."

With the fight over, the bar patrons drifted back to their beer, some counting out bills to pay up on their bets. Yup, it was a typical night at the Raccoon Saloon. Ben felt more at home by the minute.

He bent to where Lucie pushed to her hands and knees in a puddle of beer. The color in her cheeks high, she was still so pretty she made his chest hurt. He steeled himself against the onslaught of unwanted emotions and pulled her up into his arms. "Hey, Lucie."

"Ben?" Lucie blinked, her eyes widening, her face blanching as her fingers curled into his shirt. "You came back," she whispered, then flung her arms around his neck.

He held her close, the scent of her shampoo wrapping around him. This was what he'd been missing in his life. This woman and the feel of her body against his. But it was all an illusion, which would end when Lucie got her bearings. Ben steeled his heart against further pain and forced a chuckle, "Yeah, babe, I'm back, and I can see not much has changed around here. You're still giving the men of Bayou Miste hell."

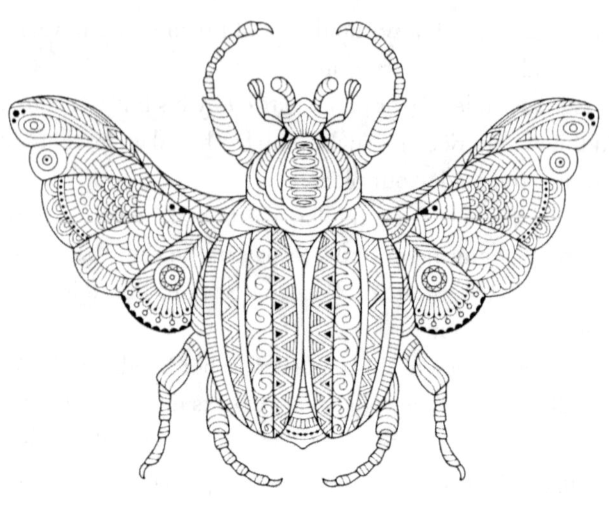

Chapter Three

Desperate times called for desperate measures.

Lucie LeBieu swallowed the wad of guilt in her throat and stretched up on her tiptoes. When her fingers wrapped around the bottle marked "Tailless Raccoon Spit," she dragged it from the shelf of her grandmother's pantry.

"Need help in there?" Alex called out from the kitchen.

"No. I can handle this myself." *Yeah. Sure.* Just like she handled her love life. And everyone in Bayou Miste knew *that* was nonexistent. But if she was caught with her hand in the proverbial cookie jar, she didn't want her two friends to catch any of the old woman's wrath.

Lucie's grandmother wasn't the normal, run-of-the-mill grandmotherly type. Oh, she had in her kitchen the usual flour, sugar, and everything necessary for a scrumptious batch of chocolate chip cookies, or even yummier Louisiana gumbo. But it didn't stop there—she had many more mysteries stashed away in her cupboards. Tailless Raccoon Spit was only one of the strangely labeled containers Lucie found as she riffled through the pantry.

Her grandmother wasn't an escapee from a mental institution, or a homeopathic healer, per se, although healing did make up the majority of her work. She was none other than the infamous bayou Voodoo queen, Madame LeBieu. And if she knew what Lucie was up to, she'd likely stir up a retribution potion that would give her granddaughter a wicked weeklong itch or something even more dreadful.

But Lucie was madder than a crab in a fishnet, and she wasn't going to let her grandmother's reputation scare her out of doing what she had to do. And her anger was directed toward one red-hot sexy Cajun. "Of all the people to turn up at the Raccoon Saloon, why did it have to be Benjamin Franklin Boyette? Why now? And the rat bastard pretty much accused me of starting that fight with LeRoy." She stomped in and out of the little pantry.

Lucie's friend Calliope opened the container on the counter and dipped a finger into a powdery concoction. "Lucie, you know Madame LeBieu would have a hissy fit if she knew you were messin' with her stash of magic ingredients."

"Stay out of that, Calliope Ostelet." Alex, the more level-headed of her two friends, swatted at Calliope's hand. "It's liable to turn your skin purple or give you boils."

Lucie ignored the two and walked back into the storage room.

Alex followed, leaning into the doorway to sniff. "What's she got in there, anyway?"

"None of your business, Alexandra Belle Boyette." Lucie emphasized the "Boyette" as if it were a nasty-tasting word. As she pushed past Alex, she redirected her guilt and anger toward her friend. She knew she shouldn't meddle in *Mamère* LeBieu's magic. But now that a foreclosure notice had been served, and worse, Ben was back in town, she had no other choice. "I shouldn't even be talking to you." She stopped on her third trip back to the butcher block in the middle of the cluttered kitchen. "You could have told me *big brother* was back."

A rosy red blush flooded Alex's cheeks. "I would have, but you were too busy waiting tables at the saloon for me to break it to you."

Lucie smacked a tin container on the counter. "Bull."

Alex sighed. "Okay, so I didn't tell you. Shoot, it has been a long time since you'd seen my brother, I wasn't sure how you still felt about him."

"I don't have *any* feelings for him." She marched back to the pantry. "None at all." Then why the hell was there moisture in her eyes, and why was her chest—and strategic points farther south—so tight and achy? She held on to her anger like a shield, praying she didn't break down in front of her friends.

She glanced around the interior of the pantry, blinking to avoid letting a single tear slip down her face. Must be all the potent herbs and cayenne pepper her grandmother kept for cooking up food and the occasional spell. Nope, she wasn't crying over that rat Ben.

"You all right in there?" Calliope peeked into to the dimly lit room.

"I'm fine. I just can't seem to find what I'm lookin' for." *Story of her life.* No matter how hard she tried, she couldn't seem to find her place in Bayou Miste. Especially since Ben left.

But now he was back. After seven long freakin' years! All the more reason to get out. *Fast.*

She spied the last canister she needed and grabbed it. Back in the kitchen, she arranged the various containers in order of the instructions she'd found in the wood-bound book marked "Madame LeBieu's Special Recipes." With the cookbook propped on a stand, she tugged a massive cast-iron stockpot from a bottom cabinet and set it on the propane-powered stove.

Alex's eyes widened and her face paled. "Ah jeez, you weren't kidding, were you? You really are going to use magic. Clear the parish!"

Lucie glared at her former friend.

"Cut the crap, Alex." Her lips pressed together, she leaned over to read the recipe, then snatched up the first container and a measuring cup.

Alex blocked her way to the stove. "Lucie, don't do it. I beg of you."

"Move, Alex."

"Madame LeBieu will be furious," Alex argued.

"Where is she, anyway?" Calliope's gaze darted around the room as if expecting the woman to appear out of thin air. "And where's Lisa?"

"Lisa went to New Orleans and *Mamère* took a poultice to Pete Pasquale on the other side of Bayou Black. He must have been poaching gators, because he got himself bit. She won't be back for half the afternoon." Lucie stared at Alex. "She'll never know I was in her pantry, if you'll move out of my way and let me get on with it."

"Any chance of Lisa dropping in?" Calliope asked.

She cringed. Her twin sister was the last person who needed to know she was attempting magic. As far as twins went, Lucie and Lisa shared looks, but nothing else. Lisa was the yin to her yang, the dark to her light. Her sister was wild, through and through. "No. She left for New Orleans this morning to visit a friend. Thank God."

"Good thing. Maybe she'll stay." With a short, harrumphing snort, Alex stepped around the butcher block and pulled up a stool. "I still think it's wrong, and I don't know what I'm doing here watching, but if this is the way you want to deal with your life, it's your funeral."

"Funeral?" Lucie wanted to laugh at how she'd shied away from the love spell her grandmother had tried to hex her with. And here she was cookin' up one of her own. If they weren't in danger of losing her home, or there was any other way to get rich quick in Bayou Miste, she'd have jumped on it. Snagging Eric Littington was her only hope of saving her grandmother's home and getting herself out of the swamp. "A little love potion isn't that big of a deal."

Alex snorted. "That's what you always say."

"Look, if you're going to watch, at least keep it quiet." Lucie ran her finger down the page, checking off her list of ingredients. "These spells have to be mixed with the appropriate words as well as ingredients, and if someone else talks, I might get things confused."

"We'll be quiet, *right* Calliope?" Alex shot a warning glare across at the redhead.

"My lips are sealed." Calliope drew an imaginary zipper across her lips and grinned, spoiling the effect.

Lucie ignored her friends and concentrated on the recipe book, her stomach knotting automatically. She recalled the last few times she'd tried *Mamère* LeBieu's magic, only to goof up every spell. She couldn't help it if she'd mistaken the Voodoo queen's canister of whole-wheat flour for ground cypress knees. So what if Mo's alligator was in love with Granny Saulnier's poodle? Worse things could happen.

But not today. She was determined to make good her escape from ruin, Bayou Miste, and Benjamin Franklin Boyette.

Ah hell, had she really added *Ben* on to the end of that thought? What did she have to worry about with Ben? Their relationship was no longer an issue—hadn't been for seven long years. A lump rose in her throat and she swallowed determinedly.

Eric was her ticket out of all her troubles and the swamp—

not Ben. Besides, Alex had mentioned that Ben was home for good. If that was the case, Lucie had no intention of staying in the bayous. What for?

Because Ben was home, a niggling voice taunted her.

With a vicious twist, Lucie wrapped her thick hair high on the back of her head and clamped it in place to keep it out of the way while she cooked up her future.

"I feel like there should be a drum roll or something." Calliope gave a little giggle. "Well? Isn't every Voodoo spell supposed to be accompanied by drums?"

Alex and Lucie glared at Calliope until she flushed and raised her hands in surrender. "Okay, okay. I won't say another word."

"Good, because I want everything to be perfect for this spell. My future with B—*Eric* depends on it." Her face warmed and she leaned over the potion book, hoping Alex hadn't heard her slip up.

Alex's eyes widened. "Are you sure *Eric's* the guy for you, sweetie?"

Lucie arched her brows at her dark-haired friend. "Let me see...Eric's the son of the richest man in the parish, not to mention he's a United States congressional candidate and the acclaimed golden boy of Louisiana politics. And from what I remember, he was always nice and might have been sweet on me at one time." She tapped a finger to her chin and stared at the ceiling before adding, "Yup, I think he's the right man to get us out of financial ruin and get me out of the swamps." Her attention returned to the book. "Now, if you don't mind, I'd like to cook up a love spell, and you're interrupting."

"Okay. Whatever." Alex shook her head. "Although I didn't hear anything about love in there. Kind of an important ingredient in a marriage, if you ask me."

After a deep breath drawn in through her clenched teeth, Lucie said, "In case you missed it, I did say 'love.' That's why

I'm here. Hel-*lo*? Love spell? Voodoo? Jeez. I'm surrounded by amateurs."

"You don't have to be so grumpy," Alex grumbled.

Her face warmed again. Alex was right. She'd been a flaming bitch since she'd run into Ben at the Raccoon Saloon. And she wasn't normally like this. Only where Ben was concerned. With a weak smile at her friend, she muttered a not-so-very-contrite, "Sorry."

"Apology accepted."

Her heart welled with a flood of emotion for her two friends. But she didn't have time for group hugs and a round of "Kumbaya." She had some fancy cooking to do. She turned back to the cookbook. "Start with stump water, dark as night. Two cups of the stuff will be just right."

From the floor, she lifted the brown glass jug marked "Stump Water" and poured it into a measuring cup until the liquid line met the two-cup mark.

"Jeez, that stuff smells like—" Calliope pinched her nostrils together and gagged.

"Stump water?" Lucie finished, then clamped her hand to her mouth. "Shoot, Calliope, you weren't supposed to say anything during the ingredient-mixing."

With hunched shoulders, Calliope pressed her hand to her lips and muttered through her fingers. "Sorry. It won't happen again."

Lucie rolled her eyes toward the ceiling. *As if!* Calliope couldn't shut up for more than thirty seconds at a stretch. She'd likely explode if she did.

Cup in hand, Lucie dumped the contents into the cast-iron stockpot, the smell triggering her own gag reflex. Back at the book, she read the next line out loud. "With the fire set low, add to the soup, a quarter teaspoon of ground alligator tooth."

Lucie twisted the knob on the stove and the acrid scent of

propane filled the air. Then, as she'd seen *Mamère* LeBieu do a thousand times, Lucie scraped a match against the rough wooden wall and the head burst into flame. After lighting the burner, she settled the pot over the fire.

Now for the next ingredient. She opened the brown jar marked alligator tooth. The odor from the jar reminded her of her last visit to the dentist—the pungent smell created when drill meets tooth assailed her nostrils. She shoved the measuring spoon inside, retrieving a quarter teaspoon, as the recipe called for.

Careful not to spill or sneeze, she dropped the powder into the water. "Then with a touch, ever so light, add a pair of crawfish eyeballs to sharpen love's sight."

"Ewwww!" Calliope squirmed and shuddered on her stool.

"Shh!" Alex jabbed her elbow into the redhead's rib cage.

A contrite-looking Calliope sat with her hand still over her mouth.

With a warning glower at her friend, Lucie moved on to the next item on the list. "Five drops of spit from a tailless raccoon will ensure the magic lasts until the ten thousandth moon." She unscrewed the cap off a small vial, and dripped five drops of raccoon spit into the stewpot.

Yuck. Some of the ingredients were really disgusting. How did her grandmother work with this stuff day after day?

"I wonder how Madame LeBieu got raccoon spit," Calliope said. "Suppose she bought it off the Internet? Or did she wrestle a tailless raccoon to the ground and knock the spit out of it?" A smile lit her face and she sat up straighter. "Maybe some of the stuffed coons in the Raccoon Saloon are from her spit-gathering."

Alex smothered a giggle.

An answering giggle leaped up in Lucie's throat, but she squelched it before it escaped. She really shouldn't encourage

Calliope's interruptions. Instead she sent a withering glance at the two seated women and moved on to the next instruction. "The fragrant blossom of the magnolia tree will enhance the romance, just wait, you'll see." Lucie opened a plastic bag filled with dried flower petals marked "Magnolia Blossoms." She dropped one petal into the pot.

Before Lucie could reseal the bag, Alex jumped up, grabbed it from Lucie and dumped the contents into the pot.

"Hey, the recipe only called for one petal, you just dumped four in there," she said.

"You're long overdue on romance." Alex hugged her and sat back on the stool.

Her vision blurred, Lucie had to blink several times and swallow the lump in her throat before she could go on with her work. God, she loved her friends. When she left Bayou Miste, she'd hate leaving them behind. But she needed a new start away from her past—especially from a past that included Ben. Straightening her shoulders, she got back to business.

"Two tablespoons of cayenne, to top it all off, as all Cajun cooking includes the stuff."

"Um, now you're making me hungry," Calliope whispered.

"Bring to a boil and then count to ten." The handwriting scrawled at the bottom of the page. Lucie had to squint to see the words "turn over" written in tiny letters. She flipped the sheet and read on.

"Turn off the heat and let the brew sit so the potion cools down a bit." As the liquid came to a boil, she counted aloud. "One, two, three, four, five."

Alex and Calliope chimed in, "Six, seven, eight, nine, ten!"

A quick twist extinguished the flame and Lucie fanned the potion, hoping to speed the process.

Alex leaned over the recipe book to read the next set of

instructions. "Says here to sprinkle the potion on the wings of a love bug."

"You mean those disgusting bugs that fly around piggy-backed, mating all the time?" Calliope asked.

Alex's lips twisted. "It says love bug. What else could it mean?"

Calliope jumped up from her stool. "I'll go outside and see what I can find. There are usually a bazillion of them making bug-gut glue all over my car."

Before Lucie could utter a word, Calliope rushed out the door. Just as well. Finding the bug would give her something productive to do while they waited for the potion to cool.

Alex bent over the recipe book. "You realize you have to turn this hexed bug loose in the same room with you and your intended target, don't you?"

"I do?" Lucie leaned over Alex's shoulder and read the scribbled words, then grimaced. "That'll be a trick to get me and Eric in a room all by ourselves."

"How are you going to manage that? Sneak into his bedroom at night? I understand they have a pretty impressive security system at the Littington mansion. I don't think you'll get by that."

"Don't worry, I'll think of something." *What*, she didn't know.

Calliope rushed back in, a frown marring her freckled forehead. "What's wrong with this place? Only last week there were hundreds, even thousands of the little creatures."

"What do you mean?"

Calliope grimaced. "No love bugs."

"No love bugs?" Alex and Lucie said in unison.

Lucie's heart sank into her shoes. "All this mixing and angsting for what? Nothing! A big fat goose egg. Great! Just great!"

Calliope held out her hand. "I did find a ladybug. I figure one flying bug is as good as the next. Can you use a ladybug?" Calliope stopped talking long enough to inhale. "Gag!" She clapped a hand over her nose. "That stuff really stinks."

"It's not the smell that counts. It's how well the potion works," Lucie held out her hand. "You couldn't find a single love bug? Jeez, I still have dead ones stuck all over the front of my 'Stang. Why is it you can find them when you don't want them, but as soon as you need one—"

"You can't find one," Alex finished. "Sounds like the story of *my* love life."

Calliope's brow furrowed. "You have guys stuck all over the front of your Jeep?"

"The way my mother keeps throwing them at me you'd think I'd be scrapin' them off my bumper." Alex leaned over the cookbook. "Does it *have* to be a love bug?"

"The recipe says, 'Sprinkle the brew on a love bug's wing and in a loud, sweet voice you must sing, "Fly little bug, fly high up above and make my lovebirds fall in love."'"

"Hey, I thought this was a love spell for people," Calliope said.

Lucie flipped the page back to read the title. "It says 'Love Spell.'"

Alex shrugged. "Whatever. You need a flying bug. All you have available is the blasted ladybug. What can it hurt?"

"Ah, jeez!" Lucie slammed the book shut. "I can see it happening already. Another Voodoo spell gone awry, courtesy of the misfit granddaughter of Madame LeBieu. This time, they might even give me the front page of the *Bayou Miste Herald*."

"Don't sweat it, Lucie." Alex slipped the ladybug out of Lucie's hand into her own. "Maybe the spell wasn't meant to be."

"Yeah." Calliope's face lit up with a huge grin. "And you can stay here in Bayou Miste with us."

With her two best friends, maybe. But top them with a dead-end job, a foreclosure hanging over her grandmother's head, and a nonexistent love life, no way. And to make matters worse, Ben Boyette had come home to stay. Lucie's heart sank into her empty belly like a lead fishing weight.

With the ladybug curled in her fingers, Alex headed for the door. "I'll just let this little guy go while you dump that mess down the sink."

Lucie's mind reviewed the options like a CD disc spinning round and round. *Marriage to a rich man or financial ruin.* Live in a mansion or out on the streets—or in this case, the swamps—of Bayou Miste. Marry Eric Littington and leave, or watch Ben Boyette parade his new girlfriends around town while she ate her heart out.

"Alex, stop!" she shouted.

Alex froze in midstride.

"Give me that damn bug." Her voice echoed in the silent room, calm and surprisingly firm.

Eyes wide, Alex slowly turned back toward her and held out her hand. "Are you sure you want to do this? Seems a bit cold-blooded of you to target poor, unsuspecting Eric with a spell."

A wall of guilt finally broke through her determination and threatened to overwhelm her. She'd never loved Eric. She'd liked him as a friend, but she'd never had any deep emotional attachment to him. Then again, her grandmother couldn't possibly live out on the streets or in the swamps without a roof over her head. Lisa wasn't a reliable source of income. It was up to Lucie to come up with a plan to save her grandmother's home and, so far, this was all she could come up with.

She drew in a deep breath past the lump rising in her

throat. "I know it sounds cold-blooded, but don't worry, I'll do right by Eric and make him a good wife. You'll see." Tears welled in her eyes as she thought of Ben married to someone else. "I have to do this for *Mamère*." And she couldn't stay in Bayou Miste, no matter what. "Alex, please. Give me the bug."

"It's your life, but don't be mad if we say 'we told you so.'" Alex uncurled her fingers, revealing the tiny red and black ladybug.

Lucie scraped the hard-shelled creature onto the wooden cutting board and settled a mason jar over it. Grasping a wooden spoon, she stirred the concoction on the stove one last time for good measure.

With her eyes pressed closed, she chanted to herself, "Please let this work. Please help me find love and happiness." Opening her eyes, she dipped the spoon into the odiferous mix, cupped her hand beneath it, and stepped back to the center island cutting board. Then she inhaled deeply and nodded at Alex. "Will you remove the glass jar?"

Her hand slow and steady, Alex reached out, her fingers hovering over the jar. "You don't have to go through with this, you know."

"Just lift the damned jar, please!" Lucie's arm shook and liquid spilled from the spoon into her hand.

The glass came up, exposing the harbinger of her freedom. The tiny ladybug opened its protective shell and flexed its wings.

Quickly, before the bug could fly away, Lucie dribbled the liquid over the board until one tiny drop touched the ladybug's wing. Then in a clear soprano, she sang, "Fly little bug, fly high up above and make my lovebirds fall in love."

The ladybug flicked its wings several times. A faint greenish glow like that of a firefly lit the tiny insect's wings.

"You did it!" Calliope clapped her hands.

"Yeah, you've done it all right." Alex closed her eyes. "All I have to say is, look out Bayou Miste, we're probably in for a helluva ride."

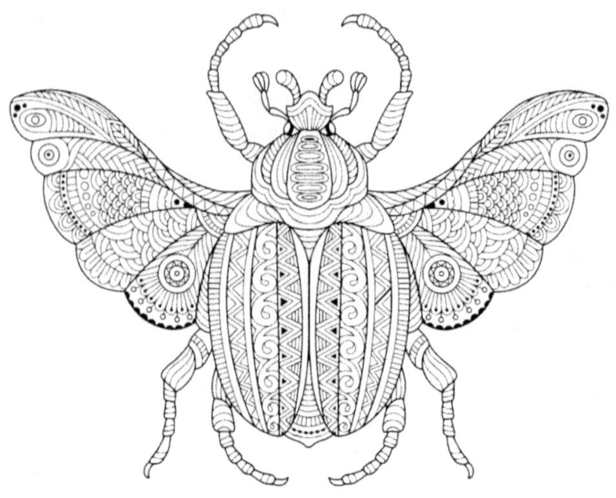

Chapter Four

"I'll need to check for bugs in every room of your office and house." Ben stood inside Eric Littington's office wearing a faded navy-blue coverall and carrying a canister of Bug B Gon.

A giant grin spread across Eric's face, and he rose from the leather chair behind his desk. "Look at you!" He rounded the desk and circled Ben, his gaze running up and down the length of his body. "I got to admit. You look like the real McCoy." Eric leaned closer and sniffed. "You even smell the part."

His lips twisted into a wry smile. "I'd better, if this is going to work."

"So, when you said you need to check for bugs, I assume you mean the mechanical ones?" Eric shoved his hands in his pocket and stepped back.

"Yeah." Ben set the sprayer on the carpet, pulled his bug detector device from his pocket, extended then antenna, switched it to vibrate, and turned it on. Then he walked slowly around the room, searching for all possible locations a wiretap or bug could be hidden. "The downside to my cover is that you'll have to pay to get your home and office sprayed."

"Not to worry. We'll manage." Eric walked to the window. "I'm glad you're the one on this case, after all that's happened in the past couple weeks. This game is starting to get dirty. I want to know who's been tailing me and who hired the dirtbag."

"We can guess at the who-hired-him part." Ben moved a chair beneath the ceiling fan in the center of the room and climbed up to examine the fixture. "Your opposing candidate has to be the one who did the hiring. But your decision to come to Bayou Miste was good. We should have no problems spotting a stranger. Hopefully, we'll have this business wrapped up in a day or two."

Ben's wishful thinking was overriding his patience and good sense. All he could think of was that he wanted out of Bayou Miste as quickly as possible.

Last night at the Raccoon Saloon had been a shock to his system. The sight of Lucie LeBieu waiting tables in her Hooters-style short-shorts and that ridiculously minuscule T-shirt had raised his heart rate to runner's speed. For the first five minutes, he'd thought she was her twin sister, Lisa, until someone shouted her name. Damn, she'd gotten even more beautiful over the past seven years. And every time he recalled those shorts and her incredibly long legs, his blood flowed south in a New Orleans minute, entering places it had no business going. Especially where Lucie LeBieu was concerned. If she didn't want anything to do with him seven years ago, she surely didn't want him now.

But those silky smooth thighs, tinged mocha by her Cajun-Creole heritage, called to him, even now. The chair he stood on wobbled, jerking him back to Eric's office at Littington Enterprises. He shouldn't be thinking about Lucie when he had a job to do. *Concentrate on the task at hand and you'll wipe her clean from your mind.*

"Enough about the case." Eric hooked his thumbs into his belt loops and rocked back on his heels. "How about that waitress last night at the Raccoon Saloon?"

The chair rocked violently. Ben waited until he had it back in control before he answered. "What waitress?" *So much for wiping Lucie from his mind.*

"Don't play dumb with me. You were there, too." Eric stared hard at him. "As I recollect, you couldn't keep your eyes off her."

Schooling his expression into his best poker face, he hopped down off the chair, ignoring Eric's words. He continued his search for hidden devices, feeling around the rim of the large oak desk dominating the room. If his stomach was a little knotted, he didn't need to share that information with Eric. He and Lucie LeBieu were no longer an item.

"Her name's Lucie LeBieu, isn't it?" Eric didn't wait for an answer. "Beautiful, just beautiful. She's one hot latte. I can't get over her."

You and me both, buddy. Hell. Did he say that out loud? Ben looked at Eric. When Eric didn't respond, he breathed a silent sigh.

"Wasn't she the kid who used to tag along behind us in school?" Eric shook his head, staring out the window. "She's grown into quite a woman. And those legs." Eric whistled. "Wow."

Ben's stomach did a flip-flop. Oh yeah, the legs. At times, deep into the night, he could still feel them wrapped around his waist. He circled the desk and dropped onto his back to look underneath. Out of Eric's view, he adjusted his coverall, appalled that the mere thought of Lucie could have him as hard as a cypress tree in no time at all.

"I think," Eric's voice drifted to him, "I'll ask her out."

Ben sat up, whacking his forehead against the underside of the desk. The room dimmed with tiny pinpricks of light squiggling through his vision. He fell onto his back and lay still, willing the miniature glow worms to go away.

"You all right under there?" Eric's face wavered into view.

"Yeah." Ben rubbed the knot forming on the right side of his forehead. "Just knocked my head."

Eric stared at him. "You're going to have a nice-sized goose egg. Want an ice pack?" He lifted a phone. "I could have the on-site clinic bring one up."

"No, I'll be fine." *Stupid, but fine.* As long as Eric didn't mention Lucie again. Ben climbed to his feet and straightened his clothes. Not that he had a hard-on anymore. Nothing like a bump on the head to kill the urge. Maybe he needed to clobber himself every time he thought about Lucie.

"So what do you think about what I said?" Eric asked.

"I think we'll find your rat, no problem."

"No, not about that. About Lucie."

He glanced around the room, looking for a mallet or something. Anything to bop against the growing lump on his forehead. Pain would help him erase her from his brain. He reminded himself that pain was the only thing she'd given him in the past.

His glance swept across Eric. The man was waiting for his response. What could he say? *Go ahead, screw the only woman I ever cared about.* He forced a shrug. "Why not? It doesn't hurt to ask."

"With every eye on my campaign, I've been afraid to ask any woman out." He shoved a hand through his thick blond hair. "Next thing you know, the papers will latch on to the relationship and make it sordid, or have me married before a preacher could say 'dearly beloved.'" Eric sighed. "I guess I'd better not. No use dragging Lucie through the media circus."

Quietly, Ben released the breath he'd been holding. "I'll just check your father's office for bugs."

"Thanks, Ben." Eric's smile was genuine, and a little sad. "I'm glad I can count on you."

"That's what friends are for." He opened the door to Jason Littington's office and stepped in. He stood several seconds, staring off into space, rubbing the lump on his head. *Did I really tell him to go for it?* With a sharp tap on the goose-egg-sized bump on his forehead, he sent pain stabbing through to his stupidity.

Hell. He'd rather poke a finger in his eye than see Lucie with another man.

***

Lucie stepped up to the guard's counter at Littington Enterprises. "Is Eric Littington in his office?"

In his crisp gray and blue uniform, Pascal Pasquale answered without looking up from his X-Men comic book. "Who wants to know?"

"Get real, Pascal." Lucie tugged the hem of her sleeveless powder-blue shirt, regretting her choice of clothing as her overlarge chest stretched the fabric all out of proportion. The matching skirt was too short and tight as well. She'd borrowed the outfit from Lisa's closet, wanting to attract Eric's attention and still look her best when he fell in love with her. "You know who I am. Is he in, or isn't he?"

When she quit fiddling with the shirt, she glanced up.

Pascal's gaze fixed on the disproportionate parts, and his mouth hung open like that of a whale trolling for plankton.

She closed her eyes and counted to five. Then she opened them and lifted Pascal's chin with the tip of her finger until his teeth snapped shut. Pasting on a flirty smile, she leaned over the top of the desk and purred, "Be a sweetie, and see if Eric is up in his office."

"He's up—he's in. Ah, hell, Lisa, why'd ya have to go and bend over like that?"

"I'm Lucie, not Lisa."

"Lucie? But you look like Lisa." Pascal's brows twisted over his nose.

Okay, so dressing like her sister might not have been the best idea.

The phone rang on the desk and Pascal fumbled to answer. "Littington Surprises—I mean Enterprises, may I help you?" He spun his chair, giving Lucie his back.

While Pascal negotiated his way through the phone call and queried Eric's office, Lucie drifted around the lobby. She checked her purse again for the clear pill bottle she'd scraped the ladybug into. The bottle was still there. The ladybug, with its strange, alien-like green glowing backside, climbed around the inside.

"Miss LeBieu."

Lucie spun toward the desk.

Pascal stood at attention, his eyes staring straight ahead, not at her.

He reminded her of one of the guards at the queen's palace in London. All he needed was the fuzzy hat and a red jacket to complete the image. Well, that and a haircut. You could take the Cajun out of the swamp, but you couldn't take the swamp out of the Cajun. "Mr. Littington will see you now. Take the elevators up to the fourth floor. First office on the right." The man had gone all business.

"Thanks." As she walked toward the elevator, Lucie caught Pascal's gaze sliding sideways, following her, his brows drawn together in a confusing mix of anger and longing. What the heck?

She stepped into the elevator, and as the doors closed, she turned to smile at Pascal. Not too much. She didn't want him to think she had any feelings for him other than friendship. In the fifth grade, she'd been nice to him on the playground. Afterward he'd clung to her like a leech. For the entire school year, he'd practically stalked her until her grandmother had threatened to put a hex on him.

No, getting mixed up in a stalker situation with Pascal wouldn't be good for her campaign to snag the bigger fish. Eric was her first-class ticket out of Bayou Miste.

And away from Ben...

As soon as the doors slid open on the fourth floor, butterflies attacked her stomach in a swarm. At the back of the elevator she hesitated. Did she really have the nerve to hex a man to get him to marry her? Had she no shame?

Guilt weighed on her conscience. Her hesitation stretched long enough that the door started sliding closed.

Did she want to stay in Bayou Miste indefinitely? A vision of Ben in the dim lighting of the Raccoon Saloon, smiling across the table at his buddy Eric swam into her head. She could just imagine him smiling across the table from his latest girlfriend, or wife, God forbid.

Her hand shot into the narrowing space between the two doors. The door continued closing, smashing her fingers. With a rush of adrenaline, she gripped the rubber edge with her free hand and pried it open, stepping through to the other side.

Well! A deep, shaky breath, a pat to the treasure in her purse, and she was ready for the next step in her journey. No doubt remained in her mind. This town wasn't big enough for her and Ben.

Her skin twitched at the thought of him moving on with his life without her. She couldn't stand it. No sir. She was better off making a clean break and starting a new life as the wife of a promising young politician on the rise. Imagine the people she'd meet, the galas she'd attend on Eric's arm.

The tight shoes and even tighter smiles she'd have to endure in the name of public appearances.

Her footsteps faltered in sympathetic anticipation of her social obligations and sore feet. If she didn't marry Eric, she'd be forced to leave Bayou Miste penniless and start over anyway—without a single familiar face or friend. Her shoulders straightened.

Her mother, Lynette LeBieu, had been content to move from place to place without money or support. Thank God she'd relented and dropped her and Lisa with her grandmother at the age of six. Otherwise, they would still be scrounging for their next meal, possibly out of a Salvation Army shelter, or worse, a trash can.

Ever since then, she had refused to leap without a net, and Eric Littington would make a terrific net. If she had to become a social icon, she could handle it. She was used to being gawked at. Her looks had garnered more than her fair share of tongue-lolling stares. She'd just have to class up her act a little.

Eric Littington. The letters were engraved in bold letters across the brass nameplate. The matching brass doorknob beckoned to her to open the door. She could hear a muffled voice through the thick oak panels. Maybe she should wait until Eric wasn't busy.

A little devil in the back of her head yelled, "Do it!"

Before she could lose her confidence, or maybe before she could regain her sanity, she knocked.

"Come in."

The brief, commanding words spurred her forward and into the room.

Cell phone to his ear, Eric stood with his back to her, speaking in short, clipped tones. "Yes, I'll be available tomorrow. Noon is fine. Please thank the mayor for me." He turned and glanced at Lucie, his eyebrows rising along with the curve of his lips. "Look, Bryan, I have someone in my office. No, I don't need you here. Take those days off I promised you. Yeah. Catch a big one for me, will ya? I'll be fine. Thanks." Eric hit the off button, shoved the phone into his pocket, and strode toward her. "Lucie, I didn't expect to see you here. To what do I owe the honor of this visit?"

She blinked twice, her mind a complete blank. Her real reason was to snag the eligible bachelor in a marriage merger, but she couldn't say that. As the silence between his question and her answer lengthened, she blurted, "I want to make a contribution to your campaign. But if you're too busy, I'll come back another time." Feet getting colder by the minute, she sensed yet another opportunity for escape, another chance to bow out gracefully before she committed another heinous Voodoo blunder. She backed toward the still-open door.

"No, of course I'm not too busy. However, my campaign manager usually handles the contributions."

"Can I leave my phone number for him?"

"Sure." Eric grabbed a card and pen from his desk and handed it to her.

After she'd jotted her number on the back, she smiled and handed it to Eric. "Call me sometime."

Eric reached out and grabbed her hands. "Please, stay. I've been thinking about you since I saw you at the Raccoon Saloon last night."

Warmth spread up her neck into her cheeks. *Just great.* He'd seen her in her waitress outfit. Not necessarily first lady or congressman's wife material...

She tried a carefree laugh that came out a pathetically nervous giggle. "Oh, that. Contrary to popular belief, I don't dress like that, normally. Nor do I engage in barroom fights on a regular basis." Wow, that sounded really bad. What congressional candidate even spoke to a woman who got into a barroom fight? She mentally kicked herself for succumbing to the need to deck LeRoy last night.

"What a shame." He smiled, his voice melting into her skin like heated butter. "It was the highlight of my evening."

Maybe there was still hope. "You mean you don't think less of me?" Lucie forced a flirty smile she didn't really feel.

With a grin smoothing across his face, he squeezed her hands. "I could never think badly of you." A devilish twinkle lit his eyes. "Not even if you took to the tabletops and stripped."

She matched his grin. "Sorry, not in my repertoire."

She hadn't known Eric well in school. Four years older than she, he'd gone off to a private boarding academy in New Orleans before she had gotten a chance to get to know him. She remembered he used to hang out with Ben at the Boyettes' house, but beyond that, he was a stranger.

His clear blue eyes smiled down at her. "Do I pass?"

For the second time in as many minutes, warmth flooded her cheeks. He was smart, but was he clairvoyant? Could he read her mind? Did he know she was after him as her future husband, the future father of her children? Her one-way ticket out of the swamps?

For once she was at a loss for words. She'd rehearsed her reason for being there, but now with the time at hand, those butterflies had turned into condors beating the insides of her belly with powerful wings. Her grandmother would say her conscience was warring with her.

The silence stretched longer and she still hadn't answered his question. "I'm sorry...what did you ask me?"

"Did I pass?"

"Oh yes! Of course!" Her brain kicked in gear and she coughed, initiating her plan. "I have a tickle in my throat. Do you happen to have some water?" She didn't have to fake the cough much. She'd almost choked on her lie.

Gran LeBieu would wash her mouth with soap if she knew Lucie was lying. Hell, she'd do a lot worse if she found out what her granddaughter was up to.

She knew her grandmother better than anyone else. Gran paraded her gruff, don't-mess-with-me attitude for the masses, but beneath her Voodoo queen persona was a heart of gold. The heart Lucie had grown to love and rely on.

Her grandmother also believed in what was right. And what she was about to do wasn't right. She knew that. But...what option did she have?

She glanced around the office, noting the solid mahogany desk, the smell of furniture polish, leather couches, and oil paintings. Her choices were simple—swamp or luxury.

Swamp. Luxury. Swamp. Luxury.

The tinkle of ice cubes clinking against crystal glass jerked her back to the present situation. With renewed determination, Lucie dug in her purse and removed the pill bottle.

As Eric, with his back to the room, poured water from a glass pitcher, she uncapped the bottle and stared down at her future.

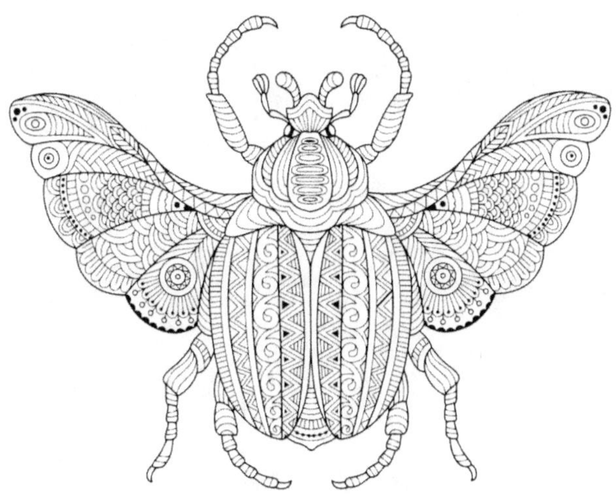

Chapter Five

Ben made a complete sweep of Jason Littington's office and found nothing. No bugs, funky wires, or miniature cameras. On his way back through to speak with his friend, he reached for the doorknob and paused. Was that a feminine voice?

Eric wasn't alone.

And he'd recognize that sound anywhere. Lucie's voice drifted through the slight opening in the doorway between Eric's office and his father's.

What the hell? Ben's first instinct was to charge in and demand to know what she was doing there. Thank God his investigative instincts kicked in. He hovered near the door, out of sight. Wouldn't hurt to know why she was there to see Eric. He considered it part of his job to know who was spending time with the congressional candidate. How better to protect him?

And if he felt a little twinge of jealousy, he wouldn't let it affect his work. No sir. He was a professional. Even where Lucie LeBieu was concerned.

Especially where Lucie was concerned.

He peeked through the doorway.

Eric stood at the bar pouring water into a glass. Lucie had her back to Ben, digging in her purse.

With the barest nudge, he opened the door a little more. The hinge creaked. He ducked out of sight and peered through the narrow slit between the hinges like a young voyeur sneaking a peek into the girl's locker room. Only he was close to thirty. And Lucie stood in the other room, doing who knew what. Though, that outfit was nearly as skimpy as underwear...

Her digging stopped and she glanced back over her shoulder toward Eric, exposing her profile to Ben's view.

One hand shot out, and she shook a small plastic bottle over the massive mahogany desk.

Ben squinted, but couldn't see what, if anything, fell onto the polished wood.

"Here." Eric held out a glass of water to Lucie.

Without missing a beat, she turned and smiled, accepting the glass with one hand, while her other hand dropped the bottle in her purse. "Thank you, Eric." She walked toward the portrait behind the desk and pointed. "Who is that man?"

What the heck was she doing? Her finger pointed at the painting, but she wasn't looking at it. Instead, she scanned the top of the desk and the surrounding floor.

"That's my Grandfather Littington. He built this corporation from the ground up." Eric's shoulders pushed back and his chest swelled. "Despite the ugliness of the chemical spill—
"

"Which wasn't your fault," Lucie cut in, a frown dipping between her eyes as she looked around.

"—the Littingtons have always strived to make this business one the community could be proud of."

Ben had heard this line before.

"Hey, you don't have to preach to me." Apparently, Lucie had heard it, too.

Eric cleared his throat and took her hands in his. "Sorry. That is actually part of the speech I'm giving tomorrow in Bayou Miste's town square."

Ben's fists tightened. Did Eric have to hold her hands so...so *much?*

Not that he cared, or anything.

The desk phone buzzed.

Eric sighed and dropped her hands. "I'm sorry, but do you mind if I answer?"

"No, go right ahead." Lucie rubbed her hands on her skirt. "Do you want me to wait out in the hallway?"

"No, stay right where you are." Eric winked, punched the speakerphone button, and stared across at her. "Yes?"

"Mr. Littington, the protesters are back at the gate." The secretary's voice called out over the intercom. "What do you want done? Should I call the police?"

"No, no. They have a right to protest." Eric lifted the receiver to his ear and punched off the speakerphone. He strode to the window and slid open the glass. A faint chant floated in. "So far, they don't appear to be violent. As long as they don't interfere with the employees coming in and out, leave them alone."

Ben didn't envy Eric's life. To deal with campaign opposition shenanigans was enough, but to answer to a swarm of irate environmentalists was double the pain-in-the-neck.

Hidden behind the door, he felt more and more the amateur sleuth than the special investigator. Where was the high-powered detective he was known as in Baton Rouge? Why was he lurking behind a door, spying on Lucie LeBieu when he should be out solving murder cases?

Fed up with himself and his grade-school techniques, he shifted to step around the door.

A movement caught his attention and he froze.

Lucie scooped a small speck off the desk and tossed it into the air over Eric's head. The spec spread its tiny wings and circled around, heading toward her, making an orbit around her head. Brows drawn together, Lucie flapped her hand, shooing the bug back at Eric.

Ben squinted. What kind of bug was it? And why was Lucie intent on directing it at Eric?

His attention still focused on the protest below, Eric remained oblivious to Lucie's erratic movements. "Did you tell him my father left for the day?" Eric said into the phone. He glanced back at Lucie.

She wiggled the fingers on her upraised arm and smiled, then clamped her arm down at her side.

Eric mouthed the word "sorry" before he turned back to the window. "No, he won't be available for comment today." His toe dug into the thick burgundy carpet, and then his foot stilled and his head shot up. "Me?" Another look back at Lucie.

She stood as still as a lurking alligator, a silly, innocent smile pasted on her face. When Eric wasn't looking, her eyes shifted upward, searching for the insect.

What was she up to? He shifted to get a better view of the entire room.

"Okay, okay, I'll be right down." Eric clicked a button on the phone and tossed it onto his desktop. Running a hand through his hair, he stepped up to Lucie. "I'm sorry, Lucie. Since my father isn't here, they want me to come down and say a few words to the demonstrators."

"Is it the group that's been carrying signs all over Bayou Miste?" Lucie asked.

"Yeah. They won't leave unless I talk with the reporter."

"Don't they know Littington Enterprises is paying for the cleanup?"

"Yeah, but any time chemical pollution is mentioned, the environmentalists see it as an opportunity for publicity." He grimaced. "If I don't say something, they could paint an unfavorable picture of my campaign."

"They could make it ugly even if you do say something."

"True, but at least I won't have ignored them." He caught her hands in his. "Will you wait here for me? I really wanted a chance to talk to you."

Her gaze swept the room, her eyes rolling upward until they fixed on the bug circling over her and Eric's heads. A smile spread across her face and she stared back into Eric's eyes. "If you want me to stay, I'll stay."

He squeezed her hands and let go, hurrying out of the office. "I'll only be a few minutes," he called over his shoulder, the elevator's beep ringing out in the hallway.

Ben took the opportunity to breathe deeply.

Good. With Eric out of the room, he had a chance to find out what Lucie was up to.

As soon as the office door swung closed, Ben eased out of the other room.

With her back to him, Lucie swung at the winged creature flying over her head. "Come here, little ladybug," she said in a fierce whisper. "Can't have you getting loose."

The bug altered directions and flew straight at Ben.

He stared at the flying insect. What was all Lucie's fuss about a harmless ladybug?

The woman in question spun on her heel in hot pursuit. When she saw him standing there, she planted both feet in the thick carpet, almost toppling over. "You!"

Her surprise was worth the tedious wait behind the door.

A deep-throated laugh rushed up from his throat and almost erupted when the ladybug collided with his forehead. The red and black spotted critter dropped to the rug, almost blending in with the maroon-and-black Persian carpet.

He squatted and scooped the bug into his palm.

"Oh crap, oh crap." Lucie danced around next to him, wringing her hands. Then she shoved her hand beneath his nose. "Give me that."

With her fingers wiggling in his face, he bunched his fist, trapping the ladybug in his palm. Rising slowly to his feet, he studied her wide-eyed, flushed face. "Now, what would you be doing in Eric's office with a ladybug, Lucie LeBieu?"

"I'm here visiting Eric, of course." She shoved her hand out to him again. "I just wanted to catch the bug and take it outside where it belonged, that's all." Bright pink flags of color flew high on her cheekbones.

"Lucie, Lucie, Lucie." Ben shook his head, his hand still firmly clutching the bug. "Your face gives you away. You're lying, aren't you?"

"No!" Dark brows drew downward. "Oh, keep the damned bug. I have to get back to work."

With an exaggerated sigh, he glanced at his watch. "At two o'clock? Raccoon Saloon doesn't open until 7:00 p.m." Ben *tsked* his tongue. "Another lie? And you just promised Eric you'd stay until he got back. That makes three."

"Shove it, Ben Boyette. If you'd just give me the darn bug, I'll be leaving."

Instead of complying with her demand, he circled around her, moving in slow, deliberate steps. "You haven't answered my question. What are you doing in Eric's office?"

"It's none of your business." Lucie crossed her arms over her chest, her chin tilting up at a stubborn angle. "Besides, why should you care?" She reached out and flicked the bright red ant embroidered on his blue uniform. "You're just the exterminator."

Score one for the swamp witch. Direct hit to the ego. "Seems like this was the same argument we had seven years ago."

"Yeah, and what did it buy you? You're back in Bayou Miste. Why didn't you stay gone?"

"Maybe—" He stepped closer until his face was only two inches from hers. Her floral fragrance assailed his senses. How well he remembered that scent. The impact hit him like a football tackle to his knee joints. He shook his head and moved closer.

She threw back her shoulders and lifted her chin. The bayou princess wasn't backing down. He almost grinned. He liked it when she was feisty. She wasn't scared of him or anyone else.

But she *was* bothered. Her breath quickened, as evidenced by the rise and fall of her breasts beneath the light-blue, low-cut shirt.

He smoothed the back of his knuckles along her neck and down to her collarbone. "Maybe I missed you."

For half a second, she stood as if transfixed, her eyes wide, her breathing halted altogether. Then she snorted, a very unladylike sound. "When alligators fly, maybe. Ben Boyette, you're so full of it." She stepped back two paces and held out her hand. "Are you going to give me that bug, or what?"

The back of his hand still tingling, he had to reevaluate his position. Perhaps it hadn't been such a good idea to touch Lucie. All the images invoked only laid open an old wound he wasn't willing to expose.

Not here. Not now.

He'd spent the better part of the past seven years trying to shake the residual effects of Hurricane Lucie from his life. Touching her, feeling the warmth of her skin against his, was like stoking an eternal flame. How the hell was he going to put it out?

She stood there, her dark brown eyes shining bright, her hair slipping from the clip holding it behind her head. If he tweaked it just once, all that long, glorious black hair would slip free and tumble over her shoulders like so many times before.

"Well?" she demanded, her hand still out, palm upward, her deep brown eyes revealing a little... What? Desperation?

His fingers loosened and he almost caved in. But he stopped himself in time and clenched his hand around his prize.

No. He wouldn't be lured into the eye of the storm again. Having weathered the turbulence once was more than enough for any man. He had to put some space between them. "If you just want to let the bug loose, let me do it for you." Ben strode toward the window. He shoved his hand through the opening, his fist still closed. "Here goes."

"No!" Lucie dove for him, slamming her body against his, grabbing for his hand.

Staggering against her attack, he opened his fingers.

The ladybug slipped free and dropped out of the window, falling...falling...

She lunged for the insect, grasping at air, her body tilting over the window ledge.

He caught her around the middle to keep her from following the bug. Like a punch in the gut, the warmth of her skin and flowery scent of her shampoo bombarded his senses once again. He fought the urge to pull her close and kiss her senseless. Just like old times.

For a moment he let his memories wash over him. Lucie in his arms felt so natural, so right. In a second, his resolve turned to mush, his muscles went slack.

Oh, no. He clenched his teeth. *Not again.* Not Lucie. *She'd* rejected *him*, not the other way around.

Thank goodness all her attention was fixed on the bug's descent. Otherwise she couldn't have missed the blatant evidence of the surge of emotions and testosterone coursing through his body.

She sagged against his arms and tipped her head backward against his chest. "Oh, no," she moaned. "Not again."

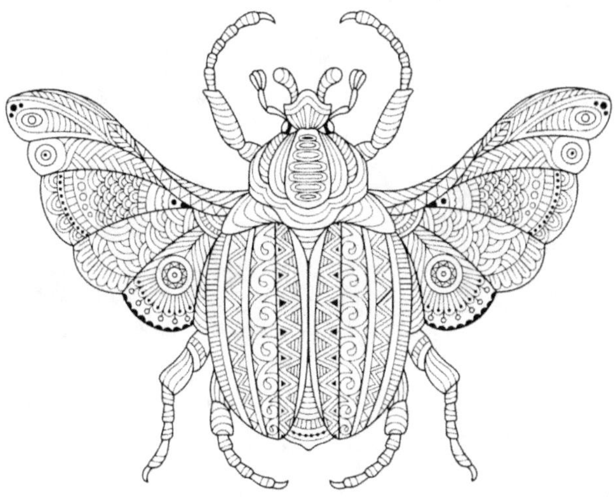

Chapter Six

All her friends' warnings pummeled against Lucie's conscience, with the ultimate mantra, *Don't do it!* reverberating through her skull.

Too late.

The ladybug had delivered its magic to Eric. Now, thanks to Ben, it was loose on the entire town of Bayou Miste.

Ben.

Holy swamp rats, Ben! Her eyes popped open and she glanced down at the arms encircling her waist. Strong, memorable arms. Arms that had held her in passionate embraces on more than one occasion. Arms encased in a bug exterminator's coverall. How ironic. She'd delivered her spell with a bug, and Ben was an exterminator. How fitting.

For a brief moment, she leaned against his chest, savoring the once-familiar warmth she'd enjoyed.

But this was Ben. Ben Boyette. The man who thought she was no better than her sister. A tease.

As if burned, she slapped at Ben's arms, shoving them away. She dashed halfway across the room and stopped, gasping for air from lungs too tight to breathe. "Don't ever touch me again."

His eyes narrowed slightly before he leaned against the window encasement. "Next time, I'll let you jump." He pushed away from the wall and strode toward her. "What were you doing with the bug anyway?"

"Nothing." Her face burned and she looked away from his perceptive gaze. Why couldn't she control her blushes?

"Tsk, tsk." Ben touched a finger to her chin. "Didn't your grandmother tell you lying gives you warts?"

Her breath caught in her throat. His hand against her skin sent fiery sparks straight to the pit of her stomach. "No, it doesn't," she whispered, the warmth of her breath bouncing off his skin to caress her cheek. Her hands rose to push him away. Instead, they rested against the solid wall of muscles.

"Are you willing to take the risk?" Ben leaned closer, his lips a mere inch from hers.

Like a hummingbird drawn to the sweet center of a flower petal, she leaned closer until her lips touched his.

His mouth covered hers, his tongue warring, twisting, tasting, and sliding in and out in a primal imitation of more intimate acts. His hands smoothed down her arms to cup her buttocks, pulling her hips against his.

She gasped into his mouth, the rigid evidence of his desire prodding her belly through the thin fabrics of his coverall and her skirt.

Her blood burned molten hot, coursing through her veins to pool at the juncture of her thighs, moistening her panties. With her heart thundering in her chest and ears, every nerve ending tautened, expectant...ready for more.

Ben broke off the kiss and pressed his lips to her temple, his racing pulse a testament to how the kiss had affected him. After a long pause, he tongued her ear, then whispered, "So, what do you want...with Eric?"

Her red-hot blood froze in midstream. Talk about your alligator pits. What was she doing, kissing *Ben?*

She jerked away and turned her back to him, buying time for her traitorous body to calm. "What's it to you?" she answered flippantly, when she felt anything but flippant. Her brain still wasn't functioning coherently. How could one simple kiss throw her so completely off track?

Who'd he think he was to come strolling in here after seven years? Did he think he could just pick up where they left off? Well, he had another think coming.

Her hands strayed across the surface of Eric's desk and she lifted a paperweight of solid brass, weighing it in her hand. This little gem could put a dent in a man's head the size of Cleveland. Her fingers curled around the cold metal. Oh, the satisfaction of bonking the oaf in the head.

Ben moved a few steps away, as if recognizing the danger of standing within range of the lethal desk ornament. A sly smile quirked the corner of his mouth, as if he knew he'd scored a hit on Lucie's sensitivities.

All the more reason to throw the paperweight at him. The louse deserved a dent in his head for confusing her so badly.

Then, as innocent as could be, he asked again, "Go home, Lucie."

"Look, I have a right to visit anyone I please."

As if ignoring her last outburst, he continued, "You can't possibly represent the protesters outside." He shook his head. "No, they're not really your style."

"Them?" Like he really thought she'd be out in some useless picket line. Ha! But she'd play his game. "Those people don't even live here. Everyone in town knows Littington Enterprises will make good on their promise."

"Then why are you here?"

Back to the original question. With a dramatic down-sweep of eyelashes, a move she'd mastered at the age of three, thanks to her twin sister, Lucie let her lips curl slow and sexy. "Do I have to have a reason to visit Eric, other than, well, he's Eric?" If that kiss had as much impact on him as it had on her, her question would find its mark.

Ben's Adam's apple bobbed once before his mouth settled into a tight line. "Leave him alone."

She'd scored on Ben and she wasn't backing down now. With slow, deliberate steps, one foot in front of the other, designed to take full advantage of feminine hip action, she stalked her prey. The vamp walk was another legacy from her infamous sister, Lisa.

Toe-to-toe, she stood before him and walked her fingers up his chest. Let him suffer a little of his own medicine. "What? Are you jealous of Eric? Afraid he might find me attractive?"

Ben grabbed her hand, squeezing hard.

"Let go." She struggled to free her hand.

He only squeezed tighter. "Stay away from him, do you hear?"

"Why should I?"

Every time she tugged, her chest bumped against Ben's arms. The tips of her breasts pushed out, forming little peaks against the powder-blue shirt she'd specifically chosen for her meeting with Eric. What had been the most subdued outfit in her sister's closet suddenly became a reminder of what she'd always tried so hard to avoid—looking like the swamp trash everyone in Bayou Miste thought she and her sister were.

Well, to hell with them, and to hell with Ben Boyette. *Eric* was her future. Her knight in shining armor, sent to pull her out of the swamp and into the life she wished to become accustomed to. And that damned ladybug better have gotten the point across!

An awful thought suddenly occurred to Lucie. In order for the ladybug to distribute its magic, it had to circle the heads of the spell's victims—er, subjects. In this bug's case, it had circled the heads of Eric, Lucie, *and* Ben. Which meant...

She'd cast a spell on not one, but *two* men. *Double* damn.

She hoped Eric would fall in love with her, but she didn't want anything to do with Ben. Besides, she didn't want his love if it came by way of magic. Wow, she could be in a very deep bayou bog if *both* men fell in love with her.

And the bug was loose on the town!

Ben dropped her hand.

Why did all her spells always end up this way? She should know better by now. But *noooo*. She *had* to try it. And then she had to go and kiss Ben, ruining seven years of attempting to forget him. She beat the heel of her palm against her forehead. "Stupid! Stupid! Stupid!"

Ben grabbed her wrist to keep her from hitting herself yet again. "What is your problem?"

She shoved her palms against his chest. "You! You're my problem." With more force than the last nudge, she shoved him again.

He clasped her hands in his. "What are you talking about?"

Anger at her sorry attempts at magic, anger at her inept attempts to make a life for herself, anger at how he'd never come back for her, all boiled up inside her. She hated that every time she got really mad, she'd do something even stupider—she'd cry.

And sure enough, tears trembled on her eyelashes now. But she refused to give in to them, to let Ben see her upset.

"Why did you have to come back into my life and mess everything up, again? Why?"

A smile quirked the corners of his mouth upward and his eyes twinkled. "Seems to me you're quite capable of messing it up all on your own."

She could fall into those eyes. Just as she had when she

was nineteen and gullible. *Get a grip!* She yanked her hands free and grabbed her purse. "Yeah, and sometimes I get a little help from so-called friends. See ya around, bug man."

Without looking back, she raced through the door. She had to catch that ladybug before it spread around more magic. All she needed was for Bayou Miste to be involved in a giant love fest. Wouldn't her grandmother be pleased?

Not!

***

"Hey, what happened in here?" Eric strode into his office, with a backward glance at the elevator door sliding shut behind him.

"I'm not exactly sure." Ben's head spun like he'd been popped by an alligator tail. What had Lucie meant by he'd messed up everything? Again? Hell, *she'd* messed up *his* life seven years ago, not the other way around. She'd toyed with his heart and left it sadly scarred.

"Something must have happened. Lucie blew by me like the building was on fire." Eric frowned at Ben. "Did she say anything? Did you?"

"No." He didn't like lying, but what Lucie had said didn't make much sense, at least not anything worth repeating. "Maybe she had another appointment."

"At least she gave me her phone number." Eric held up a business card. "I'm going to ask her out."

The punch in his gut didn't help the indigestion Ben was working on. "You sure you want to do that?"

"Why not?"

He knew he should stay out of this swamp goo, but he couldn't help himself. Something about Lucie dating Eric bothered him. Bothered him a lot. "She doesn't quite seem the type a congressional candidate would date."

"Oh, you mean her reputation?" Eric waved a hand as if pushing aside the issue. "I'm not worried about that. I think she's smart and spunky. Actually, she's just what a congressman's wife needs to be."

"Aren't you afraid rumors will spread?" Ben persisted when he should have dropped the matter.

"You and I both know how rumors have a way of being blown out of proportion." Eric grinned. "Besides, I like her and want to get to know her better. I still remember her as the skinny little girl from the swamp some eleven years ago. Wow, has she changed, or what? She's pretty amazing."

Amazing was just a part of the picture. Add to her résumé rude, mouthy, and entirely too sexy. Every man in the parish found it hard to keep his hands off her curves. As evidenced by that redneck LeRoy's attempt to grab her at the Raccoon Saloon the previous evening. But Eric wasn't listening. The man was practically drooling.

Ben clenched his teeth to avoid emitting another negative comment about the fair Lucie. If Eric wanted her, let him have her.

Why did that thought roil around in his belly like food poisoning, and make him want to punch something or someone? He needed to get out of the office and into some fresh air before he slammed a fist through the wall. "Whatever. I've made my sweep. No wires or bugs."

"Thanks, Ben." Eric held out his hand. "You don't know how much it means to me to know you're watching my back."

How could he stay mad at the guy? Anger over a woman, especially one as untrustworthy as Lucie, was ludicrous. He took the proffered hand and shook it a little harder than he meant, the lingering sting of Lucie's seven-year-old rejection still festering in his chest. Eric deserved better than Lucie. And Lucie deserved someone who could go toe-to-toe with her and not back down.

Someone like Ben.

Eric strode to the window and stared down. "What the heck is she doing down there?"

"Who?" Ben moved up beside him.

Lucie pushed through the crowd congregated in front of the gates of Littington Enterprises. From the distance, she appeared to be leaping at intervals and swatting at the air.

He suspected she was chasing the bug he'd let loose. Something wasn't right about her obsession with that bug. "I think I'll go down and find out what she's up to."

"Me, too."

"No, really. Don't you have work to do, or don't you need to manage your campaign, or something?"

"Ben Boyette, if I didn't know you better, I'd think you were trying to get rid of me. Do you have a thing for Lucie LeBieu?"

"No." His answer was short, his lips tight around the single word. At one time, his answer would have been entirely different. But not now.

"Are you sure?" Eric's brow furrowed. He stared from the erratic path Lucie followed back to Ben. "I mean, I wouldn't stand in your way, if you wanted to go after her. You probably know her better than I do."

Oh, yeah. He knew her better than he'd ever let Eric know. Besides, Eric was more Lucie's type. He had everything going for him. He'd be "good enough" for Lucie, unlike Ben. That's probably why she'd been in Eric's office to begin with. She'd set her sights on the young politician. "No, I'm sure. You can have her." *She wouldn't have me, anyway.* "You go. I'll stay here and check out a few more things before I leave."

"If you're sure." Eric grabbed the navy blazer neatly hung on the coat rack and raced for the door. "We'll talk later."

***

"Come here, you creepy little bug!" Lucie leaped as high as she could in heels and a short skirt. She'd had to leave her turquoise-blue 1967 Mustang convertible parked in the lot inside the gates of Littington Enterprises in order to chase the spellbound bug on foot.

It flew around the protesters, thank goodness, avoiding the potential for a really messy love fest. She had raced out the gates, charging through the picket line to chase the stupid creature.

And did the love bug head into the swamp like most self-respecting creatures of nature?

No.

The shiny, red, spotted insect with the alien-like greenish glow was headed straight down Highway 9 to Bayou Miste, a stretch of the legs—three miles—from the Littington compound.

A mile and a half down the road, she pulled off her shoes and started throwing them at the bug. "Die, you little beast!" The blister on her big toe and the stone bruise on her left heel slowed her progress to a crawl. Sweat trickled down her forehead into her eyes, blinding her.

The sound of a vehicle approached from behind. She inched off the road into the tall grass, hoping like hell she wasn't stepping off the edge into a muddy ditch, or worse, onto an angry water moccasin. She didn't mind snakes, except when she couldn't see them.

She brushed the perspiration from her stinging eyes and looked up.

A silver BMW sports car rolled to a stop beside her, the passenger window sliding smoothly down.

"Need a ride?"

She leaned over to peer into the dark leather interior of the car to see Eric's smiling face, shining like a ray of hope in the black world of sore feet and hopeless pursuit.

"Oh, yes, please." She melted into the cool leather seat and turned the air vents to blow full blast on her heated skin.

"Where to?"

Oh yeah, the damned bug.

Lucie stopped just short of saying, "Follow that bug!" Instead she nodded calmly, while her insides knotted like a twisted grapevine. "I was headed for town." Her cheeks warmed despite the cool air blowing on them. It was just a little white lie. After all, she was following a bug that was heading for town. Close enough.

With a confused smile, Eric stepped on the gas and the BMW shot forward.

Lucie peered through the windshield, straining to see the ladybug as they blew by. She caught a glimpse of fluorescent green. Good, the bug was still heading for Bayou Miste. If she got ahead of it, maybe she could catch it before it made it all the way into town.

"Why didn't you take your car?" Eric asked.

With an inward curse, Lucie could feel her cheeks burn in anticipation of her next lie. "I was afraid I wouldn't make it through the picket line. Besides, I felt like walking." She grimaced. "Until I went half a mile in these heels. I'll come back to get my 'Stang later."

"The blue Mustang convertible I saw in the parking lot? Nice car."

"Yeah." Lucie loved her little blue car. "My grandmother gave it to me when I learned to drive. It used to be hers."

"Where can I drop you?" Eric asked as they whizzed by the first few houses on the edge of the little community.

Her eye on the rearview mirror, Lucie squirmed around. "Park at the marina, there on the right."

As if landing a spaceship on glass, Eric slowed to a halt on the gravel parking lot outside Thibodeaux Marina.

Before he shifted the powerful sports car into park, she jumped out of the passenger seat, hopping into her high heels, one foot at a time, while lurching back the way they'd come. If she hurried, she could catch the bug before it entered town, spreading misplaced magic on unsuspecting residents.

Boy, Gran LeBieu would have a coronary if she ever found out about her itty-bitty spell.

"Wait!" Eric called out through his opened window. "Where are you going?"

Lucie stopped when she realized how nutty she must look. She turned and pasted a calm smile on the straining muscles of her face. "I see someone I need to talk to. If I don't hurry, I won't catch it—er, him. Call me tonight."

No more time. She had to find that bug. She spun on her heels, sliding a little in the gravel. Then, giving up on a dignified exit, she raced off in a cross between a power-walk and an all-out jog down the rough road leading back out of town.

Not far ahead of her, two carloads of protesters pulled up in front of the Cussin' Cajun, Bayou Miste's only diner. As the young men and women unloaded, signs and all, they stretched across the street, blocking Lucie's path.

A flash of fluorescent green winging past the far side of the diner sent a rush of adrenaline through her flagging body. "Excuse me, pardon me." She pushed her way through the crowd, her gaze focused on the ladybug.

"Hey, Lucie! Where ya goin'?" someone shouted from the steps of the diner.

She struggled to see over the tops of the protesters' signs. Alex and Calliope stood framed in the doorway of the restaurant.

"No time to talk!" she shouted back, dodging around a man pulling a huge sign off the seat of a gas-guzzling, mammoth SUV. She almost choked on a snort when he swung around, nearly clipping her with the sign that read "Down with Oil."

With her head tipped to the side, Calliope called out, "What're you doing?"

"Chasing after George Clooney. What the hell do you think I'm doing?" She didn't slow as the bug flew over the top of the little two-bedroom cottage Maurice Saulnier shared with his grandmother, heading south.

People edged past Calliope and Alex, easing their way into the crowded diner.

"I didn't know George was in town," Calliope called out over the protesters' heads.

"He's not, you idiot," Alex said. "Lucie's probably after the you-know-what."

"What?" Calliope said. "You mean George isn't in town?"

Lucie didn't have time to wait for Alex to explain to Calliope that she was chasing the love bug, nor did she have time to wait for her friends to catch up. Kicking off her high-heeled sandals, she leaped over the low fence beside the Saulnier house.

Piercing yelps erupted next to her, and she almost jumped back over the fence. At the risk of losing sight of the bug, she glanced downward and did a double take. A cotton-candy-pink toy poodle danced around her ankles, yipping at the top of her little lungs.

"Who's that out there?" Ouida Saulnier poked her head around the back screen door. Her normally soft white hair was dyed the same startling pink color as the poodle's.

"It's just me, Granny," Lucie reassured the older woman. Ouida Saulnier wasn't Lucie's grandmother, but everyone in Bayou Miste called her Granny.

"Lisa LeBieu, what are you doing in my backyard?" Granny stepped out on the porch and planted her bony fists on her equally bony hips. "You chasin' after my grandson, Maurice?"

"No, ma'am," Lucie shouted over the deafening noise of the powder puff poodle. "And I'm Lucie, not Lisa."

The bug landed on a white rose next to the porch handrail. If she could just get close enough to snatch it.

"FeFe, hush!" Granny snapped.

Without missing a single beat, FeFe turned her back on Granny and continued yapping.

Lucie inched toward the old woman. "How have you been, Granny? Is your arthritis still givin' you trouble?"

"Quit tryin' to change the subject. You know my arthritis always gives me trouble." Granny leaned forward, her eyes narrowed. "I still wanna know what the fool-darn-heck yer doin' in my backyard."

"I was—" She grasped for a reason that would satisfy Granny when the bug opened the hard casing enclosing its wings and took off past the rose bushes, the hydrangeas, and over the slats of the thigh-high picket fence. "Sorry, I can't stay and chat. Gotta go! By the way, I love the new hair color. Say hi to Mo for me."

With a smile, Granny patted a hand to her pink hair, then her mouth turned downward. "I will not tell Maurice hi for a no-'count floozy. You got no business but bad business, messin' around with Maurice. I've a good mind to tell your *Mamère* what you're up to, I do. No decent girl—"

Lucie whipped through the garden gate and chased off after the bug, leaving Granny, who was in full lecture mode, in her wake. For some reason, Granny couldn't get it through her head that Lisa was Lucie's twin, and Lisa was the troublesome twin. Usually. Although the love bug incident might prove to be equally troublesome, if Lucie didn't get it off the streets.

She rounded the corner of the Saulnier house and spotted the ladybug halfway across the road, heading toward the marina and the open swamp beyond. Between her and the bug stood Eric.

With his back to her, he leaned against his BMW, his cell phone pressed to his ear.

Good. Maybe he wouldn't see her making a complete fool of herself chasing after a stupid bug. She raced across the road, gaining ground on the insect, swatting at the air with her shoe while keeping an eye on Eric.

When the love bug flew out over the docks, she thought for sure she'd lost it. How could she manage to catch a bug in the vastness of the swamp? But the menace landed on a solid wooden post used to tie off the boats Joe Thibodeaux rented out to visiting fisherman.

If she sneaked up on the bug, she had a chance. But how to get past Eric standing in the parking lot?

Crouching close to the corner of a nearby house, Lucie chewed on her thumbnail.

"Boo!"

Lucie jumped straight up and spun around.

Calliope and Alex stood behind her, both sporting huge grins.

"Don't scare me like that," she hissed.

"Why are you hiding behind a house?" Calliope asked in a voice loud enough to raise the dead.

"Shh!" Lucie pressed a hand to her lips and pointed toward Eric. "He probably already thinks I'm a complete flake."

"Where's the bug?" Alex stepped around Calliope.

"Out there on the dock."

"Look, I'll distract Eric. You and Calliope catch the bug." Alex didn't wait for a response. She stepped out from the side of the house and strode across the parking lot toward Eric.

"Eric? Eric Littington? I haven't seen you in a coon's age." Alex strolled across the street, darting a glance backward.

Eric turned toward her, a smile curling up the corners of his mouth. He lifted a finger and mouthed, "One moment."

He turned back around and spoke into his phone, then clicked it off and once more turned his baby blues on Alex.

Lucie shook her head. Eric really was a good-looking man. A cross between Matthew McConaughey and John F. Kennedy, he had the kind of looks a girl could swoon over. In fact, any woman would be proud to be his wife.

Alex hooked his arm and managed to turn his back to Lucie and Calliope.

"Come on, let's go." Calliope slipped away from the house and ran toward the dock.

With little else stopping her now, Lucie took off after her. Maybe Calliope should have distracted Eric. She wasn't the most coordinated individual, and she was prone to disaster. Her name really should have been Calamity.

Lucie increased her pace, her bare feet taking a beating on the gravel. She reached the dock an inch before Calliope and pushed ahead toward the post where the bug still rested. As she reached out to snatch the creature, it lifted off and hovered over the water, just off the side of the wood decking.

She leaned out to grab the bug when Calliope caught up, stopping too fast to keep from plowing into her.

All her weight shifting from the dock to teetering over the water, Lucie grabbed for Calliope...and missed. Gravity took over and she fell, hitting the water in a painful belly flop that knocked the wind out of her lungs.

Water closed over her as she plummeted downward among old beer cans, plastic bottles, and a faded tennis shoe. Jeez, maybe the environmentalists had a point... Scrambling to an upright position, she pushed her bare feet into the murky green silt, cringing as muck curled around her toes. When she had her feet firmly beneath her, her lungs burning for air, she pushed off the bottom with enough force to launch her head a foot out of the water. She gasped and inhaled deeply, sucking in as much fresh air as she could before she sank below the oily surface.

When she came up this time, a white flotation ring slapped into the swamp next to her and she hooked her arm around it.

Calliope stood with her hands pressed to her mouth, her eyes wide. "Oops. Sorry!"

With a few swear words poised on her lips, Lucie glared up at her friend, rewriting the old adage, "With friends like Calliope, who needs enemies?"

And to top her humiliation, Eric and Alex pounded across the wooden planks of the dock, grinding to a halt beside Calliope.

Eric squatted on the dock and extended his hand. "Grab hold." In one smooth tug, he hauled her up and out, to stand in the circle of his arms. Strong, virile arms. Arms encased in an oh-so-expensive suit!

She gasped and backed away, her blouse and skirt no longer a smooth powder-blue, but an icky, green-slimed, fishy-smelling mess.

Holy swamp gas! What more could go wrong?

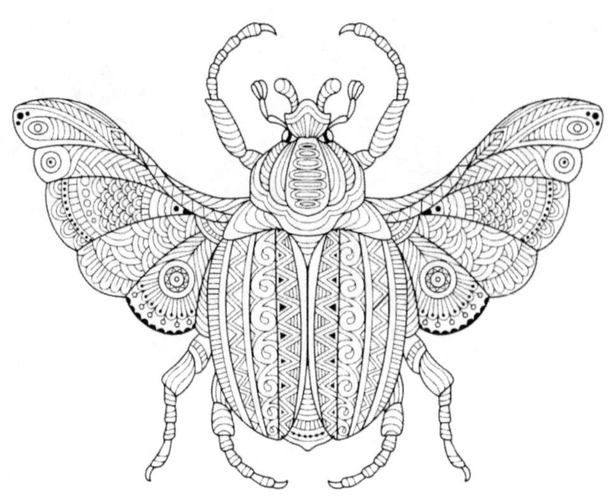

Chapter Seven

"I can't believe you knocked me into the swamp." Lucie plopped down in the wooden swing on Alex's back porch. "In front of Eric, no less." In a borrowed terry cloth bathrobe, she stared at the remains of Lisa's best shirt and skirt draped across the railing. She didn't know why she'd bothered rinsing the fishy smell out of them—the fabric was ruined. Lisa would kill her. With renewed vigor, she scrubbed at her hair with the soft white towel. No use poking at a dead crab.

"I said I was sorry." Calliope sat in a folding lawn chair several feet away, her arms crossed over her chest and a frown pushing her auburn eyebrows to a point over her nose. "It's not like I did it on purpose." Her frown disappeared and she jumped from her chair. "You want me to dry your hair for you?"

How could she be mad for long when Calliope meant only the best? The redhead couldn't help that every time she tried to assist, she ended up making things worse. Calliope had always been her friend, even in high school when other girls called Lucie the Bayou Bimbo and refused to talk to her, just because her twin was such a tease.

Lucie slid to the side, making room for Calliope. As loyal a friend as they came. Clumsy, maybe, but loyal. Calliope was a lot like Alex's golden retriever, Sport.

Snatching the towel from her hands, Calliope rubbed at Lucie's long black hair. "Sure smells better than it did before the shower."

"Anything smells better than I did before I showered," she groused, unwilling to let go of her anger.

"So, Lucie, when are you going to tell Gran LeBieu?"

She tensed at Alex's abrupt question. "I'm not."

"Don't tell me you think you can figure your way out of this mess without her." Alex leaned forward, resting her elbows on her knees, a tea glass grasped between her hands, dripping condensation onto the wooden floor. "That bug is still out there somewhere, causing who knows what kind of damage."

"I don't care." She knew she sounded defensive, but the lingering tingle of Ben's kiss just wouldn't go away. And she hated that uncontrollable surge of desire she got every time she thought about him. "I want out of this swamp, and that bug is the only hope I had. Besides, it'll surface again. I just know it."

"Yeah, after it curses half the town. No telling what'll happen." Alex set her iced tea on the table beside her and dangled her hand over the side of her chair, patting the golden retriever panting quietly at her feet. "You really should tell your grandmother."

Lucie sat with her lips pursed shut. What could she say? *I screwed up? Gran LeBieu, please bail me out, again?*

No way.

The cordless phone beside Alex rang, giving Lucie a temporary reprieve from her friend's lecture.

Instead of answering, Alex let it ring four times until the answering machine just inside the door picked up.

"Alex? Pick up the phone. This is your mother."

"As if I couldn't tell by her voice." Alex heaved a giant sigh.

"I know you're there. I saw you and your friends going into your house on my way home from getting my hair done." A pause. "Calliope, honey, pick up the phone since Alex won't."

Dropping the towel on the seat, Calliope rose to honor Mrs. Boyette's command.

Alex leaped from the lounge chair and blocked Calliope's path. "Don't you dare. You will not answer that phone."

"Why not?" Calliope backed up a couple steps, her eyes widening. "It's your mother, for heaven's sake."

"Exactly. She'll try to foist some poor unsuspecting fool on me again. She never gives up."

"Is she still setting up blind dates for you?" Lucie asked.

"Hell, yeah." Alex leaned her head back against the doorframe, rubbing her temples. "Like I said, she never gives up."

"Just tell her to back off." Calliope took up the towel again and sat beside Lucie.

With a pointed look at Calliope, Alex said, "You know my mother. Until I'm"—she crooked her fingers, making a quote motion—"'safely married,' she won't quit dragging men off the street for me."

Lucie grabbed the towel from Calliope and continued drying her own hair. "Maybe I should have your mother work for me instead of you."

"Believe me, you don't want that." Alex squatted next her golden retriever and ruffled his ears. "Right, Sport? My mamma is the matchmaking queen of the parish. Once she's set her sights on you, you either succumb and marry the latest offering, or kill yourself trying to avoid her other so-called candidates."

Sport's tail thumped against the floor and he reached his foot-long tongue out to lay a big wet kiss on Alex's chin.

Lucie squirmed. She liked dogs, but not in her face. "Have you tried talking to your mother?"

"Till I'm blue in the face." Alex straightened. "But we're not here to talk about me. You've got bigger problems. Since the love bug has hexed two men, one being my unwitting brother, I think you really need to consider calling this whole thing off and undo the spell."

"I can't," Lucie said.

"Why not?" Alex demanded.

"I think the spell is already working." Lucie ducked her head beneath the towel. "Eric seems interested."

"I'd say." Calliope practically bounced on the wooden slats of the swing. "Did you see how he looked at you on the dock? If that isn't love, I don't know what is."

"Hell, he couldn't keep his eyes or his tongue in his head. What red-blooded male could when you could see everything beneath her clothes?" Alex always had a way of bringing Lucie and Calliope back to earth.

Lucie's cheeks heated. "A good thing Eric had the decency to lend me his blazer."

"And providing a good excuse to see him again, huh?" Alex nodded, a conspiratorial smile curving her lips.

"Eric sure is dreamy, isn't he?" Calliope leaned back on the swing, her hands pressed to her chest. "I could go for that one. A regular Adonis, he is."

"Yeah, but Lucie also has that other problem," Alex said.

Lucie's stomach clenched. "Ben." That amazing kiss in Eric's office still hadn't worn off. Even after being tossed in the drink, her lips sizzled. *Damn Ben.* It had taken her seven long years to get over him for a reason, it seemed.

"Oh, yeah, Ben." Calliope tipped her head to the side, her smile soft and dreamy. "You should go for Ben. I've always liked the way that one little lock of hair falls down across his forehead. Mmm. Makes him look dangerous and mega-sexy."

"Ugh!" Alex stuck her tongue out. "You're talking about my brother."

Lucie stared out across Bayou Miste without seeing the houses and streets. Instead she remembered Ben's hair and how she couldn't keep her hands out of it when they were younger and so very in love.

Hold it! Back up, regroup. Not love, but lust. What they'd had could only be classified as lust. Wasn't it?

Considering how quickly he'd left, and how long it'd taken him to come back, it must have been.

Leaping from the swing, Lucie almost flipped Calliope over the back. "No, I'm not going for Ben. What we had seven years ago is long over."

"Yeah, except you forgot one thing." Alex crossed her arms over her chest.

"He thinks I'm pond scum, a bayou bimbo like my sister. What more do I need to remember?"

"Your little bug put a spell on my brother, too. No matter what happened when you were nineteen, Ben's going to fall in love with you, anyway."

"Falling in love won't change his opinion of me." With a moan, Lucie paced across the porch. "I don't need this complication to my plan. Not now."

"You're pretty much stuck with it." Alex plunked her fists on her hips. "You've got two men in love with you—via magic —and it's not fair to either one of them. Shame on you, Lucie LeBieu."

"You sound like *Mamère*." She hung her head for just a moment and then raised it, her chin jutting out. "I'm not ready to call in the big guns. I can handle this by myself."

Alex rolled her eyes. "Yeah, like you did today?"

"So, I fell in the swamp." She tossed the towel on the rail beside her outfit. "No one got hurt."

"You mean, not yet." Alex pointed a finger at Lucie. "And, you still don't have the bug under control."

"No, but I will. I'll go out tomorrow before work and look for it."

"Are there any instructions for undoing this spell?" Alex ran her hand through her dark brown hair, a worried wrinkle in the middle of her forehead replacing her fierce frown.

"I think so." Or at least she hoped so. But only if she decided she needed to reverse the magic.

Alex's eyebrows shot upward. "You mean you don't know how to undo the Voodoo?"

Calliope clapped her hands together and giggled. "Sounds like a song."

"I think it's the same ingredients, only you say all the words backward."

"Do you need the bug?"

Lucie squinched her eyes and hunkered low. "Probably," she whispered. "And I would have had the damned thing if your brother hadn't let it go out the window."

"Good grief." Alex shook her head, opened her mouth to say something, and clamped it shut.

Like an insect under a microscope, Lucie squirmed on the porch seat. "Why do you have to make such a big deal out of this? It's just a little love spell. The world will not come to an end."

"You're playing with my brother's heart, Lucie." Alex spun and paced the deck. "I can't believe you'd toy with him again. I'm not likely to be your friend after all this is said and done."

"But—"

Before she could form a response, the phone rang again.

Calliope was first to move.

"Hold it." Alex flicked her wrist, shoving her palm against Calliope's chest. "Let the answering machine get it."

On the fourth ring, Alex's recorded voice instructed the caller to leave a message at the beep.

"Alexandra, this is Eric Littington. I figured since you're a friend of Lucie's you could answer a few questions for me. Please call me back." He left a phone number and rang off.

Lucie stared at Alex, knowing her friend wasn't happy with what she'd done. But Alex's curiosity had to be just as piqued as hers. Would she return the call and find out what Eric wanted, despite her issues with Lucie's love hex?

Finally, Calliope broke the silence. "Well? What are you going to do?"

"You have to call him back and find out what he wants to know," Lucie said.

Alex's eyes narrowed. "What are your intentions toward my brother?"

"Oh, quit sounding so old-fashioned." She stood. "I have no intentions toward Ben. We were over seven years ago."

"Then why were you so upset the other day when he first came into town?" Alex asked.

"A girl has a right to be prepared for when her ex-boyfriend comes to town. That way I could be sure to avoid his sorry ass."

With a narrow-eyed stare, Alex considered her response. "Do you promise to undo the spell on him?"

Why did Alex have to be such a bulldog? Lucie just wanted to pursue her own path, but her friend wasn't going to let go of the issue. "I'll try," she said, without making an actual promise.

Alex gave her another one of those frowny-faced looks she used on her younger siblings. "You *will*."

"I'll *try*. That's the best you're gonna get." Lucie walked through the door and, lifting the receiver, handed it to Alex. "Are you going to call Eric back?" She held her breath and added. "Please?"

Alex grabbed the phone. "Okay, okay." She replayed the message, jotting down the number. With a long-suffering sigh, she punched it into the phone a little harder than necessary. "Hello, Eric?"

Lucie leaned close. Calliope crowded the other side of Alex.

Missing his first question, Lucie pressed her ear to the hard plastic on the back of the receiver.

"Yes, usually Lucie and I are friends," Alex responded.

Lucie jabbed Alex in the ribs.

"What's Lucie's favorite flower?" she heard Eric ask. "I'm going to ask her out, but I want to do it with flowers."

Lucie mouthed the words *white roses*. Eric was going to ask her out! Her heart should be pounding with giddy excitement. This was what she wanted, wasn't it? Yet she couldn't squelch the I'm-gonna-hurl-because-I'm-a-big-fat-liar feeling in her stomach.

"You know, why don't you ask her yourself?" Alex shoved the phone into her hands and smiled like Garfield the cat after eating the entire lasagna before Odie could get a bite.

Holy cypress knees! She had Eric on the phone. Now what?

"Lucie, are you there?" Eric's asked.

Slamming the headset to her ear, Lucie winced. "Yes, yes, it's me."

"Somehow I lost your number, but I got Alex's from Ben. Figured she'd know how to get hold of you." He stopped for a moment and laughed. "Jeez, I sound like a teenager. The reason I was trying to get you is to invite you to the barbecue my family is hosting at the parish pavilion on Friday night."

"I heard about that. I thought the entire community was invited. Why the special call?"

After a momentary pause, he answered quietly, "I want you to come as my date."

***

Ben stood in front of the window of Jason Littington's spacious study. He'd been all over the house and the grounds conducting a thorough assessment of the security system and checking for bugs. Nothing. Everything was as it should be, tight and operationally sound. Then why was he on edge and ready to jump at the slightest sound?

He refused to consider that his jitters had anything to do with Lucie LeBieu.

Jason Littington sat at his massive desk in the study of the Littington plantation house thrumming his blunt, manicured fingers against the polished surface. "I'm not so sure coming back to Bayou Miste was such a good idea for you, son."

"How else are we going to identify the creep dogging my life?" Eric paced across the Persian carpet, his progress unmarked by sound.

"You were supposed to keep a low profile while you were here, to aid in your campaign." Jason shot Eric a pointed look.

Ben settled comfortably in a brown leather chair, observing the dynamics between father and son.

"And what makes you think I'm not keeping a low profile?" Eric countered.

Jason slid a single sheet of paper across the desk.

His lips pressed into a thin line, Eric snatched up the page and scanned the contents. A smile slid up the sides of Eric's face. "So?" He laid the paper back on the desk.

Ben rose from his chair and strode across to pick up the thin white sheet.

"So," Eric repeated. "I helped pull a woman out of the

swamp today. I should think that would help my campaign, not hurt it."

The page had a badly reproduced black-and-white photo of Eric helping a sopping wet woman from the swamp by what looked like the dock at Thibodeaux Marina. Despite her hair hanging limply in her face, Ben would recognize that figure anywhere.

Lucie.

And, obvious to anyone with a pair of eyes and one of these flyers, her blouse wasn't hiding much, if any, of her luscious, fully endowed features. The caption at the bottom of the picture read, "Congressional Candidate Eric Littington in Wet T-shirt Contest With Hometown Hottie."

"You'll be the next Washington scandal if you keep seeing that woman." Not a hint of humor graced Jason Littington's countenance. A little twitch on his left jaw was the only indication of any emotion whatsoever.

"Why shouldn't I see her?" Eric stopped pacing to stand directly in front of his father's desk. "Lucie LeBieu is a very nice young lady."

"With the reputation of being a little on the loose side. She's flirted with every man in the county, and rumor has it she's slept with them all."

The back of Ben's collar heated. Although he and Lucie didn't have a future, he couldn't stand back and let Jason Littington repeat nasty gossip about her. "Lucie has a twin sister, Lisa, who has that unfortunate reputation. Lucie isn't anything like her sister."

"If I can get the rumors confused, the media will make an even bigger mess of the situation." Jason Littington picked up the page and waved it at his son. "Stay away from her if you know what's good for you and your campaign for Congress."

Ben could have predicted Eric's response. He'd seen it at least a dozen times when he'd witnessed Eric go up against his father's demanding presence. Eric always managed to come off looking like the more reasonable of the two. A quality he admired in his friend, and one that made Eric an excellent candidate for government. The man could keep calm in the most unnerving situations and make sound decisions based on facts. When he believed in something, he didn't back down.

And apparently, he believed in Lucie.

Ben remembered a time when he'd believed in Lucie, too. Until she'd shown her true colors. She'd only been interested in status.

Growing up as one of nineteen kids, Ben never much cared for status. Nor did he let the lack of status slow him down.

"Dad, I'm not a teenager anymore, and you can't tell me who I can and can't see." Eric didn't whine, he just stated the facts in a clear and concise manner.

"If you insist on seeing that woman, you'll only ruin your chances of getting elected," the elder Littington persisted.

"Now, wait a minute, Mr. Littington." Ben raised a hand to stop further testimony against his ex-girlfriend. "Lucie isn't a bad person."

"Maybe so, maybe not." Jason flicked his hand toward Ben, although his attention remained on his son. "Eric can't afford to let her bring him down."

"Lucie is a beautiful woman who's smart and determined." *Determined to marry well.* He didn't add that part. He just couldn't stand by and let Jason bad-mouth her. Lucie may have done some rotten things in the past to him, but nothing that deserved such censure.

"It's too late, anyway, Dad." Eric crossed his arms over his chest. "I like her and I want to see her again. I've asked her to be my date for the campaign barbecue Friday night."

Eric's announcement was a punch in the gut Ben hadn't been prepared for. He'd thought for sure Eric would make the right decision and stay clear of Lucie. At least, deep down, Ben had *hoped* his friend would stay clear of Lucie. Not that he wanted to start something up with her again. But, well...

What the heck *did* he want?

Jason shook his head, his mouth in a serious downturn. "Every decision you make will have a profound effect on how your constituency views you. Going out with this Lucie LeBieu woman will only bring scandal and make your voters question your judgment."

"I'll take that chance." Eric's jaw tightened and determination showed in the hard glance he directed at his father. "Lucie's worth it."

Jason stood, the color rising in his tanned cheeks. "Is she worth making her your wife?"

Ben staggered backward. Neither Eric nor Jason paid any attention to him, so wrapped up were they in their little power struggle.

Lucie, Eric's *wife?* Wow, that would be a coup on her part.

She'd turned Ben down flat when he'd asked her seven years ago.

He studied Eric across the room. His blond good looks were a stark contrast to Ben's bayou Cajun dark skin and hair. And Eric dressed for success with every item of clothing he put on, probably down to designer boxers. The man wore his success like a second skin. Hell, it probably came easy to him. Manners and diplomacy had been ingrained in him from birth. And what he hadn't inherited, Jason Littington made sure he'd learned by sending him to the best tutors and universities.

Lucie would do well to marry a man like Eric. Ben could never measure up to someone so classy.

Nor did he want to. He'd leave it to his politician friend to carry that ball and chain. He enjoyed living in the comfort of jeans and well-worn work boots. And tact was something he'd never quite mastered, neither here in Bayou Miste nor on the force in Baton Rouge.

Eric hesitated over his father's bald question. Finally, he looked straight at Jason Littington. "If I fall in love with her, I'd be more than willing to ask her to be my wife."

"It's a good thing. You might want to take a look at the New Orleans *Times-Picayune*." The older man lifted a newspaper off his desk and handed it to his son. "Your opposing candidate is blasting you about not being married, claiming you have no stability in your life and your views."

"My marital status has nothing to do whatsoever with my political views." Eric snapped the paper open and scanned the front page.

"Richard Gasson says it does." Jason tapped the biggest article splashed across the page. "He also capitalizes on his Cajun heritage and your lack of the same."

Ben almost laughed at the irony. For once Eric's money wasn't enough, and he had what Eric never could.

Eric's eyes narrowed slightly. "Not that I put any stock in Gasson's mudslinging, but it just serves to reinforce my stand that Lucie might just be good all around for my campaign."

Ben held his breath, not liking the way this conversation was going.

"How so?" Jason asked.

"If I need a wife, which I don't concede that I do, Lucie would make the ideal one. She's beautiful, she's independent, and she's Cajun. As far as I'm concerned, she's perfect. And I don't care who objects."

Jason glared at his son.

As the quiet stretched into a full minute, Ben shifted on his feet, ready to leave father and son to their argument.

Then a loud crash shattered the silence—and the huge picture window in the study. Ben spun around as the porcelain vase on the end table beside him exploded into a thousand tiny shards. A rock the size of a baseball rolled to a stop on the carpet inches from his big toe, a crumpled piece of paper tied around the middle.

"Good Lord!" Mr. Littington dropped to a crouch near the floor behind his desk.

Eric squatted low, his gaze riveted to the broken window.

All of Ben's police training and a strong dose of adrenaline kicked in to his bloodstream. He ran to the window, flattening his back to the wall beside it, then eased around the frame to stare out into the night.

Across the open lawn, a figure sped past, his legs exposed by accent lights, his face in the shadows of the giant oak trees. The man disappeared into the bushes leading toward the boat ramp where Ben and Eric had played during the summers growing up.

He jerked open the double doors leading out to the garden and leaped over the low porch railing. When his feet hit the grass, he threw every ounce of energy into gaining ground on the vandal.

Before he cleared the bushes blocking the view of the private pier beyond, a motor revved, blasting through the raucous noises of the frogs and insects serenading one another in the still night air.

A few more steps and Ben moved out into the open, charging to the end of the short wooden dock. A small skiff left a V-shaped wake as it disappeared into the dark.

"Damn." He leaped into the nearest high-powered boat and fumbled for the ignition. "Double-damn." No key. How was a person supposed to chase the bad guys when they took the keys out?

His only other choice was a rowboat flipped upside down on the shore. He'd never catch him in that.

Angry for not moving faster to begin with, he walked back

to the house and stepped through the double French doors he'd exited moments before.

"Look at this," Jason Littington shoved a crumpled paper into Ben's hands before he cleared the threshold.

As his eyes adjusted to the glare of the lights, he stared down at the block lettering.

"Go away!"

Holding the paper by the corner, he flipped the page over but it was blank on the other side. "That's it?"

A grin spread across Eric's face. "Got to give the guy credit. He's concise in what he wants.

"Unlike, say, a politician?" Ben returned the smile until the elder Littington's creased forehead caught his attention.

"My property has just been attacked and you two are making jokes? I fail to see the humor in the situation."

"Lighten up, Dad." Eric draped an arm around his father's shoulders. "It was just a rock, thrown by someone with a bone to pick."

"A rock today, a bullet tomorrow." Jason strode across to the shattered window. "This time I only lost a window—"

"And a vase." Ben interjected.

"Yes, and an expensive vase." Mr. Littington paused as if to remember where he was in his tirade. "What if this person starts shooting? Lives may be lost."

"Dad, it was only a rock." Eric glanced down at the offending stone. "But you're right. I'd like to know who threw it."

Ben grabbed a tissue from a box on Littington's desk, scooped the rock up with it, and stuffed it into his pocket. "I'll see if I can lift prints off it and the paper."

"Do you suppose it was the man who's been following Eric?" Eric's father asked Ben.

"Could be. Could also be the protesters." Ben frowned. "But since the guy got away clean into the swamp, I'd say he's someone local who knows his way around the tributaries well enough to navigate in the dark."

"Great." Mr. Littington waved his hand in the air. "Campaign crashers, protesters, and local goons. Want to add something else to that list?"

How about a very determined woman intent on marrying your son? Ben added silently to himself. No, he couldn't say that to Mr. Littington. The man was probably an alligator's hair away from running Lucie out of town, as it was. "Look, there's not much we can do tonight. I'll take the paper and see if there's anything I can glean from it. And tomorrow, we'll install additional security cameras that will take in more of the yard. In the meantime, get this window boarded up before you call it a night, if you don't want another one of these crashing through."

Jason and Eric Littington nodded.

"I'll see Mr. Boyette to the door and have the maid clean up this mess." Eric hooked a hand around Ben's elbow and led him out of the study.

He paused at the front entry, dropped his hand away from Ben's arm, and shot a quick glance over his shoulder. "Ben, do you think the message was intended for all Littingtons, or just me?"

"Hard to tell." Careful not to contaminate the evidence, he folded the paper into the tissue and slid it into his back packet. "The message was so short."

"Dad wasn't getting rocks through the window until I showed up." Not a trace of humor graced Eric's face now, only a deep frown.

"Something to be considered."

"I'm worried about my father. He doesn't need this kind of stress." Eric shoved a hand through his blond hair. "Maybe I should leave."

Ben understood family concerns. He loved his mother

and every one of his siblings. Eric's apprehension was warranted. "We don't know who did this or whether you or your father, or both, were the object of the warning. Let me do some more digging—maybe something will turn up. In the meantime, keep your eyes open."

Eric's lips twisted into a sardonic half-smile. "Okay. I trust you, man. I know you won't let me down."

As Ben climbed into his exterminator truck, his thoughts ran the gamut of possible suspects. Who the hell threw that rock? Or a better question was, what would he do next?

And if Lucie continued seeing Eric, would she be the next target?

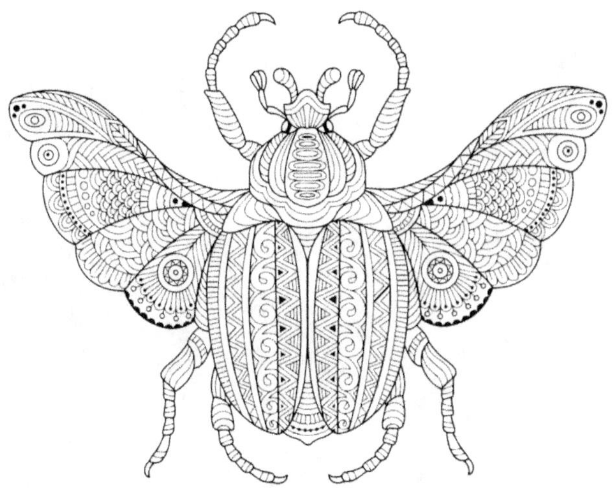

Chapter Eight

"Jean, do you think I'm a screwup?" Lucie slid her round serving tray onto the bar and hiked one butt cheek onto a stool. Business wouldn't pick up for another thirty minutes, and she was feeling pretty bummed and in need of a friend.

He handed her a dry towel and a glass. "No, I don't think you're a screwup. You're the best waitress I got."

Absently polishing the glass, Lucie thought of the mess she'd made of everything. All she'd wanted was to save *Mamère*'s house and get out of Bayou Miste. "Have you ever done something you thought was right at the time, even though your friends told you that you were out of your mind, and despite all their arguments, you did it anyway?"

Jean chuckled. "Yeah, I once ate a hundred goldfish on a dare."

"Ewwww!"

"Half my friends tried to talk me out of it. The other half egged me on. Had a bellyache for a week. These days, I can't even go to the fish store without wantin' to puke."

"That is so disgusting." Her stomach burbled in sympathy. "Did you ever feel right again?"

"No." He took the glass from her and placed it on the shelf behind him. "What I learned from the fish is that I really should have listened to my friends."

"But half of them were telling you to do it and the other half not."

"No. My *real* friends were telling me not to do it."

She sighed. He was right. Her friends had tried to stop her, but she hadn't listened. If Ben hadn't come back she might have backed down on her determination to leave. She might have looked for another way to help out Gran LeBieu. Now she was committed. "Jean, have you ever been in love?"

"Lucie." He shook his head. "You got a customer on table three."

End of conversation. What had she hoped to discover with his answer? Lucie waited the table and when she returned to the counter, Maurice Saulnier had taken up residence on the stool.

Lucie stood next to him and leaned on the counter. Jean had his back to her, pulling beer bottles from cartons, stacking them in the cooler. He glanced back once, but found something else to do that required his attention.

Definitely the end of the conversation with Jean.

"Hi, Lucie," Mo said. He tipped his bottle and swallowed a long gulp. Still in his coveralls with the Littington logo embroidered on the right front pocket, he must have come straight from work.

"Where's Larry?"

"Had to babysit his little sisters tonight. He be makin' a good wife to someone one day." Mo chuckled at his own joke.

"What about you?" If Jean wouldn't answer her question, Lucie may as well poll the only other person within hearing range. "Have you ever been in love?"

"Not Mo. Who gonna love dis big, bad boy?" His words were stated without self-pity, like a man simply asking a rhetorical question.

"Why Mo, any young lady would be happy to have you as her husband." She slid onto the stool next to him.

His shaggy black eyebrows rose an inch. "Would you?"

Gulp. She should have seen that one coming. How to let him down gently? "I'd be proud to be your wife..."

"But. Dey always be buts." Mo shrugged. "No matter, I be happy to live wit' Granny. She cooks, she cleans. What more do I need?"

"Love?"

"Who needs it? It only gives you pain." He clenched his fist over his heart. "Right here."

"Maurice, there's someone out there for everyone. Don't give up." Her heart hurt as if Mo's burly fist had squeezed it. Just as she'd felt when Ben had thrown his harsh words in her face seven years ago. "What if you could come up with a love potion to make someone fall in love with you? Would you use it?"

Maurice tipped his head to one side and squinted as if seeing into a hazy future. "No."

"No?" Was every one of the same opinion about love potions? First Alex and Calliope, and now Maurice. "Why not?"

"She wouldn't love Mo for Mo." He tipped his beer and downed the last bit in one swallow. "I couldn't live wit' de lie."

What could Lucie say to that? Maurice, who didn't have many thoughts crowded into his head, was deeper than she'd imagined. Or the answer was too obvious for even her to see. Love by way of magic was a lie. Plain as Pinocchio's nose—a big, fat lie.

Even if she managed to get Eric to pop the question,

would she accept? Could she be happy as his wife knowing she'd orchestrated the outcome?

"Hey, guys. 'Sup?" Alex, with Calliope close behind, stepped up to the bar.

"What's yer poison, ladies?" Jean tossed his bar towel over his shoulder and leaned his elbows on the counter.

"I'll have my usual," Alex said.

"One Miller Lite coming up." Jean yanked a bottle out of the cooler, tipped it under the bottle opener and set it in front of Alex. "What about you, Red?"

Calliope, bless her soul, had a finger touching her chin, and her gaze shot to the far corner.

"Give her the same, Jean, or we'll be here all night," Alex said.

"But I might have wanted something frozen or fruity." Calliope pouted, but smiled when Jean set the beer in front of her. "Thanks, Jean."

"So," Lucie said. "Are you two staking out the bar tonight or do you want me to find you a table?"

"Table, definitely." Alex shot a brief glance around the room. "I'm not man-hunting tonight."

"Honey," Lucie said, "you're never man-hunting. You've got your mother to do that for you."

"You know what they say, don't you?" Calliope lifted her bottle to her lips and swallowed.

Lucie glanced at Alex. "I give up, what do they say?"

A drop of beer trickled out the side of Calliope's mouth and she reached up to wipe it clean. "You'll only find true love when you're not looking."

Again, that little squeezing action attacked Lucie's heart. Maybe she was having a cardio-something. She hadn't been looking for love in a long, long time and certainly not now. Maybe Lucie LeBieu didn't want love—stability was more her goal—but that didn't mean she should dash someone else's hopes.

She leaned back toward the bar and whispered in Mo's ear, "Better be careful. You're not looking for love, so someone's gonna show up and knock your socks off." She kissed his cheek and turned toward her friends. "Come on. Let me find you the perfect table."

After crossing the dance floor, Calliope draped herself across her seat and nodded at Lucie. "So, what's with you and Maurice?"

"Oh, nothin' much." She dusted an imaginary speck off her black tank top to avoid eye contact. Not a chance she'd tell her friends about either one of her earlier conversations. Likely, they'd give her a whopping big, "I told ya so!"

"Someone tell you that you shouldn't have done it, or something?" Alex asked.

Damn her, damn Alex to Hell Bayou. You'd think the girl was psychic, the way she read her mind. Telltale heat crept up her neck to flood into her cheeks, right out to the tips of her ears. "No, that isn't it at all." Her ears were so hot they sizzled.

"Liar."

Busted.

"Who was it? Jean?" Calliope leaned forward. "I love playing the guessing game. I bet five bucks it was Maurice."

"Look, I haven't told anyone else about the love bug." At least that was true. "And I don't plan to."

"Have you done anything yet to reverse the spell?" Alex asked.

She scuffed the toe of her high heel against the wooden flooring. "Not yet."

Alex's lips pressed into a thin line. "Did you even find the bug?"

Lucie paced a tight line in front of the table, her hands waving in the air. "I spent the best part of my day looking all over Bayou Miste for that damned bug. I found dragonflies, beetles, flies, mosquitoes, and other really disgusting bugs, but not once did I see that hexed ladybug. It would be easier to find a needle in a haystack."

"*Coo-wee!*" Calliope sat back her eyes wide. "Do you realize how many bugs there are in the swamp? You could spend your lifetime looking for that one."

She spun toward Calliope. "Exactly!"

While she'd been talking, customers had entered the bar, seating themselves around the room. A lucky break. "I gotta get back to work."

"Don't think you're off my shit list, girlfriend. Until you un-hex my brother, you're mud." Alex's words were harsh but she tempered them with a wink. "We'll talk later."

Lucie hurried to fill orders, barely stopping to chat with anyone for very long. The usual customers had already claimed their favorite tables, and for a Thursday night, the bar was crowded. She recognized a few of the protesters gathered around tables near the door, as if they might have to make a hasty escape from the riled-up locals.

She swerved around a burly Cajun speaking with his hands. As she passed by another table, someone grabbed her arm, pulling her to a stop.

"Lucie, ain't you even gonna say hello?"

In all the bustle, she hadn't seen Pascal Pasquale enter the bar. "I'm sorry, Pascal. What can I get you?"

"I'll have a Bud."

"Anything else? You want some oyster shooters or pretzels to go with that beer?"

"No, thank you."

She swung back toward the bar only to be snagged again. With a pointed glance down at the arm Pascal held in his grip, she asked, "Did you change your mind?"

Pascal held tight, ducking his chin. "Lucie, would you consider going out with me?"

"Huh?" The question was so out of the blue, she hadn't seen it coming. Go out with Pascal? After he'd stalked her in fifth grade?

He looked up, his expression that of a puppy in the pet store. *Choose me! Choose me!*

Always a sucker for the pathetic pooch in the window, Lucie had a hard time coming up with the right words to let Pascal down easy. "No." Okay, so that wasn't so hard. Definitely blunt though, and not the least sugarcoated.

Pascal's puppy-dog plea morphed into an angry Cajun scowl. "Is it that I'm not good enough?"

"No, not at all." She twisted her arm a little trying to dislodge Pascal's hand. "I'm just not interested in going out with you."

"It's Eric, isn't it? Eric Littington. He's good enough for you, isn't he?" Pascal squeezed her arm harder.

"Is there a problem here?" A man's stern tone sounded behind her.

She'd recognize that voice anywhere. How did Ben Boyette always manage to find her in an awkward situation? She refused to turn and see his superior expression. "Thank you, Ben. I can handle this."

"I see that." His words said one thing, his inflection implied, *Like hell you can.*

Lucie bristled and struggled even harder to pry Pascal's fingers off her arm. She'd be damned if she let Ben rescue her yet again. She could get *herself* out of any tangle thrown her way. Her fingers started to cramp. Pascal's grip was like a friggin' vise.

"Pascal, let the girl go." Ben spoke in a quiet, commanding manner. *No, no, no!* She couldn't let Ben be the hero here. It would be one more reason to fall back in love with the bastard, and she wasn't going there. Ever again. It hurt too damned much.

Pascal hesitated a moment and then eased up on his grip.

Lucie yanked loose and stepped out of reach. She could have extricated herself from the situation. Just because Ben stepped in didn't mean she couldn't save herself. He wasn't some tall, dark and handsome hero she'd ever swoon over. Been there, done that, could write a really sappy love song about it. "Thanks," she spit out. To herself, she added, *But that doesn't change a thing.*

***

Ben would bet his paycheck she hated that "thanks." "I only wanted to ask her out," Pascal grumbled. "But no, I'm not good enough. She'd rather go out with that pansy, Eric."

"Know the feeling," Ben muttered beneath his breath.

Lucie darted a fierce look at him. "Ben Boyette, you don't know anything, so shut your trap." With that, she stormed away, tray and all.

Her anger enhanced the sway of her fanny in the cutoff shorts that were paired with that ridiculous black tank top. He drew a hand down his face. Lucie's figure would start a riot before quitting time.

"What did I miss?" Eric walked up to stand beside him. "Ah, I see. Did you two have another spat?"

"No, not at all." Ben pried his gaze from Lucie's bodacious buns and attempted a poker face. "Let's sit."

They found a table in a far corner and both men sat with their backs to the wall. Ben almost laughed out loud. Part of the reason they sat that way was because of the rock through the window the night before. But mostly because of one Cajun swamp siren. From their position, they could easily see Lucie moving between the tables.

"She's a beauty, isn't she?" Eric's question didn't require a response. His gaze followed Lucie's every move to the exclusion of everything else in the bar, including Ben.

"I reviewed the security cameras from the house. As I expected, the vandal was out of camera range when he threw the rock."

"Huh?" Eric turned to face Ben, his eyes glazed. He shook his head and smiled. "Sorry, I can't seem to help myself. She intrigues me."

"She has that effect on most men." Could Eric just shut up about Lucie already? The muscles in Ben's neck were already tight from the Pascal incident. He didn't need more Lucie-related stress. And having other men panting after her didn't help one bit.

"I asked Alex about her favorite flower." Eric's gaze strayed back to Lucie.

"White roses, without those little white filler flowers. Baby's breath, I think." As soon as he said the words, he could have kicked himself. His statement was way more information than Eric needed to know.

"She looks like a roses kind of girl. But why no baby's breath? And while we're on the topic, why do you know all that about her?" Eric finally pulled himself from ogling Lucie and focused on Ben.

Like a worm pinned to the dissecting tray, he fought to keep from squirming. "Lucie and I used to date."

Eric's eyebrows rose. "But you told me you weren't interested."

"I wasn't."

"But you are now?"

"No, I'm not." Ben pushed a hand through his hair and reached for his beer. Oh yeah, Lucie hadn't come by to take their order. "Want a beer? I'll get one from the bar."

"Oh, no, I'm waiting for Lucie to take my order," Eric

said. "She should make it over here soon. I'd much prefer her to bring my beer. She's better-looking. No offense."

Ben smacked his palm on the table. "Well, I'm not waiting."

A grin lifted the corner of Eric's mouth. "Ben Boyette, you're avoiding my question."

"Man's got a right." *To avoid a question and to get his own beer.*

With a shrug, the blond man sat back in his chair and crossed his arms over his chest. "Suit yourself. But I suspect there's more to your story than you're letting on."

A lot more. And you're not getting it, buddy. Ben lurched from his chair and stomped toward the bar. As he passed by folks he knew, they raised a hand and smiled in greeting, only to drop the smile and settle for a subdued *Hi.* Ben realized he was scowling like a cranky black bear and forced himself to walk like a normal person, masking his emotions in a friendly Cajun grimace.

Once again, Lucie LeBieu had slipped under his skin and made him itch.

Determined not to stare around the saloon, he kept his eyes on his goal, the bar. He ordered a beer and exchanged a few pleasantries with Jean. A moment later he didn't recall a single word of their conversation.

Longneck in hand, he turned back in time to see Lucie smiling and laughing down at Eric Littington. With her equipment, her tank top should have been declared indecent. And those shorts. Well, Ben's mamma had taught her daughters better than that. Why, every man in the room was staring at her like she was a side of slow-roasted meat. Good enough to salivate over and most definitely good enough to eat.

He groaned. His footsteps slowed and faltered until he barely moved. Every step closer raised his blood pressure another notch and his libido exponentially. What was *wrong* with him? He didn't care about her anymore. He didn't love Lucie as he had seven years ago. She was trouble now, and had been from the get-go.

But he couldn't help himself. And he couldn't stand by and let her flirt with Eric. He had to interfere. Every ounce of testosterone screamed for him to do something about it. She just wasn't right for Eric.

Then who the hell *was* she right for?

Me. The irritating little voice in his head shouted, *Me! Me! Me!*

A bellow from two tables beyond her caught Lucie's attention. She excused herself from Eric and hurried to take another order. But instead of going back to the bar she turned down the corridor to the ladies' room.

Like a hunting dog closing in on the fox, Ben slipped into the shadows of the hallway and waited for her to come out.

As he lurked at the end of the corridor, hidden in the corner, he knew his actions were bizarre and unwarranted, but he couldn't stand by and let her continue to target Eric. He had to show her how wrong she was.

Several women exited the bathroom.

He leaned on the wall and willed his blood to quit pounding against his ears. But as soon as Lucie stepped through the doorway, his heart hammered against the wall of his chest. Quickly, before she could dart out of the hall, he grabbed her from behind and pulled her to him.

She gasped and jabbed her elbow into his ribs.

Sharp pain shot out from the point of contact, but he didn't let go of his grip on her arm.

"Let me go, or I'll scream," she warned.

"Jeez, Lucie, it's just me," he gasped out.

"Ben?" She turned to face him. "What the hell are you doing lurking outside the ladies' restroom?"

"Maybe I was headed for the men's room." He dropped

her arm and pressed his fingers to his ribs. "Ouch. I think you broke my rib."

"You deserved it." After a moment, her tight lips softened and she sighed. "Here, let me see." With deft fingers, she unbuttoned his shirt down to where his hand still pressed to his rib cage. "Move."

"Yes, ma'am." Her knuckles brushed his chest, the touch doing crazy things to his erratic heartbeat. But when she reached inside and pressed her fingertips to his skin over the sore spot, he'd had all he could stand. He pinned her to the wall, trapping her hand between them.

"Do you know what you do to me?" His voice was a low growl.

Like a cornered animal, her eyes widened, and her gaze darted to either side of him. "Let me go," she said in a breathy whisper.

His raging body demanded more. He couldn't let her go if his life depended on it. He told himself he would only kiss her once, to prove Eric wasn't the one for her. But the rampaging testosterone in his body told him once would never be enough —not with Lucie.

With one hand caressing her cheek, he slid the backs of his other fingers up her bare arm to trail across her collarbone.

She shivered beneath his touch, goose bumps rising on her creamy arm. "Your skin is just as I remembered it. Smooth and" —he leaned down to inhale her fragrance, his lips lingering near her neck—"smelling of roses."

Her warmth drew him to her and he pressed a light kiss to the pulse beating in her throat. Branding a slow, deliberate path upward, he brushed his lips against her chin and across to claim her mouth. The kiss was everything he'd been fantasizing, and more. Much more.

With a sigh, she leaned into him, ever closer, her hips firmly pressed against his, her arms snaking around his neck.

She threaded her fingers into the hair at the back of his neck, pulling him even deeper into the kiss.

He felt as though he'd come home. This was where he belonged, in this woman's arms, kissing her, holding her, loving her like there was no tomorrow and no yesterday. Just here, now. Only the two of them.

His tongue dove deep, twisting and sparring with hers, their kiss taking on a frantic urgency. Her hands slipped inside his shirt, climbing up his chest to feather through the curls there and tweak his nipples.

His blood on fire, he leaned into her, pushing his knee between her legs. He wanted to shove her high up the wall and down over him, taking her right there.

"Ah-*hem*." A feminine voice sounded behind him, but he couldn't focus on anything but Lucie. His head was in a sex-induced fog.

Lucie broke the kiss first. "Ohmigod," she whispered. Then she pushed at him, fighting to be free.

"Next time you two should get a room."

He stepped away from Lucie and turned toward the source of the interruption.

Alex.

"There won't be a next time." Lucie's face was flushed, with a thin sheen of perspiration glowing in the dim light from the ancient fixtures. "This shouldn't have happened. It changes nothing." She poked a finger into his chest. "Ben Boyette, you stay away from me, do you hear? Stay *away* from me." Then she turned and fled back into the crowded barroom.

Were those tears he'd seen shimmering on her eyelashes? Imagine that. Lucie LeBieu never cried. He must really have gotten to her.

A smile curled the edges of his lips.

"I wouldn't be so smug." His sister crossed her arms over

her chest and shot him a look that reminded him of their mother.

"She still has feelings for me," he said. The thought exploded in his chest.

"Yeah, but there's seven-year-old baggage that goes with those feelings. Something to do with words said in anger." Alex tapped her chin. "Hmm. Do the words 'You're nothing but a teasing bayou bimbo' ring a bell?"

His brows furrowed. How did she know about those stupid words he'd said all those years ago? "In case you've forgotten, Lucie dumped *me*."

Alex shook her head and turned to leave. "You men are so damn clueless."

He reached out and snagged Alex's arm. "What are you talking about?" Something wasn't right with this entire picture. "Didn't you hear me? Lucie dumped me back then. Why would she do that if she still loves me? It makes no sense."

"Maybe you should ask her." With that parting shot, his sister shook off his hand and left him standing in the darkened hallway, feeling like the clueless man women were always complaining about.

Damn.

Couldn't Alex give him a break and just spell it out?

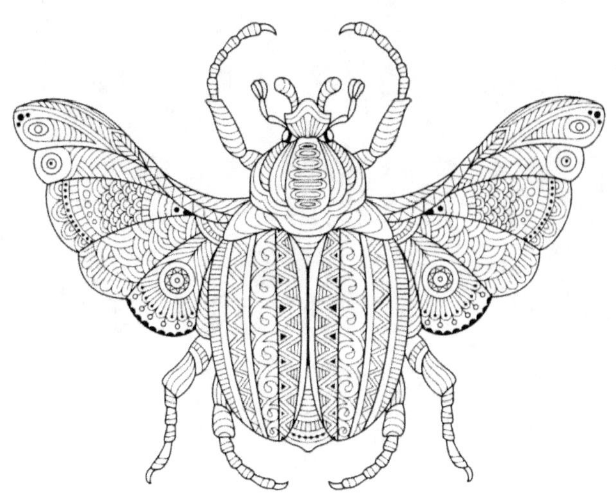

Chapter Nine

Ah, this was the life. Lucie arrived at the parish pavilion in Eric's smooth, sexy BMW. A good-looking man beside her, the smell of leather and luxury filling the air—what more could she want?

Ben Boyette, a little voice whispered in her head.

Shut up! I don't need the man. He didn't care a fig about her, so she had to get him firmly out of her head.

Somehow.

"Something wrong?" Eric asked.

Huh? Oh, yeah. She was with Eric. She sent him a dazzling smile. "No, no. What could possibly be wrong?"

"I don't know, but you looked like you were about to start a fight with your seat belt." He pulled the car into the pavilion's gravel lot, shifted into park, and turned toward her.

She immediately loosened her grip on the silvery safety strap and forced a smile wider on her lips. "I must have been daydreaming."

"Well, I hope you weren't daydreaming about me, then. If I went by the look on your face, I'd be tarred, feathered, and hung out to dry."

Lucie winced. "That bad?"

"Yes." His gentle grin lightened his response.

"If it helps, I wasn't terrorizing you in my dream. I was just thinking of work." That wasn't too far from the truth. She'd been at work when Ben had kissed her.

"Well, tonight you don't have to think about work. Just concentrate on having a good time. With me." He leaned close.

Oh, lord. He was going to kiss her. A sudden surge of panic pressed against her lungs.

He flicked the button and released her seat belt. "I have to warn you, since this shindig was an open invitation to everyone in the parish, there might be reporters here."

"Is that a problem?" Reporters were a norm around Bayou Miste, ever since the big chemical dumping issue. Protesters brought as many as they could into the bayou.

"Well, they do get in the way sometimes and ask a lot of questions," Eric said.

"I should think you would be very good at answering their questions, in your line of work."

"Yes, but since you're with me they'll be asking you questions, too."

"Oh." Why hadn't she thought of that before? Being Eric's date had inherent social obligations. Hmm. "Don't worry." She smiled brightly. "I won't embarrass you." *I hope.*

"I don't think you could ever embarrass me. I just meant for you to be prepared. They may ask some very personal questions." His lips twisted. "Sometimes they aren't very tactful."

"I'll consider myself forewarned."

He climbed out of the sports car and hurried around to open the door for her.

She'd have to thank her friends for helping her shop for

the perfect dress for the occasion. The smooth, silk crepe hugged her body from her breasts to her hips where the skirt flared out, swirling down to midcalf. The creamy white fabric complemented her black hair and deep, olive skin tones. Although she was still Lucie LeBieu inside, the clothes definitely gave her the confidence she needed to stand beside Eric.

As she hooked her arm through the congressional candidate's elbow, she fixed her smile on her face and prepared to meet her future.

"Eric, Lucie, good to see you." Ben joined them as soon as they stepped beneath the pavilion. Dressed in scrumptious black jeans accentuating the taut muscles beneath, and topped by a matching long-sleeved black shirt, he looked incredible.

Lucie wanted to stomp her high-heeled foot. Why couldn't Ben just disappear off the face of the earth? He always managed to show up wherever she was and throw off her focus.

On second thought, why should she care?

She glanced up, her gaze meeting his. Warmth spread from her chest downward. Okay, so staring into Ben's eyes wasn't such a good idea. She looked away first. Back to Eric— her future.

"Ben," Eric shook his hand. "How's the bug business?"

"Great." Ben grinned. "Neutralizing as many as I can find."

Was that a wink Eric gave Ben? She must be seeing things. Ben and Eric sure were spending a lot of time together for a potential congressman and an ordinary bug exterminator. Okay, so Ben wasn't so ordinary. But he was a bug exterminator. Not that killing bugs was a bad business to be in, especially in southern Louisiana.

"Please excuse us." Eric gave his smooth politician's smile. "I'd better make my presence known to my father."

"By all means." Ben sketched a mocking bow. A slow, sexy smile spread across his face as his gaze slid up her legs.

Damn Cajun. Didn't he know when to give up? Didn't he know they were finished seven years ago?

Then why did his kiss bother her so much?

"Lucie," Eric was saying, "I'd like you to meet my father, Jason Littington."

Oh yeah, she was with Eric. A man who resembled an older version of her date held out his hand. She had to pull herself together. She'd do well to display her best manners and behavior if she wanted to make a good impression on her future father-in-law. She took the proffered hand. "It's very nice to meet you, Mr. Littington." There, that wasn't so hard. She could do this.

"The pleasure is mine." He half-bowed over her hand in a charming, old-fashioned way. "I've heard so much about you." His suave words were a contradiction to his slightly narrowed eyes.

Instead of feeling flattered, she had a sudden attack of nerves. In the older man's firm, almost painful grip on her hand, she sensed latent animosity. And what did he mean he'd heard so much about her?

She stopped short of defending herself. That would only lend credence to whatever rumors he'd digested as gospel. With as much grace as she could hope for, she pulled her hand free and playfully batted her long lashes at the man. "Oh, don't believe everything you hear, unless it was all good. You can believe that."

Eric's face was a little pale and strained. Apparently, she had been a topic of discussion in the Littington household, and father and son had varying opinions. Interesting. A twinge of guilt rippled through her stomach. She hated to be the object of contention between the men. But if she wanted to attain her goal of saving her grandmother's home and getting the hell out of Bayou Miste, she'd have to suck it up and make it right.

"Mr. Littington, I think it's great what you're doing toward the cleanup effort in the swamp. I know you weren't responsible for the chemical dumping, and think it quite magnanimous of you and Littington Enterprises to fund the effort to remove the toxins."

Wow. She sounded as good as any politician running for office. Butter up the backers, that's how to win a campaign.

"I understand you work at the Raccoon Saloon." The elder Littington completely ignored her eloquence with a statement that wasn't a question. As if he implied her job as a barroom waitress wasn't good enough.

The hairs on the back of her neck bristled and her fighting instincts kicked in. What the heck did he expect? That she could afford to sit at home and learn needlepoint, paint her nails, and eat bonbons all day?

Eric cupped her elbow. "Dad, if you'll excuse us, I believe Miss LeBieu would like a drink, wouldn't you, Lucie?"

Before his father could protest, Eric led her in the direction of the bar.

"You warned me about reporters, but you didn't warn me about your father." She cringed at how waspish she sounded, but her nerves were just a little on the frayed side.

"I'm sorry. My father's behavior was inexcusable. His heart is generally in the right place, but he gets a little near-sighted when it comes to his only son."

"I see." She ground to a stop, pulling her elbow free of his grip. "And I'm not good enough for you?"

"Oh, you're good enough for me." He grinned. "You're great for me."

"But it'll take a little more convincing to win your father's approval." Poor Eric. Up against his father over her.

"What would you like to drink?"

"Sweet tea, please." She figured alcohol, a future father-in-law, and reporters wouldn't mix at this party.

"I'll be right back, don't go away." Eric got in line behind a number of locals intent on making the most of the open bar.

"Did you find the bug yet?" A feminine voice whispered into her ear.

Lucie turned to find Calliope dressed in a wispy floral halter dress. Beside her stood DeeDee Dubois in a very flattering cotton sundress in pastel peach. Her bushy brown hair was combed neatly and pulled back from her face, emphasizing her high cheekbones.

"Ohmigosh, DeeDee." Lucie backed up a step, her gaze sweeping over the other woman. "You look fabulous."

Well, as fabulous as DeeDee could look. Her facial features tended to resemble those of a bulldog, but with the shy smile and a little lipstick, she almost looked pretty.

"Thanks, Lucie." DeeDee blushed and ducked her head. "Calliope made me her science project for the night."

Lucie hugged Calliope, then DeeDee. "I'd say her experiment worked. You look great." She glanced behind them. "Where's Alex?"

Calliope balanced on her toes and spun in a circle. "She's here somewhere. Ah, there she is."

"Where?" Lucie asked.

"Behind the column at the dark end of the pavilion."

"What's she doing there?" DeeDee asked.

Calliope chuckled. "Her mother's here and she's snagged another man for Alex to consider."

Barbara Boyette had Larry Ezelle by the elbow, leading him around like a dog on a very short leash.

"Poor Alex." While Mrs. Boyette wasn't looking her way,

Lucie grinned and waved at her friend. "We really need to find her a man before her mother drives her nuts."

"Oh yeah, right. We." Calliope rolled her eyes. "If you get your way, there will be no 'we.' Looks like it'll be totally up to me. You'll be in DC."

"Are you going to Washington, Lucie?" DeeDee asked.

"Er..." Lucie caught Eric's gaze. That was the plan. Although, the excitement just wasn't there. "Maybe someday."

The band started a new set with a lively rendition of "Whatever Boils Your Crawfish."

"That song is one of my favorites. Come on." Calliope grabbed DeeDee's arm, steering her toward the action.

"I'll join you in a bit," Lucie called after them.

But they didn't respond. DeeDee and Calliope had already made it to the bandstand and dance floor that Eric and his father had erected for the occasion. The two women laughed, tapping their toes to the music.

The fiddle player flirted with them, jumping down from the stage to play for the two ladies before he made his way around the dance floor.

A sad smile curved Lucie's lips. She'd miss her friends and the music you could only find here in the Louisiana bayous. Washington, DC would be a lot different.

The song changed to a slow, haunting melody about a woman whose lover never returned from war. A sudden yearning, so overwhelming she could hardly breathe, filled her chest. She glanced toward Eric, still making his way to the front of the drinks line.

He shrugged at her and turned to answer a question from the man standing beside him.

Couples crowded onto the dance floor, moving into tight embraces, swaying to the strains of the song. Craig Thibodeaux drew his new fiancée, Elaine, into his arms.

Poor Craig. Lucie's twin had caused him so much grief when she'd tried to make a play for him. That Lisa was bad news. Seeing Craig and Elaine locked in each other's arms, she was glad her sister's interference hadn't worked. The couple was right together—their love practically oozed from the pores of their skin.

Must be nice.

What would it feel like to be held like that? To be loved so completely you'd sacrifice your life for another? She'd felt that way about Ben. Had sacrificed her needs for him. And for what? Only to be told she was just like her sister—nothing more than a bayou bimbo. That had been his parting shot those seven long years ago.

But before that disastrous day and those hurtful words, Ben had held her close and she had known magic.

"Dance with me." A strong arm circled her waist, the other reaching for her hand.

She melted against Ben, a natural progression from dream to reality. Her hand slipped around his neck and she leaned her cheek against his chest.

Wordlessly, she floated around the dance floor, refusing to allow rational thought to intrude and wake her from this fantasy. She and Ben had always seemed to fit, flowing together as if they'd partnered their entire lives. Her body knew his and responded to his every move in perfect synchrony.

With his chin resting against her temple, Ben dropped her hand and gathered her even closer, his hands sliding down her waist to balance on her hips. With increasing pressure, he pulled her hard against him until the ridge behind his button fly rubbed against her belly.

Liquid mercury coursed through her veins, sending tendrils of fire pulsing lower to the juncture of her thighs. Breathing grew difficult, but she didn't care. Her body rubbing against his sizzled at every contact point. Trembling, her fingers convulsing, she clutched at his hair. She wanted more. She wanted to be naked beneath him, writhing at his touch and immersed in passion only Ben could induce. Skin to skin with nothing more between them than sweat.

"May I cut in?"

Ben jerked to a halt, his head coming up, staring down at her as if asking the ultimate question.

Still dazed by what could only be considered foreplay on the dance floor, she tried to focus on Ben. Then her gaze shifted to Eric.

Holy cypress knees! What had she done?

The fire burning low in her belly extinguished, to be replaced by the warmth stealing up her neck. She glanced around to see how many people had watched her and Ben practically make love to the music. She repressed a groan when Calliope gave her a thumbs-up.

Shit! Shit! Shit!

Warm hands squeezed around her waist and she realized Ben still held her, the music was still playing, and the world, other than Calliope, hadn't stopped to gawk at her humiliation.

She jumped back, brushing her fingers down her dress, schooling her face into an innocent smile.

Ben's eyes narrowed ever so slightly, but then he turned and waved a gracious hand toward her. "Of course you can have her, Eric. I was just warming her up for you."

Anger quickly replaced embarrassment. If she had been wearing sturdier shoes, she'd have aimed one at Ben's shin. The creep! Warming her up, her fanny—setting her on fire was more the case.

With all the haughtiness of a president's wife, she tilted her nose back a bit. "Thank you for the dance." And with as much grace as she could muster, she slid into Eric's arms and danced him away from Ben.

"Hey, isn't it usual for the man to lead?" Eric laughed down at her, holding her lightly in his arms. Unlike Ben's proprietary grip.

She slowed her escape and attempted a laugh that came out sounding more like a choked giggle. "I'm sorry, Eric. Must be the stress of all those reporters lurking on the edges of the crowd."

"If this is too much for you, tell me. I'll have you home before you can say 'Louisiana.'"

"No, no. But I am a little warm." And her discomfort had nothing to do with the air temperature. Dancing with Eric didn't mesh with the aftereffects of Ben's touch still running rampant in her system. "Do you think we could sit this one out?"

"Certainly. I have our drinks on a table nearby. What say we grab them, and you and I can walk along the boardwalk?"

At this point, she would grasp at any method of escaping Ben's presence. "Perfect." She hurried Eric out of the crowd and snatched up the plastic cups filled with half-melted ice and watered-down tea. "Quick, before we're followed." She handed one of the cups to Eric, grabbed his hand, and tugged him through the gate leading to the raised walkway extending out over the swamp.

Once past the noise and crush of the masses, she slowed her pace and relaxed, allowing the monotonous drone of the bayou creatures to soothe her jangled nerves.

At the farthest point of the walkway was an observation deck, large enough to hold ten or more people. Benches allowed visitors to take a break or just to sit and enjoy the sights and sounds unique to the swamp experience. Little plaques bolted to the railing at intervals gave the reader factoids about the local flora and fauna. But in the light of a half moon, the writing was impossible to see.

And apparently Eric wasn't interested in reading, anyway. He leaned his backside against the rail and pulled her into his arms.

Too soon! Too soon! She'd barely gotten her breathing back to normal from her encounter with Ben. How could she go right into another man's arms? Especially when that man seemed intent on kissing her?

"Did you know the parish elementary schools raised the money to have this nature walk built? It took them five years to come up with enough cash," she gushed. "Not only did they raise the money, they also helped with the actual construction, clearing weeds, and cleaning up after the workers."

With a gentle touch, Eric pressed his finger to her lips, stilling her next words.

Uh-oh. He was definitely going to k—

His mouth descended on hers, warm and tender, and incredibly sweet.

The kiss started out as gentle, yet firm against her lips. Not bad, so far. His lips were warm and sensuous, not thin and rock hard.

The pressure increased and his tongue darted out to tease hers.

Okay, so she should let him in to see if his kiss was any better or worse than Ben's. She eased her lips and teeth open.

She returned his kiss, determined to find in him all the passion she'd felt in Ben's kiss the day before. She stood on her tiptoes and laced her arms around Eric's neck, pressing her body against his.

He pulled her close, deepening the pressure, sliding his tongue between her teeth, delving for, and toying with, hers.

Still...

Nothing.

But love could grow, couldn't it? Given time, she'd grow to love Eric more than Ben. At least he'd respect her. Eric made her forget the ugly rumors, the names she'd been called growing up. He'd never call her a bayou bimbo. He'd love her and take care of her. He was just that kind of man.

She pressed harder against him. Why couldn't she feel anything more for him than sincere like? He was a great guy, for heaven's sake!

The more she tried to feel it, the less she did. The kiss was not working.

A click and a flash of light pierced the gloom.

"What the hell?" Eric straightened, his hands dropping to his sides.

She jumped away from him, blinking, her night vision temporarily blinded. "What was that?" In her mind, though, she was glad for the intrusion. She needed time to think, to understand.

"Damned reporter." Eric reached out and cupped her cheek, his thumb rubbing over her bottom lip. "We need to talk."

Unable to think of a coherent response, she nodded. Yes, they needed to talk. Although with thoughts pinging around inside her head like the little metal ball in the pinball machine, she didn't have a clue what she'd say.

"Right now, we'd better get back to the party." He grabbed her hand and pulled her along the boardwalk.

The closer they got to the lights and music, the more she knew she couldn't go back. Not like this. Not after her sensual dance with Ben and her failed kiss with Eric.

Suddenly, a tiny dot of fluorescent green flashed in her peripheral vision.

The love bug!

So much for escaping the crowd, Ben, and Eric. She had

to stay and catch the damned bug before it messed up any more lives.

But first she had to ditch Eric. "I sure could use sweet tea."

"Don't move. I'll get you one." He darted off toward the bar. The crowd around the free alcohol had expanded. Poor Eric would be busy for a while. Good.

She spotted the bug just outside the pavilion, not near any people yet but closing in fast on a small group standing at the edge of the platform. Maurice Saulnier stood next to Calliope and DeeDee, all three watching as Mrs. Boyette sailed by with Larry still in her clutches. Mo's deep, rumbling laughter echoed across the open-air pavilion to Lucie.

As if drawn by his amusement, the ladybug altered course and zeroed in on Mo.

Oh, damn. If she didn't hurry, any one of them, or all three, could be hexed.

Running in high heels and dodging partying Cajuns was like negotiating an obstacle course. By the time she'd crossed the pavilion, the bug had made a complete circle around Mo's head.

Still too far to do anything about it, she was blocked by a group of rabble-rousers just starting a conga line. The line was a solid mass, a human barricade. No one would budge from his or her position to allow her to pass through.

"Calliope!" Heads turned at Lucie's shout, but the noise of the music and loud conversations continued.

Calliope stepped away from Mo, closing the distance between her and Lucie. But the conga line had expanded between them.

"The bug!" Lucie shouted and pointed at Mo.

With Calliope out of the picture, the hesitant bug made its decision and plotted an erratic path in DeeDee Dubois's direction.

"Oh, no!" Calliope launched herself at a laughing DeeDee, tackling her to the ground in an unattractive tangle of legs and fancy dresses.

From her position, trapped behind the conga line, Lucie could only shake her head.

Too late. Maurice and DeeDee could be added to the list of tragic victims of her careless meddling.

The bug had made its circle, cast its spell, and was now racing after Larry and Mrs. Boyette.

With Calliope down for the count and a bunch of inebriated, rowdy Cajuns blocking her path, Lucie could only watch, dread swishing around in her belly like stump water.

Mrs. Boyette stopped, with her hand still on Larry's arm, to talk to Elaine Smith. Where the hell was Craig, Elaine's fiancé?

Move, Mrs. Boyette! Move! Elaine scanned the room as if looking for someone and finally pointed at the far corner.

Lucie swung around to see what Elaine had pointed at. Poor unsuspecting Alex stood guzzling a beer and talking with Eric in a darkened corner.

Good. Maybe Mrs. Boyette would get Larry out of there before the bug reached—

Oh crap!

The fluorescent green dot circled Larry's head just as Mrs. Boyette grabbed his arm and marched him away from Elaine.

"No!" Lucie leaped at the conga line. "Let me through!"

Mozelle Reneau made room for her, but only enough to trap her into the dance. Swept into the bouncing, wiggling whip, she twisted to look over her shoulder. She could only watch in utter dismay as the bug rounded Elaine's curly dark hair.

When she finally broke through the line, the love bug had

disappeared into the swamp and Elaine stood staring after Larry, a dazed expression on her face.

The sudden awareness of someone standing beside her put Lucie's nerves on alert. The hairs on the back of her neck stood at attention, while a ghost of excitement trickled downward. Only one man had that effect on her.

Ben leaned close, his breath stirring her hair. "What are you up to, Lucie LeBieu?"

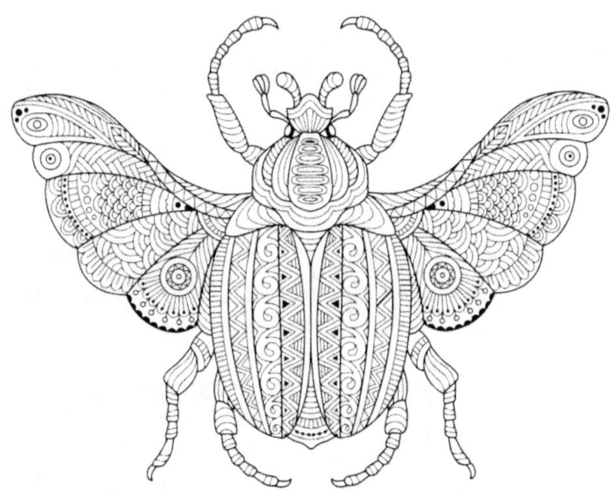

Chapter Ten

Lucie groaned. "Why can't you just go away?"

Trouble was, Ben couldn't quite figure out the answer to that very question, either.

And it bugged him.

Every time he was near her, he ached to touch her. Earlier, on the dance floor, he'd completely forgotten where he was—an easy thing to do when she was in his arms.

He was saved from answering her question when Pascal Pasquale broke through the boisterous conga line.

The Cajun security guard's angry scowl, in stark contrast with the smiling faces of the other revelers, triggered his cop instincts.

Pascal marched toward Lucie, his steps on the unsteady side, but his gaze intent, as if he were looking for a fight.

Ben stepped forward, blocking Pascal's path. "Pascal, it's been a long time. What can I do for you?"

"You can get outta my way, for one." Pascal glared up at him. "I wanna talk to Lucie."

"Why don't you let someone drive you home. You've had more than enough liquor for one night."

"I don't need no ex-cop tellin' me what I oughta do." He stood his ground, swaying slightly. "I wanna talk to Lucie."

"Guess you'll have to talk through me, then, 'cause I'm not letting you near her the way you're acting." Ben crossed his arms over his chest.

Pascal clenched his fists and glared at him, hesitating as if he couldn't decide whether to fight or leave.

Lucie touched Ben's arm. "Let him talk. I don't want a fight."

"You heard the woman, let her talk to me." Pascal smirked.

"Are you sure?" He frowned down at her.

"Sure. Pascal and I are old friends, aren't we?"

"Not in our lifetime." Pascal's words were shot at her as if he spat nails. "I saw what you did on the boardwalk."

"Pascal." She darted a glance at Ben. "You know it's not nice to spy on people."

"You've been kissing him." The guard heaved huge amounts of air into his lungs, blowing it out through his nostrils like the cornered beast at a Spanish bullfight. "Pascal Pasquale is never good enough for you—you swamp trash!" Pascal lunged for her.

Ben stepped in the middle of them, grabbing hold of Pascal's arm and wrenching it back and up between the angry man's shoulder blades. "That's enough, Pascal. No one wants a fight here."

"You won't go out with me, but you'll go out with that rich son of a bitch who doesn't deserve you. You know he'll never marry you."

"Shut up, Pascal." Ben jerked the man's arm harder until he gasped and held his tongue. "Now are you going to leave nicely or am I gonna have to call the sheriff over here? I saw him looking this way."

When Pascal refused to answer, Ben pushed his arm up higher.

"Okay, okay, I'll leave."

"What's going on here?" Eric walked up with two plastic cups in his hands.

"We were just having a little discussion, weren't we?" Ben retained his hold on Pascal.

"It's all your fault—you and your father's. You Littingtons take everything from de Pasquales!" Pascal lunged at Eric.

The congressional candidate gracefully dodged the attack, drinks intact.

"Pascal, what you be doin' both'rin' dese nice people?" Pete Pasquale, Pascal's father, stepped through the crowd. "Ain't you got no better manners 'n dat?"

"But Pappa—"

"Don't interrupt me when I be talkin', boy." Pete's reprimand cut through Pascal's protest.

Pascal's angry frown turned sullen, his chin jutting out farther.

"Now what seems to be da problem?" Wearing faded jeans and a fancy cowboy shirt adorned with mother-of-pearl snaps, Pete tapped the shiny toe of his alligator-skin boots and stared across his son's shoulder at Ben. "My boy been causin' a ruckus?"

Ben didn't like the way Pete talked down to Pascal, but he had more pressing problems, like hanging on to one red-hot ragin' Cajun ready to rumble. "He needs to go home and sleep it off."

"I'll take da boy. No need to call da sheriff over here." He smiled and waved at the sheriff standing with a group near the band, and then Pete turned a scowl on his son. "Is dere, boy?"

Pascal's lips thinned into a tight line.

"*Is* dere?" Pete asked again, his voice even more forceful than the last time.

Clearly reluctant to bow to his father's will, Pascal muttered, "No sirruh."

"I can take him from here, Ben," Pete said.

Pascal still shook beneath Ben's hold. The rage radiated heat up through his hands. "Are you going to go peaceful-like?"

"Yes, he will. Woncha, boy?" Pete answered for his son.

With a withering look, Ben said, "I was talking to Pascal." He leaned close to Pascal's ear. "Do I need to call the sheriff over here?"

"Lighten up on da arm," Pascal responded. "I'll come."

By this time, a crowd of reporters had gathered around the three, cameras clicking and flashing, adding to the noise and confusion. Ben shoved Pascal out from beneath the pavilion before he let go of the man's arm.

"What you think you be doin', boy?" Pete whacked Pascal upside the head as he climbed into the rusted-out hull of a pickup, parked nearby.

Pascal's fists clenched. "Don't hit me."

"Ain't never gonna amount to nothin', boy, if you can't make nice with important folks like our very own congressional candidate." Pete smiled back at Eric. "Why can't ya be more like him?"

Pascal collapsed into the passenger seat and slammed the door.

"That boy looks like he done bit into a green persimmon." Mozelle Reneau stood next to Ben.

He responded with a nod.

"What did he mean by the Littingtons taking everything from the Pasquales?" Lucie asked.

"I don't know," Eric said. "He works for Littington Enterprises. I can't understand why he'd turn on me like that."

"Eric," Lucie put a hand on his arm. "It was the alcohol talking tonight. You're not going to fire him, are you?"

"I don't know," Eric shook his head. "He was pretty angry. I'm not sure I can trust him at the complex if he feels like that."

She lowered her voice. "He was only mad because he saw you and me."

Ben's gut tightened. She'd left his arms to go out into the swamp on the boardwalk with Eric. "He was mad because he saw you two kissing." His words came out a lot harsher than he'd intended.

"It was none of his business who I was kissing. He had no right to accost you." Eric set the plastic cups down and grabbed both of her hands.

Ben fought the urge to step between them. *He* wanted to be the one holding her hands and kissing her.

She glanced up from beneath her lush, black eyelashes in what Ben knew was one of her best give-Lucie-what-Lucie-wants looks. "Give him another chance, Eric. I feel like it's all my fault."

"It's not your fault." Eric pressed her fingers to his chest.

The minx bit her bottom lip, staring at her hands intertwined with Eric's. "Maybe not, but I don't like being the cause of a fight."

Ben snorted.

She rewarded him with a glare.

Which only made him smile. He loved getting under her skin. His lower region twitched, reminding him there were other places on her body he'd liked to get to as well.

Apparently, Eric didn't notice their little interaction. He looked up from their combined hands and gazed into her eyes. "You have a good heart, Lucie, to be concerned about Pascal. Must be why I like you so much. I'll think about it."

If Eric got any sweeter with Lucie, Ben wouldn't be held responsible for the contents of his belly. And if he didn't like

Eric so much, he'd punch the guy for acting like a lovesick fool.

Lucie smiled so brightly Ben had to squint from the glare. "Thank you, Eric. Pascal's not so bad, he's just had a crush on me since fifth grade. I don't know why he can't get over it."

Ben knew why. Lucie was hard to shove out of your mind. Even a few hundred miles away in Baton Rouge, she'd seemed to sneak into his thoughts at least once or twice a day—and all night long.

Pascal didn't understand what motivated Lucie. She wanted only the best cut. He and Pascal both were hamburger compared to Eric's prime rib. Who'd settle for hamburger when they could have prime rib?

"Why don't we get out of here?" Eric said.

"Yeah," Lucie perched on one foot and ran the other up her leg behind her calf. "I think I've had all the fun my stiletto heels will allow for one night."

Muscles and nerves jerked to attention in Ben's body. That ankle caressing her calf set all kinds of ideas skittering across his overly active libido. *Would they please get the hell out of there before he did something stupid?*

Let Eric have her. Although that ground Ben's gut as effectively as beans in a coffee grinder. Just as Lucie had said about Pascal, Ben would just have to get over it. She wouldn't be with him if he were the last man in Louisiana—unless maybe he owned Louisiana. On a detective's salary, that wasn't likely to happen in his lifetime.

Eric pounded Ben's shoulders. "Ben, it's been fun. You'll stay, won't you? Plenty of alcohol and music." He led Lucie toward the cars.

"Yeah, lots of alcohol and music." He hadn't noticed when "Cotton Eye Joe" had started playing. Normally, it was one of his favorites. He and Lucie used to burn up the dance floor to that particular number. And just because she was leaving with another man shouldn't take the fun out of the song.

About that time the crowd yelled in unison "Bullshit!" in time to the music.

Okay, so maybe he was still hung up on the Cajun beauty, a little.

"Bullshit!" the crowd shouted again.

Okay, maybe a lot.

Eric and Lucie picked their way across the gravel parking lot to Eric's glossy BMW.

Ben had to admit, Lucie looked cool and elegant in her pale dress. No doubt, she could hold her own in a crowd of politicians.

But would she be happy?

***

Hobbling across the gravel, Lucie cursed her shoes. She was just about to lean down and slip them off to run barefoot to the car when Eric hooked her elbow and helped her along. The person who'd designed stilettos must have been a man—one who'd never had to walk across gravel in these stupid excuses for women's footwear.

She could feel Ben's gaze like a slow burn at the base of her neck, yet she refused to turn and look back. Why the hell did he have to come back to Bayou Miste now? After seven years, she'd been certain she was over him. So why did his being here bother her so much? She didn't know, but the sooner she got out of striking distance of his laser vision—and out of these killer shoes—the better.

When they reached the car, her sigh of relief turned to a gasp. "Ohmigod!"

"What the hell?" Eric exclaimed.

Every tire on the little sports car was slashed to shreds, and long scrapes marred the custom finish along the side panels. With only one spare in the trunk, the BMW wasn't going anywhere.

"Who would have done this?" She stood staring at the vandalized vehicle, stunned.

He circled the front and pointed. "Look at this."

Limping to the front, she read the spray-painted words, "Swamp Killer!"

"Good God, Eric. The protesters have gone too far with this. Don't they know you and your father aren't even responsible for the dumping?"

Eric shoved his hands into his pocket. "They may not care who dumped the toxins. Big companies make great targets. But this vandalism can't be tolerated." He pulled his cell phone out of his pocket and clicked on a speed-dial number.

"The sheriff's here, Eric. Who are you calling?"

"The auto club. The vehicle isn't fit to drive."

"I'm sure we can get a lift home from any one of the guests."

"My father left thirty minutes ago, or I'd ask him to take us."

While Eric spoke to the auto club, she balanced first on one aching foot, and then the other.

"Having problems?"

The one leg she was standing on buckled at the knee at the softly spoken words resonating next to her ear. With barely a second to spare, she got the other foot beneath her before she fell into a graceless heap. She inhaled deeply, willing her heart to a more normal pace before turning to level a we-can-handle-this-ourselves stare at Ben Boyette. "Don't you ever go away?"

His smile was smug, his eyebrows inching upward a couple hairs, like Spock's did on the old *Star Trek* reruns.

She wanted to kick his shins. Again.

Eric pressed the end button. "Oh, good. Ben, would you

mind giving us a lift home? Seems someone's had a little fun with my car."

What was Eric thinking? Her heart kicked back into overdrive, slamming blood through her veins. *Calm. Just keep calm.* "I'm sure Ben wants to enjoy the party a little longer. Why don't you fetch the sheriff while I talk to Miz Mozelle? I'm sure she wouldn't mind taking us home."

"Not to worry." Ben gave a half smirk. "I was about to leave anyway. I'd be delighted to take the two of you home."

Delighted. Lucie wanted to wipe the smug look off his face with her shoe.

"Great," Eric said. "Let me snag the sheriff first, then we can leave." Before she could protest, he'd jogged off across the gravel to find the sheriff.

Which left her stuck standing next to Ben. Alone. In the dark. Where a person could imagine all kinds of actions she wouldn't even contemplate in the daylight. A tingling sensation shivered across her nerve endings. She turned her back on the object of her confusion.

Alone with Ben Boyette was the last place she wanted to be. Her body didn't know how to respond when he was around. Or rather, her body responded just as it pleased, despite what her head tried to tell it.

"Lucie, we just heard what happened." Alex and Calliope swooped in to the rescue before she was forced into conversation with Ben.

Thank God for nosy friends and neighbors.

Eric and the sheriff were close behind. Soon, a crowd had gathered around the damaged car, insulating her from the Ben Boyette Effect.

Alex pulled her to the fringes of the crowd. "So how's the magic working?"

"Is Eric in love with you?" Calliope asked as only

Calliope could, blurting it out, loud enough only a severely deaf person wouldn't have heard what she said.

"Shh!" Lucie's cheeks reddened, but nobody seemed to be paying attention to her, anyway. "I'd rather not everyone hear about my little plan."

"Oh, I'm sorry." Calliope glanced around at the nearby onlookers, making her even more conspicuous. Then she leaned closer. "So? Is he?"

"I think so." Her gaze darted toward Ben. Was the magic working on him, too? Could that explain the close dance of a little while ago?

"Ben's been acting kinda weird all night," Alex said. "I bet the magic is playing hell with him, as well. Although I'm sure the belly-rubbin' you gave him earlier enhanced the affect."

She didn't want to think what would happen if Ben fell in love with her because of a spell. She didn't want his love if she could only get it with magic.

Then why would she settle for Eric's love when it was generated by Voodoo? She mentally smacked her forehead. *Don't get cold feet now, for chrissake.* The magic probably didn't work on a person if he hated her already. Ben couldn't be falling in love with her. No hex was that strong. *Was it?* "Maybe Ben's got an upset stomach," she suggested.

"That's how I felt last time I fell in love." Calliope sighed. "I've never had such a stomachache as when I fell head-over-heels for Rene."

Alex grunted. "That entire box of pralines you consumed didn't help, either."

"I was so in love." Calliope clasped her hands together and stared off into the night.

"And how long did that one last?" Alex asked.

"Two whole months." Calliope's head snapped up and she grinned. "My longest relationship yet."

"Point is, my brother looks like my dog, Sport, when he

eats too many sweat socks." Alex propped her hands on her hips. "The guy is an absolute case."

Lucie knew where Alex was going with this conversation, and she hurried to cut her off at the pass. "That's his problem, not mine."

Alex's brows furrowed into a deep crease over her nose. "The way I see it, it is your problem. You set that bug loose, loaded for one bear, and bagged two. You gotta let one of the bears off the hook."

"I'm not undoing the spell." Lucie crossed her arms over her chest. "I have Eric practically where I want him."

"Has he proposed?" Calliope clapped her hands. "I've always wanted to be a bridesmaid."

"Don't eat your cake before you see the shine on the ring, girlfriend." Alex grabbed Lucie's hands. "You can't leave Ben mooning over you like this. It's not right. You and he used to be a thing. What if he really has feelings for you?"

How long had she waited for Ben to come back to Bayou Miste and realize she'd only sent him away for his own good? How long had she waited for him to profess his love and apologize for his hurtful words? *Seven lonely, interminable years.*

"I'm not reversing the spell." She stood firmly on her sore feet. "I'm getting out of Bayou Miste, once and for all."

"What about Mo and DeeDee?" Alex's frown deepened. "And I think the bug zapped Larry and Elaine. What if Elaine tells Craig to shove off? Their wedding is scheduled for a week from yesterday. That's only six days away."

Lucie hunched her shoulders. "We don't even know the spell worked. Why get all worried about something that might not be a problem?"

Another giggle erupted from the swamp. Lucie, Calliope, and Alex all turned to see DeeDee and Mo walking hand-in-hand down the swamp boardwalk.

A stern look on her face, Alex poked a finger at Lucie's

chest. "Ben's my brother. Much as I think he's bossy and overbearing, he's still family, and we Boyettes look out for one another. So, if you consider yourself my friend, I suggest you fix it." Alex stomped away, her mouth set in a grim line.

Calliope glanced from Alex's retreating figure to Lucie and back. "I rode with her. I hope she doesn't leave without me." She laid a hand on Lucie's arm. "Are you okay? I mean, Alex was pretty hard on you."

She scuffed her sandal in the gravel. "Yeah, I'm okay. You go on. I don't want you to miss your ride."

"She is mad right now, but you know we love you, don't you?"

"I know, Calliope. I love you, too. Now, hurry."

Calliope scooted across the gravel to the little red Jeep Alex drove. As soon as she climbed in, the vehicle spun out of the parking lot.

Lucie stood on the edge of the crowd wondering what the hell she'd done. She wasn't happy—hadn't been happy since the moment Ben Boyette had shown up in Bayou Miste. Everything she'd tried to do from then on had only made matters worse. And now that she'd started the chain of events, how on earth could she stop it?

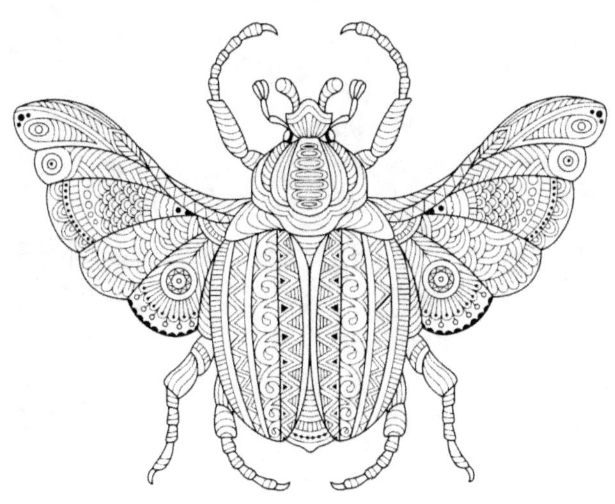

Chapter Eleven

Ben opened the screen door and knocked on Miz Mozelle Reneau's front door. He stared down at the straw mat with a bright gold sunflower and the word "welcome" painted across it. He hoped Mozelle was home. His mother said she was as good as they come for town historian or gossip. If you needed to know something, hell, anything, she knew about things as far back as anyone could remember.

And he wanted to know more about Pascal Pasquale's words from last night. What had he meant by the Littingtons taking everything? Ben had grown up in the community and hadn't noticed the Littingtons being anything but gracious and good to the people of the parish.

Mozelle Reneau was his best bet for more information. And the little fact that she happened to be Lucie's landlady had nothing to do with his being on her doorstep. Nothing whatsoever. Besides, he couldn't see the garage apartment from where he stood, anyway.

The haint blue painted door swung open. "Benjamin Franklin Boyette. Why, bless my soul." Miz Mozelle pushed the screen wide open and waved him through. "Come on in and sit a spell. Just powdered a fresh batch of beignets." She leaned close and cupped her hand around her mouth as if she was about to tell a secret in a room full of people. "Mr. Thibodeaux's favorites." She winked. "I'm sure he wouldn't mind sharin'." Mozelle took a deep breath.

While Mozelle breathed, he took the opportunity to say, "I didn't come to eat Mr. Thibodeaux's beignets. I came—"

"Nonsense." She hooked his arm with a surprisingly strong grip and ushered him into her roomy kitchen. "I always make more than the two of us could possibly eat. That's me, always making more than I need. I should have had a whole house full of children. Alas, my husband, bless his departed soul"—she made the sign of the cross over her chest—"and I weren't blessed with children. So, I give away the leftovers to the neighbors, their children, and sometimes their dogs. For that matter, I've given quite a few to your sister, Alexandra. I think she gives them to her dog, Sport. How else could she stay so slim and trim? Mind you, I'm only guessing. You tell her I don't mind in the least. That's a good dog she has. Minds his manners and doesn't dump in my yard. Occasionally sprays my rose bushes, but so far, I don't see any damage."

"Miz Mozelle," Ben blurted out, his head reeling. How could such a small woman have so much to say? "I wanted to ask you some questions. Do you mind?"

"Have a seat at the table while I get you a cup of coffee." Without stopping, she dashed around the kitchen, pulling mugs from the cabinets and filling them with the thick brown sludge the Cajuns called coffee. "You do drink coffee, don't you? Do you take it black or with cream and sugar? I even have some whipped cream, if you like the fancy kinds."

"Black is fine, thank you." Didn't this woman ever shut up? "About those questions..."

"Why certainly," Mozelle sank into the seat across from him, her eyes wide and her smile bright. "Ask away."

Before Mozelle could slip in another dissertation about beignets or dogs, he said, "Last night at the barbecue, Pascal Pasquale said something to Eric about the Littingtons taking everything from his family. Do you have any idea what he meant by that? I've lived here almost all my life, except the past seven years. Did I miss something?"

Mozelle touched a finger to her chin and stared off into a far corner of the room. "Let me see. Why would Pascal Pasquale say Eric Littington takes everything?"

"That was my question."

Mozelle's eyes narrowed. "I don't recall Eric ever taking anything from Pascal, unless..." The room fell blessedly silent for a few blissful seconds.

He actually managed to breathe two whole breaths, uninterrupted.

Then Mozelle's eyes widened and she focused on him. "Odette."

"Odette? As in Odette Littington? Eric's mother?" He had only met Mrs. Littington once before she died of cancer. He hadn't known Eric that well at the time. They must have been around fifteen years old when it happened.

Eric had taken his mother's death hard. He'd missed an entire week of school, and when he came back, he'd been a quiet shell of his former self. "What about Mrs. Littington? I can't imagine she'd take anything that didn't belong to her."

"You don't know this story?" Mozelle's smile widened and she leaned forward.

Ben almost expected her to rub her hands together like a child about to eat her favorite dessert.

"Odette was as pretty as a summer day, all golden-haired and full of sunshine. She didn't have a mean bone in her entire body." Mozelle's gaze slipped from Ben's as she slid into her memories.

"How does Odette have anything to do with Pascal? She died before Pascal could remember her."

"That might be so, but 'Stinky' never let Pascal forget."

"Who's Stinky?" Ben caught himself tapping his fingers on the table. Why couldn't she just get to the point?

Mozelle's brows furrowed. "Odette was nice to everyone, even Pete Pasquale. Everyone called him 'Stinky' back then on account he came straight to school after helping his father prepare the shrimp seines. He always smelled of shrimp and dead fish.

Ben nodded. He'd done his share of shrimping with his father before his dad traded the shrimp boat for a charter fishing rig. But even while his father was shrimping, Ben's work on the shrimp boats was confined to the late evenings, weekends, and summers. Never before school.

"The kids teased Stinky all the time, until, one day, Odette punched a boy in the mouth and told him to lay off."

Ben leaned back. "Mrs. Littington punched someone in the mouth?" He remembered her as a gentle woman with a soft voice and a sweet smile.

"She sure did. Shocked everyone. Especially Stinky."

"I still don't get the connection."

"Hold on to your britches, Ben, I'm getting there." Mozelle jumped to her feet. "Want more coffee? A beignet? I've got some shrimp gumbo if you'd like me to warm some for you."

He inhaled and counted to ten. Mozelle was only trying to be nice. "No, thank you."

Mozelle topped off Ben's coffee mug with a steamy brew. "When Stinky saw Odette punch the other fella in the mouth, he took her defense as a sign of love. That silly man thought Odette loved him."

"And did she?"

"No, of course not." Mozelle pushed a beignet in front of Ben and sat down across from him. "She was already dating Jason Littington, who'd gone off to college that year. Pete followed her around like a lost puppy for weeks. Poor girl couldn't get rid of him. After one of Jason's visits back to Bayou Miste, Odette disappeared. Her family was pert near frantic with worry. She showed up a day later with Jason. They'd done eloped and she had a shiny new ring on her finger."

"I'm still not seeing the connection. Odette didn't belong to Pete."

"No, she didn't. But Pete thought she'd been forced into marriage with Jason. He even tried to kidnap her and take her into the swamps."

Ben leaned forward in his seat. He couldn't even picture the elegant Mrs. Littington being dragged through the swamps by Stinky Pasquale. "What happened?"

"Jason found Stinky before he could get his boat started. Punched him out and threatened to have him thrown in jail if he ever so much as spoke to Odette again."

"So what does that have to do with Pascal?"

"Pete ended up marrying Frenchie Champeau, whether out of spite or what, no one knows. If it was spite, the darn fool boy only cut off his nose to spite his face. Made himself and Frenchie miserable. Frenchie got pregnant with Pascal at the same time Odette was pregnant with Eric. You'd have thought a child of his own would settle Pete Pasquale down. Instead, he compared Pascal to Eric at every turn."

Ben finished for Mozelle, "And Pascal could never live up to Eric."

"Nope." Mozelle shook her frizzy, brassy head. "Every time Eric excelled in something, Pete was sure to tell Pascal that should have been him."

"Damn." Ben had more than a little empathy for Pascal.

He'd witnessed how Pete had belittled him in front of the town last night. "No wonder Pascal hates Eric."

"Yessuh." Mozelle pleated a napkin between her fingers. "Now, I worry about Pascal falling into the same trap as his pappa."

"How so?"

"Didn't you see how Pascal was about Lucie last night?" Mozelle fixed a penetrating gaze on him. "Pantin' after her like a rabid dog, he was."

Why was Mozelle staring at him like he was just as guilty? Suddenly feeling like a rat cornered by a hungry alligator, he squirmed in his chair. Had he been just as obviously smitten as Pascal? "You think Pascal is angry enough at Eric to cause trouble?" Nothing like asking a question about someone else to deflect the scrutiny off oneself. He mentally patted himself on the back, although that squirmy feeling persisted.

"He caused a little trouble last night, didn't he?" Mozelle asked.

"Yeah, but it could have been the alcohol." Ben's job was to discover anybody interfering in Eric's campaign for Congress. Was Pascal Pasquale a threat? Would his obsession with Lucie cause problems?

Damn. He sat up straight. Would Pascal try to kidnap Lucie to keep her from seeing Eric?

"I'm not sure Pascal had the time to trash Eric's car, but he sure has a hankerin' for that Lucie." Mozelle stared hard at him again, then looked down at the napkin she'd shredded. "What happened to you and Lucie? I thought you two were in love way back when."

"That's ancient history." He didn't want to discuss Lucie with Miz Mozelle. She obviously already saw more than he'd intended.

"You two were pretty thick back before you left for the police academy in Baton Rouge. Weren't you engaged?"

"Yeah, for about two days."

"What happened?"

"I got a letter of acceptance to the police academy and she dumped me." The old pain of her rejection turned like a knife in his gut.

"Why didn't you take Lucie with you?"

For some idiotic reason, his mouth opened and answered for him, because surely he wouldn't be telling the queen of gossip about his sorry excuse for a love life. "Couldn't afford to at the time. She told me to go without her—that I wasn't good enough for her."

"Is that what happened?" Mozelle shook her head. "Huh. After you left, she moped around town for weeks as if her favorite puppy had died. Doesn't make sense."

"Did to me. She wised up. Why would she want to marry a cop? I'd never make the kind of money she wanted to marry." Ben stood. "Anyway, she wants Eric. He fits her criteria—rich and influential. As far as I'm concerned, he can have her."

A sad smile tipped the corners of Mozelle's mouth. "Still have feelins for the gal, do you?"

"Hell, no." *Liar.* He turned away from those older, knowing eyes and shook his head to clear the devil whispering in his ear. He *didn't* have feelings for Lucie. She'd dumped him. Why would he ever want to get involved with her again?

And why did he still long to hold her in his arms...?

"Sometimes people have good reasons for pushing the ones they love away. If you still have feelings for her, you ought to ask her why she sent you away."

"Seven years is a long time. I'm not going there again."

Mozelle stood up beside him and laid a hand on his shoulder. "Hurt pretty bad the first time, huh?"

"Something like that."

"Would have been hard to cart a wife around, goin'

through the academy and those first few years as a rookie cop, I suppose." Mozelle wrapped two beignets in a napkin and handed them to him.

He took the warm pastries without seeing them. Memories of those last few days with Lucie crowded into his mind. She hadn't changed a bit. Lucie was still beautiful and soft and smelled of roses.

"I see you got some thinking to do. And I got a fella to go visit. Mr. Thibodeaux and I take coffee at this time of the morning." She ushered him to the door. "If you don't eat those beignets, give them to one of your brothers or sisters. And Ben?"

"Yes, ma'am?"

"You should ask Lucie why she really sent you away. A woman's mind can work in mysterious ways."

He stepped out onto the sunflower mat, his head clouded with memories. Why *had* Lucie pushed him away? And why had she moped around after he'd gone? Could his angry words have hurt her? At the time, he hadn't thought so. She'd been pretty harsh with him, blindsiding him with her rejection.

Hell, nothing made sense when it came to women.

Why couldn't women be more straightforward, like men?

***

"*Mamère!*" Lucie stood with her door open and her mouth hanging slack. "What are you doing here?"

"Don't an old woman have de right to visit her favorite granddaughter?"

Her eyes narrowed. "Since when do you come visit me? You usually send a command for me to visit you. And grandmothers aren't supposed to have favorites."

"Be dat as it may, don't be rude and keep dese ol' bones standin' on de steps."

"I'm sorry." Lucie stepped aside, allowing the swamp's

most infamous Voodoo queen access to the inner sanctum of her one-bedroom garage apartment. She followed at a distance, wary and ready for anything. *Mamère* never paid her a visit. "If this has anything to do with the fight at the barbecue last night, I didn't start it."

Gran LeBieu worked her way through the apartment to the minuscule kitchen where she rummaged until she located Lucie's stash of tea bags. "Can't a body visit family wit'out de second degree?"

Eyes narrowed, Lucie propped a fist on one hip. "I've never known you to just go visit. Fess up. Why'd you come?"

With a teacup full of water in her hand, her grandmother fumbled with the door of the microwave, trying to pry it open. "Newfangled gadgets, can't open dem to save my life."

Lucie opened the door, stuck the cup inside, and turned the oven on. Then she leaned against the counter, her arms crossed over her chest. "*Mamère*, you're stalling."

The old woman stared straight into her eyes, her gaze direct and unflinching. "Let me get my tea, den we be settin' for a come-to-Jesus talk."

A lead weight sank to the bottom of Lucie's stomach. She felt as she had when she'd gotten caught stealing a watermelon from Charlie Hughes's watermelon patch. Had her grandmother found out about the spell? If so, who'd spilled the beans? Alex? Calliope? They were the only ones that knew. Now, here she was quaking in her slippers, fixin' to have an inch or two skinned from her hide.

The microwave binged. With a teabag in one hand and the cup of hot water in the other, the most sought-after and feared Voodoo queen in the Atchafalaya Basin made herself at home on Lucie's couch. "Come. Sit."

"I can explain," Lucie blurted.

The older woman held up a thick finger. "Don't you be talkin'. Let me tell you a thing or two." Her grandmother dipped the tea bag into the steaming water several times, dragging out the agony until Lucie thought she'd scream. "I don't know what you be up to, and maybe I don't want to know."

"You don't?" She sagged against the arm of the couch, relief filling her stomach like a cool drink of water.

Gran LeBieu gave her one of those stares that might as well have been attached to a curse.

Lucie stiffened and straightened away from the couch, her stomach churning again.

"Is dere something you be wantin' to tell your ol' *Mamère*?"

A flood of heat filled her face. "No, there's nothing out of the ordinary going on, nothing at all."

Liar, liar, pants on fire, a wicked voice called out in her head. How could she sit there and tell her grandmother a bald-faced lie? This woman had taken her in when her own mother had abandoned her.

Lucie dropped to her knees in front of the old woman, tears welling in her eyes. "Oh, Gran, I can't lie to you. My life is so screwed up, I don't know what's up from down."

Gran LeBieu patted her hands. "Everyt'ing is going to be fine. Jes you wait and see."

Lucie buried her face in her grandmother's bright-red muumuu. "Have you ever done something you wished you hadn't, but you can't undo it without hurting others?"

"You be talkin' in riddles, girl." Gran LeBieu's forehead wrinkled.

With a sigh, Lucie pushed to her feet and turned away. She really should tell her grandmother everything, starting with— "You know Eric Littington, don't you?"

"Jason Littington's boy?"

"Yes." She spun to face her grandmother. "He's handsome, smart, and going places in his political career."

"Nice young man, if I recall." The old woman's brows wrinkled. "What's your point?"

Cold feet set in, and Lucie's good intentions froze. She forced a casual shrug. "No point, I was just making a comment."

"What about dat Benjamin Boyette?"

Her heart flip-flopped. Now why would Gran LeBieu bring him up? She couldn't remember saying anything regarding Ben since her grandmother walked through the door. "What about him?"

The older woman slid a sideways glance at her. "He's handsome, smart, and going places."

"Gran, he's a bug exterminator."

The old woman's lips thinned. "It's an honest livin'."

"Besides, why should I care?" Her nonchalance had cost her with that pesky little voice inside telling her she was fibbing. She still cared.

Her grandmother's brows rose on her dark forehead. "Why, indeed?"

She fought not to squirm under her grandmother's scrutiny. "It's not like it was before he left, if that's what you're thinking."

"I wasn't thinkin' anything."

"He never loved me."

Gran LeBieu shook her head, a sad frown creasing her forehead. "You sent him away."

"It was something he'd wanted all his life. If I had married him, he would never have gone." The seven-year-old loss still hit her square in the gut. "And what do I get for my sacrifice? He called me a bayou bimbo!"

"He was hurt and angry."

"What was I? Chopped sushi?" Lucie wrapped her arms around her middle, fighting tears. She refused to shed another over that man. "Gran, he didn't come back."

"Would you? If I be recallin' rightly, you threw his love back in his face."

"He didn't come back." She repeated, her voice fading off as a damned tear spilled from the corner of her eye.

"Have you told da boy you still love him?"

"I *don't* love him. He's rude and overbearing, and couldn't care less about me. Besides, I'm going to marry Eric Littington."

Every line in Gran LeBieu's face spelled disapproval. "Do you love Eric?"

The question was the crux of all the arguments she'd had with herself and her friends. But she'd gone into this plan with her eyes wide open, and she wasn't ready to back down. "What does it matter? Lots of marriages are based on respect. Love is too hard and...messy."

"Can't have the satisfaction of making a mud pie if you don't get your hands in the mud."

Lucie pouted as she had when she was a child. "What if I don't like mud?"

"Mud is good for the swamp girl."

"That's just it, I'm tired of living in the swamp. Eric is my ticket out."

"Marriage shouldn't be a ticket, it should be all about the love between a man and a woman."

With her heart still aching from a years-old wound, Lucie couldn't hear her grandmother. Didn't want to. "Love hurts too much."

The older woman nodded once. "Sometimes. Nothing be worthwhile if you don't work hard for it."

"Love has to be equal on both sides."

"'Xactly. Think of what you be sayin', girl. Eric is a good man. Does *he* deserve to be one side to an empty equation? Dat don't add up, Lucie."

"I have thought about it." She threw her shoulders back

and stood with her feet slightly apart. "I'm going to marry Eric and we'll live happily ever after, just like a friggin' fairy tale." Her bold statement had lost its effect with the big tears that chose that moment to pop over the edge of her eyelids and slide down her cheeks.

"Then why aren't you happy, now? Don't you want to know the joy of loving and being loved?"

Her mouth moved but nothing came out. Why wasn't she happy? Wasn't Eric falling in love with her just as she'd planned? *Hell.* "I don't care if I ever fall in love again."

"Love has a way of finding you." Her grandmother touched a finger to Lucie's chin and tipped it up. "You jes got to be patient and be ready for it when it comes."

"I was patient for seven years. I can't be patient anymore." She scrubbed the tears from her cheek. "That's why I've done something stupid. Gran, I—"

Her grandmother laid a chubby finger over Lucie's mouth. "You don't have to tell me everything right now. When you be good and ready, come see me."

She smiled through her watery eyes. "You're right, Gran. I made this mess, I need to try to fix it first before I call in the big guns."

"Remember, yer ol' *Mamère* is only a boat ride away. If you be needin' me, I be dere." The old woman swallowed one more sip of tea and stood. "Now, I got a handsome young man waitin' to take me back to de swamp where I belong."

She leaned forward and kissed her grandmother's cheek. "Thanks for coming to see me, Gran."

"Don't wait too long to call on the big guns, *ma petite.*" Gran LeBieu kissed her on the cheek and let herself out the door and down the steps.

Lucie leaned against the doorframe and resisted the urge to follow the older woman out into the swamps where she could hide from all her mistakes.

Her grandmother climbed up into a rusty old pickup with Maurice Saulnier. After a few chugs and coughs, the ancient chariot lurched to life and out of the driveway.

As the truck disappeared down the narrow street, Alex's bright-red Jeep fishtailed around the corner, honking and burning rubber as if a maniac were at the wheel.

What the hell?

Lucie waited until Alex's Jeep screeched to a complete stop before she descended the stairs. No sense putting herself up as a target to the crazed driver.

Before the engine shut off, Alex and Calliope flung the doors open and leaped out.

"Did you see the front page?" Alex asked.

"Oh my God, Lucie," Calliope interjected. "It's all over the parish and clear down to N'Awlins."

"What is?" Lucie asked.

"The picture of you kissing the most eligible bachelor in the state of Louisiana." Alex ducked back into the Jeep and pulled the New Orleans *Times-Picayune* from the seat.

Lucie swallowed the wad of guilt lodged in her throat only to have it hit rock bottom in the pit of her stomach. There, occupying half of the front page, was a picture of her in a lip-lock with Eric Littington.

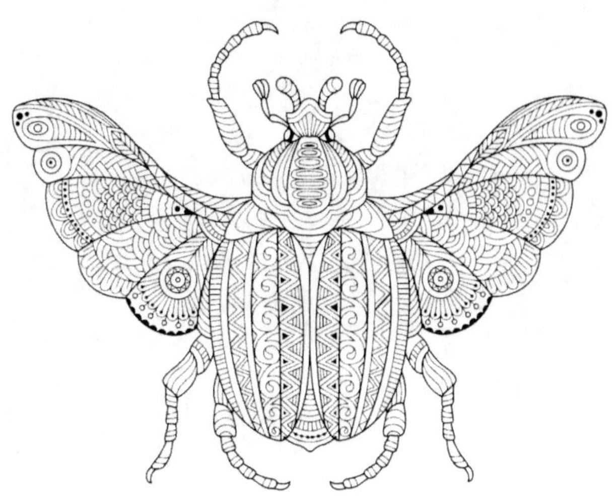

Chapter Twelve

"So, Miss I-Can-Fix-Everything-With-Magic, what are you going to do about this?" Alex tapped her finger against the picture of Lucie kissing Eric.

Lucie cringed. "Nothing."

"Nothing?" Alex folded the paper and whacked it against her palm. "You can't do *nothing*. What about Ben?"

"What about him?" She feigned indifference. But she wondered if he'd read the article, and, if so, did he give a rat's ass?

A plain four-door sedan slid up against the curb, followed by another and another, like a rental-car parade.

"What the heck's going on?" Lucie asked.

Out of the first car leaped a reporter in jeans and a tan sports jacket, camera in hand. *Snap!*

The flash blinded her and she staggered backward, suddenly all too aware of the cutoffs, tank top, and house shoes she wore. Had she even combed her hair this morning?

"Miss LeBieu, what are Eric Littington's intentions toward you?" the reporter asked.

The second car parked and another reporter dressed

similar to the first leaped out, pad and pencil poised. "Miss LeBieu, does Mr. Littington pay you for your favors?"

"What!" She stood in stunned silence as cars filled the street, and more reporters shouted questions.

"Come on," Alex grabbed her elbow, spun her around and hustled her up the stairs.

Calliope followed at a slower pace, her eyes rounded.

Lucie pushed through her doorway into the safety of her apartment, away from the shouting reporters.

"No, Eric hasn't made his intentions known that I know of," Calliope was saying at the top of the stairs.

Alex snagged Calliope's arm and yanked her through the door. Then she leaned out and shouted, "Miss LeBieu has no comments to make at this time. Please, go away."

Just inside the front door, Lucie peeked out at the crowd gathering in the driveway below. Her head spun and her stomach felt like the inside of a coffee grinder. "Where did they all come from?"

Alex shut the door, leaned her back against it, and crossed her arms over her chest. "From all over Louisiana."

Lucie pushed a hand through her tangled hair. "Why such a big deal over a little kiss?"

With an exaggerated roll of her eyes, Alex stomped into the living room. "Honey, if you haven't figured it out yet, you've been sniffing too many swamp fumes. Eric's running for high government office. Any little scandal means big news."

"Um, I like the guy with the brown hair in the denim shirt." Calliope stood next to the window and was staring out of it. "Do you think I could get him to go out with me?"

"If you promised him the scoop on Lola LeBieu here," Alex said.

Calliope turned to look at Alex, a small frown creasing her forehead. "Who's Lola?"

"Lucie, you yutz!" Alex raised her hands to the ceiling. "I was talking about Lucie!"

Lucie couldn't help the little grin that sneaked out. Calliope could be so clueless at times.

"And what are you smiling about? You could ruin Eric's entire campaign." Alex paced across the room and spun to face her. "And what about Ben?"

"Could you please leave Ben out of this?" she asked in frustration.

"I can't. He's my brother. How do you think he'll feel when he sees this?" She shook the paper at Lucie.

Why did Alex have to be so pushy about Ben? "Why would he even care? He's been away for years and hasn't spoken word one to me. Besides, we don't have a clue whether or not the spell worked."

"I sure as hell hope it didn't." Alex twisted her hair in the back and clamped it in place. "That bug flew over DeeDee Dubois and Mo Saulnier, as well as Larry Ezelle and Elaine Smith. Now wouldn't they all make fine couples?"

"Ooh, there's one with blond hair and blue eyes. *Yoo-hoo!*" Calliope yelled through the window, fluttering her fingers. Then in a conversational voice she said, "I heard Elaine left town in a hurry this morning."

Lucie's heart flip-flopped and bounced up into her throat. "She what?"

Calliope turned toward Alex and Lucie. "She left town."

"How do you know?"

"I thought everyone knew." Calliope's attention strayed back to the window.

"Apparently not." Alex walked to Calliope and grabbed her shoulders. "Focus, Calliope. How do you know about Elaine?"

"Hey, you don't have to hold on so tight." The redhead shook Alex's grip loose and brushed her hands over her arms.

"Miz Mozelle called Mirna Mae, who told Josie Ezelle, who called me."

Lucie paced in front of the couch, her head spinning with this new development. "Why did she leave?"

"Josie said something about postponing the wedding. Oh, I don't know. You know I have this short-term memory problem. I can't remember all the details. All I know is that she left town this morning."

"Did Craig go with her?" Lucie held her breath, waiting for the answer. *Please, let Craig have gone with her.*

"No. I do remember her saying Craig didn't go."

Alex glared at Lucie.

She held up her hands. "Now, don't go putting one and one together to come up with five-hundred and fifty-seven thousand, Alexandra Belle Boyette. There's bound to be a perfectly good explanation for Elaine leaving town."

"You saw the way Maurice was mooning over DeeDee last night. Eric's been all over you since bug-day, and Ben's moping around like he lost his best friend. And now Elaine's gone." Alex propped her hands on her hips. "How many lives do you have to wreck before you fix this problem?"

Her chest hurt and her eyes stung. "Oh, I don't know!" How had everything gotten so messed up? "I barely make enough money at the Raccoon Saloon to pay my own rent. How am I supposed to help *Mamère* with her mortgage? And it's been such a long time... I just wanted someone to fall in love with me and get me out of this hellhole. Is that so bad?" Tears spilled over and trickled down her cheeks. She dashed them away and turned her back on Alex's accusing face.

"Oh, Lucie." Alex's voice softened and she moved to put her arms around her. "Wanting to be loved isn't the problem. It's how you're going about it. You can't *make* a person fall in love with you by using magic."

"Magic works for Gran LeBieu." She shook off Alex's hands and walked away. "Why not me?"

Alex followed. "Do you really want to be with someone the rest of your life knowing you tricked him into marrying you?"

That thought had occurred to Lucie. Often enough to keep her belly in knots. "Eric is so nice. I think he really cares about me."

"Is it the magic or does he truly love you?"

"I don't know."

Alex could be relentless. "And how do you feel about Ben? Do you still love him?"

"How can I respond when I don't know the answer myself?" Why couldn't Alex leave her alone?

"Well, I suggest you find out." Alex strode to the door and paused. "Come on, Calliope."

"Oh, good. Let's hurry before the blond gets away."

"Good grief," Alex muttered. "You'd think you'd gone a whole day without a man in your life."

"I'll have you know," Calliope said, "I haven't been out since a week ago last Saturday."

"Wait a minute." Alex frowned. "You went out with me."

Calliope flipped her long, red hair over her shoulder and smiled as she stepped up to the door. She had that feral look in her eyes she got when she was on the hunt for a man. "That doesn't count."

"Figures." Alex stared over at Lucie. "Think about it, Lucie. I'll call tomorrow." She turned to Calliope, her hand hovering over the doorknob. "On the count of three."

"What?"

"We're going to rush through the door, down the steps, and out to the Jeep."

Her smile turned upside down. "You mean I can't stop and say hi to the nice man with the blond hair and blue eyes?"

"No, Calliope," Alex said.

With a heavy sigh, Calliope's lower lip jutted out. "Darn. Oh, well. Toodles, Lucie. Or should I call you Lola?"

"One. Two. Three!" Alex yanked open the door and shoved Calliope out.

The mob of reporters all yelled at once and camera flashes blinked like fireflies on steroids. Lucie slammed the door shut and leaned against it.

What had she gotten herself into? Did she really want to be the center of attention for the paparazzi and have her entire life laid open to the media?

Bang! Bang! Bang!

She jumped away from the door.

"Miss LeBieu, just a few questions," a reporter called through the solid wood.

With her hands pressed to her ears, she shouted, "No comment."

"Please, Miss LeBieu, we'll only take a moment of your time."

"Go away or I'll call the police."

Silence.

She breathed a sigh and pressed her fingers to her temples. Everything was happening so fast her head hurt.

Wow. The spell must really be working. How could she doubt it? The attraction between Maurice and DeeDee couldn't be explained any other way. And Eric would never consider going out with her and risking his campaign.

Holy swamp fungus! She had a date with Eric today! She glanced at the clock. In exactly twenty minutes. With a fleeting look down at her shorts and tank top, she yelped.

Bang! Bang! Bang!

"Don't you ever give up?" she yelled. "Go away!"

"Lucie, it's me, Ben. Let me in."

Ben? Her heart lurched into overtime. What was Ben

doing here? She didn't want to talk to him. Every time she did, she got more confused. Maybe if she didn't answer, he'd go away.

"Lucie, I'm not going away, so you might as well let me in."

She groaned. What was he, her punishment for crimes involving magic? She unlocked the door and walked back into the living room.

Space, she needed space.

The door opened and Ben stepped in. The tiny apartment seemed to shrink with the addition of his broad shoulders.

She couldn't breathe. Had he stolen the air as well as the space?

Ben's hair was mussed as if he'd run his hands through it several times. He used to do that when he was upset about something. Not that she remembered every little detail about him. Such as how he tapped his fingers on the steering wheel to the beat of his favorite Garth Brooks song. Or how he'd stop and stare at the sunset on the bayou. Or how he'd twirl her hair around his finger when he wasn't thinking about anything at all. Her stomach knotted into a sharp pain. No, she didn't remember every little detail. "Why are you here?"

***

"You know why I'm here." Ben took in the view of Lucie in her short shorts and bright-pink tank top and had to remind himself why he was here. *To warn Lucie off Eric.* Perhaps he was overstepping his authority, but he felt partially responsible for the success of Eric's campaign.

Lucie's shoulders slumped. "No, I don't know why you're here. You made yourself clear last time I saw you."

He ignored her words and stalked toward her. "Just tell me one thing." He stared into her eyes. "Do you love him?"

Say no.

"By him, I assume you mean Eric?" She looked away,

refusing to meet his gaze. She was stalling. If she really loved Eric, she wouldn't hesitate with her answer. Would she?

He stopped in front of her. "Do you love him?" *Uh-oh, he'd gotten too close.* Now he could smell her perfume, a soft blend of roses. The same scent she'd used seven years ago. Some women never changed. The memories invoked threatened to overwhelm him, and he swayed toward her. If he raised his hand he could brush his fingers against her breasts.

The same breasts that were rising and falling in an erratic rhythm.

What was he thinking? This was Lucie, his ex-fiancée. The woman who hadn't loved him enough to marry him seven years ago.

Lucie stepped back, and inhaled. "I don't know why everyone is making such a big deal over a little kiss."

"Was that all it was?"

"Yeah, just a kiss." She tipped her head back and met his gaze square-on, as if challenging him to argue with her.

"If I had kissed you, you wouldn't say that."

Her lips parted in a silent gasp, her eyes opening wide, before they narrowed. "You think pretty highly of your talents, Mr. Boyette."

"Do you doubt me?" He stepped closer.

She inched backward and pushed a stray hair behind her ear. "You flatter yourself. I'm not the least bit interested in you." Her gaze darted to the far corner of the room, avoiding his.

"That's not the impression I got day before yesterday." That kiss had been crazy good.

She made a face. "Temporary insanity."

He reached out and turned her face back to his. "Are you afraid of me, Lucie?"

Her chin rose out of his grip. "No, I'm not."

When he closed the distance again, her breath caught but

this time she remained in position, her shoulders stiffening as if bracing for impact. She pushed her hair behind her ear again. *Ah-ha.* She had to be only a step away from all-out panic.

He almost smiled. He liked to make her uncomfortable. She sure as hell made him uncomfortable, from the twitch next to his eye all the way down to his— Well, everywhere. "Does he make you moan like I used to?" he whispered.

She stared at his mouth, her tongue swiping nervously across her lips. "Past tense. Ancient history," she said, her voice breathy.

"Are you sure?" He ran his palm along her jawline and into the hair at the nape of her neck. God, she felt all silky and feminine. His groin tightened.

She tipped her head backward, but she didn't move away. "I'm immune to you, Ben. You're old news."

He drew her closer until his lips were only a sigh away. "Does he make you shiver in anticipation?"

Her body quivered beneath his hand as if directed by his suggestion.

All teasing forgotten, he sealed her lips with his. He'd come to prove a point. Admittedly, at that exact moment, he couldn't remember what the point was. All he knew were the touch, the feel, and the incredible scent of her. Like an erotic addiction, destined to scorch his soul.

When her lips parted on a gasp, he dove in, tasting and teasing, his tongue against hers. His hand swept down her back to cup her cutoff-clad derriere, hauling her belly against the stiff ridge of his denim fly.

She leaned against him, her fingers clutching at his shirt instead of pushing away. Her hands slid up his chest to circle his neck and she pressed her breasts to him.

His heart racing, his veins pumped blood so fast through his body he had a head rush. Which must account for *his* temporary insanity. Hell, for seven years, he'd worked hard to forget this woman. What was he thinking, kissing her?

Thinking was no longer an option. All he could do was feel. The softly frayed edges of her shorts tickled his fingers and he inched his hands lower to slide across the rounded swells of her bottom.

Her skin was silky-smooth and warm. When she drew away to fill her lungs, he didn't relinquish his hold or allow her a chance to remember it was him kissing her, not Eric.

With the ease of someone who knows the way, he trailed kisses from her lips along the side of her cheek to the sensitive spot behind her ear.

Another shiver shimmied across her frame and she moaned deep in her throat.

"Ah, Lucie," he said against her hair. "How could you say you love someone else when you make love to me like this?" He kissed her hair and sucked her earlobe into his mouth.

But her body was no longer melting softly against his. Her back had stiffened and she sure wasn't moaning any more. She removed her hands from around his neck and shoved against his chest. "Benjamin Franklin Boyette, you're about as low as a scum-sucking catfish."

He leaned back and forced a carefree grin while his heart hammered crazily inside. "Why, because I proved a point?"

Her eyes narrowed. "And what point might that be?"

"You don't love Eric."

With a quick downward sweep, she knocked his hands from around her hips. "I'm going to marry Eric Littington and there's nothing you can do to stop me."

He steeled himself from reeling backward, trying to ignore the kick in the gut he experienced from her words. So, she wanted to marry Eric. "What, is he rich enough for you, Lucie? Is he successful enough to make you finally want to tie the knot?"

With her soft, sensuous lips forming a hard line, she met his gaze with a hard-ass stare. "At least he isn't a cop dropout bug exterminator." With a quick sidestep, she ducked around him and practically ran for the door. "Leave, Ben. You're good at that."

"And you're good at throwing me out, aren't you?" The heat of desire he'd felt only moments ago surged hotter in his anger. "Well, Lucie, if a loveless marriage is what you want, I hope you get what you deserve."

She opened the door and waved her hand like Vanna White motioned toward the letters on *Wheel of Fortune.* Turning her back to him, she stared out at the street below.

If that was the way she wanted it, then to hell with her. He marched toward the door.

Just as he reached her, Lucie said, "Omigod!" and slammed the door.

His momentum carried him forward and he had to put his hands up to keep from crashing nose-first into the solid wood paneling. "Jesus, Lucie! First you want me to leave, and now you—"

"Shut up and let me think." Her gaze darted around the tiny room, and she wrung her hands. "There!"

Huh?

She pointed at the coat closet next to the door. "Get in there." Before he could move, she hooked her arm through his elbow and dragged him to the side.

"No way." Ben planted his feet in the carpet. "Do you mind telling me what the hell's going on?"

***

Lucie shot a quick glance out the window, still stinging from Ben's kiss and follow-up comments. But she refused to let him get the better of her. Did he think he could waltz in, kiss her, and make her forget about all her dreams and plans? Okay, so she forgot everything in the world when Ben kissed her. As if all the lonely years had been stripped away, she fit right into his arms. How did he do that? For heaven's sake, he'd been gone for *so* long.

A sleek white limousine pulled up next to the curb outside. The only person she knew who could and would drive around Bayou Miste in a limo was Eric. The chauffeur climbed out and opened the back door. Eric emerged dressed in a sexy black tuxedo.

Lucie wondered how he'd gotten away without a swarm of reporters following him but talk about a knight in shining armor charging in to rescue her on his trusty steed—okay, limo. Eric was everything a girl dreams about—sophisticated, charming, incredibly handsome, and loaded. Everything Lucie needed to be happy.

Except love, whispered that pesky voice in the back of her conscience.

So, she'd grow to love him, and he would love her. She had the spell to thank for that.

Like eating raw persimmons, her success wasn't sitting so well with her. Eric was such a nice man. Didn't he deserve more?

The man in question leaned into the car and pulled out an embarrassingly large bouquet of white roses.

And he was romantic. Definitely Prince Charming to her Cinderella. Only she was feeling a little more like one of the wicked, conniving stepsisters than the sweet-tempered soon-to-be-princess.

Ben leaned over her shoulder. "Oh, so that's how the cookie crumbles."

Drat the man. Why did he have to come back to Bayou Miste and confuse her so? Well, she just had to shove a little steel into her backbone and do what she'd set out to do. Ben no longer had a place in her future.

Then how could she explain how unraveled she'd gotten over one kiss?

Ben was smiling all superior-like.

She'd show him. "Yeah, I told you I'm going to marry Eric Littington, and I don't need you messing things up for me. Now, are you going to hide in the closet, or am I going to have to scream?"

"You wouldn't."

She sucked in a deep breath and opened her mouth to scream.

Ben clapped a hand over her lips and glanced out the window. "Okay, okay. I'll get in the closet."

"Good." She held the door for him. If only she had a key to lock the big oaf in. It would serve him right.

Just as he stepped inside, a knock sounded on the door. "You better get that, you don't want to keep your future waiting."

She slammed the door, narrowly missing his nose.

With a smile plastered on her face she didn't really feel, Lucie opened her front door to what could only be described as a bush full of lovely white roses.

"Eric, what a surprise." She stood blocking the doorway. "I must have lost track of the time."

"I'm sorry. Should I have called ahead?"

Add considerate to his list of attributes. Unlike the jerk in the closet.

"No, no, I should have remembered. Could you give me a few minutes to change into something more appropriate?"

"Certainly, take all the time you need."

Lucie started to close the door in his face.

But Eric stuck his hand out. "Do you mind if I wait inside?" He grinned. "I've had a group of reporters on my tail all day. I put some diversionary tactics in place before I left the house. I don't know how long that will last."

"Oh, yeah. Come on in." She spoke loud enough to get the message across to Ben in the closet. Double drats! How was she going to get rid of Eric so that she could shove her unwanted closet guest out the door? "I guess you saw the papers."

"I think everyone in Louisiana saw the papers." His gaze scanned the interior of her little apartment. "Do you have a vase to put these in?"

"No, but I have a glass I think would work just fine. Why don't you have a seat on the couch?" She raced for the kitchen and found the biggest plastic cup she could and filled it half-full of water. With the cup balanced in her hand, she ran back to the living room, all five steps, and held out the cup. "Could you put the roses in this while I go change?"

"Sure."

She set the cup on the table and made a dash for her bedroom. Her nerves were screaming by the time she shut the door between them.

"So what do you think we should do about the picture?" Lucie asked through the door panel.

She riffled through her clothes until she found a figure-hugging, strapless red dress. She called it her go-to-hell red dress because when she wore it she felt like she could rule the world and everyone else could go to hell if they didn't like it. The dress gave her a sense of power. And right now she could use an infusion of confidence. Especially when she felt as if her entire world was in the midst of crashing down around her ears.

And if Ben just happened to see her in it, maybe he'd regret what he'd left behind so many years ago.

"I've been thinking about what to do," Eric's muffled voice drifted through to her as she stripped out of her cutoffs, tank top, and bra. "I've come up with a plan."

"Yeah?" She slipped the slinky red dress up over her hips

and zipped the back. Then she slid on her black stilettos, fluffed her hair, and feeling very go-to-hell, threw open the door to her bedroom. "And what plan is that?"

Eric turned toward her, his mouth opened to say something but his jaw dropped to his chest instead.

Lucie basked in the self-satisfying moment of silence, congratulating herself on her choice of dresses.

"Wow, Lucie." Eric's head swayed from side to side. "Wow."

Anxious to get out of the apartment and away from Ben, she grabbed her purse and headed for the door. "I'm ready to go. You can tell me about your plan on the way to the limo." She raised her volume as she stood next to the closet.

"Oh, the plan's simple." Eric opened the front door and held it for her.

Just another reason to love Eric over Ben. Eric knew what chivalry meant. The bug man probably couldn't even spell it. "How sweet of you to open my door for me." Again she spoke a little louder than necessary.

"I'd crawl to the ends of the earth for you, Lucie." He lifted her hand to his lips and pressed a kiss to her knuckles. "Which brings me to my plan."

Her heart did little flip-flops. Not many men had ever kissed her knuckles. The sensation was not unpleasant. With time, she was sure she could grow to love Eric. And to hell with Ben! As Eric lingered over her hand, she started feeling a little uncomfortable. "You said you had a plan?"

"The plan? Oh, yes. I think we should announce our engagement."

"What?" She staggered backward at the same time as a loud *whomp* could be heard from the vicinity of the closet.

"What was that?" Eric peered over her shoulder at the closet.

"Nothing. Aren't we late for dinner? We should be

going." She hooked her arm through Eric's and dragged him through the door.

"No, I'm sure I heard a sound coming from that closet."

"It's b-bugs. I have a serious bug problem. I've been fighting them for years."

He frowned, resisting her tugs on his arm. "Then maybe we should call in an exterminator to take care of the job? I know one you might use."

She almost laughed hysterically. "I definitely don't need an exterminator to fix my problem. He'd probably only make it worse. Really, come on. I'm finished here."

"Okay, if you're sure." He opened the door a crack. "Coast is clear of reporters, let's go."

When they'd settled in the backseat of the luxurious limousine, Lucie heaved a huge sigh. Juggling two men was absolutely exhausting. Perhaps she should consider breaking the spell, after all. She was beginning to think men were too much trouble.

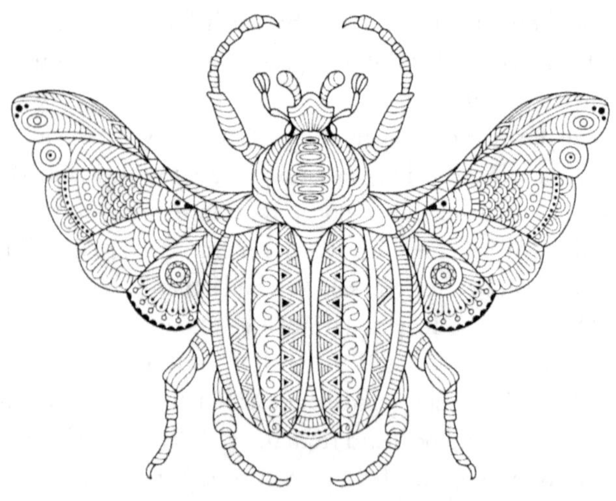

Chapter Thirteen

ngagement!

Ben stumbled out of the closet into Lucie's empty living room. His head smarted where he'd banged it on the hanging bar, but it didn't feel nearly as pained as his heart.

Eric and Lucie were not right for each other—he barely knew her. He didn't know that when she slept she snored softly. What kind of politician's wife snored? Eric would drag her all over the country and leave her alone often as his schedule demanded. Lucie didn't do alone very well. Ever since her mother dropped her and her sister Lisa on her *Mamère* LeBieu, she'd done everything in her power to always be with someone. She belonged in the swamp with people who knew and understood her. People like Alex and Calliope.

And me?

Ah, hell. He'd sworn he wouldn't get involved with her again and here he was all eaten up by Lucie and Eric's engagement. He ought to be happy for her. She always wanted financial security and a real family.

She could have had all that with him. Okay, so maybe the

financial security hadn't been there seven years ago, but he had it now. As a detective for the state police, he made decent money and he'd even managed to put away a little nest egg.

He pushed his hand through his hair and winced. So what? Lucie wouldn't marry him—hell, she'd rejected him once. Why risk a second rejection? Besides, she'd made it perfectly clear what she wanted. Or rather, whom she wanted. And he wasn't in that picture.

He strode for the door and paused with his hand on the knob.

The taste of Lucie still lingered on his lips. Her soft curves had fit perfectly against him when he'd held her. What happened all those years ago to make her go from hot to cold and break off their engagement? Maybe Mozelle was right— he should ask Lucie. At least he'd know the real reason and could put the issue to bed.

He groaned. Bed was exactly where he wanted to be with Lucie. But she was out with Eric, possibly getting engaged and making a commitment to another man when she couldn't make that same commitment with Ben.

Give it up, Ben Boyette.

As he jerked the door open and strode out, his cell phone chirped.

He hit the talk button. "This is Ben."

"Ben. Jason Littington. Could you get over here right now? I believe Eric's campaign has reached a crisis point."

"Sure. Do you want me to bring Eric?"

"No. He's part of the problem. So, can you make it?" His words were clipped and angry, as they used to get when Eric was in trouble as a kid.

Ben wondered what else could go wrong. "I'll be there in five minutes."

Click.

As promised, five minutes later, he entered Jason's home office.

Mr. Littington stopped drumming his fingers against the solid mahogany desk and rose to greet him. "Thank God you're working to protect Eric and his campaign. I didn't know who else to turn to."

"What's the problem? And why isn't Eric here to discuss it with us?"

Jason tossed the front page of the *Times-Picayune* across the desk to land in front of him.

The kick in his gut was only slightly less painful than the first time he'd seen the picture of Eric and Lucie kissing. "Is this what you called me over to discuss?"

Jason's brows rose. "Did I underestimate you, Ben? Do you not see the potential this LeBieu woman has to ruin Eric's run for Congress?"

He bristled at Jason's reference to "this LeBieu woman." "What's wrong with Eric seeing Lucie?"

"She's not the kind of woman a congressman marries." Jason strode across the floor and stood at the window staring out at the night. "I knew she was trouble when he brought her to the barbecue. Now he's taking her out to one of the more exclusive restaurants in Morgan City."

"So?"

"So? The public will have them married before the first constituent casts a vote. I knew he should have married a respectable woman before he started this campaign. Single candidates have too much stacked against them. The public wants to know the candidate is stable and ready to assume responsibility. Not gallivanting around the swamps with a bayou bimbo."

Ben counted to ten to keep from blasting Jason. But the ten count didn't help. "Lucie isn't a bayou bimbo." He couldn't ignore the irony of his defense. Hadn't he used those very same words in anger on Lucie when they'd broken up?

Mr. Littington snorted. "She works as a waitress in a bar wearing skimpy outfits that show more than they cover. What else would you call it?"

"A living." Littington was usually so tolerant of the people of Bayou Miste and would gladly sink money into the community to keep it alive. But when it came down to his son, Jason lost all perspective.

"My son cannot marry a bar waitress. It'll ruin him."

"Being a waitress isn't a bad thing." Why was he sticking up for Lucie and Eric? He didn't want Lucie to marry Eric any more than Jason did.

Jason smacked his palm on the desktop. "You have to stop Eric from making a huge mistake."

His head jerked up. "*Me?*"

"Yes, you. Sources say you and this Lucie woman used to be an item."

"That's history. Old history."

Jason strode across the room and stood directly in front of him. "I'll pay you double what you make on the force to make your affair with Lucie current news."

"I can't do that to Eric or Lucie."

"I'll pay you triple."

Triple was a lot of money. "No, I can't. For one, it's against my ethics. And if Lucie and Eric really love each other, more power to them."

"Then I'll pay you to convince them they aren't in love." Jason spun and paced across the Oriental carpet. "The polls indicate that Eric stands a real chance of winning against the incumbent, Gasson. A scandal could blow this opportunity. Ben, they've only known each other for a few days. How could they possibly be in love?"

He pondered Jason's statement. If Eric and Lucie weren't

in love, he'd be doing them a favor by breaking it up before they made the ultimate mistake of getting married. "If I decide to test them, and they prove they are really in love, will you step back and let Eric and Lucie make their own choices about marriage?"

Jason chewed on Ben's question, his brows drawing together into a straight line over his eyes. "I don't believe Lucie is the right woman for my son."

"That wasn't the answer I was looking for." Ben stuck out his hand. "It's been nice talking to you, Mr. Littington. I'll show myself out." When Jason didn't take the proffered hand, he shrugged and turned toward the door.

"Wait!" Littington grabbed his arm.

He stared down at the hand, then back over his shoulder at his friend's father. "Yes, sir."

"Okay, I'll step back. But you have to make an effort to interfere with their romance. A real effort to come between them."

"I can do that." He wanted to know whether Lucie really loved Eric anyway. "And I don't want your money for this job. I'll do this on my own. If they end up getting married, I'll consider it my wedding present."

Jason opened his mouth to protest.

Ben held up a finger. "If they aren't meant to be together, hopefully Eric will understand I did it to save him from a future divorce."

The older man nodded. "Fair enough."

"Now, if that's all you needed from me, I'll get back to work."

Ben's thoughts were already miles away at a fancy restaurant in Morgan City. He had a few ideas on how to "test" Lucie and Eric's love for each other. He couldn't wait to put the ideas in motion.

***

Lucie sat in back of the limousine with Eric's arm draped over her shoulder. They'd been to the perfect restaurant, eating steak and lobster cooked to perfection, drinking the perfect wine for the meal, and Eric had been perfectly romantic the entire evening. Then why the hell was she thinking of Ben's kiss?

"A penny for your thoughts?" Eric squeezed her arm, his thumb brushing against her breast.

Lucie turned so that he couldn't quite reach the front of her dress and forced a laugh. "You'd be wasting your penny."

"Is there something troubling you? Was the food not to your liking? Have I said anything to upset you?"

"No, not at all. Everything about tonight was"—she struggled to hide a grimace—"perfect."

"Lucie, being with you has made me so happy. It's as if you've brought the magic back in my life."

A lump of cold guilt settled in the pit of her stomach. Why did he have to go and mention magic?

He hugged her close against him. "Lucie, I've felt pretty lousy all evening about my earlier suggestion."

A sudden weight lifted off her chest and she smiled up at Eric. "You, too?"

He grinned. "Yeah, I realize how badly I handled it."

She laughed. "Oh, thank goodness. I thought you were serious."

The limousine pulled up in front of her apartment, effectively ending their conversation while the chauffeur climbed out and opened the door for them.

She slid out first and turned to Eric, who'd straightened behind her. "Thank you for a wonderful evening. It couldn't have been nicer." *Now will you please go so I can think?*

"I'll walk you to your door. You can never be too careful." He snatched her hand in his with a surprisingly strong grip.

"Aren't you afraid the press will see us together?" She

glanced around, realizing for the first time she hadn't seen any the entire evening. "Speaking of which. I haven't seen a single one all evening."

Eric's chest puffed out. "I made reservations in Morgan City and tipped off the reporters so that we could go the opposite direction. I wanted time alone with you. Now, let me escort you to your door."

"Okay." But only to the door, then she'd go in alone. She led the way to the top of the stairs of the white clapboard garage apartment. When she reached the top, she faced Eric. "Thank you again for a wonderful evening." *Now please, please, please, please go.*

Instead, he raised her hand to his lips and pressed a kiss to her fingers. "Lucie, I was serious about my earlier suggestion. It was the delivery I regret."

Oh, no. Her heart tightened in her chest. *Please just go home.*

"I think I've loved you, Lucie, from the very first moment I saw you in the Raccoon Saloon. I would be so honored if you would marry me."

Like a movie where the sound was out of sync with the video, Eric's lips moved and his words sank in a second later. And a full speechless half-minute later, her brain engaged. "Eric, we've only known each other for three days. How can you be so sure?"

He laughed and pressed her hand to his chest. "I don't know. All I know is the enchantment I feel being in your company, and I don't want to lose that."

Her heart did a sliding plunge to the bottom of her belly. "Are you sure? Marriage is a huge step. One you should make with the person you want to spend the rest of your life with." *Like I wanted to do with Ben.*

"I've never been more sure of anything before in my life."

"What about your campaign? Will this make things worse

for you?" She grimaced. "I don't have the right credentials to be a politician's wife."

"I don't care." His brows furrowed. "Would you be terribly disappointed if I didn't get elected?"

"No, of course not."

"I wouldn't care as long as I had you."

Oh man, had that bug's magic worked, or what? Eric had it bad.

"Eric, I think you're smart, sweet, and so romantic." She fought for the right words. Hell, she fought for *any* words. What did she want to say to him? Here he was presenting her with exactly what she'd schemed to win—a marriage proposal from the most eligible bachelor in the bayou. And all she wanted was for him to disappear.

"I feel a 'but' coming on." He lifted both of her hands and kissed them. "Please don't say no. Give it some thought. I'll wait. I know this is sudden, and, like you said, we've only known each other for a few days. Just promise me you'll think about it?"

Eric was offering her everything she dreamed of—financial security, a lavish lifestyle, and his unconditional love. Why couldn't she say yes? "Okay. I'll think about it."

He blew out a long breath, as if he'd been holding it, waiting for her answer. "Great. Then I'll leave you to your thoughts."

Finally. She had a lot to think about, and the sooner he left the sooner she could get started thinking. She tugged on her hands.

He didn't let go. His blue eyes shone bright in the soft glow of her yellow porch light. He stepped closer until her hands were crushed between their chests. Then he dropped them and pulled her into his arms.

She braced herself, knowing a kiss was expected after a marriage proposal. And maybe, if she kissed Eric, it would shake the taste of Ben's earlier kiss from her mind. The Cajun bug man shouldn't have any bearing on her decision whether or not to marry Eric. She closed her eyes and tipped her lips upward to meet Eric's.

Eric skimmed the edges of her teeth and dove in deeper, his hand sliding from the small of her back to cup her rump, snuggling her closer. The hard ridge of his zipper pressed against her go-to-hell red dress. The man had it *seriously* bad.

She leaned into the kiss, dancing her tongue against his, trying to capture the "magic" he said he felt.

After several rounds of dueling tongues, she sighed. The magic just wasn't there for her. Had the bug only worked on Eric and not her? Or had the magic only worked for her on Ben, since he was the last one the bug had circled? Whatever the case, she had to extricate herself from this embrace as gracefully as possible.

She tipped her head away.

Eric leaned closer, nibbling her lower lip. "Oh, Lucie, I can't believe I found you." He trailed kisses down her neck, his hands siding up her sides to cup her breasts.

How in hell did she get out of this? She couldn't shove him away and risk his falling down the steep steps. She needed some way to distract him.

Bang!

The porch light over their heads exploded into a zillion shards of paper-thin glass, showering down over them.

"What the hell?" Eric clapped his hand on her head and shoved her to the wooden planks of the landing.

"Ouch!" Tiny slivers of glass were embedded in her hands and knees. "Why the hell did you do that?" She tried to rise, but Eric held her down, crouching next to her.

Bang!

Her heart leaped into high gear. The first bang she'd

attributed to the glass exploding, but the second one had nothing to do with a faulty lightbulb. "What was that?"

"Gunfire. Give me your key."

"I can't."

"Why?"

"My purse fell down there," she pointed to the ground ten feet below. "Damn, and this was my best dress." She tugged at her skirt to keep her butt cheeks from lighting the evening sky. Then she reached up to pull the top securely over her breasts to keep them from falling out.

So much for her go-to-hell red dress. She'd hate to die all exposed. Why didn't they make sexy dresses for dodging bullets? She should design an all-purpose dress for today's woman. Built to last under the worst conditions, rain, snow, bullets—

"Gerald? You okay down there?" Eric called out to the chauffeur below.

"Yes, sir," he responded from somewhere beneath the stretch limousine.

Eric fumbled in his pocket for his cell phone and punched 9-1-1. "This is Eric Littington. Someone is shooting at us. We're at Lucie LeBieu's apartment. You know the place? Fifteen minutes? That long? Yes, we'll stay low." He hit the end button and looked sideways at Lucie. "Stay low? We're perched on a friggin' deer stand, prime targets for anyone with half an aim. Are you okay? Not hurt, or anything?"

Lucie's lips twisted in a wry grin. "Nothing but my pride." And her dress.

He smoothed her hair out of her face. "Sit tight, I'm going to find out who was shooting."

Her hand reached out to hold his. "Don't, Eric, it's dangerous."

"I can't just stay here and wait. The guy might get away before the police get here."

"Is that such a bad thing?"

"Are you kidding?" Eric grabbed her shoulders and held her away from him, his knitted brows a big indication of his concern. "You could have been killed!"

"And you could be killed."

He shoved his cell phone at her. "Hit 5 and the talk button. I'm going after the guy."

"But—" Eric ran down the stairs and across the narrow driveway to the bushes on the other side. "Come on, Gerald. Let's catch us a prankster."

"Yes, sir." The chauffeur rolled from beneath the car and raced after him.

"Eric!" Lucie climbed to her knees and stared after his disappearing figure.

Bang!

Down on her stomach again, Lucie remembered Eric's instructions and dialed 5.

After barely an entire ring, a curt male voice answered. "Boyette."

"Ben? Oh, thank God!" A sudden sense of relief washed over her, quickly followed by confusion. "Why does Eric have you on speed dial?"

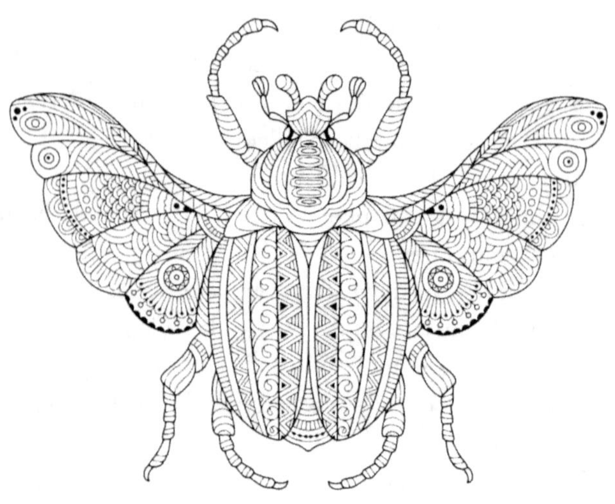

Chapter Fourteen

Ben slowed his exterminator truck, pressing the cell phone to his ear. He'd been halfway back from the restaurant in Morgan City, kicking himself for missing Lucie and Eric, and consumed by thoughts of the two together. Had he been so entrenched in images of Lucie in Eric's arms that he'd conjured this call? He held the device away to glance at the phone number. Eric's name was written in digital letters across the white screen. "Lucie? Why are you dialing from Eric's cell?"

"Because he's off in the bushes chasing after some nutcase with a gun." Was that a sniffle? "You didn't answer my question."

Ben's heart thumped against his rib cage, his cop instincts and adrenaline kicking into overdrive. "What do you mean, a nutcase with a gun?"

"Just what I said. Someone took a couple potshots at us, and I ruined my best dress ducking the bullets."

The kick in his gut made him pull his foot off the accelerator. "Holy shit! Lucie, where are you?"

"At my apartment."

He jammed the accelerator to the floorboard. "Stay put. I'll be right there."

"Tell me you're not going to take fifteen minutes like the sheriff?" Despite her complaints about ruining her dress, her voice shook.

"Make it two, sweetheart." He was still four miles from Bayou Miste, but the fear in her voice spurred him to go faster.

She sighed into his ear. "That's more like it. Now, hurry, before Eric gets hurt."

"Don't hang up, darlin'."

"Are you kidding? You're stuck with me."

His heart surfaced from his apprehension for her safety to let her words wash over him. *You're stuck with me.*

If only she meant for life...

As he skidded into her driveway, his heart lodged in his throat. Other than Eric's limo, the driveway was dark and appeared deserted. He leaped from his bug exterminator truck and shouted, "Lucie!"

"Ben?" A shaky voice sounded from the top of her landing and her dark head peered out from between the railings.

"*Merci Dieu.*" He released the breath he'd been holding and raced up the stairs.

Lucie eased up to her knees, tears glistening in the moonlight like the shards of glass littering the landing.

Without a thought for Eric, he pulled her into his arms and held her close. Her warmth dispelled the cold, sick feeling he'd had in his helter-skelter race to get here. He smoothed his hand over her hair and down to her bare shoulders. Her skin against his made the old flame in his heart burn even higher. *Lucie, Lucie. Why did you send me away?* his heart cried out. But his mouth remained mute, pressed to her temple.

When her body shuddered against him, he set her away

and pushed the hair from her eyes. "You have glass in your hair."

She smiled shakily up at him, tears pooling in her eyes. "That's not the only place I have glass." She held up her hands, where tiny slivers had cut into her tender skin. Blood oozed from the miniature wounds.

His stomach clenched. He was used to seeing blood from more extensive and sometimes mortal wounds. But not on her. He pulled her hand close and stared down at it. "We need more light."

"My hands can wait, I'm more concerned about Eric and the chauffeur."

His tender thoughts exploded in a rush of apprehension. Oh yeah, Eric. His responsibility and his friend. How could he forget? "I'll find them. You go inside."

She frowned and hesitated.

"For once, don't argue, Lucie." His fingers tightened on hers. "I can't go after Eric until I know you're safe."

Her frown disappeared. "I wasn't going to argue. It's just that I can't get in. I dropped my purse below the steps when the light exploded."

He kissed her forehead. "I'll find it. You stay here. But stay down."

Without protest, Lucie crouched in her red dress, her eyes going round again as she peered into the darkness.

He took the steps two at a time, and scrambled among the gravel and weeds until he spotted a thin black shadow that proved to be an evening bag.

Ten seconds later, he had her door open and Lucie escorted into the apartment. He pressed a brief kiss to her lips when he would rather have folded her in his arms and drowned in her. "I'll be back as soon as I find Eric."

"Someone looking for me?" Eric's voice called out from the bottom of the steps.

Lucie stared up at Ben for a moment, her lips poised as if for another kiss. Then she blinked and her face flushed a rosy pink. The moment was gone.

"Eric!" She rushed out the doorway and met Eric halfway down the stairs, hugging him tight as if he were the only person she could ever love.

Ben stood at the top of the stairs telling himself the sight of Lucie in another man's arms didn't bother him. But it did. "Ah-hem. Think you two can knock it off enough to tell me what happened?"

Eric circled Lucie's waist with his arm and walked her up the stairs. "Sorry, Ben. Shall we go inside where I can fill you in while we wait for the sheriff?"

"Only if you get your hands off my girl," Ben wanted to say, but couldn't. Lucie wasn't his girl anymore. Hadn't been for a long time. And by the looks of it, she was Eric's girl now. But that didn't stop the surge of possessiveness flooding through his body. He needed to hit something, preferably his friend Eric.

As Eric and Lucie climbed the steps, Ben heard a siren in the distance. Eric paused with his foot on the last step and shook his head. *"Now* they come."

The wailing increased until a sheriff's sedan slid sideways into Lucie's driveway.

Lights went on in windows of the nearby houses. Mozelle Reneau opened her front door. "Lucie, what the fool-darn-heck is going on?"

"Don't worry, Miz Mozelle, I'll fill you in tomorrow," Lucie called down to her landlady.

Mozelle squinted. "That you, Ben?"

"Yes, ma'am."

The deputy leaped from his squad car, weapon drawn. "I'm here, everyone just stay calm."

"I'd be a heap happier if you'd point that pistol at something besides me, Billy Ray," Mozelle called out.

"It's okay, deputy," Eric said. "Whoever did the shooting is long gone."

"And how do I know *you* didn't do the shooting?" the deputy asked, turning his pistol to point at Eric.

"Because he was the one being shot at!" Lucie stomped her foot. "Put the gun away before someone gets hurt, Billy Ray."

As if disappointed he didn't get to shoot anyone, the deputy dropped the muzzle of his Glock. "You sure he's gone?"

"Yes. I chased him past the marina before I lost him."

"Damn. I always wanted to apprehend a perp." Billy Ray shoved his weapon into its leather holster.

"Maybe next time," Ben said from the top of the stairs.

Billy Ray took a deep breath and blew it out on a huge sigh. "Someone want to tell me what happened here?"

Eric looked up at Lucie, standing on the landing. "Will you be all right?"

Lucie nodded.

Eric turned and descended the narrow steps. "I'll fill you in."

"You'll need to come down to the sheriff's office to fill out a report."

Eric looked back at Ben. "Could you take care of Lucie while I follow the good deputy to file my report?"

"Don't worry," he said, his night suddenly looking less grim, "I'll take care of her."

"Lucie, I'm sorry the evening turned out this way. I'd planned it to be very special, really unforgettable."

Lucie laughed uneasily. "Mission accomplished. I guarantee I'll never forget tonight."

"See you tomorrow?" Eric gazed up at her with that lovesick-cow plea in his blue eyes.

Ben wanted to puke.

Especially when Lucie nodded.

Eric turned back to the deputy. "Let's get this over with." Then he climbed into the rear of the limo, Gerald assuming the driver's position. After the deputy backed out of the driveway, the limousine followed.

"You two sure you're okay?" Mozelle asked again, hope in her voice. "I got some beignets I can warm up in a jiffy."

"No thanks, Miz Mozelle." Lucie pushed her hair out of her face with the back of her hand. "I'm so tired I can't see straight."

"Thanks, but I think we'll pass, Miz Mozelle. Good night," he said with added emphasis.

Mozelle disappeared behind her door, leaving him and Lucie alone on the landing.

"Come on, let's clean you up." He hooked Lucie's elbow and guided her back into the garage apartment, wondering how the evening had ended up in his favor yet again. Hell, why was he looking a gift horse in the mouth? Eric had asked him to take care of Lucie. Ben had every intention of doing just that.

***

"Damn, damn, damn," Lucie muttered. Her world was knocked askew from earlier that day when she'd known what her goal was and had pursued it relentlessly. Eric was her future, Ben was her past.

Past, past, past.

Why did Eric have to be so nice and trusting? How could he not have a clue about Ben and his impact on her resistance?

Didn't he have even an inkling of how hard she was trying not to feel it? She wanted to marry Eric, not Ben. Then why the hell did she feel more secure and at the same time completely off-balance when around Ben?

And now, just when she was most vulnerable, she was stuck with the jerk.

The jerk smiled. Not an I-got-you-cornered-smile, but a gentle one. Why? Why? Why did he have to go and get all kind and sweet? She was doomed. *Doomed!*

She felt her walls crumbling. But she had to make an effort to forestall the inevitable. "Look, Ben, I can handle it from here. You don't have to stay."

"I made a promise to Littington. I keep my promises."

Ouch. She cringed. That barb hurt more than the glass shards in her hands. She knew he was referring to their broken engagement. But hell, she'd had reasons to break it off. Damned good reasons. But he still hadn't gotten it, and he probably never would. No use rehashing ancient history. "If I ask you to leave, would you?"

He shook his head. His smoldering gaze bore into hers, sending tiny warning signals to her melting brain cells. *Make him leave, before it's too late.*

Then he took her hands in his and raised them palms upward. "Come on, I'll help you pick the glass out of your hands and anywhere else you may have gotten splinters."

The low voice and tender look was her undoing.

He led, and she followed like a lamb to the slaughter. She hadn't been able to resist him in the past—what made her think she could now?

All thoughts of Eric receded into the back of her mind, and all she could think of or feel was Ben. He led her to her little bedroom and sat her on the edge of the bed.

"Where do you keep your first aid kit?"

Too overwhelmed by images of what she and Ben could do beneath the sheets, and keyed up from her near-death experience, she had to remind herself to breathe. "In the medicine cabinet behind the mirror."

He ducked into the bathroom.

She could have jumped up from her questionable perch on the mattress and strolled back into the living room—putting distance between her and the bed. But she didn't. She waited for him to return, and he came back with the first aid kit, cotton balls, and a wet washcloth in hand.

He paused for a moment and gazed at her as if he'd never seen her before. Seven years earlier he'd seen every inch of her, including a few nooks and crannies she'd blushed about.

"What?" She reached up to brush her hair from her face and winced when a shard of glass pressed deeper into her flesh.

He shook his head and hurried forward, laying the items he'd collected on the nightstand. "Nothing. Let me see those hands." He pulled a pair of tweezers from his pocket and sat next to her on the bed. "Let's get those bad boys out of there before your hands get infected."

She sat in numb silence, inhaling the scent that was so very Ben. "You still wear the same cologne." Her eyes suddenly widened. "Did I say that out loud?"

He chuckled. "Yes, you did, and yes, I do. A gorgeous young woman gave it to me a long time ago and I haven't found anything I like better."

Her heart skipped a beat. Was he talking about fragrances, or did he mean he hadn't found another love as great as hers in all these years? "That's a long time stuck with the same-ole-same-ole."

"Some things are good enough to keep for life." He removed one shard of glass at a time until all the little pieces were fished out of her palms. Then he looked up. "Any other places?"

She gulped and gazed longingly into his eyes. She started to shake her head, but she nodded instead, and held out her leg. Her short red dress crept up her thigh, exposing a considerable amount of skin.

A sharp intake of breath indicated that he wasn't as unaffected as he pretended. As his gaze swept the length of her leg from hip to toe, he dropped to one knee. "This—" His voice broke. He cleared his throat and started again. "This won't hurt a bit."

"Promises, promises," she muttered. Getting over him had hurt more than anything. Was she up to getting over him a second time?

His hand circled her ankle and slid up the back of her calf.

No, definitely not. Based on the explosion of her senses at his slightest touch, she wasn't up to washing Ben from her mind. She was a mere mortal, not prone to acts of selflessness, or able to hold up under the pressure of masochistic torture.

When his fingers connected with the sensitive zone at the back of her knee, she moaned.

He darted a worried frown up at her. "Hurt that bad?"

"Oh, yes." He had no idea what he was doing to her or the repercussions that would reverberate through her life afterward. *She* did, yet she still did nothing to stop him. Oh, no, our little swamp girl didn't even try.

His frown deepened. "I'll kill the bastard." With the tips of the tweezers, he eased the slivers of glass from her knees, one at time. His gentle touch, combined with the little prickle of pain, fired her nerves to a screaming pitch.

"That's all of them." He pressed a cotton ball to the mouth of the bottle of rubbing alcohol and tipped it upside down. "This may sting a little."

She was already clamping down hard on her tongue trying to hold back her desire to moan aloud. Or was it to hold back her desire? She'd lost track.

When he pressed the sopping cotton ball to her knee, she jerked forward, pain jolting her temporarily back to her senses.

He blew gently on her knee to ease the fire, only to create a far more destructive burn in her lower abdomen. He pressed a kiss to her knee and another to her inner thigh.

Without conscious thought, she spread her legs ever so slightly, allowing him greater access—to that wet, delicious place.

Ben glanced up at her, as if gauging her resistance.

She should call a halt right here. He was giving her the opportunity. But she couldn't begin to stop the inevitable, and frankly, she didn't want to. Her knees dropped apart, her dress riding higher until the thin line of her black string bikini panties peeked from beneath.

Light flared in Ben's eyes. He leaned forward and, with feathery flicks, glided his tongue in a lazy trail up her thigh, alternating between tonguing and nipping until he was wedged between her legs, his broad shoulders pressing them wider. With a pause, he glanced up at her, his brown eyes reflecting the light from her nightstand, intensifying the gleam in them.

She laced her hands through his curling black hair, urging him closer. "Oh God, Ben, don't stop now."

"As you wish, baby. You're calling the shots." As he spoke, his breath blew against her inner thigh, already highly sensitive to his touch. He backed away enough to close her legs, hook his fingers into the lacy black elastic of her panties, and slide them down her legs. With a flirty flick, he slung the scrap of lace to the far corner.

As cool air hit the moist area between her legs, she tried to spread her legs again.

"Not yet." He held her legs together, then rose from his kneeling position, pulling her off the bed to stand in front of him. "I want to see you."

A warm shiver rippled across her skin and she reached behind her back, lowering the zipper of her strapless red dress until it slid off her breasts and down over her hips to pool at her ankles.

Naked, exposed to the man she'd never stopped loving, she felt no shame in her own skin, just a deep longing.

The fire in Ben's eyes enveloped her, clothing her in the moment.

"Your turn." Lucie stepped forward until her bared breasts rubbed against his jumpsuit, the uniform of his newly chosen profession. So he wasn't a cop anymore. His choice of jobs didn't make him any less of a man. A very desirable one, at that. "I love a man in uniform," she said, "but I like it even better when he's out of uniform." With her fingers firmly wrapped around the pull-tab, she ran the zipper down to the bulging point between his legs.

Ben gasped, his head falling back, his body tensing. "You're killing me."

"Oh, baby, I've only just begun." Her hands dipped inside the open edges of the jumpsuit, settling on the taut muscles of his midsection. Waves of excitement pulsed through her body, diving southward. Liquid oozed from her, making her moist, ready for him to enter her. But she still had work to do.

With her fingers weaving their way through the wiry curls on his chest, she ran her hands up to his shoulders. Then she pushed the fabric over and off, exposing a darkly tanned wall of rippling sinew.

"*Ooo-la-la.* Let me taste you." Her distended nipples rubbed across his chest as she rose up on her tiptoes and pressed her lips against the vein in his neck—the vein pumping warm blood through his body at an alarming speed. She sucked the salt from his skin, liking the taste and texture, perhaps a little too much. When her mouth came away, the light purple evidence of a love bite remained.

Her lips curved. She'd marked him as hers. Now it was his turn to mark her.

She stepped away, dropped her eyelids to half-mast and crooked her finger. In her most seductive voice, she asked, "Are you just going to stand there? Or are you going to make love to me?"

She turned her back and climbed into the bed, knowing full well her bottom was exposed to his view, her moistened cleft practically begging him to take her.

The rustle of clothing, the thump of a shoe, followed by another, were all the indication she needed that he would follow. She lay full out on her stomach, her legs slightly apart, waiting for him to join her.

Which he did, in less than thirty seconds.

She knew, because she'd counted as she held her breath. That small niggle of doubt had crept back in, only to be swept away when he straddled her, draping his body over hers. "I thought you'd never come," she whispered.

"I thought I'd never get here," he breathed into the back of her neck. He kissed her nape and worked his way downward, tickling her spine with the tip of his tongue until he reached the crease of her buttocks.

He slid off the end of the bed, spread her legs, and pressed his cock between them, his hands palming her rounded cheeks, massaging the muscles, moving downward to the line between buttocks and thigh. With a gentle glide, he traced that line inward to her aching center.

She hunched upward, trying to make that connection between her swollen nether lips and his long, work-hardened fingers. She wanted to feel the sexy abrasion of his rough skin inside her. More than that, she wanted him filling her to full, completing her. Her bottom hiked higher, pressing backward.

Ben's finger found her center, and dipped inside.

All the Voodoo magic in the world couldn't conjure the explosion within. This was more than magic, more than anything she could have dreamed. Tension built in every muscle and nerve ending, begging for release. "Oh, Ben, you're killing me!"

"Honey, I've only just begun," he said, echoing her own words. Then his finger slid out and his tongue slid in.

She practically jumped off the bed, the feelings so intense she thought she'd die of pleasure.

She pressed her face into the comforter to muffle her screams. Every flick he inflicted on her clitoris rent another scream until she writhed in the sheets. "Please, oh God, Ben. Come inside me, now."

The exquisite torture ceased, leaving her teetering on the precipice of orgasm.

He grabbed her hips and pulled her against him, nudging his cock against the opening of her swollen entrance. But he hesitated. "What about protection?"

"Damn." How could she have forgotten?

She climbed to her hands and knees and reached inside her nightstand, groping for a foil package she was sure was there. Her little bit of hope stashed away for, how long was it —two, maybe three, years? About the time she'd given up on Ben ever coming back. But he was here now and she couldn't wait.

Her fingers closed around a stiff square. "Oh, thank God!" She twisted and collapsed on her back in the middle of the mattress holding up her prize. "Quick!"

Ben snatched the treasure from her hand and ripped it open.

She stole it back vand eased it down over his magnificent cock. "Oh yeah, baby. I remember you." She lay back, her knees dropping wide.

A wicked glitter in his gaze, he leaned over her and pressed his lips to her opening, darting his tongue inside. His head lifted and he grinned naughtily. "Just testing."

"Oh, I'm more than ready." She'd been ready for this moment for a very long time.

One agonizing kiss at a time, he slid up her body until he lay over her, his penis pressed to her core.

"Ben!" she squealed. "Hurry!"

"I'm coming, I'm coming," he reassured, smoothing the back of his hand along her chin. Then he drove home, filling her in one hard thrust.

With a gasp, she curled her legs around his waist and clenched, holding him close as she absorbed him, stretching to accommodate his size and length.

Then he pulled away until the velvety smooth tip was a breath away from falling free of her.

She flexed her legs, drawing him back in. "Please, don't tease me." Were those tears in her voice? Was she that desperate for him she'd cry? Did she still care that much? Man, she was going to be in big trouble. "Do it, Ben. Do it, like before."

"Ah, Lucie. I've missed you so damn much." He pressed a kiss to her lips and rammed home. In and out, he rode her hard.

She met him thrust for thrust, planting her feet on the bed to give her added lift. She climbed that precipice and toppled over the edge, exploding into a million glittering fragments of light.

He jerked to a halt, his body rigid, his cock pulsing. His lips pulled back over his teeth in a groan with the strain of his release. Then he collapsed on top of her, squashing the air from her lungs.

She didn't care. Ben was with her—inside her—as she'd dreamed of for so long. Everything would be all right. Tomorrow she'd wake up and all would be right with the world.

He shifted to his side and lay down next to her, pulling

her into the circle of his arms. "Ah, Lucie. You feel like heaven." He smoothed a hand over her naked skin.

She basked in the afterglow of being loved by him. Surely, after what they'd just shared, he loved her. She snuggled closer, pressing a kiss to his bare chest.

"See?" Ben whispered into her ear, teasing her lobe with his tongue. "You can't possibly marry Eric. Besides, you'd never be happy as a congressman's wife. You belong here, in the swamp.

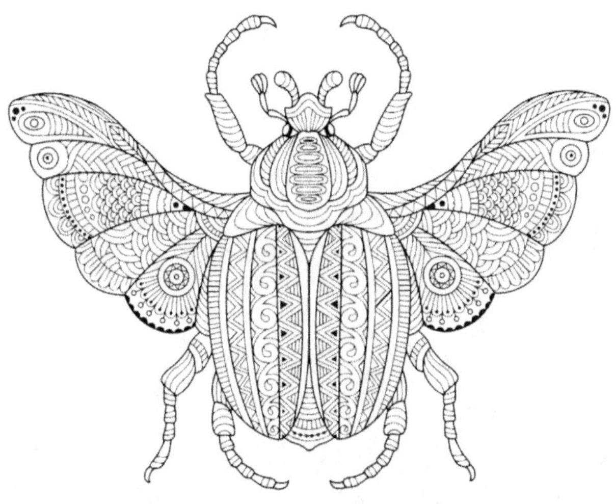

Chapter Fifteen

"Lucie! Ohmigod!" Bursting through the doors of the Shear Safari Beauty Salon, Calliope, with DeeDee Dubois in tow, made a beeline for Lucie's chair. "We're so glad you're here."

Josie Ezelle, the young beautician wearing the salon's skintight leopard-print uniform skirt, dropped the strand of Lucie's hair she'd been cutting and stepped back. "Hi, ladies."

Lucie cringed and forced a casual smile to her lips. "Hey. I didn't realize you two had appointments today." Otherwise she would have rescheduled. She didn't feel up to the inquisition, no matter how well-intentioned.

She sure as hell didn't want to discuss the lapse of sanity that caused her to sleep with Ben. After last night's faux pas she had a lot to think about, and couldn't possibly complete an entire thought with Calliope's incessant chatter blasting through her brain cells.

Whatever. Her life was already so screwed up, what more could go wrong?

"I'm giving up my appointment for DeeDee, if that's okay with you, Josie?" Calliope hugged the cosmetologist.

"Fine by me." Josie held her scissors far from her body to keep from poking the effervescent redhead. "What's it gonna be? Cut, highlights, facial?" Josie turned back to Lucie and snipped another lock of dark hair.

"The works!" Calliope threw her hands in the air, smiling ear to ear. "DeeDee has a date."

"That's wonderful news." Josie's hand paused and then continued combing through Lucie's hair. "Who's the lucky guy?"

Lucie cringed for the second time in one morning. She knew the answer.

DeeDee blushed, the fiery red burning a mottled trail up her neck into her cheeks. She giggled and whispered. "Maurice Saulnier."

Josie leaned closer. "Who?"

"Mo," Lucie interjected, her tone flat, her happiness for DeeDee decidedly absent.

DeeDee's little brown eyes rounded. "Do you think it's crazy? I know Mo is much too handsome for a girl like me, but he did ask me out, and"—she nibbled her lip—"I want so much to go."

Immediately, guilt set in and Lucie softened her response. "Oh, DeeDee, of course I'm happy for you. Maurice is a really nice guy and so are you. Girl, I mean. You're a nice girl."

DeeDee's smile returned, lighting up an otherwise doggish countenance. The poor girl's face was too long, her eyes closely set and beady, and her nose big enough to be considered manly. DeeDee had been born with the title of "Dog-Faced DeeDee" through no fault of her own. But she did have pretty hair, the deep brown of a chocolate lab. And her glow of happiness softened all her harsh features to almost pretty.

Lucie's own natural optimism became more and more elusive, to the point she felt downright depressed. Because of one simple spell, she'd caused this transformation in DeeDee. That was the upside. The downside was that the unfortunate woman would be absolutely heartbroken if she reversed the magic.

Calliope herded DeeDee into the chair beside Lucie. "DeeDee wants a mani, pedi, facial, cut, and style for her date. Don't you, DeeDee?"

DeeDee nodded.

"Mirna Mae?" Josie called out.

A chair scraped in a back room and a diminutive older woman wearing a leopard-print skirt and bony-rib-hugging tank top matching Josie's appeared in a doorway. "Whatcha need?"

"Could you do a manicure while I finish up Lucie?" Josie asked.

"Guess I could. Got nothin' better to do than eat Mozelle's beignets and drink coffee. Come on, girl, let's skin this alligator."

DeeDee frowned at Calliope and hesitated. "You aren't gonna skin my hands are you?"

"I will"—Mirna Mae raised an eyebrow— "if you don't get yer buns in my chair afore I count to three."

Lucie smiled at DeeDee. "Mirna's bark is much worse than her bite. And she does a fabulous job on fingernails. Go on. We want you perfect for your date."

Her frown disappearing, DeeDee scooted into the little chair across the table from Mirna Mae.

"Well, well, DeeDee," Mirna Mae arranged bottles of polish and nail files. "Since when are you and Maurice an item?"

Lucie stared in the mirror, trying not to be too obvious about her interest in the woman's answer.

The same mottled flush stained DeeDee's cheeks. "Oh,

we're not an item." She ducked her head and murmured, "Yet."

"Yet, huh? So when did the boy ask you out?"

DeeDee sighed, all but melting in her chair, a smile lifting the corners of her lips. "At the barbecue. I tell you, it was like magic."

Lucie's gaze darted to Calliope and she frowned a warning.

But Calliope wasn't the sharpest tool in the shed. "Yeah, Lucie's bug—"

Lucie kicked out hard, the pointed toe of her high-heeled shoe connecting with Calliope's shin.

"Ouch!" Calliope reached down to rub her injured leg, while shooting an accusing frown at Lucie. "What did you do that for?"

"I'm sorry," she smiled at Calliope and shook her head. "My foot must have slipped." She made a slashing motion across her neck and pressed a finger to her lips. "Ixnay on the ugbay."

"Ixnay?" Still rubbing her shin, Calliope's brows drew together, then her eyes widened and a grin spread across her face. "Oh, yeah. Gotcha."

Apparently oblivious to Lucie and Calliope's charades, DeeDee continued, "If it hadn't been for Calliope knocking me down, none of this would have happened."

Calliope beamed proudly. "That's me all over for ya. Chalk it up to these clumsy feet." She winked at Lucie.

Lucie groaned and struggled not to roll her eyes. *Lord, save me from my friends.* Keeping secrets was not one of Calliope's strengths.

Josie leaned close to Lucie's ear. "I get the feeling there's a lot more to the story. Wanna spill?"

Her gaze met Josie's in the mirror. Man did she need

someone she could talk to, but... "No, there's nothing more to say. As far as I could see, it was just as Calliope said."

Josie's lips tightened briefly, then she asked over her shoulder. "So how did Calliope's knocking you to the ground bring you and Mo together?"

"It was like a complete fairy tale." DeeDee sighed again. "He helped me to my feet, and when Calliope got up, she knocked me into Mo's arms." She stared dreamily out the window. "It was so romantic and thrilling. Next thing I knew, we were walking out on the boardwalk and he was asking me out. Me!"

As Josie snipped away at her hair, Lucie's heart sank further and further into her belly. What a mess she'd made. DeeDee would be devastated. The first guy to pay any attention to the woman, and all because of a little Voodoo snafu on her part. Not to mention the mess she'd made of her own situation. She was supposed to marry Eric, but she'd slept with Ben.

"There." Josie set her scissors on the counter and fluffed Lucie's hair. "You're all done. Take a look."

She peered at her reflection without seeing the glorious black tresses falling in luxurious waves. How the heck was she going to undo the disaster she'd created? "It looks great, Josie. Too bad you can't fix problems as nicely as you fix hair."

Fists on her hips, Josie gave her a narrow-eyed look. "Girl-friend, I can't fix what I can't see."

The back door burst open and Alex skidded in, gasping for breath. "Lucie!" She pressed a hand to her chest. "You gotta get out of here, quick!"

Her heart bouncing from the pit of her belly into her throat, she leaped from the chair, cape and all, and ran to her friend. "What's wrong, Alex?"

Alex laid a hand on her arm and panted as if she had been running. "The press, the demonstrators, all hell's broken loose." She stepped aside and motioned to the glass doors and windows at the front of the Shear Safari salon.

Outside, she could see cars pulling up in the few parking spaces lining the busy streets of Morgan City. A news van with a rotating satellite antenna on top of it double-parked, blocking Lucie's and Calliope's cars.

"I thought the press was in Bayou Miste clambering around the Littington estate." Lucie's stomach knotted. "What are they doing here in Morgan City?"

"That's what I was trying to tell you." Alex grabbed her arm and ushered her to the back of the salon. "Someone got wind that Eric Littington is here at the local jewelry store having a family ring fitted for a certain young lady he hopes to marry."

Lucie planted her feet and stood firm against Alex, stalling. "Wait just a minute. And why do you think this has anything to do with *me*?"

Alex gave her *the look*. "Don't play dumb with me, Lucie LeBieu. This is just what you wanted, what you planned. Hell, what you cooked up!"

She winced. "Okay, so it is, but that doesn't necessarily mean I said yes."

Alex's eyes widened. "So he *did* ask you?"

That icky feeling crept across her skin. The same feeling she'd had when she'd lied about stealing from Charlie Hughes's watermelon patch. She'd gotten away with it then because Charlie'd had a soft spot for the Voodoo queen's granddaughter. Or maybe he'd been afraid of what Lucie's grandmother might do to him if he pressed charges.

Calliope and Josie crowded around Lucie, blocking her escape through the front door. Was it just her, or was the air getting scarcer in the little shop? She couldn't lie her way out of this tight spot. These girls weren't Charlie. Lucie sighed. "Yes, he did ask me to marry him."

"Ohmigod! Lucie!" Calliope grabbed her hands and jumped up and down. "I'm so happy for you. It worked! It worked!"

"What worked?" DeeDee asked from her position at the manicure table with Mirna Mae. "What's going on? Tell us, please."

"Yes, tell all. My ears must be getting old," Mirna Mae groused. "I only heard about every fifth word. Gotta get a dad-blasted hearing aid so I can keep up with my eavesdropping."

"Nothing worked." Lucie pushed through the suffocating group of women.

"Eric Littington asked Lucie to marry her." Calliope clapped her hands together.

"Congratulations, Lucie," DeeDee said, her face wreathed in smiles. "I'm so happy for you."

"That's wonderful, Lucie." Josie hugged her close.

"Good catch, if you ask me," Mirna Mae said, without looking up from the fingernail she was filing. "Man's got money and political aspirations. Probably the most eligible bachelor in the parish."

The only person who didn't congratulate her was Alex. Her face was set in a deep frown. "What about Ben?"

The knot in Lucie's gut clenched until she felt like she'd toss her meager breakfast all over the shiny linoleum floor.

"Ooh, that's right." Josie's eyebrows rose. "Weren't you and Ben a thing some years back?"

"*Were.* Past tense. Back before he left for the academy," she said. If only he was still a part of her distant history. But his role in her life was all too fresh. Why did he have to be so sexy, and why did she have to be such a pushover and sleep with the man?

"That's what I thought." Josie ducked to glance at her own reflection in the mirror and run a comb through her hair. "Geez, with Craig Thibodeaux and Eric Littington snatched up, that's two less eligible bachelors for us poor girls of Bayou Miste."

"There's still Ben, Larry, and Maurice," Calliope offered.

DeeDee's stricken gaze darted toward the group.

"DeeDee here seems to have snagged Mo, not that I'm interested." Josie smiled over her shoulder at DeeDee. "He and my brother, Larry, have been friends for so long, I can't think of him as anything but another brother. Good thing you're marrying Eric, and Ben's free and back in town, Lucie. I'm thinking about going after him myself."

Lucie's heart flipped over and landed with a thud in her gut. Holy swamp muck! Josie was a pretty girl with big blond hair and pale, creamy skin. Completely opposite of her own dark haired, dark-skinned looks. Ben was bound to find her more attractive. The thought made her feel like the nails on her fingers should lengthen into claws. She had a sudden urge to scratch Josie's eyes out. "I haven't agreed to marry Eric."

"No?" Calliope's brows shot upward.

"No?" Alex's frown deepened.

"No?" Josie grinned.

"Why not?" Mirna Mae asked.

"Yeah, why not?" DeeDee echoed.

Good question. She wished she could answer it.

A reporter, followed by a cameraman, stepped through the front door. "Is there a Miss LeBieu in here?"

Josie tossed her comb to the counter and strode toward the reporter. "Sir, do you have an appointment?"

"No, I just want a word with Miss LeBieu." The reporter pressed a handheld digital recorder to his mouth. "I'm inside the beauty salon where Miss LeBieu has her hair done. Miss LeBieu, is it true congressional candidate Eric Littington proposed to you last night?"

Dread washed through her intestines like a moldy milkshake.

How the hell was she going to undo this fiasco? The whole world knew. Or at least all of Louisiana would know Eric had proposed by the time the five o'clock news aired. Would they also know she'd slept with Ben Boyette the same night Eric had proposed? Where was Saint Jude, the patron saint of lost causes, when you needed him? Who else had the power to bail her out of this mess?

"Don't answer," Alex said.

"Don't worry, I'm not about to." Feeling like a big fat fraud and totally unworthy of her friends, Lucie shifted to make sure Alex stood directly between her and the cameraman.

"Miss LeBieu, is it also true you make your living as a waitress and a stripper?"

Rage burst through her veins and she tried to shove Alex aside so she could get to the reporter and punch him in the teeth. "No, that is not true!"

"Leave it, Lucie." Alex, with Calliope's help, restrained her and kept her from making a bigger scene.

"Sir, if you don't have an appointment," Josie stepped in front of the cameraman and held her hand over his lens, "you'll have to leave."

"In that case," the bigmouthed reporter said, "I'd like to make an appointment for right now."

The unflappable Josie, stood her ground. "The only opening I have is for bikini waxing. If you'll just step into the back room and drop your drawers, we can get to work."

The reporter's eyes widened. "Uh...I don't think so."

Lucie smothered a giggle at the man's horrified expression. Served him right. She'd like to wax his body for his rude insinuation.

"Then you and your shutterbug friend here better leave before I call the police." With the threat of being waxed hanging over them, the two men didn't resist. Josie, as smooth as you please, ushered them out of the shop and locked the door with an exaggerated *click*.

Alex and Calliope loosened their hold on Lucie and stepped away.

"Thanks, guys." She rubbed her hands over her bare arms. "I don't know what I'd do without you."

"Yeah. That's what friends are for." Alex gave her a twisted smile and glanced out the window, where a growing crowd of reporters swarmed around the salon. "I'm afraid this may be one mess we can't get you out of. Only you can do that. And by the looks of that mob, it ain't gonna be easy."

***

Ben paced the sidewalk across the street from the jewelry store Eric had entered thirty minutes earlier. Who'd tipped the reporters off about Eric's proposal? And why the hell was Eric already having a ring fitted? Lucie hadn't said yes. At least that's what she'd told him. Had she lied?

Last night had nearly put him in the grave with a heart attack. Or was that with a broken heart? When he'd responded to Lucie's frantic call, he'd been hit with a double whammy.

Someone had taken a potshot at Lucie and Eric. His stomach still flip-flopped when he thought of the possibility of Lucie lying in a pool of blood because of some fanatic with a gun.

He had a sinking suspicion he'd screwed up last night. Why couldn't he keep his big foot out of his mouth when he was with her? By sleeping with her, he'd really thought he'd convinced her not to marry Eric. Then he'd gone and opened his stupid mouth and made her madder than a wet hen.

She'd kicked his ass out of her apartment so fast she'd had to throw his clothes out with him. Thank goodness Miz Mozelle hadn't come out to witness his humiliation.

Now, with Eric on the verge of making the biggest mistake

of Ben's life, he couldn't even begin to think straight. Tough, nothing-but-focused Benjamin Franklin Boyette was in a tailspin and he couldn't pull out. All he knew was that he had to stall this business with the ring. And he had to get Eric out of town before the reporters converged on him, and his friend made some stupid announcement about his intentions to marry Lucie.

But how could he stall him without looking like a jealous ex-lover, which he was feeling more like with each passing step?

"There's his car!" a man shouted.

Ben recognized him as one of the protestors from Bayou Miste. Apparently, they'd followed the reporters to Morgan City. A mob of people dressed in white T-shirts with green lettering and cartoon pictures of dead frogs and fish scattered all over them moved en masse toward the jewelry store.

Ben crossed the street and ducked in before the crowd got there.

"Eric, you got trouble brewing." He glanced over his shoulder and pulled the door closed.

"What's this?" The sales clerk blinked twice behind his owlish glasses before straightening. "Sir, you can't hold that door, this is a place of business."

"Ah, Ben." Eric turned and smiled across at him. "I'm glad you're here. I need your opinion."

"No time for that." He braced himself for the first protester, who reached for the doorknob. "You need to go through the back door if you want to avoid the mob outside."

"What mob?" Eric squinted and then his brows rose. "More demonstrators?"

"That and reporters." He leaned back, his hand gripping the knob as the man on the other side of the door attempted to pull it open.

"Don't worry about them. They have just as much a right

to shop here as I do." Eric continued smiling, much to his annoyance. "Let them in, Ben."

"They aren't here to shop, Eric, and you know it." He didn't relinquish his hold.

Other demonstrators knocked on the windows, their muffled yells falling on Eric's deaf ears. The man was completely befuddled. Ben recognized the Lucie effect. Hell, he had it himself. Problem was, he didn't know how long he could hold out against the growing crowd. His hands were starting to sweat.

"Do you think Lucie would like my mother's engagement ring or a new one all her own?"

Ben groaned. He had to stop Eric from getting a ring and keep him safe all at once. How the hell could he do that when Eric was floating on cloud nine? "Why don't you wait until the woman says yes?"

Eric leaned against the counter and sighed. "I hope she says yes." Then he frowned at Ben. "Can you think of any reason she wouldn't?"

Because she doesn't love you, she loves me! He bit hard on his tongue to keep from saying what was in his heart. Hell, he didn't know what she was thinking. Never had. But Eric was an honorable man and she couldn't find a better one to marry. As rough of a life as she'd had, she deserved someone like Eric to wrap her in silk and diamonds. "No, I can't think of any reason for her to say no."

How could he hope to compete with Eric? His heart sank to a new low, pretty much at bottom-clinging pond silt. Especially after what he and Lucie had been up to the night before. Eric was his friend, yet here he was betraying him by omission—and by deed last night.

"I think she'd like one of her own." Eric leaned over the counter and pointed at the glass. "I'll take that one in a size six."

Damn, Eric even knew her ring size. Ben remembered it from all that time ago, when he'd asked Lucie to marry him. He still had the ring tucked away in a drawer at his mother's house.

The door shook as yet another protestor struggled to open it. *Get a grip, man. She's not yours, never has been.* Last night had meant nothing to her.

But the world to him.

"I'll have to have it sized," the clerk said, glancing nervously at Ben. "Really, sir, you should step away from the door."

"How long will it take?" Eric asked, completely oblivious to Ben's struggles or the clerk's distress.

The man behind the counter shot a desperate look toward Ben. "It could be ready by tomorrow."

"That's good." Eric smiled. "I have just the place I want to take her." Eric handed the clerk his credit card.

Just as the congressional Romeo was signing the credit slip, Ben's hands slipped off the knob. "Ah, hell. Look out, here they come."

Eric tucked the receipt in his pocket and turned as half a dozen people in frog T-shirts spilled into the store, carrying signs and chanting, "Clean the swamps!"

They were followed by reporters armed with cameras and microphones.

Ben edged in front of Eric, creating a physical barrier between the demonstrators and the candidate.

With a hand on his shoulder, Eric spoke softly into his ear. "Ben, you can't keep them away, let me handle this."

Fine. He stepped aside. It was Eric's funeral.

As he shifted, he noticed a man standing among the demonstrators, dressed in a white T-shirt with "I Love LA" written in green letters. Ben wouldn't have noticed, except he didn't quite fit with the others. He didn't have the "I want to save the world one seal pup at a time" look about him. He was older and he sported deep frown lines around his narrowed eyes.

Ben recognized the man as the leather-jacketed stranger in the bar the first night he'd met with Eric. As this realization struck, the frowning man reached into a satchel.

Was he going for a gun?

Ben tensed. Before he could react, the man removed his hand from the bag and lobbed a bright green balloon through the air, straight for Eric.

"Get down!" Ben yelled so loud the demonstrators around him ducked. Without thinking, he reached out to catch the balloon. When rubber met flesh, the balloon burst, splattering thick paint the color of shamrocks all over his hand and down his arm.

"What the hell?" Eric said.

Ben spun toward his friend and the reason he'd been assigned this mission.

With a puzzled frown denting his forehead, Eric rubbed at the paint on his cheeks. He looked like a victim of an alien massacre with green blood spatter from the waistband of his wrinkle-free khaki slacks up to the top of his neatly combed hair.

A collective gasp rose from the demonstrators gathered around Eric. Cameras flashed like so many strobe lights, temporarily blinding Ben.

Then a single voice shouted, "Save the frogs!"

A moment later the roof shook with the combined voices of a dozen demonstrators chanting, "Save the frogs!"

Ben grabbed Eric's elbow and ushered him to the back of the store where the nervous salesman stood rubbing his hands together as if working up a lather. "Oh dear, oh dear." His gaze locked on Eric's shirt.

"Where's the back door?" Ben asked.

The salesman threw his hands in the air. "In the back. Where else?"

He pushed Eric around the counter toward the rear of the small building.

The worried clerk surfaced from his stupor long enough to protest, "Sir, you're not allowed in the stockroom!"

Ignoring the man, Ben led Eric through the maze of boxes and jeweler's worktables to the back door.

"Come on, let's get out of here." He took off at a trot down the alley behind the store, listening for Eric's footsteps behind him.

After passing several buildings, he slowed and looked around.

Eric caught up and grinned. "This campaign is getting more interesting by the minute. How are we supposed to get to our cars?"

Ben was just trying to figure that out when he noticed the bright-red Jeep parked in the alley a few buildings down from where they stood. "Alex."

"Alex? As in your sister, Alex?" Eric asked.

"Yeah. I think we have a ride back to Bayou Miste."

Just as they reached the Jeep, Alex burst through the back door, followed by Lucie.

His stomach clenched. She looked stunningly beautiful, her long black hair falling in shiny waves around her shoulders, framing her face.

"Ben! What are you two doing here?" Alex asked.

Eric strode straight up to Lucie and grabbed both hands. "Lucie, my dear. You're gorgeous."

Her gaze darting from Eric to Ben, her cheeks flushed, then her eyes widened as she focused on the green splatters. "Good Lord, Eric, what happened?"

Eric held up his hands. "It's okay. A few overzealous

protestors and a balloon full of paint. Nothing a new shirt and shampoo won't take care of."

"But that's awful!" She dropped one of Eric's hands to reach up and wipe a spot of paint from his brow. She darted a look at Ben, her lips tightening around the edges.

If he'd thought she'd gotten over her anger from last night, he was sadly mistaken. Yet his gut tightened as she tenderly caressed Eric's cheek. She obviously cared about the guy. *But how much?* And how could she love another man when she'd made such passionate love to him last night?

He pulled his keys from his pocket and tossed them to Alex, then held out his hand. "Let me have your keys. You can take my car. It's parked in front of the jewelry store a couple blocks down."

"But you're covered in paint!" Alex wailed.

"Don't worry, I'll have your seats professionally cleaned," Eric reassured her.

"But— But..." Alex's brows met over her nose and she looked ready to cry. "My Jeep's my baby."

"We'll be careful. Now quit blubbering and hand over the keys." Ben held his hand palm upward, crooking his fingers impatiently.

Calliope stuck her head out the back door of the hair salon. "Hey Lucie, Alex, you better hurry, they're going around— " she stopped midsentence and stared at Ben and Eric. "Hello guys, where's the party?"

"Hi, Calliope." Eric grinned. "The party is down the street, only I don't recommend the decorations." He slid into the passenger seat as if he were sliding into a limousine.

Calliope giggled. "Me, neither. Although I do look good in green, I don't fancy that particular shade."

Ben climbed into the Jeep and tapped his fingers on the steering wheel. "If you two are through discussing color choices, maybe we could get the hell out of here?"

"Testy, aren't we, Mr. Boyette?" Lucie turned to Calliope. "What were you saying when you came out?"

"I was saying something?" Calliope scrunched her eyebrows together. "Oh, yeah. That crowd is leaving the front door as we speak. I suspect they might be headed around here to the back to catch you."

"Get in, Lucie," Ben ordered.

"Yeah, come with us," Eric reached out and caught her hand.

"Damn," Lucie muttered.

Ben figured the last place she wanted to be was anywhere near him. But the rising hum of a dozen voices spurred her into action. She yanked open the back door of the Jeep and hopped in.

He fought to keep from busting out with a smile, and his heartbeat sped up in anticipation. After he dropped Eric off at his house, he could pick up where he left off last night with Lucie.

If he could get her to forget about what he'd said...

After what they'd shared, Lucie couldn't be serious about marrying Eric. And he fully intended to remind her why.

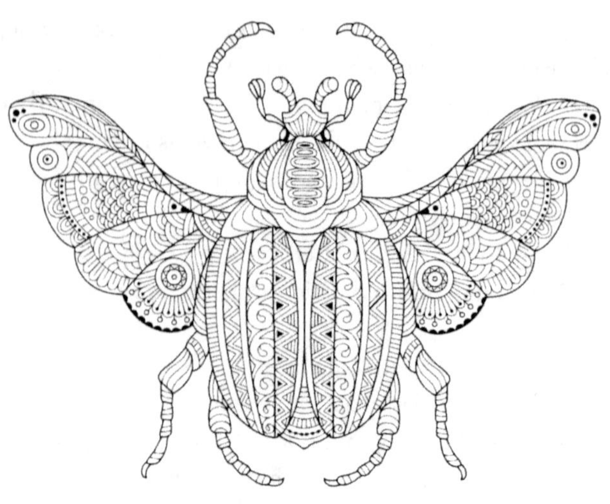

Chapter Sixteen

Lucie hunkered down in the back of Alex's Jeep, as much as a person could with her knees jammed into the back of the seat in front of her. *Ben's seat.* For every bump, she banged her knees into Ben's back through the cushion. Deliberately? Maybe. She held onto the roll bar and set her teeth against the jolting ride—mad because she'd been chased out by reporters, madder because she had to leave her Mustang, and maddest because she'd had to ride in the same car as Ben.

Holy swamp goo! What the hell was she doing in the same vehicle as the man she'd made love to *and* the man she planned to marry? Sadly, they weren't the same person. Guilt wadded in the back of her throat like an old sock.

Could her life be any more difficult?

Eric craned around to look at her, his boy-next-door face and sincere smile making her feel more like a heel by the minute. "Darling, would you like to join me for lunch?"

Panic filled her belly with butterflies. She couldn't be in the same room alone with Eric. Not after last night. Surely her face would give her away, or she'd say something equally revealing. No. She couldn't. Not yet. Eric was too nice a guy to lie to. She had to find a way to fess up before the hole in her gut turned into a genuine ulcer. Eric deserved better than two-timing swamp trash.

She wanted to sink through the floor and disappear. *My God.* She'd become her mother and her sister! Sleeping with any man who'd call her pretty.

She shot dagger looks into Ben's back. And prayed he could feel them. Oh, for a Voodoo doll to stick full of pins!

Just as she was projecting daggers into him, he looked up into the mirror and smiled at her. That smirky, I-know-what-you're-thinking look. She kicked her foot under his seat hard enough to make him jump, causing him to swerve onto the shoulder.

Eric grabbed the dash. "What's wrong?"

Ben's brows lowered, practically connecting over his nose. "Thought I saw a skunk."

"Great. All I need to top off the paint on my shirt is to smell like a skunk. Not candidate material, if you ask me. You sure it was a skunk?"

Lucie couldn't resist. "Takes one to know one, huh, Ben?"

Eric laughed and jabbed his elbow into Ben's rib. "I believe she just called you a skunk. Are you going to take that from her?"

"I've taken a lot more than that." Ben glanced back at her. "Would you care to expand on that, Lucie?"

He wouldn't dare kiss and tell. She narrowed her gaze at him. *Would he?*

"What has my friend Ben taken from you that you didn't willingly give?" Eric asked, still oblivious.

"See, that's just it." Ben slowed to take a corner. "I only took what she more than willingly gave me."

"Sounds mysterious." His teasing tone belied his serious look. "And here I thought you two weren't even close after your breakup so long ago. What else don't I know about you, Lucie, darling?"

She gulped and choked on her own spit, bursting into a fit of coughing.

"Are you okay?" Eric turned in his seat, all teasing gone. "Ben, perhaps you should pull over. I think she can't breathe."

She coughed and coughed, tears running down her cheeks, her face burning with the effort to breathe. Between fits, she choked out, "No need to stop. Just take me home." She swallowed in spasms and finally got her throat under control. Whew! She couldn't have timed that any better. With all her sputtering, Eric hadn't noticed she never answered his question.

A musical jingle sounded from the front seat.

Good, maybe Eric would get involved in a long conversation on his cell phone and not ask her any more revealing questions that would make her spill her guts like an eviscerated pig. No, that wouldn't do. She still hadn't made up her mind whether to say yes or no to Eric's proposal. But she knew she'd have to come to grips with sleeping with Ben. And probably confess.

Oh, man, oh, man. What had she *done?*

"Hey Neal, what's up?" He listened for a moment. "At the house? Now? I'm in no condition to meet with a contributor. Okay, okay. I'll sneak in the back door. Stall him until I can duck into the shower and get the paint out of my hair. Aren't you going to ask me what paint? Oh, you've heard?" He shook his head. "Great."

Finally, she was getting a break, Eric had an appointment to keep. Yay! That could buy her a little time to figure out her dilemma.

And her future.

Eric turned around in his seat, a crooked smile lifting one side of his mouth. "Lucie, I must apologize. My campaign manager insists I speak immediately with one of the chief contributors to my campaign fund. Apparently the paint incident has made it around and I need to show my game face." He laughed out loud. "*Without* the paint. Could we reschedule lunch to dinner?"

Another break! Thanks to heaven and cypress knees. "I'm sorry, Eric, I have to work tonight."

His blond brows furrowed momentarily, then shot upward. "Even better. We can go out tomorrow night. There's something I have to pick up in Morgan City, anyway." A secretive smile curled his lips.

What was that look for? "I'm sorry, Eric, I have to work tomorrow night, too." Could she be lucky enough to avoid him for another entire night? She held her breath.

"Then I'll pick you up from work."

Her breath shot out in a whoosh. "But that's two o'clock in the morning!"

"All the more reason to see you home." His smile widened. "We can go to Morgan City for breakfast."

Wait. Breakfast? Or *breakfast*?

Damn!

Okay, so she'd have a little more than thirty-six hours to make up her mind. That was doable. Wasn't it? Deciding whether or not to marry Eric should be easy enough in that amount of time.

His grin was so infectious, she couldn't say no—at least to the date. Nor would she give Ben the satisfaction of thinking he had anything to do with her reluctance to go out with Eric. She pasted a happy smile on her face and met Ben's gaze in the rearview mirror. "Sounds wonderful."

Ben's brows furrowed and the Jeep lurched forward.

Ha. Let the man stew. He didn't own her or have any right to tell her whom she could or couldn't marry. Or have breakfast with.

When she glanced out the window, she was surprised to see the sweeping driveway leading to the Littington estate. The trip from Morgan City she'd thought would be endless was almost over.

"Pull around back, if you would." Eric ducked low in his seat as they passed a black Lincoln Navigator.

As soon as the vehicle came to a halt, Eric jumped out and reached in to assist Lucie to the ground so she could switch seats. For a moment he held both her hands in his and gazed lovingly down at her.

Guilt washed over her in waves. Eric was so nice. Perfect husband material. And by the look in his eyes, he was smitten. She'd gotten what she wanted; all she had to do was to reach out and take it. Why was that so damn hard? Why wasn't she the least bit happy?

"Do you realize how much your hair glistens in the sunlight? You're beautiful, Lucie. And every moment away from you is an eternity."

She tugged against his grip, uncomfortable with his pretty speech. How strange, when she'd always dreamed of a man saying such things to her. "Don't, Eric."

He chuckled. "What? Am I embarrassing you?" He turned to Ben. "I can't believe I'm embarrassing a woman who can hold her own at the Raccoon Saloon."

Ben snorted. "Yeah, hard to believe." His words were for Eric, but his enigmatic gaze rested on her.

Eric stared down into her eyes. "I'm sorry you got dragged into what's turning out to be a dirty campaign, but I'm not sorry I met you."

"Eric—"

He pressed a finger to her lips. "Sadly, I have to go. But I will see you tomorrow when we can have a nice, long talk. There's so much I want to say." He kissed her knuckles.

"Until then." He helped her into the front seat and stepped back with a bow.

Ben revved the engine and pulled away—a little faster than she thought was necessary.

Eric stood for a moment, waving, then disappeared into the house. Poor, poor Eric. What had she done to make him so besotted?

Oh, wait. The love bug.

"Very touching." Sarcasm dripped from Ben's two words.

"At least he isn't rude and degrading, like some people I know."

"Namely me?"

She glared at him. "That's where I would start the list."

"What do you want with Eric? The man's in the middle of a heated campaign. He doesn't need distractions."

"So, now I'm just a distraction?"

"You've always been a distraction, Lucie." The soft look he shot her way tempered his harsh words. "You're hard to forget."

She crossed her arms over her chest and stared out the window, willing the sudden tears not to spill from the corners of her eyes. After having cried an ocean of tears over this man, she didn't need to shed another. Especially in front of the oaf. No sirree, not one.

"Not for *some* people," she gritted out.

Warm liquid made a trail down the cheek closest to the window. *Oh no.* Why now? After seven years, she should be well over Ben. She reached up on the pretext of pushing her hair from her eyes, scrubbing at the tear before it made it to the bottom of her cheek.

He would *not* see her cry.

***

Ben knew what she was doing, had seen the glistening

tears pooled in her eyes, and his heart cracked a little more. "What's wrong with us, Lucie?"

"Nothin'. Because there isn't any 'us.'"

Well, that pretty much put him in his place. He pulled into her drive and shifted into park.

Lucie grabbed the door handle.

Before she could open it and jump out of his life again, he placed a restraining hand on her shoulder. "Sweetheart, we need to talk."

She stared down at the hand on her arm and then up into his eyes, her frown expressing her anger, her watery eyes the hurt. "You should have thought of that seven years ago. Let go of me, Ben."

"Let go of you, as in your arm? Or let you marry Eric?"

"Both." Her face was set, but her bottom lip trembled. "Why did you come back to Bayou Miste, Ben? You don't belong here anymore than I do."

"I came back for the job."

Lucie snorted and flicked the collar of his bug exterminator uniform. "Yeah, right. And I'm the queen of England." She shrugged out of his grip and slid from the Jeep. "Leave me alone."

As she walked away from him, he called out his window, "Do you love him?"

Her footsteps halted and for a moment she stood with her back to him. Then she turned. "If I told you I did, would you leave me alone?"

Not quite the answer he wanted. He let all the air out of his lungs like a deflating tire. "If you really love Eric, as he seems to love you, I'll step aside."

"Then step aside." One eyebrow rose in challenge.

"You didn't answer my question."

"I feel under no obligation to answer any question from

you, Benjamin Franklin Boyette." She spun, her hair flipping over her shoulder as emphasis, and walked away.

He sat for a moment, watching her hips twitch side to side as she climbed the steps to her garage apartment.

She hadn't said she loved Eric. In fact, she'd deliberately avoided the question.

The lump of a heart that had been parked in his chest for seven long years suddenly felt lighter. His blood flowed freely through his veins after having been clogged for way too long. Clogged with unanswered questions, and a love long lost. The blood flowed so freely, he almost felt light-headed.

Lucie had not admitted to loving Eric.

Another thought slowed his dizzy brain. Even so, that didn't mean he stood a chance with her. She'd shown him the door once; why did he think he could win her over a second time around?

He slammed his hand against the steering wheel. Why did women have to be so damn complicated?

###

"Why do women have to be so damn complicated, Jean?"

Ben sat across the bar from Jean Dupree, the bartender. He'd gone about the business of protecting Eric all day when he would rather have been shaking a few answers out of Lucie's head. He couldn't get her off his mind, not for a single moment, and he was sick to death of being rattled by a woman.

"Do you think if I had the answer, I'd be tending bar in Bayou Miste?" Jean dried a mug and set it on the shelf behind him. "Take that one," he nodded at Lucie. She was weaving her way through the crowd, a smile on her face, her skimpy T-shirt showing enough belly to keep the predominantly male customers happy and horny. "She's worked for me the last seven years and she's still not married. Every other waitress got married. Some several times. But not my Lucie."

She hadn't made it back to the bar since Ben came in. He was looking forward to her reaction, while at the same time dreading it. How many times did she have to tell him to get lost before he got the hint? Still, after last night, he couldn't help but have hope. She couldn't have faked her abandon during their lovemaking. Hell, she wouldn't have let him do what he'd done if she didn't care a little.

Would she?

Perhaps all the sly comments of some of her customers were true and she'd become a slut like her sister Lisa since he'd left town. He shook his head. No. He knew better. Lucie's flirty act was a cover for a sad, lonely young woman whose promiscuous mother had dumped her and her sister when they were little girls. You didn't get over something like that. Not ever.

Only Ben and maybe a few of her closest friends knew her background. She was so afraid of ending up like her mother, she flirted but never followed through.

Except with him.

Then why the hell hadn't she married him, as she'd promised?

He downed his second beer and swiveled to face the room. "I just don't understand women."

"Me, neither." Pascal Pasquale claimed the seat next to Ben.

"Want the usual?" Jean Dupree asked.

Pascal shook his head. "No, I need something to numb the senses. Make it a whiskey."

"Hey, Pascal, sorry I had to get rough with you the other night." Ben stuck out his hand.

Pascal took it and shook. "I deserved it. I acted like a damned fool."

Jean set a glass of whiskey in front of Pascal. "Love has a way of making us humble."

"Yeah," Ben and Pascal said at the same time.

Ben stared down into his beer. "Doesn't help, either, when the competition looks better than anything you got to offer."

"No shit." Pascal tossed the whiskey back and swiveled on his seat to stare out into the crowd. "Makes you wish the competition would just go away."

"Yeah," Ben said. "But even without any competition you don't always get what you want." As well he knew. He hadn't had any competition seven years ago, and Lucie had still pushed him away. "Having the competition out of the picture doesn't always mean the lady will fall for you."

Pascal frowned. "Gives you more of a chance, though."

"Only if there are feelings there to begin with." So, if Eric were out of the picture, would Lucie reconsider being with him—Benjamin Franklin Boyette, bug exterminator?

Hell, she'd told him he wasn't good enough once, why would she think any more highly of him now?

Because they'd had great sex last night. Wasn't that enough to convince her he was the only man for her?

Although he'd changed out of the uniform of his under-cover profession, as far as the lovely Lucie knew, he was still nothing more than a bug man hanging around pesticides. It stank. If she'd ever loved him, she'd be able to look past that and love him for who he was inside, regardless of the outer shell of a navy blue uniform with a giant ant on the front.

But then again, Eric had everything going for him, especially with his classic good looks—not that Ben considered himself a slacker. Eric was rich—however, money didn't buy everything, as Eric himself could tell you from his childhood experiences. But to top it all off, Eric was well known and climbing the political ladder. Hell, he could be president someday—the leader of the friggin' nation.

That sinking feeling hit Ben's belly like sour beer. *Damn.*

Pascal banged his empty glass on the counter. "Hell, some folks get all de breaks!"

"Whatcha bellyachin' about now, Pascal?" Lucie walked around Ben to the other side of Pascal and laid her tray on the counter. "I need a Coors, two Bud Lights, and a rum and coke."

Jean slid a mug full of beer her way and stuck another under the tap. "Gotcha."

"Ah, Lucie," Pascal said. "If you'd just marry me, I wouldn't have such a bellyache."

"Pascal, I told you back in the fifth grade, I like you, but I just don't love you. Can't we be friends and call it a day?"

She hadn't said two words to Ben yet. But he knew she was aware of his presence by the way she completely avoided making eye contact. And the way she was flirting with Pascal as if tossing her avoidance in his face.

"I love you, Lucie." Pascal grabbed her hand. "Always have, always will."

Now, there was a sentiment Ben could relate to.

"No, you don't." She tugged her hand loose. "It's just a crush. You'll find someone who curls your toes, and you'll forget all about me." Her words were gentle, her smile genuine.

He had to admire Pascal. The guy had a lot of balls to up and spit it out so publicly.

Ben scratched his head. Hmm. He hadn't tried that tactic. But based on her response to Pascal, he wasn't so keen on the technique. Unlike the redneck Cajun, public humiliation wasn't his style.

Well, at least he wasn't alone in the boat called *Lucie's Conquests*. But the old saying "Misery loves company" was as empty as his life.

Tired of her cold shoulder, he straightened and smacked his hands together. He preferred anger to indifference.

Perhaps he could stir her up a little. "What are you going for, Lucie, a record of notches on your bedpost for all the hearts you've left broken in your wake? Chalk up another for Hurricane Lucie!"

She didn't respond with words, but if her glare had been a fillet knife, she'd have sliced clean through him in one long, painful stroke.

He smiled. *Now we're getting somewhere.* At least she'd acknowledged his existence.

"Give it up, Pascal." He patted the Cajun on the shoulder. "She's not interested in the likes of us. We're just homegrown swamp gators and she has bigger fish to fry. Besides, she's in love with someone else."

Having thrown the gauntlet, he awaited her response. Now maybe she'd answer his question.

"What do you know about love, Ben Boyette?" she snapped. "I bet you wouldn't know love if it slapped you in the face." She didn't wait for a response, just lifted her tray and flounced off. Her cutoff shorts showed a whole lot of leg to the rest of the world, as evidenced by the appreciative whistles of the patrons of the Raccoon Saloon.

"Try me, honey," he called after her, although she'd already gone out of earshot.

Pascal emitted a low whistle.

He turned to face the other man and noted how he, along with everyone else in the room, watched Lucie's progress across the crowded floor.

Ben was appalled. Did *he* look like that? With the sad, kicked-puppy eyes and mouth so far down he could have passed for a basset hound? *Holy shit.* Was there no cure for the woman?

He spun back to Jean. "I'll take a whiskey, too."

Jean handed him a glass of amber liquid and stared at him through the smoky haze. "You feeling all right, Ben?"

"Not really."

Pascal turned to Jean as well. "Give me the same."

"Pascal don't look any better," Jean said. "Must be something goin' around."

"Of that, you can be sure." Ben tossed the drink back, searching for that numbing feeling Pascal had spoken of earlier. Maybe he should take his own advice and give up.

Why should she be interested in mudbugs when she could have lobster?

***

The night had been interminable. Lucie had smiled and flirted with the customers as always, but her heart wasn't in the light banter and careless conversation, and her tips showed it.

How was she supposed to come to a decision about Eric when Ben kept showing up and confusing her even more?

She'd breathed a huge sigh when the bane of her existence finally left the bar. Now she could concentrate on her work and getting through the night without collapsing into a sniveling crybaby. Pascal still sat at the bar, his sullen gaze following her around until well after midnight, when he also gave up and left.

Every muscle in her body flagged and she counted the minutes until the bar closed at 2:00 a.m. She swept, filled napkin holders, and scrubbed tables until the last waitress left and only she and Jean remained. She was exhausted, emotionally and physically. All she wanted was a hot shower and cool sheets. When the routine cleanup was complete, she looked around for the bartender. "Jean?"

No answer.

Her heart scudded to a groaning low. "Jean? You better not have left without me!"

"I told him I'd lock up." Ben stepped out of the shadowy doorway that led to the back stockroom.

"But my Mustang is still in Morgan City. He was my ride," she wailed, very near bursting into tears.

"Now I'm your ride."

"And that's supposed to make me feel better?" She threw her hands up into the air. "I'd rather walk."

"It's two miles to your apartment. Are your feet up to the task after you've just spent the past six hours on them?"

His raised eyebrows nearly got him a flyby with the napkin holder she still held.

"So are you going to swallow your pride and ride with me or not?"

Her feet really did hurt and she didn't have the strength to walk. "Damn you, Ben."

He grinned. "I'll take that as a yes."

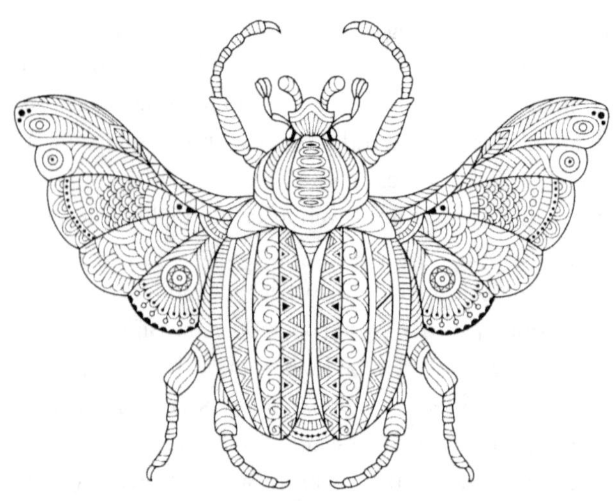

Chapter Seventeen

"If you're going to try to talk me out of marrying Eric, save your breath. That particular topic is not up for discussion." Lucie climbed into the front seat of the bug exterminator truck and let her head drop back against the headrest. All she wanted was a hot bath and bed.

Alone.

"We don't have to discuss anything if you don't want to."

"Good, because I don't."

He shifted into reverse and backed out. "Fair enough."

"Then why did you offer to take me home?"

"Because I couldn't get you off my mind."

She emitted a very unladylike snort. "Like I buy that."

"No, really. I'm having a really hard time concentrating on my work since I got back to town. All because of one dark-haired Cajun hottie. I think your grandmother must have put some kind of hex on me."

Every previously relaxed muscle in her body tensed to alert. *Had he guessed?* Did he know about her unfortunate spell? Her heart did flip-flops in the pit of her stomach, threatening to upend the bowl of Jean's famous gumbo she'd eaten four hours ago.

With a stolen look at Ben's calm profile, she shook her head. No. No way. Her friends were all sworn to secrecy. But what about Calliope? Had she inadvertently let it slip?

Only one way to catch a fish—go fishing. With a deep, steadying breath she asked, "What makes you think magic was involved?"

"Why else would I be completely distracted?"

Her laugh sounded forced even to her own ears. "How much concentration does it take to spray houses for bugs?"

A smile quirked at the edge of his lips. "You have a point. But I wouldn't want to miss and spray Granny Saulnier's prized poodle or Mo's alligator. Even though Granny Saulnier wouldn't mind T-Rex out of the picture, she's kinda attached to FeFe. By the way, what color is she today?"

"Granny Saulnier's hair or FeFe?"

"Both."

"Lilac." Lucie laughed despite her previous fear of being caught in her little stint at playing Voodoo queen. Ben's teasing comments about FeFe and T-Rex defused her worries and had her leaning back against the seat again, her lids drifting shut.

Although her eyes were closed, her other senses were at full alert. Despite the chemical odor of the truck, she could smell the sandalwood and whiskey on him. She could hear every breath he took, and hear the rustle of his button-down chambray shirt as he maneuvered the narrow streets of Bayou Miste. If she let the last seven years of loneliness slip from her mind, she could almost imagine she and Ben were still together out on a date. He was even driving at a slug's pace to prolong their time together, just as he had when they were young and in love.

Just like old times.

But that was a long time ago. Too long.

"This reminds me of the good old times." Ben's voice covered her like a liquid blanket, warming her in places she'd only dreamed about until last night.

"Some of them were." She'd give him a little leeway without getting snippy.

He chuckled.

She peeped through one eye. "The comment wasn't meant to make you laugh."

"Sorry. I was recalling the time we rode the Ferris wheel twenty times at the Shrimp and Petroleum Festival in Morgan City. We wanted to break Craig Thibodeaux's record of most minutes spent kissing on a Ferris wheel."

"Yeah, I had motion sickness for a week." She smacked his arm. "To this day, I can't ride on a Ferris wheel without getting queasy."

"I forgot about that." His brows dipped for a few moments, then his face brightened. "Do you remember the time I brought you water lilies from the bayou? I spent five hours beating off the mosquitoes and alligators to get them."

"Yeah, I remember. I was so excited until I stuck my nose in one of the flowers and a red wasp stung me. My nose swelled up like a baseball and I ended up in the Morgan City ER overnight. And that was the same week as my senior class pictures. I thought I'd never live it down. Come to think of it, I still get comments from old classmates."

"Oh, yeah." The truck was crawling now. At this rate of speed, she wouldn't get to her home, shower, or bed for a week. Yet she didn't protest. Reminiscing, although sadly nostalgic, was fun.

"I know," Ben burst out. "How about the time we went skinny-dipping in Bayou Black. You gotta admit that was a blast."

"Until the alligator ate my clothes." A smile sneaked up

on her and for a moment she forgot all her worries. "I had a helluva time explaining to Gran LeBieu why I was wearing your shirt and nothing else. Next thing I knew she was handing me a box of condoms. 'Use them!' she said."

"Think that alligator choked on your swimsuit?"

"At the time, I sincerely wished he had. That was my favorite bikini." She sighed. "I guess that was my punishment for being stupid."

"A pretty small sacrifice if you ask me. Could have been your skin he bit into." Ben shuddered. "Scared the crayfish out of me."

"Ben Boyette, now I know you're lying. Nothing ever scared you. You were always running around with your hair on fire, driving too fast, pulling dangerous stunts—except when you were with me. You couldn't have been scared of a little ol' alligator."

"Little, hell! He was twelve feet long and only ten feet away from where you stood in the water."

Warmth filled her at his admission. "So, why were you scared, Ben?"

***

Ben's heart mimicked the pace it had beat when Lucie had stood naked before him, the water swirling around her hips. Rivulets gleaming in the moonlight had trickled off her hair and down over breasts bathed blue by the moonbeams. He'd been so entranced, he hadn't seen the alligator until it was almost too late.

He sucked in air and blew it out through clenched teeth. "I was an idiot to let you talk me into swimming in the bayou to begin with. Especially Bayou Black." He gripped the steering wheel until his fingers turned white. "I could have lost you forever."

He'd been so upset at the thought, he'd asked her to marry him the next day.

And she'd accepted. How happy he'd been, imagining himself in love and Lucie loving him, too.

His elation had lasted all of two days, until Lucie dumped him.

"Why did you quit detective work?" Lucie asked.

He stiffened, surfacing from the mire of his past. "Why do you want to know?"

She glanced down at her hands. "Just curious. When you left Bayou Miste, you were hell-bent on a career in law enforcement. What changed your mind?"

He didn't answer right away. What could he say without telling her the truth? He was undercover and no one was supposed to know the real reason he was in Bayou Miste. The only thing he could think of was an incident that had almost made him resign from the force. "On a routine stakeout, I made a mistake. A bad one."

"Did you get fired over it?"

"No." He hoped his clipped response would put off her natural curiosity and make her too uncomfortable to dig deeper. Years had passed since he'd talked about his partner, Skeeter.

But she wasn't willing to drop the matter yet. "I've never known a Boyette to give up on anything. Why did you leave?"

"The mistake cost my partner his life." All the old pain and guilt rushed over him, making him relive the horrible moment he'd held Skeeter's lifeless body in his arms.

"I'm sorry."

"I didn't have the stomach for law enforcement after that. I didn't want the responsibility of another person's life in my hands." If not for his lieutenant's support and confidence in him, he would have quit three years ago when it happened.

She sat in silence, her face reflecting the meager light from a half moon shining through the truck window.

He pressed his foot to the accelerator, uncomfortable with

spilling his guts to her. The rest of the short trip to her apartment flew by. As he turned into her driveway, he slammed on the brakes before he hit the car already there. Or rather, the ancient boat.

The license plate was from California.

Lucie stiffened beside him. "Don't even park, Ben."

"Why? What's wrong?" He stared at the car in front of them, his hands clenching into fists, ready to take on anyone who dared to hurt her. "Does this car belong to someone you know?"

"No!" Lucie inhaled sharply and blew it out, her eyes glistening in the light from her porch. "Yes! I think... Hell, could you take me to Alex's house, please? I can't go in there. I just can't." Her voice broke on the last word and she buried her face in her hands, her shoulders shaking with silent sobs.

Although he'd much rather stay and face whoever had made her cry, he shoved the shift into reverse and pulled out of the driveway.

Her hand shot out, touching his arm. "Wait."

"What do you want to do, Lucie?" He pulled against the curb, put the truck into park, and turned to face her. "Do you want me to go with you to face this person? Are you scared? Is he dangerous? Tell me!"

She hung her head, gulping hard, making a valiant attempt to stem the flow of tears. "No, not dangerous. And no, I don't need you to protect me. This is something I have to do myself." She reached for the door handle and swung the truck door open.

"Wait! Are you sure?" He frowned. He was about to insist on accompanying her to her apartment, when she looked up and gave him a watery smile. A very unconvincing smile.

"Yes, I'm sure. You can go home. No one is going to hurt me. Not anymore. Really, I'll be okay." She gave him the same shaky smile. "Thanks, Ben." After stepping down from the truck and closing the door, she strode across the driveway and stood at the bottom of the steps for a moment, as if gathering her chaotic thoughts.

He waited at the curb, uncertain whether to wait in the truck or ignore her protests and go after her.

As he sat in frustrated indecision, she trudged up the steps and entered her apartment.

He sat a moment longer, wishing he'd gone with her.

Who the hell could it be, who had her so panicky one moment and so depressed the next?

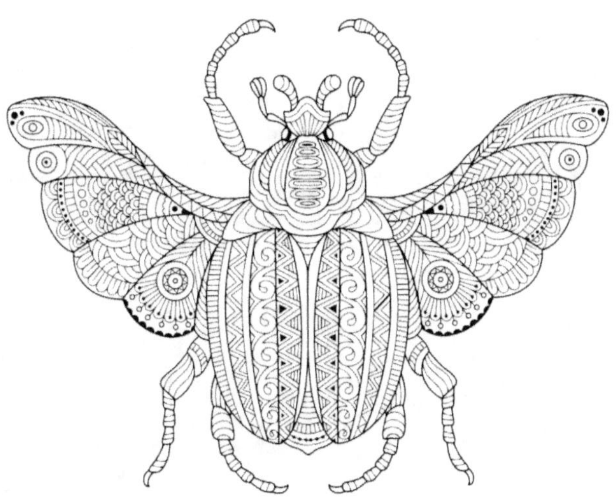

Chapter Eighteen

The woman lying on the couch could be no one else but Lucie's mother, Lynette.

Lynette pushed up to a sitting position, shoved the shoulder-length black hair from her face, and blinked several times. Then her eyes widened, and a smile spilled across her face. "Lucie? Omigod, Lucie!" She leaped to her feet and ran forward, her arms outstretched. "Look at you, you're all grown up."

Lucie raised her hands in a defensive block and stepped backward before her mother could throw her arms around her. After schooling her face into an unreadable mask, she asked, "How'd you get in?"

The older version of herself came to a halt two feet in front of her. Her mother's shoulders sagged and the light in her eyes faded. "Miz Mozelle let me in."

After waiting all her life to see her mother again, she just couldn't see past the years of loneliness and heartache she'd been forced to live through because of her.

This was the woman who'd abandoned her.

"Why are you here?" She didn't soften her question. All

twenty years of pain and anguish pushed her words out in a harsh rasp.

"I wanted to see my girls." Her mother's eyes filled with tears.

After twenty years? *Give me a freaking break.*

"Lisa's in New Orleans, why don't you go there?"

"I missed you." Lynette hung her head. "I wanted to tell you I'm sorry."

Lucie spun away, laughing to keep from crying. Yet she didn't quite succeed. She choked back an unwilling sob, swallowing hard. "After twenty years," she whispered.

"I know. There's no excuse for what I've done to you. I'm not here to give you excuses."

"Don't bother." Furious, she turned toward the woman who gave birth to her. "Nothing you say now can give me the mother I didn't have growing up."

Tears welled out of eyes rimmed with wrinkles. "I don't deserve it, but would like you to hear me out."

"I'm tired, Lynette. And I really don't have the energy to deal with this." Hell, she had problems enough, without having more turn up on her doorstep.

"I know you're angry." She put her hands up when Lucie would have jumped in. "And you have every right to be. What kind of mother would leave her child?"

"The worst kind."

"Yeah, you're right. The worst." She nodded, swiping away traces of tears from her cheek. "I know. I made so many mistakes, I gave up counting."

After all this time, Lucie would have thought she was immune to a kick in the gut from the one person who could have made a real difference in her life, but had chosen not to. But the kick found its mark. Whether it was intentional or not, Lucie didn't care.

"And I was one of your mistakes." She straightened her

shoulders and leveled a look as devoid of emotion as she could muster at her biological mother. "You've said you're sorry, now leave. You're good at that. Good-bye, Lynette. Maybe we can do this again in another twenty years."

Her mother stared at her for a moment and nodded. "I deserve that, and I can respect your desire to kick me out. I'd really like a chance to talk, but I can see you're not ready. I'll be around for a while, in case you change your mind. I'm staying at Mamma's."

"Thanks for the warning." Lucie walked to the door and yanked it open. "I'll be sure to avoid it."

Lynette gathered her purse and closed the distance between them. She paused in the doorway and glanced into Lucie's eyes, her own filled with tears, again. "I didn't want to leave you and your sister. But I loved you so much, I had no other choice." She reached up to touch her cheek.

Lucie jerked away as if stung.

Her mother's hand fell to her side. "I'm very sorry I hurt you." She turned and left.

With a hefty shove, Lucie slammed the door after her, the ceiling rattling with the force of the impact.

In a numb stupor, she found her way to her small bedroom and fell flat on her back across the bed, clothes and all. She didn't have the strength to deal with all this, much less to breathe. She was tired of trying to make the right decisions, tired of making mistakes, and tired of trying to find love in a world filled with pain. All she wanted to do was crawl under a rock and hide until it all went away.

With one hand grasping the comforter, she rolled into a fetal position, dragging the blanket over her. Naturally, the bed linens still held Ben's scent.

God, she couldn't get away from that man! And now her mother had come back to Bayou Miste. What the hell was she going to do?

Blessed exhaustion claimed her and dragged her into a dream-filled sleep where Voodoo drums beat a haunting echo in her head and Gran LeBieu stood over her, shaking her head.

***

Ben knocked on Miz Mozelle's blue door the following morning, hoping like hell Lucie wasn't up and moving about where she could see him. He'd parked his bug truck a block away and walked, just to make sure. What he was about to ask Mozelle Reneau was none of his business, but he needed to know more about the visitor who was at Lucie's last night.

Miz Mozelle opened the door, and a smile lit her finely wrinkled face. Her bright, unnaturally red curls were a riot of color against her pale skin. "Why Benjamin Boyette, it's a pleasure to see you. Come in. Come in!" She stepped aside and held the door wide.

The sweet smell of freshly fried beignets wafted through the opening, wrapping around his empty stomach and yanking him across the threshold. "Miz Mozelle, your kitchen smells great! Are you making beignets again?"

"Sure as shootin'! Get your heinie in here and sit a spell, while I fry up the last batch." She moved ahead of him to the homey kitchen filled with early-morning sunlight. "What brings you along so early this morning, Benjamin?"

How did he broach the subject without sounding like a jealous lover? "Frankly, I was curious about Lucie's visitor."

"Ah, yes." She paused to concentrate on her task. With the expertise of many years of experience, she attacked a ball of pastry dough with a rolling pin, leveling it in a few efficient strokes to an eighth of an inch thick. "That would be Lynette."

"Lynette? As in Lynette LeBieu? Lucie's mother?" Ben rose halfway from his chair. "Damn! When did she come back to Bayou Miste?"

"Yesterday." With a butter knife in hand, she sliced the thin dough into two-and-a-half-inch squares.

Ben sank into his chair at Mozelle's dinette set and shook his head, trying to picture how Lucie might have reacted to her mother showing up after a twenty-year absence. "Man, Lucie's not going to be happy."

"Maybe not, but she needs closure, as my shrink would have said." Miz Mozelle looked up. "I let her in to wait for Lucie last night."

Ben leaned to the left to glance out the back window to see if the Cadillac was still there.

As if reading his mind, Mozelle said, "Oh, she left shortly after Lucie got home. By the way, I saw that you dropped her off. What happened to her car? Break down or something?"

He shook his head. "No, it's in Morgan City at Josie's shop. Long story." One he didn't want to get into. "Any idea what went on over there?"

Mozelle glanced over the pot of bubbling oil as she dropped a thin wafer of dough in. The hot liquid hissed and spit as eruptions of oil popped out of the pot and landed on the stovetop. Within a few short minutes she fished a golden brown beignet out of the vat and laid it on a paper towel. She sprinkled it with powdered sugar, scooped it onto a sandwich plate, and handed it to Ben.

"None whatsoever. But I had a nice long chat with Lynette yesterday evening while she was waiting for Lucie to get off work."

The delicious, sweet scent of the beignet filled his senses, calling out to him, reminding him he hadn't eaten breakfast. Without waiting a reasonable amount of time for the confection to cool, he gingerly lifted it by the corners, burning his fingers in the process. But he didn't let go. Instead, he blew on one side and bit into the featherlight pastry. A dusting of the powdered sugar drifted onto the front of his shirt, but he didn't care. "Miz Mozelle," he moaned. "This is heaven."

She beamed. "Thank you kindly. My Joe thinks I'm trying to fatten him up. Gained fifteen pounds since we started going out."

"I can feel my arteries clogging as we speak. But if I drop dead of a heart attack, I'd die a happy man."

"That's pretty much how Mr. Thibodeaux puts it." She laughed and pulled another fluffy treat from the hot grease. "So, when are you going to marry Lucie?"

Blindsided, Ben inhaled sharply, dragging powder sugar into his lungs. He burst into a fit of coughing, thanking his lucky stars he was choking so he didn't have to answer Mozelle's question.

She shoved a glass of water into his hand and thumped his back with surprising strength. "Got yer breath back now?"

He gulped water until he'd emptied the glass and set it on the table. When his breathing was pretty well back to normal, he polished off the rest of the beignet and started to get up.

"You got so busy coughing, you never answered my question." Miz Mozelle planted her hands on her hips. "When are you going to marry Lucie?"

Ben cursed silently. "I told you, she turned me down last time I asked."

"You talkin' about that mess when you were kids?" The older woman clucked her tongue. "Remember the ol' saying, 'That was then, this is now.'"

"She told me I wasn't good enough for her. As far as she knows, I'm nothin' more than a bug man."

"What do you mean?" Mozelle's brows sank low over her nose and she stared into Ben's eyes. "Is there more to your return to Bayou Miste than yer lettin' on?"

He realized his mistake and answered the best he could. "Even if there was, I wouldn't be at liberty to say."

"I knew you couldn't have come back with yer tail tucked between yer legs like some kicked dog." She grinned and smacked him on the back again.

"Is that what people are saying?"

"No, but it sounded good, didn't it?"

"You're a case, Miz Mozelle."

"Damn straight, and I don't apologize for nothin'." She squinted her eyes. "Well, maybe if it's important, I do. Speakin' of which, did you ever ask Lucie why she dumped you?"

Mozelle could shift so quickly in midstream she created a whirlpool effect, sucking him under. He shook his head. "I didn't need to. She'd already told me once I wasn't good enough."

"And you believed her, I suppose." Mozelle rolled her eyes. "I keep forgettin' how downright thickheaded men are."

"Thanks a lot." He stepped into the living room. "It doesn't matter anyway. She's going to marry Eric Littington. And he's a much better choice for her."

"How do you figure?"

"He's not bad-looking, he's loaded, and he's a rising star on the political scene. What more could a woman want?"

"Ben, I usta think you were a smart man. Now, I'm not so sure." She heaved a big sigh. "What about love?"

Love. That elusive emotion he thought he had experienced just once, only to have it slip away. "Eric's got that covered. He's so hung up on her, he's practically losing sight of his campaign."

"That's Eric." Mozelle retrieved another beignet from the sizzling oil. "What about Lucie?"

He walked through the living room and leaned against the back of a bright floral-print couch. "I don't know. He proposed two days ago. She hasn't given him an answer, but he's bought the ring."

"Stall them!" Mozelle exclaimed.

He swung toward her. "How can I? He has a date with her tonight after she gets off work. He's expecting an answer."

"What do you think she'll say?"

His chest tightening at the thought, he shoved his hands in his pockets and stared at his shoes. "I don't know."

"So what are you waiting for? Go find out!"

"How?" He glanced up at the older woman.

"Le'ssee... Ask her?"

"She'd tell me to go jump in the swamp."

"Men!" She wiped powdered sugar off her hands with a dish towel. "If you want something done, get a woman to do it. Hell, I'd ask her myself, but I promised Joseph I'd go fishin' with him today." She dug around in a duffel bag of a purse and pulled out a cell phone. "What did we do before these little jewels?" She punched the keys.

"Who're you calling?"

She held up a finger. "Hello, Alex?"

"Alex?" His frown cleared and he smiled. "Damn. Why didn't I think of that?"

Mozelle's raised brows told him clearly. *Because he was only a man.* "Alex, your brother needs to know if Lucie's going to say yes to Eric's proposal tonight."

Mozelle listened for a moment, and frowned at Ben. "He's a man. Do I need to say more?"

As an ex-cop, then a detective, and now a member of the elite Criminal Investigator task force, Ben thought of himself as a pretty tough guy. Miz Mozelle was making him out to be a lightweight wimp next to his sister.

"So you'll do it and report back to your brother?" She paused, listening.

Ben leaned closer. Despite his disgust with himself, he wanted to know if Alex would get the information from Lucie.

"What condition is that?" Mozelle asked.

"*Condition?*" he wanted to yell into the phone. "*Alex, for God's sake, don't be stubborn!*" But he held his tongue.

Mozelle laughed. "You got it. I'll send him over with two beignets just for Sport. Thanks, Alex. See ya in church Sunday." She ended the call and winked at him. "Be nice to your sister. She's doin' you a favor."

"I don't need favors from you or my sister. I can ask Lucie the question myself."

"And she'd tell you?" One of Mozelle's eyebrows crept upward. "Sometimes you ain't got the sense God gave a gnat." She patted his cheek. "But I love ya anyway. Now get on outta here. I have a date."

He headed for the door, stopped, and looked back at the amazing Miz Mozelle. "Thanks."

"Thank me when you have a ring on that girl's finger, not a minute sooner."

He stepped outside and inhaled the heady scent of honeysuckle and magnolia blossoms. If he could convince Lucie not to marry Eric, could he convince her to marry him, instead? His batting average wasn't so good with oh-for-one. Did he have the fortitude to step up to the plate again with the possibility of being struck out a second time?

Did he love her enough to risk going through all that pain again?

Hell, yes!

Then why not start now? He didn't have to wait for Alex. He could do some snooping into Lucie's psyche all by himself. Besides, she could probably use a shoulder to lean on about now, what with her mother returning after a twenty-year absence.

No time like the present. He marched around Miz Mozelle's house and up the steps to the garage apartment. He knocked and waited.

Nothing.
He knocked again, this time louder.
Still no answer.
Damn! How had he missed her again?
***

About the time Lucie pulled her pillow over her head to block out the banging on the door, her phone rang on the bedside table.

She let it ring five times before she reached out lifted it and slammed it back on the receiver. "I'm not home! Not to Eric, not to Ben, and especially not to mommy dearest!" She pulled the comforter up to her chin and her pillow back over her head, pressing it into her face until she couldn't breathe. Maybe she could smother herself out of this pickle.

When her lungs began to burn and panic set in, she flung the pillow aside and gasped.

Jeez. Well, she could rule out that method of suicide. Sleeping pills were out of the question as she didn't have any, nor had she had a need for them, until now. She didn't own a gun, and knives were too messy. Carbon monoxide poisoning was out of the question since every appliance in her apartment, including the water heater, air conditioner, and heater, ran on electricity.

Damn. She'd just have to live through another day.

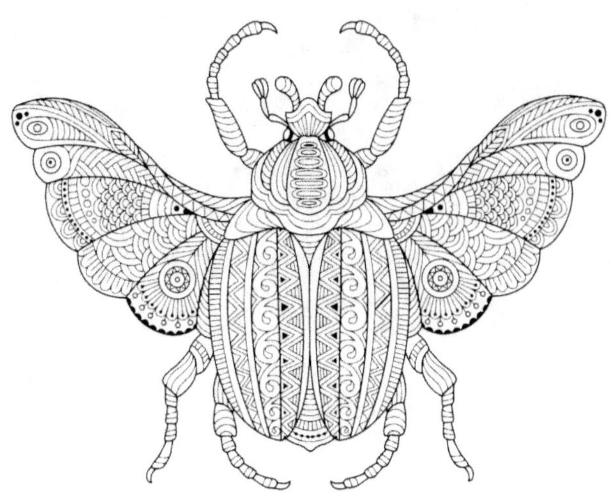

Chapter Nineteen

Lucie's head and feet hurt, but most of all her heart hurt.

Time was running out.

She'd avoided the phone, company, and any contact from human beings all day long. Finally, she'd unplugged the telephone and buried her head beneath her pillows once again.

When she'd tried to call in sick, Jean told her Brandy had beaten her to it. He was counting on her as the only waitress at the Raccoon Saloon that night. She couldn't call in sick or she'd be fired.

Great.

With a heavy heart she slipped into the "uniform" that would make any Hooters waitress proud, and hitched a ride to work with Maurice's grandmother and her poodle. Her mood reflected the color *du jour* of Granny and FeFe's matching hair. Blueberry, Granny informed her. To Lucie, it was blue funk.

"Hey, Lucie, what's gotcha so down?" Jean set two frothy mugs on her tray and went back to the tap for two more.

"Nothin'."

Everything.

Her whole damn life!

"Well, try smilin' a bit. You're scarin' the customers."

"Right. Smile." With her teeth bared at the bartender, she lifted the tray to her shoulders and set off in the direction of the beer-drinking customers. As she snaked her way through the usual crowd of rowdy Cajuns, she plunked the beers on the table so hard golden liquid slopped over the sides.

"Hey, watch it!" A lumberjack of a Cajun scooted back and cursed at the damp spot on his lap.

"Oh, Amos, I'm sorry." She dabbed at his jeans with a bar towel. How much worse could it get? Her life was in the crapper and she couldn't even do her job right.

"*Coo-wee*, baby! Spill some of dat on me." The man next to Amos waved her forward.

Heat suffused her cheeks when she realized what she was doing, dabbing at the man's crotch. "Oh hell! I'm sorry, Amos. This one's on me."

"Oh please, Lucie." The man next to him pressed his palms together in prayer. "I don't mind wearing a little beer if it means you'll wipe it off." He sat back from the table and spread his arms wide. "I'm all yours, honey, spill away."

Despite the weight of her worries, Lucie managed a smile. "Keep your shirt on, Marcus. I'm not gonna spill beer on you."

With his hands clutched to his chest, he heaved a big sigh. "My heart's broken."

"Get in line, buddy." Luc whacked him in the belly with a backhanded swing. "You and every guy in this joint are heartbroken."

Lucie tipped her head, frowning. "Why?"

"Rumor has it you're marrying Littington," Marcus said.

"Rumor, hell!" Amos picked up a copy of the *Times-Picayune* and smacked it against the table. "Says so in the paper."

"And you believe everything you read in the newspaper?" She snorted and placed empty bottles on her tray.

Amos grabbed her free hand. "You mean it isn't true?"

Marcus dropped to his knees on the floor. "Bless my soul! There is a God!"

"Get up, Marcus." She swiped her rag over the table and straightened. "I didn't say I *wasn't* marryin' him."

"Then what did you say?" A low voice asked behind her.

Lucie's heart turned a complete cartwheel and landed with a thunk against her rib cage.

"Ben!" she swung around, tray and all, and bumped into his chest. Empty bottles teetered and toppled over side. She reached out with her free hand to grab for the bottles, upsetting the others. Before she could utter an ugly curse word, five bottles had crashed to wooden floor, four of them bouncing, and one, unfortunately, shattering. "Damn!"

Ben's warm hand on her bare arm stopped her from stepping backward. "Don't move."

"Let go of me." His fingers seared through her skin, creating havoc with her heart rate. "I have to clean up this mess."

"No, the glass could go right through those crazy high-heeled shoes you're wearing. Let me."

"No way, Ben." She yanked her arm free. "This is my job. I'll do it myself."

"If you'd stop being so damn hardheaded for just one damn moment, you could see straight. You're not wearing proper shoes, any idiot can see that."

"So now I'm an idiot?" She lifted the tray in front of her like a shield. "You're one to be talking—a man who couldn't see the nose on his own face!"

Ben's brows twisted into a frown. "What's that supposed to mean?"

"If you ever bothered to look past it, maybe you'd know. Now, move!"

"Lucie, you're talking in riddles and I'm not in the mood to figure them out."

Before she could emit another scathing retort, Ben scooped her up into his arms and marched across the floor to the bar, plunking her down on an empty seat. "Stay, or else."

She started to push off the stool only to bump into his chest. "Or else what? You'll turn me into a toad?"

He leaned close and whispered loud enough for only her to hear, "Stay, or I'll kiss you in front of God and everybody."

Her breath caught and she almost choked on how much she wanted just that. Until she realized he'd only meant it as a threat. But she didn't want to tempt him. No telling how she'd respond. And wouldn't that be a pretty sight. Kissing Ben when she was supposed to marry Eric—not good.

She shut up and let him clean up the glass. That was the least he could do for rattling her. Besides, if he hadn't sneaked up on her, she wouldn't have dropped the bottles in the first place.

If she were honest with herself, she'd admit she was a little on edge. Had been all day. And who wouldn't be, with the kinds of decisions she had to make?

Alex and Calliope showed up out of nowhere and slid into the seats on either side of her. Ganging up on her, no doubt.

"Hey, girlfriend," Calliope said. "Takin' a break?"

Lucie harrumphed her answer.

Alex squinted through the smoky haze. "Is that my big brother cleaning the floor? I'll be damned. Never saw him do that at home."

"Damn right," she answered.

"Isn't that your job?" Calliope asked.

"Up until a minute or two ago, I'd have agreed." Lucie

turned her back to the room. "Jean, I'm on break for the next five minutes. Could you hand me a Miller Lite?"

"You know I don't like my girls to drink while they're on duty."

"I'm on break, so technically I'm not on duty. Are you going to give me that beer, or am I gonna have to crawl across the counter and get it myself?" Her voice rose with each word she uttered until she sounded like a nagging housewife.

"Okay, okay. You don't have to bite my head off." Jean slammed a mug frothing with foam on the counter.

"My, my. Aren't we the growly bitch tonight?" Alex said.

"I'm not in the mood, Alex." She downed half the contents of her mug in one long swallow.

"I noticed." Alex gave her a long, penetrating look. "Along with practically everyone else in the bar."

"If you're here to promote your brother's cause, save it." She tipped her mug and poured the rest of the icy liquid down her throat. "I don't need another person questioning my decisions tonight."

"Jean, Miller Lite, please." When Jean set the mug in front of her, Alex lifted it and turned toward Lucie, a sly smile slipping across her face. "And have you made any?"

"Any what?" Lucie eyed her empty mug and pushed it away, almost sending it over the opposite edge of the bar.

"Decisions?"

She closed her eyes and tilted her head back. "If you were my friend, you wouldn't ask."

"I am your friend," Alex said. "And as your friend, I'm worried about you."

"Don't be. I can take care of myself."

"I'm not so sure lately." Alex laid a hand on her arm. "You're really tense, you've got circles under your eyes, and you're as cross as a trapped ringtail."

"Yeah," Calliope said. "You haven't been as much fun to

hang around lately." She smiled and patted Lucie's arm. "But I'll hang around you no matter how bitchy you get. That's what friends are for."

Lucie looked from Calliope to Alex, then groaned. "Am I getting that bad?" She dropped her forehead to the edge of the bar and banged it twice. "I'm so confused, and feeling guilty and, well, I don't know what to do!"

Alex pulled her into her arms and hugged her tight. Calliope hugged her from behind.

"We love, you sweetie." Alex smoothed her hand over Lucie's hair. "Everything will be okay."

"First there was Ben, then Eric, and...and that damned bug!" She sobbed into Alex's shirt.

"I know, sweetie." Alex pushed Lucie's hair out of her face. "Shh. It's okay."

"And now, my mother's moved back to Bayou Miste!" She leaned back and stared into Alex's eyes, her own filling with tears. "What am I supposed to do?"

"Dry your eyes, honey. You're a tough ol' bird. God never gives us more than we can handle. You'll see." She pulled a tissue from her purse and dabbed at Lucie's eyes, then handed her the tissue.

"I'm not handling this very well." She blew her nose and straightened.

"No, you're not."

With a pout, Lucie said, "Hey, you're supposed to be supportive."

"I am, when I think it's right. And some of the stuff you've been doing lately just isn't right."

She crossed her arms over her chest, bracing herself. "All right. Go ahead, say it."

"Say what?" Calliope asked.

"I told you so," Lucie said. "I can tell Alex is dying to."

"I'm not going to rub your nose in your big, fat mistake. I

love you, Lucie. I want you to be happy. I just don't think you've gone about it the right way."

"And you would have done it better?" she asked, some of her hurt pushing her to add, "And how long has it been since you've had a decent date?"

Alex stiffened. "That's hitting below the belt."

"Do you like your mother picking your men for you?" She felt compelled to go there.

"No. But we weren't talking about me, were we?" Alex poked a finger to her chest. "We were talking about *you*, Lucie. *You* got this ball rolling. Or should I say, bug flying? Now, *you* have to make the big decisions."

"Wait, whoa!" She raised her hand. "Did anyone ever tell you you're a freakin' bulldozer, Alex?"

Alex had the grace to blush. "Well, yeah, but—"

"No 'buts.' However, you're right. I got this bug flying. I have to make the tough decisions."

"Lucie, are you going to marry Eric?" Calliope asked.

"I don't know!" Overwhelmed, Lucie jumped off the stool. "Jean, my break's over. If you need me, I'll be waiting tables." Without another word to her friends, she snatched up her tray and dove into the crowd.

Avoiding Ben and the bottle mess, she headed toward the entrance, debating a quick escape, yet knowing she couldn't leave Jean without a waitress. Just when she thought she might catch her breath, a strikingly beautiful older woman stepped through the doorway.

Holy swamp gas, her world was blowing up in her face! Of all nights, why did her mother have to go and show up at the Raccoon Saloon?

***

Ben scraped fragments of glass into the dustpan Jean had provided, keeping one eye on Lucie and the other on the guy in the dark corner. If he wasn't mistaken, the man in the back was the same one who'd tossed paint on him and Eric in the jewelry store in Morgan City.

What was he doing here? And why was he watching Lucie?

His blood boiled on high heat. He was used to all the guys in Bayou Miste ogling the swamp princess. Not that he liked it. But a complete stranger had better keep his distance. After the man's performance the other day, he deserved close scrutiny. The man had been arrested, but must have been let out on bail.

As he carried the broken bottles to the trash can, Ben glanced at the clock over the bar. Midnight. The place didn't close till two, and the crowd looked as though they were settling in for the long haul. Smoke hung heavy and stale in the air, the music and laughter loud enough to damage eardrums.

Half a dozen guys stood around the bar, shouting for beer. As the only waitress on duty, Lucie couldn't be expected to keep up with everyone.

She looked dead tired.

He wished he could whisk her away from the smell of spilled alcohol and cigarettes. Out into the fresh night air to hold her under the moonlight. Maybe if he kissed her, and this time told her he loved her, she'd tell Eric to get lost.

When he noticed a woman, who could have been Lucie's clone, step through the door, his heart squeezed hard in his chest. She was older, but every bit as beautiful as her daughter.

Lucie's face blanched and her mouth tightened, but she didn't so much as acknowledge her mother.

She had to be hurting. He could have wrung Lynette's pretty neck for waiting all these years and then having the gall to show up and expect Lucie to welcome her home.

He wanted to go to Lucie and hold her in his arms, kiss

away her heartache. With that in mind, he stepped toward her, only to stop when another person entered the bar.

Eric Littington.

Too late. He should have stolen her away earlier. Now he was obligated to let her make up her own mind about his friend. Damn! Once again, his timing was off. He'd do well to keep his focus on the stranger and make sure he didn't pull another stupid stunt with Eric. His desire to make things right for Lucie would have to wait.

"Ben!" Eric strode across the room and settled into the chair opposite him. He was all smiles and in a good mood.

Ben wanted to snarl his greeting. Instead, he stuck out his hand. "Hey, Eric."

"Didn't expect to see you here." He glanced around the room, his gaze following Lucie's every move.

The blood in Ben's veins moved like molten lava on a slow crawl. He wanted to hate Eric for everything he had, for everything he was. But he couldn't hate him. He'd been his friend for years. Yet how much was a guy supposed to suck up before he exploded?

"So, tonight's the big night, huh?" It took every ounce of his determination to speak the words out loud. He held his breath waiting for Eric's answer, hoping by some stroke of fate, Eric had changed his mind.

"Yes, sir!" Eric patted his trouser pocket. "Made it back to the jewelry store in Morgan City today to pick up the ring. I'm ready."

"The question is, is she?" His gaze drifted to Lucie. Even tired and worried, she was beautiful. He'd give his left nut to be with her as he had the other night. The raw knot of guilt flared in his belly and he glanced back at Eric.

Obviously, Lucie hadn't shared their secret with him. Otherwise, he wouldn't be sitting so happily next to the man who'd screwed his potential fiancée. He had mixed feelings about Lucie telling Eric about their stolen night together. If Lucie chose to marry Eric, the confession would only ruin their chance at a happy future. On the other hand, maybe if Eric knew, he wouldn't marry Lucie. She'd be free to marry him.

Ben sat forward, his heart thudding against his chest, the temptation to tell driving his mouth open.

Eric chose that time to wave at Lucie, a joyful smile on his face.

With a sickening realization, Ben sank back in his seat. He couldn't ruin Lucie's opportunity for happiness. She deserved a chance at the good life.

His biggest regret was that she hadn't chosen him. Marriage to Lucie would never have been peaceful, but he was sure it would have been a helluva ride. She'd have kept him young into his old age.

"You're getting a terrific woman," he said.

With a laugh, Eric ran a shaky hand through his hair. "She hasn't said yes, yet. God, I hope she does."

On the outside, Ben nodded and agreed with his friend, while on the inside, he prayed she'd say no.

Please, God, let her say no.

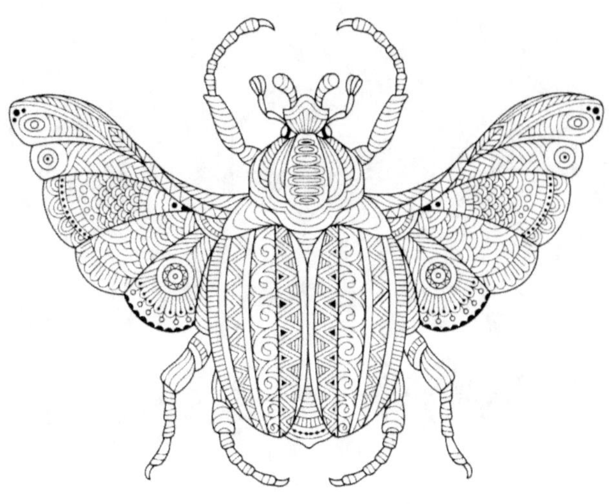

Chapter Twenty

B y the time Jean escorted the last customer from the bar, Lucie was as jumpy as a flea on a dog, her stomach tied in one huge, nervous knot. With Alex, Calliope, Ben, Eric, and Lynette all staring at her for the last two hours, she felt like raw steak in a room full of hungry vultures.

Sheesh!

At least Eric had offered to wait out in the car while she switched from her "uniform" to decent clothes. Jean would lock up, so all she had to do was change into the shirt and slacks she'd brought along for her breakfast date with Eric.

The two-hour effort to ignore her friends, ex-fiancé, potential fiancé, and long-lost mother had taken its toll. She was balancing on her last nerve and in no mood to go out. What she wanted was a long hot bath and an even longer night's sleep.

Would Eric understand if she asked him to take her home?

One look at his handsome, eager face, and she'd known she couldn't put him off another night. Somehow, in the next hour or so she had to make a decision whether or not to marry Eric.

As she slipped into her slacks, she weighed Eric's pros for the hundredth time in the past few days. He was handsome, wealthy, a political climber, completely in love with her, and incredibly nice—and don't forget romantic.

Tugging a ribbed-knit coral T-shirt over her head, she had to give the cons equal consideration. *Okay, so list the cons already!*

She stood for a moment, staring at her reflection in the mirror. "Come on, girl, Eric has to have some cons."

He wasn't Ben.

The longer she thought, the more frustrated she became. Eric didn't have any cons? Holy crab cakes—the man was perfect.

So what are you waiting for? Go get him.

An image of Ben lying next to her in her bed popped into her mind. "Because you haven't told him about Ben—and the teensy little fact that you slept with him the night Eric proposed," she said to her guilt-ridden face in the mirror.

She'd been looking at it all wrong. She'd been thinking only about what *she'd* get out of marrying Eric. What would *Eric* get out of this marriage?

She stepped into her high-heeled sandals, one at a time.

He'd get *me*.

She thought about that for a moment. She wasn't so sure that was a pro for him. More likely, it was a huge con in the scheme of all that had transpired in the past week. She'd resorted to magic to lure him in. Kinda like a black widow luring her ill-fated mate in for the kill. Her natural aversion to eight-legged beasts had her shivering in the heat. Then, after he'd proposed to her, she'd slept with his friend...and hadn't had the decency to enlighten him.

And she came with baggage. Loads of it! And her biggest

bit of baggage had just moved back to Bayou Miste with *her* baggage, wanting to work her way back into her daughter's life. Like that was going to happen. *Not!*

A knock at the door made her jump.

"Lucie?" Jean's voice called out. "You coming out or do you want me to lock you in?"

Jean's comment was too close to the truth. She glanced at her watch. Shit! She'd been in the bathroom for fifteen minutes! Eric would be getting worried.

"No, Jean, I'm coming out." Her hands shaking, Lucie left the safety of the bathroom and the stale smoke of the bar, and stepped out into the night.

With a deep, cleansing breath of humid swamp air, she marched across the parking lot to meet her fate, still without a clue what it was going to be. If only everyone hadn't ganged up on her, showing up in force to keep her mind in a jumble.

She needed to focus. *Remember, Eric is perfect and Ben is not an option.*

The perfect man stepped out of his BMW and met her halfway. "Lucie." One word. Spoken like a parched man holding out his hand for life-giving water. Eric wrapped her in his arms and hugged her close. Then he steered her to the passenger seat and held the door open as she climbed in.

Perfect. The man was absolutely perfect.

She had no idea why the repetitive thought was making her less happy by the minute.

"I thought you might be too tired to go all the way to Morgan City, so I packed a snack. I have a special place I'd like to take you that's a little closer and a lot more private, if that's okay with you?"

She leaned back against the leather seat and closed her eyes, willing herself to relax. *You're not going before a firing squad.* "That would be...perfect."

The engine hummed to life with barely a sound.

Wrapped in the quiet cocoon of the car's interior, her numb ears reveled in the stillness. She loved Cajun music, but hearing the blaring noise night after night got old, and her ears would probably pay the price. For the moment, she was content to let the silence lull her to calmness.

Like the calm in the eye of a hurricane.

***

Ben had left the bar a few steps behind the man in the leather jacket. As much as he wanted to follow Eric and Lucie, he needed to learn more about this stranger who'd tossed paint on him and Eric. If he was the one sabotaging Eric's campaign, he had to catch him.

Leather Man climbed into a navy-blue Ford Taurus and pulled out of the parking lot.

With the car in his peripheral vision, Ben sauntered casually to his Audi, which he'd left in the parking lot earlier. After all, it was considerably less conspicuous than the exterminator truck. Once in the car, he jotted down the license number.

When the man's rental car turned onto the highway, Ben jammed the Audi into drive and spun out after him. He didn't have far to go. The Taurus had backed into an overgrown side road, just a few yards past the entrance to the bar's lot. He would have missed it if he hadn't seen the brake lights flash once before blinking out.

Okay, what are you up to? He drove past and around a curve in the road. Once out of sight, he executed a U-turn, switched his lights off, and sneaked around the corner at a snail's pace. He found his own hidey-hole in the bushes a tenth of a mile from his quarry. Two could play this game.

Now, they'd wait—Leather Man for Eric—probably—and Ben for Leather Man. And waiting gave him way too much time to think.

His mind drifted to Eric and Lucie and what he knew was

going to take place this evening. He wanted to stop it. But only Lucie could do that. She had to decide whether Eric was the man for her, or if he, after a seven-year absence, still had a place in her life and heart.

Then a sickening thought occurred to him. *He hadn't offered her a different choice.* He hadn't offered her anything, because he was afraid she'd reject him as she had so long ago. Hell, she was going to make a decision based on only one offer.

Damn! He'd screwed it up again.

Cursing his own stupidity, he pulled out his cell phone and punched one of the autodial numbers. Might as well do some work, since that might be all he had left after tonight.

"Hey, P.J., this is Boyette."

"Boyette! Long time no see! Wassup in the swamps?"

"Same ole, same ole. Loads of fish, too many bugs to count, and a few alligators to wrestle."

"Boring, huh? Sure could use you back at the department."

"How's the new guy working out?"

"Okay, but he's not you."

"He'll get the hang of it. And I'll be back before you know it." Ben stared out at the dark shadow tucked in the bushes ahead of him. "Hey, P.J., need your help."

"Shoot."

"Need a license check on a rental." Ben gave P.J. the license plate number, a description of the vehicle, and his cell phone number so P.J could call him back.

"Got it. I'll get back with you when I have something. You take care. When you get back to Baton Rouge, the wife wants you to come by for some jambalaya."

"Will do. Thanks, P.J." He clicked the phone off and settled back to wait. Such was the life of a detective. Hurry up and wait. Sometimes he'd wait all night long outside a residence and nothing would happen. Other cases were more interesting. The trick to investigation was to keep a low profile and observe.

A stream of cars and pickup trucks paraded in both directions away from Raccoon Saloon. The bar was closing. Jean and Lucie would be the last to leave, Lucie in Eric's car. He waited to see what Leather Man's next move would be.

The moonlight gave him an added advantage. He could see the occasional glint off the shiny metallic finish. Five minutes passed, then ten. His cop instincts kicked into heightened alert. Not long now. Fifteen minutes after the last customer left, lights speared the darkened road as Eric's BMW pulled onto the highway, heading away from him and Leather Man.

Just as he anticipated, Leather Man pulled onto the highway behind Eric and Lucie. *Lights off.* The navy Taurus was a shadow tailing the unsuspecting congressional candidate. If not for the occasional brake lights, Ben might not have seen the car at all.

As he slid onto the road behind Leather Man, his pulse increased. Not because he was a predator on the prowl, but because he didn't know if this was the same guy who'd taken a shot at Eric and Lucie a few nights earlier. If he was, they could be in trouble tonight.

He closed the distance to within a hundred yards, afraid to get too far behind in case he lost them. The moonlight helped, but tall trees crowding the roadsides cast inky shadows over the pavement for long stretches.

When Eric turned off the main highway onto another smaller road, Ben knew exactly where he was going. His heart bottomed out. Eric was taking Lucie to one of Ben and Lucie's old haunts. *Jesus.* The place he and Lucie had made love for the first time. Would she remember?

Even more disturbing, Leather Man was right behind

them. This was a particularly lonely stretch of road. Nobody lived out here and only the occasional teenagers came out here to drink or make out. He hoped some of those teenagers were out here tonight. Perhaps that would discourage Eric and Lucie from staying. If the place was deserted, Eric would propose to Lucie—and Leather Man might pull some stupid stunt.

Great! Should he turn his headlights on and let Leather Man know he was back here? Perhaps the Taurus would turn around and leave if he did. But then Lucie would see his car and wonder what the hell he was doing following her. She might even think he was there to ruin her chances with Eric.

Eric parked his BMW at Make-Out Point on the edge of Bayou Black. The lights blinked out.

A few car lengths behind Eric, the Ford Taurus had come to a halt, its brake lights glaring red beneath the canopy of trees overhanging his position.

What was the guy doing?

Ben shoved his Audi into park, turned his interior light switch to the off position, and climbed out. Hell, maybe he'd just ask. But he'd keep it quiet so as not to interrupt Eric's little talk with Lucie.

As he approached the rear of the Taurus, the red taillights blinked off and the car spun out, spitting gravel into his eyes.

He blinked the dust from his vision in time to see the car heading straight for the BMW.

Good God.

"Lucie!"

***

Eric had been gracious enough to remain silent throughout the short drive. The reprieve from the storm of mindless inner chatter had lulled Lucie into a state of near calm. Until the car halted and the engine switched off.

She opened her eyes. Before her, moonlight spread over

the bayou like a silvery cloak. Although she hadn't been here in a while, she instantly recognized this place and her stomach turned a flip.

Talk about an unwanted jaunt down memory lane.

He'd brought her to freaking Make-Out Point? The point was a small pullout area where tourists could come to see the swamp during daylight hours. The kids used it at night for necking. She and Ben had made out here on more than one hot, steamy night. One particularly beautiful moonlit evening with Ben, she'd lost her virginity.

Not a good reminder, considering Eric's intention. How could she say yes to Eric when they were in a place filled with such amazing memories of Ben? Jeez! All her calm flew out the window.

She turned to Eric to ask if they could go somewhere else, but he was staring at her as if she'd hung the moon over the swamp. "I found this place today while I was out driving around, and I knew it was perfect for what I want to say to you."

There went that word again. Perfect!

Her pulse quickened and her chest tightened to the point she felt as though someone was sitting on it, squeezing the air from her lungs. Well on her way to a full-scale panic attack, she wasn't ready for Eric's next words.

Eric's eyes widened as he stared into his rearview mirror. "What the hell?"

Huh?

"Lucie!" A shout outside the vehicle alerted her they were not alone.

She glanced into the mirror on her door. Headlights flared to life, blinding her.

Wham!

The BMW lurched over the low earthen rise, throwing Lucie forward. Her seat belt tightened, catching her in time to save her head from smacking the dash. Eric wasn't so lucky. His head whacked the steering wheel with a dull *wonk*.

As if in a B horror movie, Lucie saw bushes and small trees race by the window as the BMW plunged toward the murky waters of the bayou.

Helpless to stop the forward momentum, she willed herself to be calm. They were going in. She prayed to God and her grandmother's Voodoo magic the water wasn't deep.

The front of the BMW dived beneath the surface and jammed into the soft silt of the bayou bottom. Water spilled in through the floorboard, rising fast to her knees. She fumbled to release her safety belt.

"Eric!" She felt next to her for Eric. Slumped over the steering wheel, he didn't respond when she shook him. The water was rising at an alarming rate.

She had to get him out! With her hand on his seat belt, she followed it to the safety catch and pressed the button. The lock didn't release. She jammed her thumb on it, shaking and tearing at the metal clasp. Water was up to her chest now, if she didn't hurry, they'd both drown. "Eric, wake up! Please, wake up!"

With barely enough time to take a deep breath, the fetid smell of the murky swamp water, now rising to her neck, pressed against her senses. Eric would die if she didn't get him out. She tipped his head back to keep his nose from submerging.

She pushed away from him, sucked in air, and dived for the door handle. Her hand smoothed across the door until her fingers closed around the little lever. She tugged. It was locked. She tugged again and the locking mechanism released, but the door wouldn't open. She tried to pound her fist against the window, but her hand bounced back like dandelion fluff in the wind. She surfaced inside the car and gulped in precious air. Then she dived down again, braced her feet on the console, her shoulder against the door, and shoved. *Move, damn it!*

***

When the Taurus hit the back of the BMW, Ben was fifty yards away. His heart stopped for a split second before it raced to fill his veins with adrenaline.

The bastard was trying to kill Eric and Lucie! Ben raced forward, ready to rip Leather Man apart.

When he reached the Taurus, the white reverse lights lit the night. He didn't have enough time to move out of the way. The car backed right into him. He flung himself over the top of the trunk, crashing against the back windshield. He hit with enough force that the windshield cracked into a million pieces, the safety glass the only reason he didn't fly through into the backseat.

When the car slammed to a stop, he slid off the trunk onto the gravel, rolling to the side, out of the tires' reach.

Before he could catch his wind, the Taurus skidded out of the parking area and disappeared into the night.

Head spinning, he lurched to his feet. Pain shot through his shoulder, and his lungs hurt when he breathed. But he didn't care. Lucie and Eric were in the BMW and he couldn't see it anymore. With a hand pressed to his side, he limped to the edge of the bayou.

The rear end of the BMW was barely above the surface. Steam and bubbles percolated from where the engine had submerged. No sign of Eric or Lucie.

His breath hitched. *Oh God. Please let Lucie be all right.* He kicked off his shoes and plunged into the swamp. He had to get them out before they drowned. He no longer cared if Lucie married him or Eric. He just wanted her alive.

His hands skimmed the passenger side of the car until he reached the door. The water was five feet deep at this point. He tugged on the door handle. The heavy metal door didn't budge. The force of the water on the outside of the car wasn't equalized with the interior. Which meant the inside wasn't completely full yet. Until the pressure equalized, the door would be impossible to budge. But he couldn't wait—they could be drowning.

With his foot braced on the back door, he grabbed the front door handle and pulled as hard as he could. The door opened enough to let a flood of water race in.

"Help!" Lucie's voice cried out once, right before the water filled the rest of the interior.

He wrestled the door open, reached in, and grasped her slim hand flailing in the water. He pulled until she surfaced, sputtering and coughing. She clung to him, her legs wrapping around his waist.

"You can stand in the water here," he said into her ear.

"Omigod. Eric!" She dropped her feet to the bottom and pushed off Ben and moved to dive back into the car.

"No." He caught her before her head disappeared beneath the murky water. "You get to the shore. I'll get Eric."

"But—" She tugged against him, her gaze sweeping the water's surface.

"Just do it! You're wasting time and we don't know if there are alligators out here."

She darted a quick look around. "Okay, but he's uncon-scious. Hurry!"

"I'll get him. Now go." He didn't wait to see if she followed his orders. He dragged in a deep breath and slipped beneath the surface, feeling his way across the passenger seat to the driver.

Eric was slumped over the steering wheel, held in place by his seat belt.

Ben worked at the belt's clasp until he realized he was wasting his time. With one hand holding the steering wheel, he dug in his own pocket, his lungs burning with the effort to stay submerged. He realized he couldn't stay down a moment longer, and he backed out of the vehicle, surfacing to catch his breath. While he inhaled another breath, he dug in his pocket again until he found his pocketknife. Thank God. No Cajun worth his salt would be without one.

Back in the swirling, murky water, he pulled himself over to Eric, sliced through the constricting belt, and freed Eric's arms. The unconscious man floated toward the ceiling.

With a hand full of Eric's shirt, he pushed backward toward the passenger door, dragging his friend with him. He surfaced, immediately bringing Eric's head above the water.

But Eric wasn't breathing. His lungs had to be full of water given the amount of time he'd been under.

Ben dragged him to the shore and pulled his body out of the swamp enough to work on him. He flipped him onto his stomach and straddled his hips. With both hands, he pushed against Eric's ribs, forcing the water up and out of his lungs.

He leaned into Eric's back. "Come on, buddy! Out with the old, in with the new. Breathe!"

***

Heart in her stomach, Lucie dropped to her knees next to the still man. "Spit it out, Eric!"

Ben pushed again.

This time, water erupted from Eric's mouth and he coughed.

"Eric, oh my God, Eric!" She pushed the hair off Eric's forehead. "He's breathing!" She smiled up at Ben in the moonlight.

But Ben's face was an unreadable mask in his own shadow. "Help me turn him over, will ya?"

Together they rolled Eric onto his back. "Lucie?" he said, his voice a hoarse whisper.

Ben got to his feet. "I'm going for my cell phone." He paused for a moment. "You gonna be okay?"

"Yeah." Eric coughed and gave a weak excuse for a smile. "Really. And thanks."

Ben turned and loped to his car.

Eric's eyes drifted shut, and he lay still.

Heart still thundering, she leaned close to listen for the steady rhythm of air moving in and out of his lungs.

"Lucie?"

She jumped. "I'm here, Eric."

"Scared for"—he coughed—"you."

She laughed and lifted his hand to her face. "I'm the Voodoo queen's granddaughter, what could possibly happen to me?"

He smiled and curled his hand around her cheek. "Did I ask you?"

"Ask me what?" she asked, before she could think. *Oh yeah.* Her heart leaped from her belly to her throat. *Don't do it, Eric,* she cried inside.

"Will you marry me?" He gripped her hand.

As she stared down at him, wondering what she could say, the hair on the back of her neck stood up. Ben stood behind her. He had to have heard Eric's question.

Eric's hand slipped back into hers. "I love you, Lucie."

With the word "no" poised on her lips, she felt weak pressure on her fingers.

"Don't say no," he whispered. "Please."

How could she say no? The man could be dying, for all she knew. She inhaled air to the bottom of her lungs, squeezed her eyes shut, and answered, "Yes, Eric."

Behind her, she heard a sharp intake of breath. Though Lucie's heart cried out for him to protest, Ben didn't say a thing. He didn't plead with her to change her mind. No protestations of love or offers to sweep her off her feet.

What did she expect? He'd offered for her once. A man wasn't likely to risk getting burned twice by the same fire.

For a girl who'd finally gotten exactly what she'd wanted, why was she so miserable?

What a mess.

And Eric wouldn't have asked her in the first place if it hadn't been for her magical spell and one tiny bug. She was a complete fraud, a louse, a low-life Voodoo queen wannabe without compassion and love for anyone but herself. She'd never be truly loved by anyone.

In the meantime, she sat with Eric's head in her lap, afraid to face the only man she'd ever really loved for fear of witnessing his disappointment—or worse, his contempt.

Fifteen minutes seemed like forever, waiting for the emergency medical service to arrive.

With a smile curving his lips, Eric drifted in and out of consciousness.

She wished she could drift out with him. With Ben's car the only other available transportation not under five feet of water, she was glad when Eric surfaced long enough to ask, "Will you ride with me in the ambulance?"

When the EMS arrived, she climbed in beside Eric and played the dutiful fiancée all the way to the hospital.

The press must have been listening to their scanners, because when the ambulance arrived at the small hospital in Morgan City, they were mobbed.

Thanks to the state police who'd followed along as an escort, they made it inside with minimal delay. She found herself scanning the crowds for Ben. He'd said he'd follow them. Had he changed his mind?

Eric's father met them at the ER entrance and followed them inside, demanding a private room and any specialist money could buy to ensure Eric's survival.

Once Eric was diagnosed with a small concussion, bruised ribs, and fluid on the lungs, they settled him into a room and loaded him with antibiotics and painkillers.

Finally, able to get close enough to speak to Eric again, Lucie leaned over him and said, "If you don't need me anymore, I'm going home."

Eric grasped her hand. "Did you have the doctors look you over?"

"Yeah, no harm done, other than a broken nail."

"Dad?" Eric leaned back, his eyelids drifting closed over drug-glazed eyes.

Jason Littington moved to the head of the other side of the bed. "Yes, son."

"Lucie and I are engaged. Be nice to her, will you?"

The elder Littington stared across his son at her. Instead of contempt or snobbery, he gave her a gentle smile. "Welcome to the Littington family, my dear. I'm sure I'll love you like the daughter I never had."

She would rather have had his contempt. With Jason Littington being so cordial when his son's fiancée had tricked him into falling in love with her, she felt lower than a scum-sucking snail.

She wanted to crawl beneath the rock she'd slithered out from under. Her chest tightened, her heartbeat fluttered like a skittish cat, teasing her system into thinking it was delivering life-giving blood to her body. But her pulse was so shallow it made her light-headed. She had to get outside. Now!

Eric was out cold; he wouldn't miss her.

After some lame-ass excuse to his father, she practically ran out of the hospital room.

She stopped at the nurse's station and asked for a pen and a sheet of paper. She scribbled a note and handed it to the nurse, knowing it was cowardly, but it had to be done. "Could you please give this to Jason Littington before he leaves?"

Without waiting for a response, Lucie hurried out of the hospital. She stood on the concrete sidewalk and inhaled deep breaths of thick, humid Louisiana air, trying to tamp down the rising panic. When she'd regained a tentative level of calm, her brain engaged and she realized she didn't have a ride home.

She was about to turn and reenter the hospital to find a telephone, when a silver Audi slid to a stop in front of her.

Her stomach knotted and all her hard-won calm skittered down the sewer drain. She'd rather face an entire firing squad of reporters armed with cameras than the one man with the ability to break her heart.

Ben.

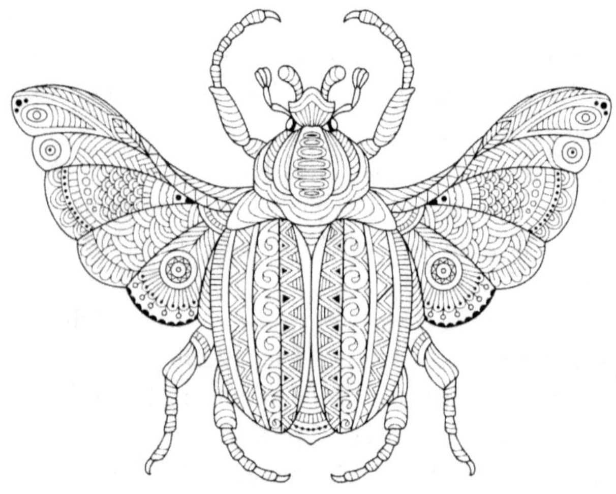

Chapter Twenty-One

Why he couldn't leave well enough alone, Ben hadn't a clue. He tried to rationalize that Lucie would need a ride home after the ambulance had delivered Eric to the hospital.

Deep inside, he knew he wanted to ask her, "Why?" Why had she pushed him away all those years ago; why did she say yes to Eric and not to him?

She stood looking at the car, her face strained as if she were afraid of him.

"Get in," he said, a little more brusquely than he'd intended.

When Lucie climbed into his car, he fought to keep from pulling her into his arms and shaking her to within an inch of her life. How could she marry Eric? Didn't she know she was supposed to love *him*?

Oh, yeah. She'd told him he wasn't good enough for her.

"If we're going home, it helps to put the shift in drive," she murmured.

Heat filled his cheeks. He'd been so buried in his misery he hadn't realized the car was still idling in the hospital parking lot. He jammed the shift in drive and floored the accelerator.

Lucie gasped, a hand fluttering over her heart.

He shot a glance her way and immediately let off the gas. Her face had drained of color.

"Sorry." *What was wrong with him?* Hadn't she been through enough without him scaring her by driving like a sulky teen?

Her laugh was more a breathy sob. "No. I'm a bit jumpy."

Damn! He should have known she was fragile. Hell, she'd almost drowned! His blood ran cold. *Lucie had almost drowned in that car.*

His lips pulling into a tight line, he concentrated on the road back to Bayou Miste, keeping his speed to five miles an hour under the posted limit. Hunkered in her corner of the front seat, she stared out the window into the inky black night. The moon had disappeared behind clouds.

They drove in silence until he pulled into her driveway. He expected her to leap out and race up to her apartment.

Instead, she sat staring up the stairs, a shimmer of tears reflecting light from the brand-new bulb glowing over her door.

The man who loved Lucie more than life itself screamed inside him, urging him to action. *Say something! Tell her you still love her. Tell her you don't want her to marry Eric. Do something!*

Then the logical man who'd regulated his life for the past seven years overruled him.

Lucie had made her choice. She would marry Eric. He would go back to Baton Rouge and that would be the end of any stupid dreams he may have conjured while at home in the swamps.

Why the hell wasn't she getting out of the car?

Finally, she fumbled for the door handle. After her second

attempt, he sighed and stepped out. By the time he got around to open her door, she had pushed it wide and stood up.

When he grabbed her elbow, he felt the tremors. She was shaking so hard her teeth rattled as she collapsed against him.

Ah jeez! She was going into shock. He should have recognized it when she wasn't talking. Lucie always had something to say.

He scooped his arm under her legs and lifted her as easily as if she were a child. But her luscious curves were anything but childlike. As the side of her breast rested against his chest, he sucked in air.

A sob escaped her lips and she pressed her face into his damp shirt, wrapping her arms around his neck. He had to put her down quickly—before he couldn't let her go at all. He strode to the steps and took them like he was in a race for his life. He was in a battle to retain his sanity. With Lucie clutched against his body, his gray matter scrambled. He couldn't think beyond the next step until he reached her door.

A giggle erupted from her, ending in a sob. "I don't have my key."

"Where is it?"

"In the swamp?" She sniffed and stared up at him.

"Think you can stand?"

She nodded. He dropped her legs, still holding her around her middle.

When her knees buckled, he held tight to keep her from falling. "Yeah, sure you can stand." One hand holding her, he reached into his pocket and pulled out his trusty pocketknife. He unfolded the blade and jammed it between the door and the frame, jimmying the door handle with the knife until the door swung open.

"I can take it from here," she said, not even frowning at his handiwork.

Beneath his hands, he could still feel her tremors. She

needed someone, and the only person immediately available was Ben Boyette.

Sucker. How could he maintain control when she was so soft and sweet? How could he respect her choice and his friend's trust, when she clung to him as though he was her lifeline?

As soon as he pulled her into his embrace, lifted her off her feet, and moved across the threshold, all his control crumbled.

"Don't leave me, Ben." she leaned her face into his chest.

He inhaled and blew his breath out slowly, fighting the rising surge of desire flooding his veins. "I can't stay."

"Please."

"What about Eric?" he ground out.

Her fingers clenched against his chest. "I was going to say no."

"But you didn't." And she'd broken his heart as he stood watching her promise herself to another man.

"I couldn't." Her head hung low. "He was hurt."

"You chose *him*, Lucie."

"I want *you*." Her voice was the barest whisper he had to lean closer to hear.

"But I'm not good enough, am I?" The old hurts bubbled up and he stepped away.

She swayed, her brows furrowing. "This has nothing to do with what happened seven years ago."

"It has everything to do with what happened."

"Tell me." She dragged in a deep breath. "Would you have gone to the academy if I hadn't made you leave?"

"Hell no, I wouldn't!"

"Exactly. It was your dream, Ben. Ever since we were kids playing in the bayous." She shook her head. "I couldn't take away your dream."

He blinked, her words taking a long moment to sink in.

"I don't believe this." He turned his back on her, his gut clenching at her revelation. "You're lying. You told me you'd always wanted to marry up. Had you married me, we'd have been poor. You couldn't stand that, could you?" He spun toward her, wanting to hurt her as she'd hurt him all those years ago. *"Could you?"*

All the color drained from her face and her shoulders sagged. "What's the use, Ben? You don't want the truth. So why are we discussing history? Just go away."

"Yeah, I should." He pushed his hand through his hair, but he didn't make a move for the door. He strode toward her until they stood nose to nose. "I should, but I can't."

She gazed up at him, her eyes widening.

When her bottom lip trembled, he lost control and crushed his lips to hers. He plundered her mouth, his tongue pushing past her teeth. The warmth of her beneath his hands fired his soul, a soul he'd long thought dead.

Lucie belonged to him!

And her response matched his, passion for passion.

When he finally broke the endless kiss, he grabbed her arms and shoved her back. Her eyelids drooped, her lips were swollen with his kiss.

"Does he make you feel like this? Does he make you come alive in his arms?"

"No."

Triumph swelled briefly in his chest.

Everything he felt was so right and so wrong at the same time, his gut tightened into a knot. Lucie was the woman he loved, yet she'd promised to marry his friend. How could he betray his friend by kissing his fiancée? What had started as a means to comfort her after her frightening experience had snowballed into something he wasn't sure he could stop.

Just then, her hand slipped up the front of his chest to rest against his heart. "I know it's wrong, but I don't want to be alone tonight." Her hand circled his neck and she pulled his lips back to hers. She kissed him, claiming his mouth, his heart, and his soul. With one hand entwined in his hair, her other hand slid beneath his shirt, lacing through the hairs on his torso.

She shivered, and he realized they both still had on the wet clothing they'd worn in the swamp. He broke off the kiss and stepped back.

Her hair hanging limp around her shoulders, her shirt clinging to her body in damp places, she very much resembled a drowned rat. But her eyes shone bright, and she was still the most beautiful woman he'd ever known.

Once again, he lifted her from her feet and carried her, through the tiny bedroom to the attached bathroom. When he set her down to lean in and turn the shower water to hot, she clung to him.

"I'm going to regret this later." He tipped her face up to his. "But I can't stop myself now." With a frustrated sigh, he tugged her shirt up over her head, tossing it to the linoleum floor. His hands on her waistband, he slowly unzipped her slacks, then slid them—well, maybe yanked—until they dropped to the floor in a sodden heap. In nothing but a lacy black bra and bright-red string bikini panties, her hair hanging like dreadlocks around her face, Lucie was stunning. Her deep olive complexion complemented the midnight black of her hair and her root-beer-colored eyes.

Then a shiver shook her from shoulders to hips. Goose bumps stood out on her arms, while steam filled the small bathroom. "Have you ever gone swimming fully clothed in the swamp at night before tonight, Ben Boyette?" She trembled again and crossed her arms over her breasts. "I don't recommend it. Especially if you're trapped in a sinking car." She laughed, her voice shaky, uncertain.

He pulled her to him, bent, and caught her beneath her

thighs, wrapping her legs around his fully clothed waist. Then he pushed the shower curtain aside and stepped beneath the spray, clothes and all.

"But you'll get your clothes wet!"

"Hey, I was swimming in that swamp, too. Besides, I don't care." Her breasts bobbed beneath his nose and he gave in to temptation, smoothing his cheeks between the tawny mounds pushed high by her bra.

She threaded her fingers into his hair and pressed his face against her skin.

Blood rushed from his limbs to his groin in a mad race. He stiffened against the tight confines of denim, groaning at the sweet pain.

"Not fair." She pressed a kiss to his temple. When he bit through the lacy material of her bra, she arched her back and moaned. Apparently frustrated by his slow progress, she reached behind her and unsnapped the hooks, her straps sliding down over her shoulders, the cups falling forward.

He nuzzled the black lace aside and sucked in a full, round areola, tonguing, laving, and suckling until it beaded into a hardened tip. He gave equal attention to the other until she squirmed against the hard ridge of his cock.

Water ran down her back and over his shirt and jeans, quickly making him hot and sticky, and entirely overdressed for the shower.

He set her on her feet and pulled his black T-shirt over his head, flinging it behind him. It landed with a splat on the side of the tub.

Before he could work on the rest, she ran her hands from his shoulders downward through the thick hairs on his chest. Her lips followed her hands, teasing and tasting both of his hard brown nipples.

He couldn't strip out of his jeans fast enough. Tangled in

the soggy mess, he hopped on one foot and almost fell on the slippery surface of the porcelain tub.

While he maneuvered out of his jeans, she slid her red panties over her hips and kicked them off.

When they finally stood naked in the spray of the shower nozzle, they came together like ravenous creatures, too long starved of each other's bodies.

He reveled in the silky smoothness of her skin rubbing against his. He soaped his hands and ran them over her full, jutting breasts, tempting the nipples to matching peaks. She leaned back to allow water to run over her shoulders and down through the suds. Narrow streams dripped off the tips of her breasts and slid down the corridor of her cleavage to disappear into the curly mound of dark, springy hair.

His hands following the trail of soap, he cupped the juncture of her thighs, opening her nether lips like a flower to pluck at the petal within. She arched against him and moaned. Her fingers trailed down his arm to the hand tempting her to the edge. She pressed him deeper. One, then two fingers slid inside her and back out to trace her creamy essence over her most sensitive spot.

With his hardened cock pressed to her hip, he inhaled the soapy, fresh scent of her, and swooped in to claim her lips.

The more he stroked, the more tense she became until she grabbed his hand.

"Stop!" She gasped, her shoulders stiff, her eyes squeezed shut. Then she pressed his hand over her mons and rocked against him. "Oh, God, Ben." Her cream wept onto his fingers. "I need you. Now!"

Her hands circled his neck and she climbed up him to wrap her legs around his waist. He steadied her to keep her from sliding off, their bodies slick with soap and water. Then he lowered her, sheathing his shaft completely in the warm, pulsing center of her. *God, she felt good.*

With her legs locked behind him, he turned her to press her back against the cool tiles. Then in a primitive, natural rhythm, he slid in and out of her. The rising tension that had been building all along burst in a fiery explosion of sensations. He sank into her and held steady as wave upon wave of mind-blowing orgasm consumed him, sucking the very soul from his heart and breath from his lungs, shooting him into clouds of pleasure he'd only dreamed of.

When he fell back to earth, he leaned his body against her, crushing her between him and the shower walls. "I swear I just had a near-death experience." He groaned and nuzzled her neck.

She lay against him, her head drooping on his shoulder. "If that's what death feels like, I should have died a long time ago."

***

Lucie slipped from Ben's arms early the next morning. After a short, dream-filled night plagued with ghosts of ancient Voodoo queens, she gave up any pretense of sleep. Awakening before Ben had its advantages. She could fill her heart and memory with the sight of him resting peacefully in her bed. Lying on his side, his broad shoulder loomed over her, beckoning her to smooth her hand over the muscled planes.

The sheet had slipped below his waist, allowing her a glimpse of his magnificent cock, slack now in slumber. How she'd ridden him through the night, climbing the peak to bliss more than once, only to fall back into his arms. He caught her every time and snuggled against her, spooning her in his embrace, his shaft pressed to her bottom only to rise for another round of beautiful sex.

She ached to touch him, awaken him tenderly with a gentle caress, a kiss, her hand sliding down his body to grasp him.

Her own body quickened and oozed liquid desire. She wanted him again, and again—to wake beside him for the rest of her life. But she couldn't, knowing she had unfinished business to take care of, a spell to undo, and apologies to make to her almost-fiancé.

With costly determination, she remained hands-off, choosing to admire without disturbing his sleep. Dark shadows smudged the skin beneath his eyes. He hadn't been asleep long. Their unwanted swim in the swamp and their to-die-for mattress calisthenics had taken their toll on his body as well as hers.

With the gray light of dawn squeezing through the cracks in the blinds, the room lightened.

If she planned to make a break for it, she'd have to go soon. He was likely to wake at the slightest sound and expect to find her lying beside him.

She padded barefoot and naked across the room to her dresser. Easing drawers open, she selected the appropriate undergarments, jeans, and shirt, and quietly made her way into the living room. After dressing in record time, she ran a brush through her tangled mop, tied her tennis shoes, and peeked one last time at the man she'd always loved, wishing things had turned out differently.

He slept on, blissfully unaware of her stealthy escape. Next time she saw him, he'd no doubt wonder why the hell he'd slept with her in the first place.

Unable to live another day with the lie she'd created, she knew she had to find a way to break the spell. Eric deserved to find someone he really loved. As nice as he was and as much as she liked him, she didn't love him.

And as much as she *did* love Ben, she couldn't continue a relationship with him, knowing he might only return her love because of a selfish spell she'd concocted. If she couldn't have him with his love given freely, she didn't deserve to have him at all.

Having screwed up her own chances, she prayed she wasn't going to ruin Maurice and DeeDee's chances at love and a happy life together.

Either way, Lucie had to break the spell. But first, before her guilt overwhelmed her and the reporters got wind, she had to officially break off her engagement.

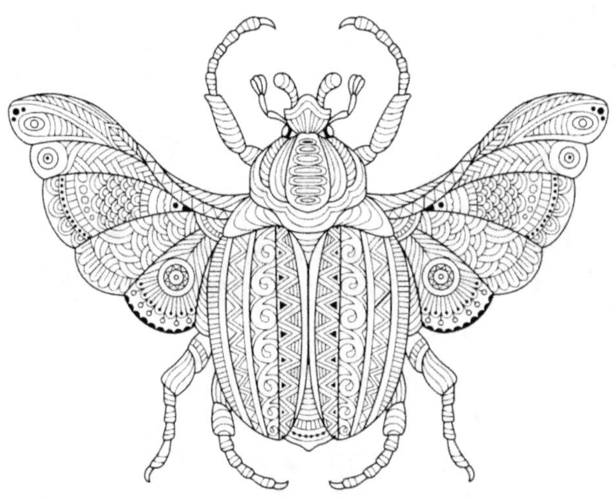

Chapter Twenty-Two

"You put out an APB on the guy?" Ben wanted to get his hands on the bastard who'd tried to kill Lucie last night and almost killed Eric and him.

"We did. I'll let you know as soon as we have him in custody."

"Good." He scrubbed a hand through his hair. "Get Ron to conduct the interrogation. I bet he'll spill his guts in fifteen minutes flat."

P.J. laughed into the phone. "I bet he doesn't last ten."

"You're on for twenty bucks."

"Get anything back from forensics on that slug you found at the girl's apartment?"

"Not yet. I'll give them a call this afternoon.

"Let us know. If the two incidents are related, we'll have more evidence to nail the guy with in court."

"You bet." He would use every talent in his arsenal of detective skills to catch the guy from last night and whomever he worked for.

Ben clicked off his cell phone just as he pulled into the hospital parking lot. He felt as if he had a wad of swamp silt sitting at the bottom of his belly. How could he face Eric when he'd slept with his fiancée last night?

How could he not? He'd been assigned to protect Eric, and report on what little he'd found out about the murder attempt.

But if he could slip in a little plug for Eric to reconsider his engagement, more power to him. Although, how he'd bring up the subject, he didn't have a clue.

But more than anything, he wanted to bust up the engagement and take Lucie for himself. He just wished he didn't like Eric so much. If it were anyone else, he could just punch him out and tell him to get the hell away from his girl!

Eric was sitting up in bed, his ear pressed to a cell phone, when Ben walked in. "Yeah, I think the doctor would have released me this morning, but my father insisted I stay around for additional observation. I think he wanted the press to have time to cool their heels and me to get my strength back before I'm bombarded with questions."

He listened for a moment and grinned. "Yeah, he's probably right. After swallowing a bayou full of swamp water, I didn't feel like facing a media swarm. I should be right as rain by tomorrow, so don't cancel my Daughters of the American Revolution speech. They've been real good to me and I'd hate to let the ladies down. Look, Neal, I got company." He nodded at Ben. "We'll talk later."

"Sorry to interrupt." Ben hesitated in the doorway. He'd never liked the antiseptic smell of hospitals. That, and the huge amount of guilt he had weighing him down, made for a nasty combination in his gut.

"Not at all." Eric waved him in. "We'd been at it for fifteen minutes. I was getting cauliflower ear." He rubbed at the ear he'd had plugged into the cell phone. "I don't know which is worse, being on the phone for hours, or having to wear a hospital gown that doesn't quite cover my ass." He tugged at the strings behind his back, but soon gave up and leaned back against the pillow.

Ben forced a smile. "The gown, definitely."

"Noticed you had some of the local cops guarding my door. What's up with that?"

"After last night's attempted murder, I didn't want to take any chances." He leaned against the wall, just inside the door.

Eric nodded. "That's what I figured. Thanks."

With a nod, he dismissed Eric's gratitude. He didn't deserve it. "Ever heard of a guy named Robert Davis?"

"No." Eric shook his head. "The name doesn't ring a bell. Why?"

"The car that bumped you into the swamp last night was rented by a man named Robert Davis."

"I haven't heard of him, but maybe my campaign manager has." Eric lifted his cell phone. "Want me call him back and try the name out on him?"

"In a minute." Ben strode across the room and stared out the window, struggling with how to broach the subject of Eric's engagement.

"Lucie left a few minutes before Neal called."

Ben swung back to face Eric. "She did?" *Dilemma solved.* Since Eric had brought her up, he might as well plunge in and get it over with. *Okay, smartie, how?*

Eric's eyes narrowed slightly. If Ben hadn't glanced up right when he did, he wouldn't have noticed.

"Ben, are you still in love with her?"

When he should have felt a rush of relief for the opening, his throat clogged. He wanted to shout, Yes! Yes, he still loved her, more than life itself.

But the frown on Eric's face brought him back to reality. As far as Ben knew, Lucie still planned to marry Eric.

"You don't have to answer my question." Eric looked away.

"It's just that you get tense every time she's around or I mention her."

"Yes, I still love her." Ben turned his back to Eric and stared out the window, without seeing the parking lot below. "I don't think I ever stopped."

"She kinda gets under your skin, doesn't she?"

"Yeah. I let her get away once and I've regretted it ever since." He spun toward Eric. "If you love her half as much as I do, you'll hold on as tight as you can. Don't let her get away. Because if you don't snap her up, I'm going after her. And this time, I won't let her go."

Eric's lips twisted into a wry half smile. "Yeah. She's pretty special."

Images of Lucie's naked body flittered through his thoughts. Her teasing smile and gentle touch still tingled along his nerve endings. "You don't know the half of it."

"I just wonder if she can handle being a congressman's wife." Eric scratched his chin and slid a glance up at him.

Lucie? A congressman's wife? Although he'd told her differently, he knew she could do anything she set her mind to, and do it well. "Lucie's tough, she can handle anything, and she'll make a beautiful addition to your campaign and life."

Had he really told her she wasn't cut out to be a congressman's wife? No wonder she'd been so mad. It ranked right up there with his stupid, angry words of seven years ago, when he'd called her a bayou bimbo. He'd said that to draw blood. To match the blood she'd drawn when she'd given him his ring back and told him he wasn't good enough for her. She'd struck him right through the middle of his heart.

"I don't know." Eric rubbed his chin.

His heart leaped. "Are you having second thoughts?" *Please say yes!* He held his breath.

Eric shook his head. "I love her, and I'd marry her in a heartbeat."

"But?"

"But nothing." Eric crossed his arms over his chest and grinned. "She's terrific."

"Yeah, she is." Ben sighed. *So, it was over.* Lucie was going to marry Eric, and he would go back to Baton Rouge and try to piece his life together for the second time. "Congratulations."

"Don't congratulate me yet," Eric said. "I haven't gotten her to the altar. Who knows, she may change her mind, like she did with you."

Ben could only hope.

***

"Bless my wrinkled ol' soul! I swear I be seein' de ghost of my granddaughter, Lucie." Gran LeBieu clutched her ample breast and staggered backward.

"Gran, I'm in trouble, and I need your help." Lucie stepped past her grandmother and strode through the door that hadn't seen paint since 1957.

Despite the shabbiness of the furniture and the curling paper with the roosters and hens on the kitchen wall, Lucie loved this house. It had always been her safe haven, her home when no one else wanted her. She and Lisa had come here as little girls and grown up with the bayou as their playground. When she'd sent Ben away, she'd retreated to her grandmother's house to grieve her loss. And God bless her wise old soul, Gran LeBieu hadn't pressed her for details, but let her tell her story when she was ready.

She ducked her head into the small guest bedroom, searching. "Where is she?"

"Who?"

"Lynette."

"Your mama was very upset the night before last."

"She's not my mama, and I'm not responsible for her happiness. She never felt responsible for mine." She stood facing her grandmother with her fists propped on her hips. "Is she here?"

"Dere be many things you don't know about your mama."

"I don't want to know her. She didn't bother to get to know me." Although she'd come for her grandmother's help, she couldn't stand the thought of facing her biological mother. The pain was still too fresh.

Gran LeBieu rested a hand on her shoulder. "She had her reasons for staying away."

"There's no reason good enough for a mother to dump her daughters and not come back for twenty years." She jerked away and searched the other room.

"Did you bother to ask her?"

She chose to ignore her grandmother's question. "She's not here."

"She took de boat to Bayou Miste for a few groceries. She won't be back for an hour."

"Good, 'cause I need your help." Lucie let out a sigh and let her hands fall to her sides. She might as well jump in. "Gran, I've done something stupid."

"And you think stupidity belongs only to the young?"

"No. I believe it belongs only to me."

"Come sit, girl." Her grandmother grabbed her hand and led her to the threadbare sofa and sat, motioning for Lucie to sit beside her. "Unburden your soul with ol' Gran LeBieu."

"I really need *Madame* LeBieu's help."

"Dat bad?"

She hung her head, bracing herself for her grandmother's wrath. "Worse."

"And what could be so bad you are afraid of your *Mamère?*" She held Lucie's hand in her chubby brown fingers, stroking her in a gentle, soothing rhythm.

Lucie took a deep breath and held it. "I cast a spell." She squeezed her eyes shut and waited.

The older woman's hand stopped in midstroke. She didn't say anything for a few moments—long enough that Lucie risked a peek from beneath her eyelids.

Gran LeBieu sat with her lips pressed together and turned downward in a slight frown. When she met her gaze, she shook her head. "You know how I feel about you practicing de magic."

Her grandmother's disappointed tones were more lethal than her wrath. Lucie's eyes clouded and tears spilled down her cheeks. "I'm sorry, Gran. I know I shouldn't have done it. But I couldn't stay in Bayou Miste. Especially when he came back."

"Ben?"

"Yes, Ben." Her tears trailed down to her chin and dropped into her lap. She scrubbed at them, but they wouldn't stop.

Her grandmother lifted her chin, forcing her to look her in the eye. "Voodoo be powerful magic, something not to be taken in vain or for selfish reasons."

"I know." She pressed her cheek against her grandmother's hand. "I was so wrong, and I couldn't have made a bigger mess if I'd tried."

Gran LeBieu pulled her into her arms and hugged her close. "Tell me."

Between sobs, she poured out all the sordid details of her magical mess. Her grandmother kept her supplied with tissues until her story and her tears ended.

The Voodoo queen sat in silence for several moments, her forehead creased in a frown. When she looked up, her potent gaze seared into Lucie's most secret thoughts. "Who do you love?"

"Oh Gran, I don't know who I should love." She wrapped

her arms around her belly and rocked back and forth. "Eric is everything a girl could want for a husband."

"But you don't want him." Her words were a statement, not a question.

"No, I don't." She sighed. "I've tried, but I can't love him."

Her grandmother's gaze had the same effect as pinning her to a wall. "You can't because you still love Ben."

Lucie buried her face in her hands and cried tears she didn't think she had left. "I do."

"Then why do you think you have to undo this spell? If Ben loves you, you have what you be wantin'."

She looked up. "I'd thought about that, but I can't leave the spell in place."

"Why?"

"I have to let Eric go to live his life and find a woman to love. One who is more deserving than me."

"But if you undo the spell, Ben may or may not be in love wit' you anymore."

Lucie pushed off the couch and walked to the window where sunlight and warmth spilled through. Closing her eyes, she soaked in the rays, hoping to thaw the chill in her heart. "I know." She turned to her grandmother. "I can't have Ben if he doesn't love me of his own free will. If he only loves me because of a spell, I won't find the happiness I've always wanted."

"Looks to me like you have all de answers den." Gran LeBieu stood. "You have to undo de spell."

Lucie nodded. "That's why I came."

"You want Madame LeBieu to fix what's broke?"

Hope and dread filled her chest. "Could you?"

Mamère crossed her brown arms over her chest. "No, I cannot."

Her heart thumped around in her chest, then fell to her stomach. "You can't or you won't?"

"Both."

All Lucie's hopes crashed around her ears. Her grandmother had always helped her through tight spots. Why not now? "Then what am I to do?"

"You have to find de bug."

"I've tried, but it's been all over the place."

The old woman smiled. "That's where I might be able to help."

"Oh thank you, Gran." She hugged her grandmother. "How? How will you help?"

"I have just de potion you need to catch de bug."

"You do?" She clapped her hands together. "How soon can I have it?"

Her smile faded to a stern line. "As soon as you make me a promise."

"I promise not to play in Voodoo without your permission from now on."

"Dat's not de promise."

She frowned. "What do you mean?"

"I want you to promise me you'll talk with your mother and actually be listenin' dis time."

Her gut clenched as if she'd been sucker punched. "I can't."

Her grandmother cocked an eyebrow at her. "Can't or won't?"

"Both."

"No talk, no potion." Gran LeBieu turned her back on Lucie.

How could her grandmother ask her to do this? "She left me," she said in a hoarse whisper. "Twenty years ago."

Gran LeBieu turned back to her, one eyebrow raised. "Is it a deal, or not?"

Lucie pushed a hand through her hair. She didn't know which was harder, forgiving her mother or losing Ben. But she knew she couldn't live her life regretting the choices she made.

She reluctantly stuck her hand out. "It's a deal."

***

"What are we doing out in Alligator Alley in the middle of the night?" Alex asked. "What's the big secret?"

Lucie reached beneath the pirogue's seat and pulled out the antique glass perfume atomizer her grandmother had given her earlier that day. "Gran said the potion would only work when exposed to moonlight."

"The moon shines in my backyard just as well as it does out here," Calliope grumbled.

"I know, but the reporters have been swarming all over the parish." She held up the bottle and prepared to spray. "I didn't want them to see what I'm about to do."

"And just what are you about to do?" Alex pulled the paddle out of the water and rested it across her lap.

"I'll bet you five dollars, she's frog-giggin' for a man." Calliope giggled at her own joke.

Lucie glared at her in the light from the half moon. "Look, I appreciate both of you coming out to help me." She drew in a deep breath and blew it out slowly. "I'm going to catch the love bug."

Both women gasped.

"So you're finally going to do it?" Alex clapped her hands together. "You're going to undo the spell?"

"Oh, Lucie. Are you sure?" Calliope clutched her arm. "But DeeDee and Maurice are sooo in love!"

"I know, I know." She hated hurting the new lovebirds. "But it can't be helped. The magic was wrong." She raised her palm to Alex. "I know. You told me so. Maurice and DeeDee will have to take their chances. I can't leave the spell in place."

"But DeeDee will be devastated. And we just had her hair

straightened." Calliope's pale face shone sad in the moonlight. "She's never been happier."

The lead weight of her heart slowed to a morbid beat. She was going to remove a spell that had quite a few people in Bayou Miste living a lie. "And what if the bug contaminated Elaine and Larry? Elaine's supposed to marry Craig in just two days. Has anyone seen Elaine?"

"No." Calliope's shoulders slumped.

"Your sister would have been happy to bust them up a couple months ago," Alex said.

"She was wrong and had no business interfering in their lives. They love each other and deserve to be together. And I don't deserve to marry a man who can only love me because of a spell."

"Omigod!" Alex threw her hands in the air. "Lucie's growing up!" She plunked her fists on her hips and frowned. "Frankly, sweetie, it's about time!"

"Alex, you're getting on my last nerve." Lucie glared at her. "I'm not *that* heartless."

Alex snorted. "You've sure been acting like it lately."

"Well, I mean to change that." She handed Calliope and Alex each a butterfly net, then raised the bottle and wrapped her fingers around the bulb. "I'm not exactly sure what'll happen when I spray this stuff. But Gran LeBieu said it would help me catch the bug."

"Do you have to say anything, a spell or incantation?" Alex asked.

"Oh please, don't!" Calliope held her net in front of her. "I don't relish the idea of being a bug."

"I'm not chanting any spells or changing either of you into bugs, so get a grip." Lucie raised the atomizer higher, into the air above her head. "Ready?"

Both Alex and Calliope squinted and hunkered low in their seats.

With a determined pinch, Lucie squeezed the bulb of the atomizer, sending a spray of what smelled like sleazy French perfume into the night air.

Calliope covered her nose. "Ewww! I smelled it." She glanced at her arms. "I'm not turning into a bug, am I?"

"No, silly," Alex said, but she glanced at her arms in the light from the moon. "Actually, it smells like the cheap perfume my great-aunt Rachel used to wear."

Lucie ignored them and squinted into the night. Where was that darn bug?

"I wonder how long it takes to work?" Calliope held her net up and scanned the sky.

A mosquito landed on Lucie's arm and sank its greedy little pointy thing into her. She smacked it and another that landed not two inches away.

"Hey, I'm being attacked here." Calliope swatted at her arms and neck.

"Me too," Alex said. "And it ain't by a love bug."

Lucie scrambled for the can of bug spray that was kept beneath the seat of the boat and sprayed herself then tossed the can to Alex. What was taking the love bug so long?

A bright light bumped into her forehead and dropped into her lap. Her heart jumped. Was this it? She stared at the bug in her lap.

"Did you find it?" Alex leaned close.

"No. It's just a firefly." Lucie lifted the bug and tossed it high. It circled and bumped into her again. "What's wrong with you?" She *shooshed* it away only for it to return again, followed by another and another.

"Oh! Oh! I have a ladybug on me!" Calliope bounced up and down on her seat. "Is it the one? Is it?"

Lucie and Alex peered at the bug.

"No." Lucie shook her head, disappointment filling her belly. "The love bug had a kinda greenish glow."

"Suppose it faded?" Calliope swung at half a dozen bugs flying around her face.

What did Lucie know about magical bugs? "I don't think so."

"Hey, I've got one." Alex's voice shouted into the night. But when she stared down at the ladybug on her arm, she sagged. "No glow."

Within seconds, ladybugs, mosquitoes, june bugs, fireflies, and every bug known to southern Louisiana swarmed them.

"Holy bug bath!" Lucie swatted the creatures away. "This stuff must have called the entire population of bugs in the swamp!" A bug flew into her mouth. *Bluh!* She spit it out, coughed, and sputtered. With her eyes squinted as closed as she could get them and still see, Lucie cried out, "See it yet?"

"Not a damn thing," Alex muttered through clenched lips.

"There it is. *Bluck!* I swallowed a firefly!" Calliope gagged. "*Ewww!*"

"Don't just sit there, catch it!" Lucie dove for the ladybug with the greenish glow. Without a net, she couldn't quite reach it and almost tipped the boat.

"Let me." Alex leaned out and batted at the air with her net. "I caught something!"

"Let me see." Lucie grabbed Alex's hand and pulled the net close. Inside were two-dozen bugs of varying species, including a handful of ladybugs. But no greenish glow.

Alex shook the net free of her catch and all three women squinted at the sky again.

Bugs coated their clothing, bare arms, and hair.

"*Ewww!* I have bugs everywhere. I can feel them crawling around." Calliope tossed her net to the floor and flipped her red hair from side to side, combing her fingers through to shake the bugs loose. "*Ewww!*"

"There it is." Alex pointed above Lucie.

She dove for Calliope's abandoned net and spun to look at where Alex still pointed. About five feet above her head, the hexed ladybug circled in an erratic pattern.

Lucie stood straight up and swung her net through the myriad bugs whizzing around her and buzzing her ears.

Unfortunately, Alex stood and swung at the same time. The little pirogue tilted one way. When Lucie leaned the other to compensate, so did Alex. Their combined weight flipped the boat, Calliope, and all.

Lucie plunged into the swamp and sank beneath the surface. At first, she panicked. The last time she'd been in the swamp, she was trapped inside a car. When her feet touched the bottom, she scrambled to stand. Within seconds, she was standing in water a little over four feet deep. And she still had her net in her hand.

A quick scan of the contents sent her heart racing. "I caught it!"

"At least we know where your priorities are." Alex waded over to where she stood.

Calliope joined them. "Thanks, you two. If I'd known we were going for a swim, I'd have worn my swimsuit instead of my favorite pair of Gap khakis." She grabbed Lucie's hand. "Let me see."

Jumbled among twenty or so other wet bugs lay a ladybug, glowing a faint greenish color, its hard red shell closed tight.

A small amount of weight lifted from Lucie's shoulders. At least she had the bug now. It couldn't do any more damage.

"Quick, do the spell before you lose it again," Calliope said.

Despite being up to her neck—well, maybe her chest—in swamp water, Lucie thought back over the words her grandmother had her memorize.

"Come little creature, 'tis time to be free
Let go of your past and then you will see

Life can go on as fate did intend
Love given freely finds you in the end
Reverse the bad magic that led you to be
With a green shiny heinie for all who can see
All will be well by the mystic Voodoo
When those who know not, bow to those who do."

"That's one funky spell." Alex inhaled and blew it out. "Well, let's hope it works."

All three women leaned over the wet net full of creepy-crawlies and stared down at the one brightly glowing ladybug.

"Look!" Calliope hopped up and down, splashing water in their faces. "The green glow is going away."

Just as she said, the ladybug's aura dimmed until they could no longer distinguish it from the other ladybugs caught in the net.

The rest of the worry hanging over Lucie lifted. *The spell was reversed!* Eric could get on with his life, and Craig and Elaine would get married. The little bit of elation was quickly followed by a deep sense of sadness. DeeDee and Maurice would be devastated. Not to mention her own little problem—she was totally, head-over-heels, hook-line-and-sinker in love with Ben.

And ending the spell would have erased any chances of Ben loving her back.

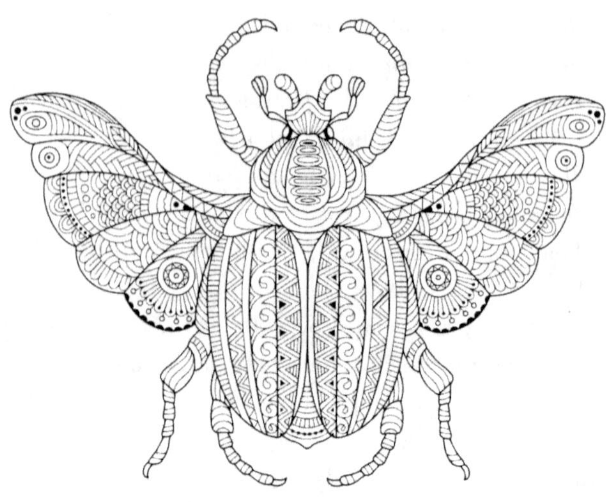

Chapter Twenty-Three

The more Ben thought about it, the more he wasn't okay with standing by and watching Lucie marry a man she probably didn't love. How could she love Eric when she'd slept with him? Not once but *twice* in the past week. He could still feel her moving beneath him, crying out his name in the heat of passion.

The images haunted him. Haunted him so much he'd do anything to win her back.

Thus, the trip to Madame LeBieu.

He'd caught Joe Thibodeaux as he was closing up shop at Thibodeaux Marina, and rented a boat. With darkness quickly cloaking the bayou, he'd taken the twisting channels to the old woman's house in the swamps. He could have found it in the dark, as many times as he'd visited it when he and Lucie were dating. Now as he stood on the porch, his hand raised to knock, he didn't know if he could go through with his plan.

The door swung open before he could change his mind.

"Benjamin Franklin Boyette! What you be doin' on my porch at dis time of de night?" Madame LeBieu's deep Cajun accent fascinated him and gave him the chills at the same time.

He'd heard a rumor that she'd changed his old buddy Craig Thibodeaux into a frog a few months back. How much truth there was to the rumor, he didn't know. Craig had been at the bar several nights ago getting close to a nice-looking lady. He hadn't noticed anything green or froggish about him. Still... The woman knew things about Voodoo that kept most sane people away.

But times were desperate, calling for desperate measures. If he wanted to win Lucie back, he had to do it before she up and married Eric.

"Madame LeBieu, I need your help."

Her eyes narrowed. "You have no called me Madame LeBieu since you and Lucie dated. Are you here for de Voodoo?"

He took a deep breath and sighed. "Yes, ma'am."

She stepped back into the house and opened the door wide. "Come in, boy."

Once inside, he stopped short. A woman, the spitting image of Lucie, rose from the couch. For a moment his heart leaped into high gear. Upon closer review, fine lines around her eyes and mouth gave her away.

"Nice to see you again, Lynette." He stuck out his hand.

"Ah, Ben." She smiled, Lucie's smile. "Good to see you, too. I've heard a lot about you."

Ben's heart warmed to this woman before he remembered her history of having left Lucie to be raised by her grandmother. He dropped her hand abruptly. "I'm sorry, I haven't heard much about you." He didn't disguise the contempt in his voice. This woman had hurt his Lucie. A deep scarring wound she might never overcome.

"You've heard enough to condemn me, I see."

"You left your children. What do you expect?"

She shrugged. "I didn't expect anything. But I'd hoped I could at least tell my daughter why. Look, you've obviously got business with my mother. I'll go to my room." Lynette LeBieu disappeared into a small bedroom and softly closed the door behind her.

Alone with the formidable Madame LeBieu, he didn't know how to begin. He'd been so determined when he'd marched up her steps. But having met Lynette reminded him of Lucie's reasons for wanting to leave Bayou Miste, and why she deserved a better life than the one she'd been given growing up. Suddenly, his own desires and needs seemed selfish. Unwarranted. He turned to Madame LeBieu. "I shouldn't have come."

"Let me be de judge of dat." She pointed to the couch. "Sit."

Like an obedient dog, he did as he was told and perched on the edge of the worn floral cushion, elbows propped on his knees, fingers threaded together in front of him.

The Voodoo queen, in her bright-red muumuu, sat beside him, her broad bottom taking up half the seating area. "Now, what be de problem?"

"Lucie."

"Dat pretty much narrows it down. Could you be more to de point?"

He ran his hand through his hair, standing it on end. "I love her."

The old woman's head tipped back and she stared down her nose at him. "Ahh. My lovely granddaughter."

"Lovely, and frustrating, and completely insane." He leaned back and waved his hand in the air. "Yeah, Lucie."

"Why did it take you so long to come back to my Lucie?"

Ben pushed to his feet and strode across the floor. "I didn't think she wanted me. Hell, she told me I wasn't good enough for her!"

"Up until dat moment, did she give you any reason to doubt her love?"

He paused in midstride and thought back through seven years of hurt pride and pain. He'd thought Lucie loved him as much as he loved her. "I'd have given up everything to make her happy. I thought she would have done the same."

Madame LeBieu raised her eyebrow. "And didn't she?"

Ben stared at her, trying to comprehend that look and knowing he wasn't getting it. "I don't understand. You'll have to spell it out for me."

The old Voodoo queen rolled her eyes. "Men can be so foolish and blind." She took his hands in hers. "Lucie gave up everything because she loved you more dan you deserved. She gave up her happiness for you to follow your dreams."

Ben reeled. Madame LeBieu's words echoed Lucie's, only he hadn't listened when Lucie had said them. Hell, he'd thrown them back in her face.

Could they be true? Could she really have done that...for him?

And for all this time, because of his stupid pride, he hadn't seen what was painfully clear now. She'd sent him away to allow him the chance to follow his dreams.

And he hadn't come back for her.

No wonder she was so pissed. She'd sacrificed her happiness for him to have the life she couldn't give him. And he hadn't even given her the opportunity to explain. He'd let pride get in the way a second time, and he could well have lost her for good.

No.

That's why he'd come out to the old witch's house tonight. "I've made too many mistakes to deserve her, but I love Lucie more than my own life." His grip tightened in Madame LeBieu's hands. "I can't lose her again. I need a love potion to help her change her mind about marrying Eric. I want her to marry me."

The old woman tipped her head to one side. "Have you bothered to ask her?"

"She'd laugh in my face. She wouldn't believe me. Why should she? I've been too stupid to believe her." He never thought he'd do it, but Ben dropped to one knee in front of Lucie's grandmother. "Madame LeBieu, I want to marry your granddaughter. Will you help me win her back? Will you give me a love potion or something to make her love me as much as I love her? Please?"

Okay, so he was begging. Sometimes a man had to do what a man had to do.

"After such a very pretty speech, how can dis ol' woman not help?" Madame LeBieu dropped his hand and disappeared into the other bedroom. Within seconds, she returned and handed him a fancy perfume bottle with a bulb at the end of a tube. "Be careful with dis potion. Spray a little on you before you see Lucie. Don't talk to any other female first. It must be Lucie."

Hope filled his chest. "Will it make her love me?"

"If she doesn't love you after dis," Madame LeBieu raised her right hand, "I'll give up making de Voodoo."

Whew! That was an endorsement, if he wasn't mistaken. "Thank you, Gran LeBieu." He leaned over and kissed the old woman's cheek. "You're the best Voodoo queen in the bayou."

"Damn right! I be de only Voodoo queen."

Ben didn't wait. He was out the door and into the johnboat before the screen door could slap closed behind him.

He couldn't wait to try the potion on Lucie. The sooner she realized she loved him, the sooner he could return to sanity.

***

After a fitful night's sleep, Lucie climbed into her car and drove the short distance to the agreed-upon location. Though she was already twenty minutes late, her thoughts were so centered on what impact the reversal spell would have, she almost missed her turn.

Alex and Calliope stood outside the Cussin' Cajun, waving like fans at a celebrity. She was past them before her brain engaged and she realized they were waving at her. Without thinking, she slammed on her brakes and the rear end of her car skidded sideways and stopped two inches from Granny Saulnier's prized poodle, FeFe.

The little dog yelped and all three pounds of bright-orange fluff leaped straight up in the air.

Seemingly out of nowhere, Maurice and DeeDee rushed to grab the dog. DeeDee got there first and snatched FeFe into her arms, shooting a glare at her. "You should drive more carefully, Lucie LeBieu." She cooed at the little dog. "It's okay, FeFe. I won't let that meano Lucie hurt you."

Maurice stepped up behind DeeDee and slid his arm around her waist, nuzzling her neck.

"Sorry!" she called out the window. She completed her U-turn and crept to a parking place next to Alex and Calliope.

"Lucie, you're late." Alex rushed to the driver's door and yanked it open. "We're so glad you got here, though. I tried calling your cell phone, but you didn't answer."

Lucie dragged her body out of the car and stood rolling the kinks out of her tense shoulders. "It's at the bottom of the swamp in my purse."

"Oh, yeah. I forgot." Alex nodded toward the happy couple and the orange poodle. "You saw Maurice and DeeDee?"

"Yeah." She sighed, staring at them, their happiness making her queasy. "I guess the spell didn't work on them. Have you heard anything from the Elaine-Larry-Craig front?" Lucie hoped at least one of the problems would be cleared up.

"Yeah," Alex said. "I talked with Joe Thibodeaux. He said Craig and Elaine had some big argument and decided not to get married."

"Oh, no!" Lucie's queasy stomach dipped and roiled. "Did he say what it was about?"

"No, he just said they decided not to get married." Alex said. "Read into it what you will. The man was too busy with customers."

Lucie sank to sit on the curb, and buried her head in her hands. "This is all such a mess. Do you think there's any chance it could have worked for some and not others?"

Calliope grabbed her arm and pulled her back to her feet. "Only one way to find out."

"I know, I know." A dull throbbing beat against her temples. Too much swamp water and worry. "I better get it over with."

"Don't you want breakfast first?" Calliope asked.

Her dipping, roiling, burbling belly rebelled. "No way! I'd rather face the music on an empty stomach. Girls, wish me luck."

***

"I'm sorry to say that since the night you were bumped in the swamp, the police haven't seen hide nor hair of one Mr. Robert Davis," Ben said.

"I don't like it," Eric strode across the room to the liquor and water decanters. "The man tried to kill me once, maybe twice, if you count the shot-out lightbulb. Both times, Lucie was with me. She could have been killed."

"I know." Ben's gut had been in a permanent knot since the swamp-swim incident. "No one wants to nail this guy more than I do. Unfortunately, he's disappeared for the moment. I've got the local sheriff's department, state police, and a few of my buddies in the FBI looking for him."

"Damn it!" Eric slammed his fist against the counter,

rattling the crystal glasses. "What do you think I should do? I can't put Lucie at risk." He turned to face Ben. "Maybe I should withdraw from the congressional race."

"No. You can't. That's exactly what this guy wants."

"I can't let my running for Congress endanger those I love. And who's to say he won't target Lucie to get to me?" Eric jammed his hands in his pocket. "I have too many speeches and dinners to attend to keep an adequate eye on Lucie."

"So what are you suggesting we do to protect her?" Ben asked.

Eric swung toward the window and stared down, silent for a moment. Then his shoulders stiffened. "Ben, I want you to be Lucie's bodyguard."

Eric might as well have punched him in the gut.

The congressional candidate faced him. "You're the only one I trust to protect her."

"I think you should hire a professional bodyguard for that one. I've been tasked to protect you."

"I can take care of myself." Eric strode toward him. "I'm more concerned about Lucie."

"I am, too, but—"

"You're the perfect choice. You already know her and no one would think you were a bodyguard."

"But—" He couldn't be around Eric's fiancée and not touch her. Torture like that would either unman him or make him insane.

"Do it, Ben—for our friendship." Eric held out his hand. "For Lucie."

As if reaching for a snake, he placed his hand in Eric's. "Okay. But only until I can get someone we both can trust in place. In the meantime, I'll have Billy Ray tag along with you."

"Deal."

They shook hands.

"Now I have work to do. I'd really like you to check out Dad's office again. I'm worried that someone might have it bugged."

"Sure." Ben spun toward the door connecting Eric's office and Jason Littington's. Before he stepped through, he turned back. "Eric, I'll take care of her."

"I know." Eric nodded, his mouth twisted in an ironic grin. "I know."

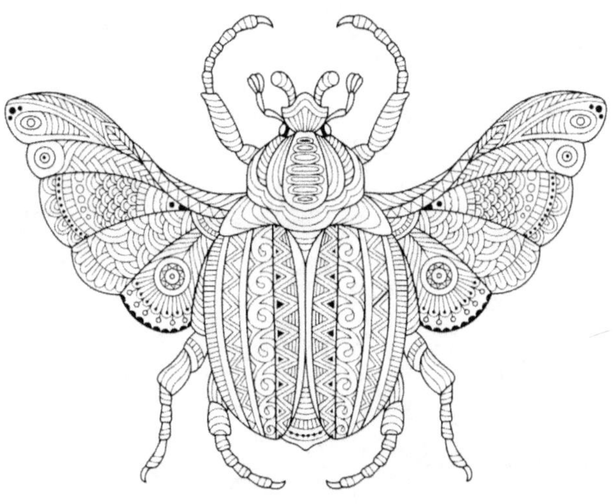

Chapter Twenty-Four

"Pascal, could you please ring Eric's office and ask if he has time to see me?" Lucie tapped her high heels on the smooth granite floor, her nerves screaming to get this over with.

Pascal jumped to his feet, knocking over a cup of pens and pencils. "Lucie, you can't marry Eric. You should marry me and be my wife."

"I don't love you, Pascal." She gathered the spilled items and placed them on the counter. She didn't love Eric, either, and she hoped he didn't love her. That's why she'd come to see him at his office. She'd have gone to his home, but she'd been told he'd already returned to work.

"I won't let you marry him," Pascal said.

"Get over it, Pascal, you don't have a chance with me. I thought I made myself clear back in fifth grade." Why did men have to be so dense?

"You were nice to me then." He reached across the counter and grasped her hand in his. "You have to have feelings for me."

"I do. I feel like you could be a friend—nothing more." Her

heart squeezed tight in her chest, hating the hurt look in Pascal's eyes, knowing the feeling of loving and not having that love returned. But she was tired of the same argument. With a yank, she pulled her hand free. "What do I have to do to get through to you? Now, will you get Eric or do I have get him myself?"

"Are you looking for me?"

Lucie spun toward the deep voice.

In his business suit, Eric looked elegant, incredibly handsome, and every bit the congressional candidate. The light-gray silk-and-wool-blend suit complemented his blond hair and blue eyes. He was as close to a Greek god as Lucie had ever come to marrying, and she'd given him up.

What kind of stupid had she become?

"Could we go to your office?" she squeaked.

"No! I will not let you take my Lucie." Pascal came out from behind the front desk and cocked his fists at Eric.

To his credit, Eric didn't show fear, he pressed his fingers to his temples and sighed. "Pascal, it's okay. She already called off the engagement. Now, put your fists down before I have to fire you. Your threats are starting to get on my nerves."

"You aren't going to marry him?" Pascal looked to Lucie for confirmation.

She shook her head. "I'm not marrying Eric."

"Then you can marry me!"

"No, I'm not going to marry you, Pascal. Not now, or ever." She wanted to reach across and wring his idiot neck. She hooked her arm in Eric's and pulled him toward the elevator. "Come on, before I inflict violence upon him."

Eric chuckled. "Remind me not to make you mad."

"I will."

Once in his office, she didn't know how best to ask Eric if he still loved her. He might answer yes to keep from upsetting her.

With a quick look toward his father's office, Eric strode across and pulled the door closed, leaving a slight gap. "So, what brings you here today, Lucie?"

She could think of only one way to prove whether or not the potion had worked for him. She dragged in a deep breath and turned to face him. "Eric, kiss me."

"Huh?"

She waved him forward. She didn't have time to play around. "Kiss me."

"I thought we were through. You said you didn't want to marry me."

She stomped her foot, frustration building by the moment. She had to know if the spell worked. "Humor me, just this once."

Eric frowned but moved forward until he stood directly in front of her—within kissing range. "I don't get it."

"Just shut up and kiss me." She grabbed the lapels of his tailored suit and yanked him toward her, her lips crashing against his.

Without hesitation, his hands circled her waist and pulled her against him.

To Lucie's dismay, Eric deepened the kiss, until his tongue pushed past the barrier of her teeth and tangled with hers.

He didn't push her back, didn't stop the kiss until a full two minutes later. When he did come up for air, he rested his cheek against her hair and held her in his embrace. "Nothing?"

Tears welled in Lucie's eyes. "Nothing. As much as I wanted to, I can't love you like you deserve." She kissed his lips gently. "I think you're a special man and deserve someone who loves you with all her heart."

"Well, thank you for your honesty." Eric smiled down at her.

"You'll be okay?" Lucie asked.

"I'll be fine." Patting his chest, he winked. "It'll mend."

"Thanks, Mr. Littington, I'll just check Eric's office—" The voice came from the connecting door Eric had closed only moments before. "Oh, excuse me."

She jumped out of Eric's arms and spun to face the intruder. She stopped short of smacking her forehead. Of all the people to witness her in Eric's embrace, her luck would make sure it was Ben.

"Sorry to interrupt. I didn't realize you had company." With his hands shoved in his pockets, Ben stared at her, although his words were directed at Eric.

"Not at all." Eric grinned. "We were through, weren't we Lucie?"

Only she would know Eric's crooked smile was a strained attempt at looking normal. Her gut twisted. Damn! Why hadn't the spell worked? Then another thought occurred to her and she stared at Ben. Had it worked on him?

One thing was certain. She couldn't conduct the "kiss test" on him here. Not in front of a heartbroken Eric. She may be stupid, but she wasn't totally insensitive.

She touched Eric's arm and smiled gently. "I'll go." Without a backward glance, she dashed for the elevator and punched the down button, praying the doors would open and swallow her before Ben or Eric could join her. Already embarrassed at being caught kissing, she didn't have the heart to "test" Ben yet.

Or was she chicken? Did she really want the love spell to be broken for Ben? Had the spell worked for Ben, but not Eric? It hadn't worked to undo Maurice and DeeDee's match, nor Elaine and Craig's problem with Larry. She just had to know about Ben, and the sooner she found out the better.

But not now.

The elevator slid open and she stepped in, collapsing with her back against the far wall.

A hand shot in when the doors were only inches from closing, forcing them open again. In stepped Ben, and all Lucie's troubles seemed to multiply in intensity to screaming-meemie level.

They rode down in silence and stepped out of the building through the glass double doors.

When she should have been testing whether the undo spell had worked, she'd stood tongue-tied in the elevator. Instead of asking Ben if he still loved her, she'd walked outside. His bug truck stood next to her Mustang in the parking lot. It was now or never.

"Lucie."

"Ben."

They both spoke at once.

"Go ahead," Ben told her.

"The other night." She paused, her gut clenching in a painful knot. "When you stayed with me," she gazed up at him, her eyes narrowing, "you never said you loved me. Do you?"

Ben pulled her into his arms and crushed her to his chest. "Oh Lucie, I thought I could love you no matter what. But I can't. Not now, not with the situation the way it is."

Lucie almost wept. The undo spell hadn't worked for Eric, but had for Ben. Why? Was this fate's way of fixing her mistakes by making her pay for them for the rest of her life?

For a moment she reveled in his embrace, loving the feel of his arms around her, breathing in the smell of him. She sniffed. What was that? Cheap perfume? Kinda reminded her of the stuff she'd used last night to attract every bug in the swamp. Why did Ben smell like perfume?

She pushed away from him.

"I can't live this lie," he said. "I can't love you, knowing it's wrong."

Huh? "Why is it wrong?"

He turned away and shoved a hand through his hair. "Lucie, you have to make the decision about what's important in life. Whether it's money, position, love, or forgiving your mother—you have to do it. No one else can." He spun to face her, his gaze boring into hers. "If you can straighten out your life and still have room left in it, come see me. Until then, I can't love you."

An emptiness so vast she couldn't put her arms around it filled Lucie. Ben was telling her he didn't love her. Or as he put it, couldn't love her.

Well, that was that. The undo spell had worked for one out of the four hexlings.

She fought the tingling prelude to tears welling in her eyes. "Thanks, Ben. I understand."

"Lucie—"

"No, Ben. You're right. I have to fix my life." With a forced smile, she climbed into her car and shut the door.

Ben stood where she'd left him, his gaze never leaving her as she cranked her engine. Couldn't he get into his bug truck and out of her sight? He was done with her, why did he have to linger? Was it some grotesque kind of punishment?

Her entire body shook as if she'd been tortured. With her hand on the gearshift, she shoved it into reverse and slammed her foot onto the accelerator. She couldn't get away fast enough. Unfortunately, she didn't look in her rearview mirror in time to stop herself from slamming into Eric's BMW.

Kaboom!

An explosion, of greater magnitude than merely bumping a car in the parking lot, rocked Lucie's Mustang, throwing her against the steering wheel. Pain stabbed through her head before blackness darkened her vision.

***

The blast knocked Ben to the ground, the concussion reverberating through his ears. After several seconds, his mind reengaged. What the hell happened?

Flames leaped from the crumpled remains of Eric Littington's BMW. In front of it stood Lucie's little turquoise Mustang convertible pockmarked with shrapnel from the explosion.

"Lucie!" He shouted, and raced to pull her from the wreckage before the flames from the BMW could consume the Mustang.

Adrenaline kicked in as he lifted Lucie in his arms and carried her back into the building.

"Call 911!" he shouted at Pascal. "We need an ambulance."

The Cajun stood there with his mouth open, staring at Lucie, making no move to do as Ben had told him.

"Do it!" he shouted.

The sharp order broke through Pascal's shock and he fumbled through the call, before he hung up and joined Ben.

Gently, he laid her on a couch in the lobby, bending close to feel for her soft breath against his cheek.

Thank God, she was breathing. With a cursory glance all over her, he noted a few cuts and bruises, but nothing life-threatening. What he couldn't see worried him more. She'd been unconscious now for several minutes and he couldn't tell whether or not she had internal injuries.

He wanted to gather her close to him, but he was afraid of causing more injury. If not for the fire, he'd have left her in the car for the emergency medical technicians to handle. If she'd suffered spinal injuries, he could have exacerbated them.

"Wake up, Lucie," he called out to her, pressing a kiss to her ear. "Wake up, sweetheart."

"Oh my God!" Eric cried out from across the room.

"What happened?" He strode across the granite tiles in the lobby, followed by his father.

"She backed into your car and it exploded," Ben said, his voice flat, the gravity of what had happened not at all lost on him.

Eric sank into a chair across from the couch and dropped his face into his hands. "Oh, sweet Jesus. Lucie, what have I done to you? That explosion was meant for me."

"I didn't do it!" Pascal cried out, his eyes wide, his face pale beneath his Cajun swarthiness. "I only wanted Eric to leave Lucie alone. I never tried to kill him."

"What are you talking about, Pascal?" Eric asked. "No one is blaming you for the explosion."

"I didn't do it." Pascal dropped to his knees in front of Lucie. "I never meant to hurt anyone."

Eric started to say something, but Ben put a hand out to stop him.

"Tell us about it, Pascal," he said softly, when he'd rather reach out and wring a few answers out of the distraught man.

Pascal sobbed into his hands. "I threw the rock through the window, and I shot the light out when Eric was kissing Lucie. But only because I wanted him to leave." He looked up, his face wet with tears. "I never wanted to hurt him and I definitely wouldn't hurt Lucie." He stared down at her, his face softening into a weak smile. "I love Lucie."

"Seems like quite a few of us do," Ben muttered.

Pascal's brow furrowed and he stood. "I may not like Eric Littington," he said, his mouth twisting into a snarl. "But I didn't blow up his car."

Ben stared up at Eric. "You need to have security sweep the compound. I'll bet Davis is out there somewhere. He must have planted the bomb after you arrived this morning."

Jason pressed a hand to Eric's shoulder. "I'll take care of

it." He strode to the communication console and radioed security. "Get everyone out there. I want that man caught."

Not as much as Ben did. The man had hurt Lucie. Anger burned deep in his veins. If he could, he'd tear the bastard apart limb from limb. But first, he had to know Lucie would be all right.

Sirens could be heard through the thick glass windows, and moments later, emergency medical technicians rushed in, some carrying medical kits, others pushing a stretcher.

"Over here!" Ben shouted. He moved aside to let the professionals take care of Lucie. But he didn't let her out of his sight for a second. He would be by her side no matter what. That's where he belonged, not Eric. He looked across at his friend and noted a reflection of the anguish he felt himself. Eric really loved Lucie. But they weren't married, yet.

Ben's lips tightened. As much as he liked Eric, he wasn't going to give up on Lucie without a fight. He loved Lucie enough to make the ultimate sacrifice. He wouldn't be wearing that stinky love potion Madame LeBieu gave him for any other reason.

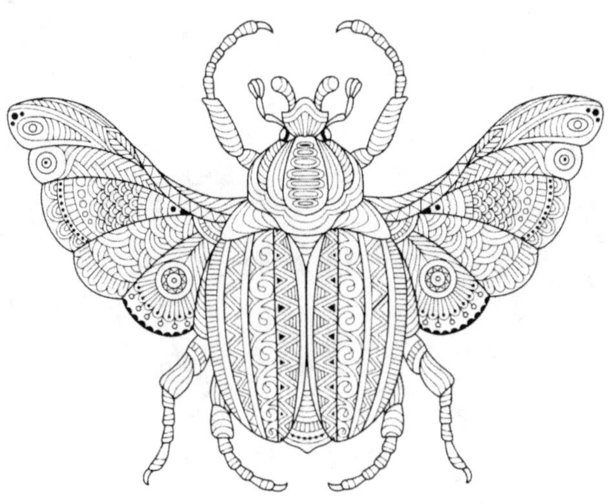

Chapter Twenty-Five

"I don't know why I have to stay here when I feel just fine." Lucie hated lying in bed and liked it even less in a backless nightgown.

"My, aren't we the fusspot." Alex slid down in the vinyl-covered seat next to Lucie's bed and flicked the television remote. "Wonder if the news is on." She flipped through the channels until she found the local newscast.

"That's Eric!" Lucie leaned forward. "Turn it up!"

"In today's news, congressional candidate Eric Littington is in New Orleans to speak with the Daughters of the American Revolution. Mr. Littington, tell us about the car bomb that exploded at the family refinery in Bayou Miste, yesterday.

"The bomber was taken into custody by the Louisiana State Police."

"Thank God," Lucie said.

The report continued, "Rumor has it the bomber was hired by your opponent, Richard Gasson. Do you have any comments on that?"

Eric chuckled. "Only that it's a heck of a way to run a

campaign. In most states, they let the constituents decide elections."

"Sir, we heard your fiancée was hurt in the explosion."

"Yes, she was." The smile slipped from Eric's face. "Only she's no longer my fiancée."

"What?" The reporter stepped back a moment as if shocked by the news. "Would you care to elaborate?"

"Miss LeBieu is doing much better, but we've decided not to get married after all." His smile returned. "Which leaves me more time to handle the issues of the state."

"Did she break it off, or did you?" the pesky reporter asked.

Eric's lips thinned, but he never lost his very charming smile. "That's up to the lady to tell. Now, if you'll excuse me, I have a speech to give."

Alex turned to Lucie, a frown between her brows. "I thought he was going to wait until after the election to announce your canceled engagement?"

Lucie sighed. "That's just the great kinda guy he is. He'd sacrifice his chance to win to release me from the engagement."

"You should have married him," Calliope said. "I bet five bucks he'll win anyway. Who wouldn't vote for him? He's so damned sexy."

Alex tipped her head to the side. "Wonder what Ben will think about that."

"Probably nothing," Lucie said. "I told you, he said he didn't love me."

"*Couldn't* love you," Alex corrected. "There's a difference."

"Yeah." Lucie lay back against the pillows. "Whatever."

"I bet you five bucks you didn't know he was here all last night sitting where Alex is, holding your hand." Calliope rocked back on her heels, a smirk on her face.

Alex kicked her foot at Calliope's shin. "Enough with the betting. Besides, you weren't supposed to say anything."

Lucie's heart kicked into high speed. Ben spent the night here? Why hadn't he said anything, woken her up, kissed her? Anything!

The redhead wrinkled her nose. "You know how well I keep secrets."

"Yeah, not at all," Alex grumbled.

Calliope took the remote from her and flipped through the channels. "Hey, I haven't seen *I Love Lucy* reruns since I was in grade school." She sat forward from her perch on the windowsill.

"Who cares?" Lucie smacked the sheets and blew out a huffy breath. She couldn't get on with her life from a hospital bed. "I really need to see my grandmother."

"And you will," said a voice from the doorway. Lynette LeBieu stepped through, a little hesitantly. "Do you mind if I see you first?"

Alex popped out of her chair. "Here, you can have my seat. Come on, Calliope, we have giant-sized coffees with our names on them somewhere in this Popsicle joint."

Calliope gave her a confused look. "Alex, you know I don't drink coffee."

Before Lucie could protest their desertion, Alex grabbed Calliope and they were out the door, leaving her stuck with the woman who'd ditched her twenty years ago.

Somehow, all the hurt and anger wasn't quite as intense as the first time she had seen her mother. After all that had happened and the mistakes she herself had made, she wasn't nearly as resentful. People made mistakes. Some bigger than others.

For a few awkward minutes, neither woman spoke.

Lucie grabbed for the remote and punched the mute

button, silencing Desi Arnaz in the middle of "Lucy, you got some 'splainin' to do!"

"How appropriate." Lynette snorted softly. "That's exactly how I feel. I have some 'splainin' to do. I don't suppose you'd listen while I do it?" Hope shone from her eyes.

With a shrug, Lucie stared at the television without seeing it. "Might as well. I'm a captive audience until they give me my clothes and marching orders."

Lynette's smile slipped from her face and she laughed one of those laughs that conveyed little humor, but a lot of pain. "Now that I'm here, I don't know where to start."

"Try twenty years ago when you dumped me and Lisa on Gran LeBieu." Her words were delivered with slightly less of the anger she'd felt a few days ago.

Her mother winced. "I'd rather go back a little further than that."

"Suit yourself." Lucie was listening, but she wasn't feeling charitable enough to make it easier for the woman.

"I was seventeen when I met your father. He was eighteen. But we fell in love so deeply, we knew we had to be together, no matter what."

Despite her reluctance to hear her mother out, Lucie wanted to know more about the mystery man who'd been her father. "So what happened to him?"

"We were on the way home from a football game when a drunk driver ran us off the road. We crashed into a tree. I was thrown from the car, and Richard was killed instantly." Lynette looked away, but not before Lucie saw the tears trembling on her lashes.

"It was all so horrible," she continued. "One minute we were planning a wedding for after graduation, the next I was going to his funeral." She stared out the window, her gaze far away from the parking lot below. "I remember that day like yesterday. It rained. Not a surprise for southern Louisiana. I was so sad, I threw up on the way home." She wiped a tear from her cheek and turned back to grimace at Lucie. "I didn't know until later that I was pregnant.

"Your grandmother was wonderful. She helped me all along the way, even came with me into the delivery room. But I couldn't get over your father's death.

"I couldn't go back to my old life. Everywhere I turned, I could see Richard there. I dropped out of high school and went to work to support you and Lisa. I didn't want my mother to be burdened by me and twins. So I moved away, hoping it would make me stronger. I'd wanted to stand on my own two feet. We went to Texas, where I worked as a waitress in a bar. It was the only place I could make enough to support us and pay for a sitter."

Lucie didn't want to feel empathy for this woman who'd left her for so long. But her heart ached for the young mother desperately trying to make a life for herself and her children.

"I couldn't make it on my own. Babysitting costs were too high, and I missed your father so much it hurt all the time. I started drinking to numb the pain. One drink led to another, and another, until I couldn't climb out of the bottle long enough to care for the little girls I loved more than life itself."

Tears welled in Lucie's eyes as she remembered the little six-year-old she'd been, lapping up any crumb of attention her mother would throw her way.

Lynette kept talking as if the floodgates had finally opened. "One day, I was driving somewhere, I don't remember where. You and Lisa were in the car with me. I was half-stoned from the liquor I drank at all hours. I didn't see the car until too late. I broadsided it, killing the driver." Lynette doubled over as if the pain was fresh. "She was just a teenager and I killed her! And I almost killed you."

"Oh, God." Her hand sneaked out and she touched her mother's arm. Here she'd been feeling sorry for herself because Ben didn't love her. How awful to know you'd killed someone out of your own carelessness and couldn't give that person her life back.

"You and Lucie went to live with your grandmother on that day. I was charged with vehicular manslaughter and spent six years in jail. I had time to dry up, but the guilt never went away."

A deep well of sadness opened up and Lucie fell in. "Why didn't you come back after you'd done your time in prison?"

"I couldn't forgive myself for what I did. I didn't want you and your sister to know what a horrible person I was. Believe me, I didn't want to kill that girl. If I could, I'd give my life to bring her back." Tears ran freely down Lynette's face and silent sobs shook her frame. "I couldn't face you two knowing what I'd done. I was better off dead." Her voice faded away into a whisper.

Lucie remembered looking out at the swamp, hoping beyond hope her mama would come for her. All those years other girls had their mothers to love and be loved by. Not Lucie and Lisa. If not for Gran LeBieu, she would have died of loneliness. "Why now?"

Again, her mother laughed, more of a hiccupping sound of self-derision. "I needed so badly to see you, to tell you I was sorry, and that I never stopped loving you. I had to tell you...before the cancer takes me." Her voice faded off into a room gone completely silent.

Lucie sat stunned, unable to utter a word. She'd just gotten her mother back. How could God take her away again?

"Look, I've said what I wanted to say. More than anything, I'd like to get to know you, but that's completely up to you." Lynette stood and slid her purse over her shoulder. "Your grandmother is waiting out in the hallway. I'm sure she'd like to see that you're all right."

With a numb nod, she stared after her mother as she slipped through the doorway.

Holy swamp turtle. She wished she could crawl under a rock. Her emotions threatened to overwhelm her. After twenty years, her mother had come back to die. How unfair was that?

Gran LeBieu stepped into the room, her eyes filled with the pain Lucie was only beginning to feel.

"Oh, Gran!" she cried.

The old woman sank onto the side of the bed and gathered Lucie in her arms and together they wept.

"Why, Gran? Why?" Lucie sobbed into her shoulder.

"De magick works its own agenda, my girl." She squeezed her hard and then set her away.

Gran LeBieu yanked a tissue from the box on the nightstand and dabbed at Lucie's cheeks and her own. "Aren't we a pair?"

Lucie laughed and the tears welled up again. "And I thought *my* life was a mess."

"Sometimes it takes other's troubles to show us de way with our own."

Which brought Lucie back to her love spell dilemma. "Gran, the undo spell didn't work."

Her grandmother frowned. "Did not de ladybug stop glowing?"

Lucie nodded. "Yes, but Eric still loves me, Maurice still loves DeeDee, and Craig and Elaine broke up. The only one it worked on was Ben." Her chin dropped. "He doesn't love me, Gran."

Her grandmother stared at her for a long time. "What did you learn about castin' Voodoo spells?"

Lucie snorted. "Like you said in your spell, leave it to the pros."

The old woman propped a fist on her hip. "What else?"

"You can't make someone love you with a spell. If they don't love you without the spell, it's not real love and it's not yours to keep."

Gran LeBieu nodded. "Very good. Dat's all you needed to know."

"But what can I do to make the spell go away?"

With an upturned hand, Gran LeBieu smiled. "What spell?"

"The love spell I used on the love bug?"

"Oh, dat one." Gran stood and straightened her muumuu. "Not to worry. It did not work in de first place."

"What do you mean?" Her head reeled as if she were about to pass out.

"Jus' what I say. It did not work." Gran grinned. "You used de wrong bug. Every good Voodoo queen knows you have to follow all de directions or de spell doesn't work."

Lucie flopped back against her pillow. "You mean I didn't have anything to do with Elaine and Craig splitting up?"

"Nope."

"And the love bug didn't make Maurice and DeeDee fall in love?" All this worry, all this time she'd thought she's screwed up so many lives.

"Nope, again."

"*Wooweee*! So Maurice and DeeDee found each other on their own." She'd been lifted up by joy after all the sadness she'd been feeling, only to crash to the earth again. "Then Eric really does love me."

"Dat's right."

"And Ben doesn't and never did." She sank even lower in the mire of anguish.

"Oh, I wouldn't say dat." Her grandmother smiled her wickedly mysterious smile that left people guessing.

Her eyes narrowed. "What do you know, Gran?"

The old Voodoo queen drew herself up to her full height

and stared down her nose at her granddaughter. "What is told to Madame LeBieu in confidence, stays in confidence." She winked. "But I know someone dat came lookin' for a love potion of his own."

Lucie's eyes widened and her heart tripped several times before settling into a speedy pitter-patter. "Ben?"

Her grandmother crossed her arms over her chest. "I'm not sayin' one way or de other. But you best get yer heinie out of de bed. De doctor said you could go."

She flung the sheets aside, jumped up and threw her arms around the old woman. "Thank you, Gran. Thank you!"

"Don't be thankin' me yet." She handed Lucie a bag of clothes and *shooshed* her toward the bathroom. "Hurry up, dis ol' lady and your mama will be waitin' outside for you."

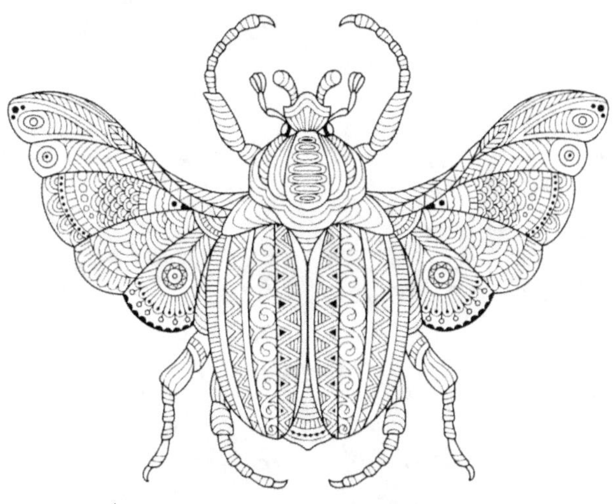

Chapter Twenty-Six

"Y ou can't make me go to work. I'm calling in sick." Lucie plopped on the couch and refused to budge.

Calliope and Alex ganged up on her and, each grabbing an arm, hefted her off the couch and into her bedroom.

"Get your clothes on," Alex said, "you're going to work!"

"Yeah, how else will I get a free beer if you're not there serving?" Calliope smiled. "It's one of the perks of having a friend working at the Raccoon Saloon."

"And we're not letting you louse it up," Alex planted both fists on her hips and stood with her legs apart, blocking the door out of the bedroom. "Now move it."

Lucie popped a salute. "Yes, ma'am!" She trudged to her dresser and pulled out a shirt and skimpy shorts. "But I'm warning you...payback's a mother."

"Yeah, yeah," Alex said. "Big talk for a woman who hasn't been outside her apartment for two days."

"We thought you were going to grow mushrooms under your toenails or something," Calliope flopped onto the bed and frowned at the black T-shirt and frayed shorts Lucie flung onto the comforter. "You're not wearing that, are you?"

"Yeah." She strode into the bathroom, squirted toothpaste on her toothbrush, and made a loud production of brushing her teeth to avoid any attempts at conversation with her so-called friends. Didn't they know she no longer had the will to live, and all she wanted to do was wallow in her own self-pity?

She spit, rinsed her mouth, and spit again.

"All right already, enough with the spitting." Alex appeared in the doorway. "Get your fanny out here and get dressed. We're not going to get our usual table if you make us late."

Lucie snarled at her nemesis. "I'm beginning to see why your mother wants you married. You need someone else to boss around besides your siblings and friends."

"And you need to get over whatever bug crawled up your ass." Alex's harsh words were tempered by a huge grin. "Oh, come on. It won't kill you to go back to work. You'll feel better before the night's over, I promise."

"And if I don't?" How could she? Ben hadn't been by to see her, despite what her grandmother had said. Which went back to Lucie's original hypothesis—Ben didn't love her. Now she knew how her mother felt when she'd lost the love of her life. Pretty much like sucking scum off the bottom of a pond.

When she dragged herself back into the bedroom, Calliope had a silly, sneaky smirk on her face. What the hell was she up to? Lucie bent to pick up her shorts and ratty T-shirt only to find her favorite floral skirt and matching coral sleeveless blouse in their place. "I can't wear that to work. Where'd you put my shorts?"

Alex gave her another sneaky smile. "I hid them."

"Fine, I have more." Lucie turned back to her dresser, only to find her shorts drawer empty.

Calliope held out her hand to Alex. "You owe me five bucks."

"Fine," Alex said. "The first round's on me."

"Fair enough," Calliope responded.

"Hey, what the hell's going on?" Lucie stood in her panties and bra, getting madder by the minute.

"I bet Alex you'd go right back for more shorts," Calliope said. "I was right."

"I'm not wearing that skirt or shirt, so cough up my shorts."

Alex and Calliope stood with their arms crossed.

Surrounded and not up to a fight, she gave in. "Fine!" She grabbed the skirt and jammed her legs into it, pulling it up over her hips. The shirt went on just as fast. "Let's go."

"What about your hair?" Calliope dashed into the bathroom and returned with her hairbrush and proceeded to yank every knot and tangle out by the root.

"Ouch! Give me that before I'm bald!" She snatched the brush from Calliope and dragged it through her hair until it hung springy and shiny. She glanced at her reflection in the mirror. "What's the use? I'm still in Bayou Miste and I'm destined to die an old maid."

"Not after— *Yeeouch!*" Calliope jumped away from Alex, clutching her arm. "Why'd you go and pinch me, you freaktoid?"

"Look, blabbermouth, shut up." Alex turned to Lucie. "Quit whining and let's go."

Lucie stared from Calliope to Alex and back. "Okay, what gives?"

"Nothing." Alex glared at Calliope. "Right, Calliope?"

A guilty blush spread across Calliope's cheeks. "Uh, right. Nothing." She shot for the door. "Let's go before we're late."

Alex followed Calliope.

"Before we're late for what?" She retrieved her purse from the kitchen counter and trotted to keep up with the other two girls.

"Since your 'stang is still in the shop, you can ride with us."

"But you two never stay until closing. How am I supposed to get a ride home? I really should stay home." She turned toward the stairs. "I'm calling in sick."

"We'll stay until you close. All right? Satisfied?" Alex hopped into her Jeep, turned the ignition, and revved the engine to maximum rpms. "Sheesh! What does it take to get you to work?"

"I don't want to work. If I did, I'd get myself there." She climbed into the backseat and stared up at her apartment, wishing she could go back inside and bury her head under a few dozen pillows.

All the way to the bar, she couldn't shake the nagging suspicion that Calliope and Alex were up to something. "If you're planning on fixing me up with some loser, forget it. I'm not interested in dating."

"Not to worry. We couldn't care less whether you ever date again," Alex said.

Calliope giggled.

They were definitely up to something. But what, Lucie hadn't a clue. How unlike Calliope to keep a secret for more than five seconds. Must be a whopper. Lucie hoped at least it didn't involve her. She settled into the backseat and lost herself in her own morbid musings.

Ben hadn't called, hadn't stopped by, and hadn't breathed a word to her since her little incident with the car bomb. Was he truly finished with her?

The acids in her belly burbled, a reminder she hadn't eaten in a while. She thought back. Hell, she hadn't eaten anything since lunch yesterday! Whoever said love didn't kill you didn't have her stomach.

The parking lot was still fairly empty, as the big crowd never arrived before nine. The regulars would already have taken up their favorite seats and eaten their way through several giant bags of pretzels, popcorn, and peanuts.

Same ole, same ole. She sighed. Did nothing ever change in this Podunk town? Was she destined to be a wrinkled old waitress and die at forty because she'd tripped on some Cajun's big feet? She climbed out of the Jeep and straightened her skirt and shoulders. She was in the dumps, but there was no use having everyone else join her. With a job to do, she might as well do it right.

"Lucie!" Jean rushed out from behind the counter to greet her with a bear hug that took her breath away. In shock, and not exactly sure how to handle Jean's unnatural exuberance, she patted his back.

"It's okay, Jean. I've only been gone two days." When he let her go, she put a few feet of space between them.

Jean lifted his bar towel and dabbed at his eyes. "I'm just so happy you're back and you're okay. Excuse me." His face bright red, he took up his position behind the bar, head down to the task of polishing glasses that didn't need polishing.

What was up with him? Something was way off about tonight, but she couldn't quite put her finger on it.

Brandy was already hard at work when Lucie arrived, and soon people filled the room to overflowing. And it wasn't even nine-thirty! Lucie had to hustle to keep up with the drink orders. When the crowd kept growing, her nerves clenched and she doubled her effort to stay on top of the work. Jean had hired a new waitress while she was gone. Her name was Toni-with-an-I, and she was from Morgan City. Even with all the assistance, Lucie couldn't help the rising sense of panic.

"I'm not up to this," she admitted to Alex and Calliope

when she stopped by their table to drop off two longneck Miller Lights.

"Oh, you can handle it, just hang on a little longer." Alex peered toward the door.

"Who are you looking for?" Lucie shook her head. "Oh, who cares, I don't have time to think, much less ogle men." She spun toward the bar, trying to remember if she was supposed to get a Guinness or a Bud Light.

That's when she heard the sirens. What the hell?

"Jean? Are we in violation of something?" She leaned her back against the bar, a prickle of fear creeping across her skin in a trail of major goose bumps.

More sirens joined the first. The band trailed off to the electronic screech of a microphone too close to the speakers.

"Uh, Jean?"

"Yeah, Lucie?"

"What's going on?" She stared around the room at the crowd that had suddenly gone silent, all eyes riveted on the door.

"You're about to find out," Jean said.

The door burst open and a Louisiana State Trooper in full uniform, including his mirrored sunglasses, stepped in. He marched halfway across the floor and stopped, planting his hands on his hips, looking tough enough to toss alligators.

A chill snaked down her spine. She'd hate to be on the wrong side of this cop.

Behind him streamed in no less than a dozen more troopers and the entire local sheriff's department. Even Billy Ray stood staring straight ahead, a serious-as-sin look on his face.

Numero uno cop cleared his throat. "Is there a Lucie LeBieu on the premises?"

Her breath caught in her throat. "Me?" she squeaked.

"Are you Lucie LeBieu?" The trooper turned toward her.

What had she done? Her gaze darted around the room.

Jean's mouth twitched at the corners. Was that humor or fear?

Whatever. Jean was no help. She squared her shoulders and faced the officer. "Yes, sir. I'm Lucie."

"Ma'am, please come with me." He marched up to her. "You can come along quietly or I can handcuff and frisk you."

"I'm for frisking." LeRoy Le Due yelled out. "Let me."

"Shut up, LeRoy," Lucie yelled into the crowd, then to the trooper she asked, "What am I being charged with?"

"Tampering, ma'am," he said in his deep monotone voice.

"Tampering with what?" Her heart thumped wildly against her chest.

"You have the right to remain silent," the officer's hand circled her elbow and he pulled her toward the door.

Holy cypress knees! What had she done? Was she being charged with bombing Eric's car? "I didn't do it!"

"Yes, ma'am, we have it from a reliable witness that says you did."

"Did what?" she cried.

The crowd fell in behind her as the trooper led her through the entrance out into the parking lot.

Lights from a dozen squad cars blinded her and she raised her hand to cover her eyes. Once outside, the state trooper dropped his hold on her elbow and stepped away.

An electronic squealing noise ripped through the air followed by someone talking through a loudspeaker. "Is it on? It is? Oh. Okay."

"Can someone tell me what's going on?" Lucie cried.

"Lucie LeBieu, step away from the bar!" The disembodied voice sounded over a loudspeaker.

"What am I being charged with?" Her empty stomach was no match for the flock of butterflies beating inside. She had no desire to go to jail. Especially when she didn't understand why.

"You're being charged with tampering with a man's heart." The giant voice, laced with static, was familiar.

A strange tingling battled with the butterflies in her belly. "And whose heart would that be?"

"Isn't it enough to know you tampered and you're going to be held accountable? What have you got to say in your defense?"

Her heart sang. *Yes!* She knew that voice. It was the voice that plagued her dreams, day and night. "I plead guilty. Am I allowed to have a lawyer?" She squinted against the lights. Where was he?

"No, you won't be allowed a lawyer."

"So you're to be the judge, jury, and executioner?"

"That's the idea. Miss LeBieu, by your own admission, you've been found guilty of tampering with a man's heart. You're being sentenced to life."

"Life?" She stepped forward, a smile lifting her lips. "Isn't that a bit harsh?"

"Possibly. If you consider it harsh to be sentenced to a life with me." Ben stepped forward, dropping a bullhorn to his side.

She closed the distance between them. "I'd consider it a pleasure to be sentenced to life married to the bug exterminator."

He cocked his head to the side. "You mean you'd consider me good enough even as a bug exterminator?"

"I'd take you even if you were the honey hut cleaner." She gazed up at the man she'd dreamed of for seven long years. The man she'd never stopped loving and never thought she'd ever see again. "On one condition."

Ben's eyebrows rose. "Since when is the accused allowed to make deals?"

"Consider it a plea bargain." She walked her finger up his chest.

Ben held the bullhorn out to the side. "Somebody take this. I think I'm going to have my hands full."

She gave him her sexiest smile. "You can count on it."

Billy Ray ran up to take the bullhorn. "Does she need convincing, sir?"

"No," Ben said without looking up from Lucie's gaze. "I think we've put the screws to her. She's talking."

"If you say so, sir." Billy Ray ran back to join the circle of people surrounding her and Ben.

"Well, I'm sorry to say, you don't have the choice of honey hut man *or* bug exterminator."

Her heart dropped like a lead ball into the pit of her empty belly. "You don't want me?"

"Oh, I want you, all right, but I'm not a bug man or the honey hut man." He shook his head, his lips thinning into a straight line.

"Then what kind of man are you?"

"Let me introduce myself." He held out his hand. "Benjamin Franklin Boyette, criminal investigator with the Louisiana State Police."

"You're with the state police? You're living your dream?" Her chest swelled with pride.

"Yes, ma'am." He tipped his head in a nod. "And I'm living my dream in Baton Rouge, but if you want to stay here in Bayou Miste, I'm sure I could work it out."

"I don't care where I go or stay, as long as I'm with you." She wrapped her arms around his waist and pressed her cheek against his chest.

But Ben pushed her back. "Wait, I'm not done." He turned around in a circle. "Can I have a little intro, please?"

Sirens roared to life, blasting every eardrum for miles

around, animal or human. When Ben sliced his hand across his throat, they all silenced.

He turned, a grin spilling across his face. "Love the sirens."

Her brows furrowed. "Intro for what?"

"This." He dropped to one knee and took Lucie's hand in his. "Lucie LeBieu, will you marry me?"

Her heart exploded with joy and she almost did a Snoopy dance there in front of half the Louisiana State Police force. But she tamped down the smile threatening to break through. "Ben, you haven't met my condition."

"Oh yeah, you did mention a condition." He held his arms wide. "You name it."

"Hand over the love potion my grandmother gave you."

"Love potion?" His innocent look was a bit too innocent.

"Don't play dumb with me, Benjamin Boyette. I've got your number."

He pressed a kiss to her hand. "Honey, you've got my heart."

"And you have mine." Her eyes narrowed. "I just want to make sure I don't have any competition."

"Hey Lucie, my beer's getting cold," Alex yelled from the doorway to the Raccoon Saloon. "What's it going to be? You gonna marry that baboon of a big brother of mine or not? He's been driving everyone nuts."

"Have not!" Ben retorted.

"Have too!" The crowd disagreed in unison.

Ben had the grace to look sheepish.

"Well, Lucie?" Calliope asked.

"Yes!" She yelled loud enough for everyone to hear. "Yes, I'll marry him."

As Ben wrapped her in his arms and swung her around, a cheer rose higher than the treetops, echoing across the waters of Bayou Miste.

The sound carried to a cabin deep in the swamp where a wise Voodoo queen stood in her bright-red muumuu.

A lone ladybug buzzed past her nose in an erratic pattern until it landed on the porch rails, folding its wings beneath its hard shell.

Madame LeBieu winked at the tiny creature. "And dat, my little love bug, is de way it's done."

Thank you for reading Voodoo For Two. A Cajun Magic Mystery Series continues with Deja Voodoo. Keep reading for the 1st Chapter.

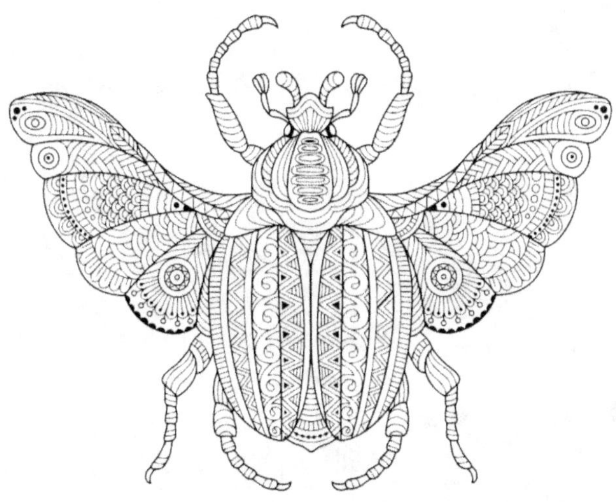

DEJA VOODOO

A Cajun Magic Mystery

Book Three

New York Times & *USA Today*
Bestselling Author

ELLE JAMES

Deja Voodoo
A CAJUN MAGIC MYSTERY
NEW YORK TIMES BESTSELLING AUTHOR
ELLE JAMES

Chapter One

BAYOU MISTE, LOUISIANA

"Boyette, I hope this idea works." Edouard Francois Marceaux scrunched his smartphone between his ear and shoulder as he sat on the bench by the back door of the rental cottage. With his hands free, he pulled off a muddy boot and dropped it to the porch planks. "If it doesn't, we may have us one dead witness on our hands, and that bastard Primeaux will get away with murder."

"Don't worry, it'll work," Ben Boyette, his partner in the Special Criminal Investigations Unit in Baton Rouge, reassured him. "Did you have any trouble finding the old trapper shack?"

"Did anyone ever tell you GPS devices work best on roadways, not waterways? Still, we managed with a few dead ends and switch-backs. If I lose this thing, I'll have to hire a tracking dog with gills to find them. Holy Jesus, that swamp is a freakin' maze! Marcus and I counted no less than nine alligators while we were out there. And those were the ones we could see."

"Did you point them out to our witness?"

"You bet." Ed shifted the phone to the other ear and attacked the laces on his left boot. "That ought to make even her stay put."

"You think? After the drug-running, backstabbing, mafia thugs she's been shacking up with, the alligators probably looked tame."

"Good point." One-handed, he tugged at the remaining muddy boot. The phone slipped, and he grabbed for it. "Tell me again why we're playing babysitter to a witness and why you didn't take this assignment?"

"Number one, I don't trust anyone else to get our witness to the courthouse alive. I suspect we have a mole in the force. And I'd have done it, but I'm up to my neck in trials over the serial rapist case." Ben sighed. "Since I did all the legwork, I'm the one in court. God, I hate courtrooms. But, we have to nail this guy so it sticks. Otherwise, I'd be there in a heartbeat. Oh, and I have a pregnant wife at home."

"Oh, yeah. That. Guess you're right. Although, I'd switch with you in a second. You're the one with all the experience wrestling alligators."

"You'll survive. Hopefully, the only alligator you have to wrestle is my moth—" Ben stopped in mid-sentence as if he changed his mind about what he was going to say next. "By the way, how are your digs? Mom buy your story?"

"Yeah." Ed padded through the small cottage, appreciating the homey feel of it. This was the kind of house he'd always pictured belonging to his grandmother. If he'd ever known her. "I hate lying to your mom, though."

"She'll get over it. Did my share of fibbing to get out of doing the lawn a couple times growing up." He chuckled.

"Come to think of it, I can still taste the soap. That woman could see right through every lie. She always caught me. But she loved me anyway."

"Yeah. She had to love you, you're her son." And Boyette was damned lucky to have her.

"I'm sure your mom did the same."

"Don't bet on it. Never knew her." His voice was a little harsher than he'd intended. A twinge of longing flickered across his subconscious, which he quickly squelched. No use pining after something he never had.

After all these years, he hadn't realized how much he missed having a mother until he'd met Ben's. Barbara Boyette was the consummate maternal figure. Care and concern written in every smile, wrinkle, and gray hair.

Ben cleared his throat. "Oh, by the way, do you like kids?"

Ed pushed his boots to the side and stood. Did he like kids? "Never thought about it. Why?"

"No reason. Did mom invite you to dinner already?" Ben asked.

"Nope."

Ben laughed. "Don't worry, she will."

"Is that bad?"

"Uh, no, not at all." Ben's answer was a little too swift for his comfort. "She moves quickly with single men."

"I'm not single, I'm divorced. There's a difference. Is there something you're not telling me?" He tamped down a sudden urge to get out of town. Fast.

"No, no. Nothing at all." Now Ben's voice sounded entirely too cheerful.

He should definitely run from this small town stuff as fast as his Nikes could take him.

"Mom's a great cook. She just sometimes cooks up more than her guests are ready to swallow."

Now he knew for sure Ben was keeping something from him. "What the hell do you mean by that?"

"Okay, so you're all set, then." Ben ignored his question. "Lay low and go fishing enough to keep Marcus and our girl fed and happy."

"Gotcha." He looked around the tiny cottage, the walls closing in on him already. "One question."

"What's that?"

"What the hell am I supposed to do with my time for the next few days?"

"Keep an eye open for suspicious characters. Otherwise, make like a vacation, and relax."

"I don't think I've ever taken a vacation." He scratched his head and thought back. No, he'd hung out at the office even on annual leave. All that use-or-lose vacation time got lost each year. "What do you do on a vacation?"

"Sleep until noon, girl-watch, you know, the usual thing."

"Maybe on Cocoa Beach, but in Bayou Miste? I'd go so far as to say the alligators outnumber the people. I don't think I've seen one live human besides your mother and the marina owner. Tell me, Ben, do they count the alligators in the census?"

Ben's outright laughter blasted Ed's ear. "Bayou Miste isn't that bad. Think about it, you arrived in the middle of the day, right?"

"Yeah. So?"

"School and work should be getting out by now." Ben chuckled again. "Just wait."

He didn't like the sound of his partner's laugh, it had a devilish quality. "Wait for what?"

"To meet the family. You're gonna love them."

"I thought it was just you and your mother."

Ben snorted. "Oh, no. I have eighteen brothers and sisters."

He fumbled the phone and almost dropped it. "Holy hell!"

"Yeah, that's what it's like around my house after school."

The introverted halls of Monti-Ed-zuma crashed around his ears.

Nineteen children in one family? What were his parents thinking? Obviously, they hadn't been thinking, they'd been—

"What have you gotten me into, Boyette?"

"You're a tough guy, you can handle it."

~

As the tune to "When the Saints Go Marching In" played on Alexandra Belle Boyette's phone for the sixth time in thirty minutes, she lay down on the couch and crammed a pillow over her ears. "Please leave me alone."

"Why don't you answer it and get it over with?" Calliope sat across from her, scraping the silver coating from a scratch-off lottery ticket, her long wild, light red hair fanning across her shoulders like a cape. She wore a halter top and an ankle-length, tie-died peasant skirt, her legs tucked under her. No matter the circumstances, she always looked relaxed and carefree.

"No way." Alex sat up and leaned her face in her hands. "She'll ask me again if I've been seeing anyone, or she'll invite me to dinner at the house and drag some poor slob to the table with the family."

"So? What's wrong with that?"

"Even if I liked the guy, one look at my family and he'll run screaming into the bayou."

"Damn." Calliope frowned at the lottery ticket and tossed it onto the table. Then she looked across at Alex with a smile. "Your family's wonderful."

"Yeah, all nineteen of them." She rolled her eyes. "In this

day and age, who in their right minds would have nineteen children?"

Calliope grinned "Your parents."

"Yeah, and what did it buy them?" She sat up. "An early grave for my father and insanity for my mother." Despite her flippant words, she still felt the pain of loss. Her father had been the rock in their lives and she missed him terribly, even two years after his passing.

"Alex, your mother loves every one of you and only wants to see you happy."

"I wish she could love me a little less."

"You don't mean that."

"Yes, I do. She won't leave me alone about love and relationships. I'm happy with the way things are. I have my own business, I'm in the best shape of my life. I have this great house. What more does she want?"

"Grandchildren?"

She snorted. "Big Brother Ben has that market nailed. She'll have her first grandbaby in three months. Lucie's getting as big as the bayou."

"Speaking of Lucie, I saw her yesterday when I was in Baton Rouge. And you're right. She is getting big." Calliope smiled. "She looks great. Pregnancy must agree with her."

"Yeah, and Ben's over the moon. His chest is swelling so much, I doubt they can find shirts to fit him." Alex was happy for her brother. At the same time, a stab of intense longing hit her right in the gut. She had to suck in air to relieve the pressure.

"Oh, I almost forgot." Calliope jumped from her seat on the couch. "Lucie asked me to give you something."

She cringed. "Oh God, what now?"

Calliope fished in her pocket and dug out a small red velvet drawstring bag.

When Alex peered inside, she almost gagged. It smelled

like something the cat dragged in from the swamp. "What is this stuff?"

"She didn't say. I bet five bucks it's some Voodoo remedy."

"Egad!" She dropped the bag on the end table. "You remember the last time she dabbled in Voodoo she almost had the entire town of Bayou Miste under her wacky love spell."

"But it all worked out in the end. Lucie married Ben, Maurice and DeeDee scheduled a Christmas wedding and Elaine and Craig eloped. The whole magic thing couldn't have turned out better. And, she's been taking lessons from her grandmother."

"Maybe that spell worked out all right, after a considerable amount of bad luck and a few murder attempts. But the one she put on Mo's pet alligator gave the poor beast a bad case of puppy love for Granny Saulnier's poodle. T-Rex still hasn't gotten over it."

"I don't know what it is. She asked me to give it to you the next time I saw you. I did and now my duty is done." Calliope blinked, all innocence. "Maybe it's a sachet you're supposed to put in your drawer to make your clothes smell good."

She wrinkled her nose "Not this stuff. It could make a grown man weep. I swear it has that rank odor of stump water." She shoved the bag toward her friend. "Take it back to her. I don't want to risk getting caught up in one of her crazy spells."

"Oh, no." Calliope held up her hands. "I'm not carrying that thing around. It might give me hair in places I have no business growing hair. Or worse, maybe it'll make me lose hair that I shouldn't. No, if you want her to have it back, you'll have to give it back yourself."

"Fine, I will. Next time I'm in Baton Rouge." She frowned at the sachet bag. "In the meantime, I have to put up with it. I hope it isn't anything dangerous."

The phone sang again and she flopped down on the couch

pulling the pillow back over her head. "Why couldn't I have had Lisa and Lucie's mother, who stays gone for twenty years at a time?"

Calliope stood at the sound of the third ring. "Because your mother loves you, and you should be nicer to her." She reached for the phone.

"Don't do it, Calliope," She warned. "If you value our friendship, you won't touch that phone."

Calliope cocked an eyebrow and punched the talk button. "Hello?" She listened. "Yes, Mrs. Boyette, Alex is right next to me. Sure. I'd be happy to relay the message. Seven o'clock? I'm sure that would be fine. Me, too? That would be nice. Good to talk to you, too, Mrs. Boyette. Bye, now."

"What did she want?"

"You and I are invited to dinner at her house at seven tomorrow night. Oh, and put on that slinky red dress you wore to Lucie's bachelorette party."

"My mother said that?"

"Well, most of it." Calliope grinned. "I added the part about the dress."

"Thanks, Calliope. Don't know what I'd do without you." She dripped sarcasm. "But I'm willing to try it."

Her friend dropped into the chair and tucked her legs underneath her. "I heard Lucie's Grand-mère LeBieu has been coaching her on Voodoo, again."

She punched her pillow and set it against the arm of the couch. "Should we consider moving to another state?"

The redhead tipped her head to the side as if considering her jest. "Possibly."

"Geesh. I just got the gym operating in the black, I hate to sell and start somewhere else."

Calliope's eyes lit up. "We could move to Biloxi."

With a very unladylike "Ha!" Alex stood and paced around the room. "That's the last place you need to move."

"Why?"

"Don't play dumb with me." She stopped in front of Calliope, planting her hands on her hips. "Biloxi would be entirely too much temptation for you. What, with a casino on every corner, it would be like navigating a minefield."

"I'm not that hooked on gambling. Besides, I could get a job in one of the casinos." Calliope's eyes twinkled and an excited grin spread across her face. "The pay and tips would beat what I get at the Raccoon Saloon."

"You should be happy you landed Lucie's old job. She got great tips."

"I guess moving is out of the question." Calliope's smile turned downward and she heaved a sigh. "I miss Lucie."

"Me, too," Alex said. "Why do things have to change?"

"Yeah," Calliope sighed again. "Why do people have to get married and move away?"

"Although, Lucie seems very happy." She could still picture Lucie's glowing face at the wedding. How had she lucked into finding the love of her life here in Bayou Miste?

Calliope's eyes got all dreamy. "Do you think we'll ever find someone to love as much as Lucie loves Ben?"

"Not me. I only date the guys from hell."

"Like Theo?"

Alex rolled her eyes. "Why can't that bonehead take the hint?"

"Still botherin' you?"

As if to prove her point, her phone sang the theme for Jaws, the da dum, da dum sound grating on every last one of her nerves. She launched herself across the coffee table, snatched the phone, and cocked her arm to throw.

Calliope grabbed the device from her hand before she could let go. "Hey, don't ruin a perfectly good cell phone because of a guy."

She drew in a long breath and let out the tension with her

exhale. "You're right. You're right. I'd miss my phone more than Theo."

"Not all guys are like Theo, you know," Calliope pointed out.

She snorted. "You haven't seen the ones my mom keeps throwing at me." She settled back on the couch and hugged a pillow to her chest. "I don't know where she gets them, but they've all had major 'me' hang-ups."

"What do you mean?"

"It's all about the guy." She wandered around her tastefully decorated living room where everything had a place and everything was in it. "Why can't I find a guy who thinks I hung the moon? A partner who will love me even when I'm majorly PMSing. Someone who will love me unconditionally, no matter how bad a day he's had."

As if he sensed how upset she was, Sport, Alex's golden retriever, trotted across the room and sat at her feet, his tail sweeping the floor in a steady rhythm. He stared up at her, mouth hanging open like he was smiling at her, his eyes pleading, "pet me".

She reached down and scratched behind his ears. "I don't think I'll ever find someone to love me like that."

"Sport loves you like that." Calliope giggled.

She laughed. "You know, Calliope, you're right. I need a guy like Sport. One who will greet me at the door, always happy to see me. Someone who can forgive me for forgetting his birthday. Someone who's happy no matter what I feed him or how fat I get." She squatted next to Sport and hugged him around his neck.

"Wouldn't it be neat if Sport were a man?"

"Yeah." She loved the silky feel of Sport's coat against her cheek. He loved her no matter what. "I wish he were a man. Then maybe my mother would quit trying to set me up."

"Hey, Sport." Calliope snapped her fingers. "Come here."

The dog laid a long wet tongue across Alex's cheek and wiggled loose to go to Calliope.

"How would you like to be a man?" The redhead rubbed her hand in his thick fur. "I bet you'd be really sexy, huh, boy?"

Alex stood and brushed the dog hair off her workout pants. "I have to get ready for work. Would you mind taking Sport out for a walk?"

"I'd love to." Calliope leaped from her chair. "Wanna go outside, boy?" She reached for the leash hanging on a hook inside the coat closet.

"Just don't let him whiz on Miz Mozelle's rose bushes. She never says anything, but I'm sure she doesn't appreciate it. I don't know what it is about her rose bushes that inspires him to grace them."

"We'll steer clear." Calliope snapped the lead on Sport's collar.

"And watch out for Granny Saulnier's poodle."

"FeFe?"

"Yeah. Sport has a thing for her. If you're not careful, he'll yank your arm out of its socket going after her."

"I'll be careful." Calliope paused with her hand on the front doorknob and looked back with her eyebrows raised. "Anything else before we go for a nice walk?"

"Get out of here." Alex lobbed a pillow at Calliope as she and Sport exited.

～

Later that night, Alex lay in her bed, Lucie's Voodoo pouch lying on the pillow beside her. She'd had a particularly tough aerobics session at the gym and her muscles ached.

She lifted her cell phone and dialed.

"Hello?" Lucie's sleepy voice answered.

"Did I catch you doing something I only dream about?" she asked.

"Sleeping?"

"Never mind." She stroked the red velvet bag. "Is Ben home?"

"No, he's putting in a late day with the prosecuting attorney. You know, his criminal investigation stuff."

"What, and leaving his pregnant wife to fend for herself? Who's going to make the run to the convenience store for your latest cravings of sardines and pickles?"

"He's got orders to pick some up on the way home. How are you, Alex?"

"Great. I'm in the best shape I've been in a long time, I'm healthy, my business is booming and I've never been happier." Geez, she sounded like a broken record. A pathetic broken record, at that.

"Lonely, huh?"

That empty feeling gripped her belly and she automatically reached over the side of her bed to pat Sport's head. His wet nose nuzzled her hand. Was she lonely? Was that why she'd called Lucie in the first place? "Yeah, a little."

"Consider yourself hugged."

"Thanks." But a real hug would have been much warmer. From a real man—even better.

"Did Calliope give you the present?"

"Yeah. Actually, that's why I called." Alex lifted the pouch in her hand. "What is it?"

"A little Voodoo good luck for one of my best friends."

She grimaced. "Uh, gee thanks, Lucie. I can't tell you how happy it makes me."

"Relax, Alex." Lucie laughed into her ear. "You won't wake up as a frog or anything. My grandmother helped me with it, so don't worry."

"I can't tell you how relieved I am." Only slightly. Madame

LeBieu knew her stuff. As the well-renowned Voodoo queen of the bayou, her spells always worked the way she intended. Unlike Lucie's.

"I can tell you're not thrilled." Lucie laughed. "Gran watched me every step of the way. She loves you like another granddaughter. Why would she propose something that would hurt you?"

"Let me remind you, she turned Craig Thibodeaux into a frog," she said, her voice flat.

"Yeah, but it all worked out in the end, didn't it?" Lucie sighed. "I love you, Alex. I just want you to be happy."

"I'm happy." Her hand tightened on the phone. "Why can't everyone figure that out?"

"Maybe you protest too much?"

"I'm not protesting." Alex realized, as she said it, she was doing just that. Her lips clamped shut.

"Is it a crime to want all my friends to be as happy as I am?" Lucie's voice drifted off.

She could imagine Lucie patting her swelling belly, and a sudden surge of maternal longing struck her right between the breasts. Why was she mooning over having a baby? Hell, she'd helped raise all her younger brothers and sisters. "I'm happy. Really." Even to her own ears, her voice wasn't very convincing.

"Give the Voodoo charm a chance, Alex. That's all I ask."

Lucie's voice cut through her ill temper and she relented. "Assuming I give it a chance, what is it supposed to do?"

A long pause met her question. Not a good sign. "I'm not exactly sure. Gran LeBieu said it would bring you good luck."

"In terms of what?" A chill swept down Alex's spine.

A whimpering sound rose from the floor beside her. Sport must have sensed her unease.

"It's okay, really. Gran LeBieu wouldn't give you anything that would hurt you."

"I'm shaking in my sheets here."

"Look, if you don't want it, bring it back with you the next time you're in Baton Rouge."

"I will."

"And when will that be?" Lucie demanded.

"As soon as I can break free from the gym." She knew that was an excuse. The thought of visiting Lucie in all her happy, pregnant glory made her own life look boring, lackluster, and downright sad.

"You're working too hard, Alex. Let Harry take over for a weekend. You need some down time."

She straightened her shoulders, refusing to give into downheartedness. "No, I like being busy."

"And you like going home alone?"

"Yes."

"Alex, it'll happen for you," Lucie said. "When you least expect it, love will knock you over."

"Like it happened with you?" She snorted. "I don't want to fall in love because of a Voodoo love potion. I want a man who loves me for me."

"Much as I'd like to take credit, my love spell never worked. Gran LeBieu confirmed, it had to be cast by a love bug, not a lady bug. If you remember, we couldn't find any love bugs, so we used a ladybug. She let me think it worked to teach me a lesson."

"What?" She shook her head. "You mean my dumb brother didn't need a kick in the pants to tell you he loved you?"

"Maybe he needed that kick in the pants, but he didn't need the love spell."

"I knew that," Alex said. She didn't know whether Lucie's news was good or bad. If the love spell didn't work, what were her chances at love? She fingered the velvet bag. "So, Lucie, what is this bag, really?"

"Gran LeBieu said it would help make your wishes come true."

Alex shuddered. "Kinda like my genie in a bottle?"

"I'm not entirely sure. I just thought you needed a little push, a boost to get you started."

"Look, Lucie, just because you're in love and that makes you happy, doesn't mean I have to be in love to be happy." But she had been pretty lonely since Lucie left. And she hadn't had a decent date in...When her visual memories started dating back to high school and she couldn't name a single unforgettable—happily they'd been forgettable—date, she grimaced. "Okay, I'll keep your gift for now, but I'm still not convinced I need it."

"Which makes me all the more convinced you do."

"I have my own business, my own home and a wonderful, if a little meddling, family. I don't need a love interest."

"Oh, Alex. You're my best friend in the world and I only wish you could feel how I feel."

"That's you, honey. And I'm happy for you." She didn't add, and I miss you like crazy. Why mar Lucie's happiness?

"Oh, Ben just walked in," Lucie said. "Hey, mon cher, anything you want to say to your baby sister?"

The distinct sound of smacking noises carried across the line and Lucie giggled. "Beeennn, I'm on the phone with your sister." Another giggle.

A pang of longing twisted in her gut. Again. What the hell was going on?

"Alex? That you?" Ben's voice blasted into Alex's ear.

"Yeah, bro."

"Lucie's gotta go now."

More giggling erupted in the background and an indignant, "Ben! What about the baby?"

"Look, I have some ironing to do," she said. Suddenly, she couldn't stand listening to their playful antics on the phone.

"Yeah, okay," Ben said, obviously distracted.

"Tell Lucie I'll call tomorrow."

"Gotcha—damn..." A loud clunk was followed by dead air of being disconnected.

Alex plugged the phone into the charger on the night-stand and turned off the light.

She fought the strange pressure in her chest. What was wrong with her? She was happy. She sniffed. Was she coming down with a cold? Were her glands swelling in her throat, choking off her air?

A tear slid down her cheek. Oh hell. She didn't need this. Self-pity was for weenies, not for black belts in karate or really kick-ass business owners.

She flung her hand out, bouncing it off the empty pillow beside her. The velvet pouch bumped against her fingers.

"Sport?"

After a brief pause, a cold, wet nose poked up over the side of the bed.

"I'm so lucky to have you." She ran her hand over his velvety snout. A long tongue snaked out and licked her fingers.

Sport was always there for her without being annoying or obsessive. Alex shivered. She'd had her share of boyfriends and stalkers. She'd rather remain celibate than go through that again.

But deep down, she ached for that closeness. And hell, she hadn't had sex in so long she wondered if she remembered how. Was she going to die one of those frigid old maids destined to read erotic romance novels to get her jollies?

I'm Pathetic.

And her mother would drive her stark-raving mad if she didn't quit shoving fresh meat at her every chance she got.

"Oh Sport, I wish you were a man. That would solve all my problems." She settled against her pillow and closed her eyes. "It would take a lot of magic to get my mother to back off. I'm not even sure having my own choice of a boyfriend will satisfy the woman." She yawned and snuggled in, pulling the comforter up to her chin to ward off the chill of the air conditioner.

As she drifted into a half-awake, half-asleep state, the bed sank down on the far side. Sport had leapt up beside her.

Too tired to tell him to get down, she gave up and let go.

A thrumming sound filled her dreams, building into a full bass echo of drums. Somewhere in the back of her sleep-numbed mind, she recognized the drums as those played at the Voodoo ceremonies Madame LeBieu conducted on those rare occasions when a little extra umph was needed to initiate one of her spells.

Just as she succumbed to oblivion, an eerie chant echoed through her head, "Wishes come true. Wishes come true. Wishes come true."

Alex sighed and gave in to the magic.

If only wishes really came true.

Get ∼ DEJA VOODOO ∼ NOW

About the Author

ELLE JAMES also writing as MYLA JACKSON is a *New York Times* and *USA Today* Bestselling author of books including cowboys, intrigues and paranormal adventures that keep her readers on the edges of their seats. When she's not at her computer, she's traveling, snow skiing, boating, or riding her ATV, dreaming up new stories. Learn more about Elle James at www.ellejames.com

Website | Facebook | Twitter | GoodReads | Newsletter | BookBub | Amazon

Or visit her alter ego Myla Jackson at mylajackson.com
Website | Facebook | Twitter | Newsletter

Follow Me!
www.ellejames.com
ellejames@ellejames.com

Also by Elle James

Brotherhood Protectors International

Athens Affair (#1)

Belgian Betrayal (#2)

Croatia Collateral (#3)

Dublin Debacle (#4)

Edinburgh Escape (#5)

Brotherhood Protectors Hawaii

Kalea's Hero (#1)

Leilani's Hero (#2)

Kiana's Hero (#3)

Maliea's Hero (#4)

Emi's Hero (#5)

Sachie's Hero (#6)

Kimo's Hero (#7)

Alana's Hero (#8)

Nala's Hero (#9)

Mika's Hero (#10)

Bayou Brotherhood Protectors

Remy (#1)

Gerard (#2)

Lucas (#3)

Beau (#4)

Rafael (#5)

Valentin (#6)

Landry (#7)

Simon (#8)

Maurice (#9)

Jacques (#10)

Brotherhood Protectors Yellowstone

Saving Kyla (#1)

Saving Chelsea (#2)

Saving Amanda (#3)

Saving Liliana (#4)

Saving Breely (#5)

Saving Savvie (#6)

Saving Jenna (#7)

Saving Peyton (#8)

Saving Londyn (#9)

Brotherhood Protectors Colorado

SEAL Salvation (#1)

Rocky Mountain Rescue (#2)

Ranger Redemption (#3)

Tactical Takeover (#4)

Colorado Conspiracy (#5)

Rocky Mountain Madness (#6)

Free Fall (#7)

Colorado Cold Case (#8)

Fool's Folly (#9)

Colorado Free Rein (#10)

Rocky Mountain Venom (#11)

High Country Hero (#12)

Brotherhood Protectors

Montana SEAL (#1)

Bride Protector SEAL (#2)

Montana D-Force (#3)

Cowboy D-Force (#4)

Montana Ranger (#5)

Montana Dog Soldier (#6)

Montana SEAL Daddy (#7)

Montana Ranger's Wedding Vow (#8)

Montana SEAL Undercover Daddy (#9)

Cape Cod SEAL Rescue (#10)

Montana SEAL Friendly Fire (#11)

Montana SEAL's Mail-Order Bride (#12)

SEAL Justice (#13)

Ranger Creed (#14)

Delta Force Rescue (#15)

Dog Days of Christmas (#16)

Montana Rescue (#17)

Montana Ranger Returns (#18)

Brotherhood Protectors Boxed Set 1

Brotherhood Protectors Boxed Set 2

Brotherhood Protectors Boxed Set 3

Brotherhood Protectors Boxed Set 4

Brotherhood Protectors Boxed Set 5

Brotherhood Protectors Boxed Set 6

Iron Horse Legacy

Soldier's Duty (#1)

Ranger's Baby (#2)

Marine's Promise (#3)

SEAL's Vow (#4)

Warrior's Resolve (#5)

Drake (#6)

Grimm (#7)

Murdock (#8)

Utah (#9)

Judge (#10)

Delta Force Strong

Ivy's Delta (Delta Force 3 Crossover)

Breaking Silence (#1)

Breaking Rules (#2)

Breaking Away (#3)

Breaking Free (#4)

Breaking Hearts (#5)

Breaking Ties (#6)

Breaking Point (#7)

Breaking Dawn (#8)

Breaking Promises (#9)

Hearts & Heroes Series

Wyatt's War (#1)

Mack's Witness (#2)

Ronin's Return (#3)

Sam's Surrender (#4)

Hellfire Series

Hellfire, Texas (#1)

Justice Burning (#2)

Smoldering Desire (#3)

Hellfire in High Heels (#4)

Playing With Fire (#5)

Up in Flames (#6)

Total Meltdown (#7)

Take No Prisoners Series

SEAL's Honor (#1)

SEAL'S Desire (#2)

SEAL's Embrace (#3)

SEAL's Obsession (#4)

SEAL's Proposal (#5)

SEAL's Seduction (#6)

SEAL'S Defiance (#7)

SEAL's Deception (#8)

SEAL's Deliverance (#9)

SEAL's Ultimate Challenge (#10)

Texas Billionaire Club

Tarzan & Janine (#1)

Something To Talk About (#2)

Who's Your Daddy (#3)

Love & War (#4)

Billionaire Online Dating Service

First Responder (#5)

Cowboys (#6)

Silver Soldiers (#7)

Secret Identities (#8)

Warrior's Conquest

Enslaved by the Viking Short Story

Conquests

Smokin' Hot Firemen

Protecting the Colton Bride

Protecting the Colton Bride & Colton's Cowboy Code

Heir to Murder

Secret Service Rescue

High Octane Heroes

Haunted

Engaged with the Boss

Cowboy Brigade

An Unexpected Clue

Under Suspicion, With Child

Texas-Size Secrets

www.ingramcontent.com/pod-product-compliance
Lightning Source LLC
Chambersburg PA
CBHW070756120726
47910CB00001B/193